JUL 2006

CH

Divas of
Damascus Road

Also by Michelle Stimpson

BOAZ BROWN

Divas of
Damascus Road

Michelle Stimpson

West Bloomfield, Michigan

WARNER BOOKS

NEW YORK   BOSTON

Published by Warner Books with Walk Worthy Press™.

Warner Books
1271 Avenue of the Americas, New York, NY 10020

Walk Worthy Press
33290 West Fourteen Mile Road, #482, West Bloomfield, MI 48322

Visit our Web site at www.walkworthypress.net.

Printed in the United States of America

First Edition: July 2006
10 9 8 7 6 5 4 3 2 1

Library of Congress Cataloging-in-Publication Data
Stimpson, Michelle.
    Divas of Damascus Road / Michelle Stimpson.— 1st ed.
      p. cm.
    Summary: "A family of Christian women battle issues of unwanted pregnancies, overeating, mental illness and traumatic childhoods, hoping that—like Saul's encounter with God on the road to Damascus—their lives will turn around."—Provided by the publisher.
    ISBN-13: 978-0-446-57746-5
    ISBN-10: 0-446-57746-4
  1. African American women—Fiction. 2. Christian women—Fiction. 3. Life change events—Fiction. I. Title.
    PS3619.T56D58 2006
    813'.6—dc22   2005035365

Book design by Charles Sutherland

For my friends and family, who put up with
laugh with me, fuss with me, and pray with me.
You show me what it means to love

Acknowledgments

First and foremost, I give all honor and glory to God, from Whom all blessings flow. I continue to be amazed at how He uses me (of all people) to do His will through such an awesome medium. I pray for continued strength as I often find myself typing until two in the morning, but He gives me strength to carry on the next morning as though I had a full night's rest in Him. Thank you, Father!

Next, to my family, both immediate and extended. Stevie, Steven, and Kalen, you all continue to be part of my anchoring system. When it's all said and done, it is nice to have people to share life with, people who remind me that relationships are priceless, people who have more faith in me than I have sometimes. It's nice to be able to borrow.

To my parents and my brothers, thanks for all you have done to proclaim, "That's *my* daughter/sister!" and get the word out about my first novel, *Boaz Brown*. And to my extended kinfolk, the Williams, Smith, Music, Stimpson, and Lenear families, thanks for all your support via e-mail, coming to book signings, phone calls, and prayer.

I also want to thank my morning commute buddy and confidante, Kimberly "Kim James" Scott, for her listening ear and wise counsel. We have both grown so much in the Lord, and it's nice to have someone who will laugh with me and cry with me. Also to my prayer partners who continue to hold me up— even when I ain't ackin' right. Thanks for loving me anyway just as I love you, too, Jeanne and Opal. And Shannon Green, girl, what can I say? We go a long way back. I look forward to a long way forward, too.

My coworkers at Region 10 Education Service Center have been invaluable. From my original crew of cheerleaders/editors/saleswomen/advertisers/marketers (Jayne Knighton and Dr. Denni Scates) to my more recently added sources of inspiration and critique (Ellen Kimbrough and Nancy Wyatt), you cannot know how much you have blessed me to become a better person. We are growing up! Aside from the ELA team, there are so many more coworkers who have wished me well, spoken encouraging words into my life, and supported me in so many different ways. Even the teachers and administrators we serve throughout the region have been so supportive in letting me know in no uncertain terms that they, too, have been blessed and continue to pass the word along. I thank you!

Thanks to all the book clubs who so graciously selected *Boaz Brown* for reading and discussion. I can't even begin to name all the book clubs and organizations, but I owe special thanks for your fine hospitality in making a sister feel right at home, to Girlfriend 2 Girlfriend (Phoenix, AZ), Spiritual Nuggets (McKinney, TX), Garbo Hearne and her staff at Hearne Fine Art (Little Rock, AR), CushCity (Houston, TX), Sista 2 Sista (Fort Worth, TX), Kym Fisher and Family/Friends (Houston, TX), and the servicemen and women who meet regularly at the Navy Mid-South Chapel (Millington, TN). Thanks to the Sorors of Delta Sigma Theta who keep showing up and showing me love!

For the bookstores who have been so accommodating (especially JoKae's, Dallas, TX), I give thanks for all you do in communities across the world in supporting the move of God through Christian fiction. Thanks, also, to Carol Mackey (blackexpressions.com) for putting *Boaz Brown* front and center.

My big sister in Christ, Karen Bradford—I know we haven't talked much, but you are always in my prayers. For my OCBF family, I thank you for all the opportunities to serve and worship with a body that is growing higher and deeper.

To my partners in Christ, the faithful writers in my writers' group, especially Vivi Monroe Congress, Chris Howell, Elaine Flowers, and Shaundale Johnson, it's nice to share our growing expertise in faith and in the love of God. This is only the beginning!

Again, I found a great deal of help in putting together *Divas of Damascus Road*. So many people made themselves available to me and selflessly gave of their knowledge and expertise. My publisher, Denise Stinson, thanks again for partnering with me and believing in me. To Frances Jalet-Miller for your insightful editing remarks. To all the other experienced writers who give of themselves to me, Francis Ray and Stanice Anderson especially, I appreciate you!

To my readers who have e-mailed me and signed my guest book letting me know how this gift God has given me has in turn blessed you. Now, *that* is the real proof in the pudding. To know that what I do (the nights I wake up and write down an idea, the days I spend thinking through the plot, the times I stop in the middle of a conversation and write down what I just heard) is all for His glory, I tell you, it is marvelous in my eyes. For as many times as I have been inconvenienced by this writing bug, someone has e-mailed me and given me a word of encouragement—"Keep writing"; "You made me think"; and more important, "I want to know God the way LaShondra knew God"; "I asked God to remove the hate from my heart"; or "Your book helped me to heal"—I cannot tell you how many times I just sat and cried after reading your messages. Thank you for allowing God to use you to strengthen me in the same way He used me to strengthen you. Isn't that just like Him?

In His love,
Michelle Stimpson

Divas of Damascus Road

Prologue

Dianne woke from ten minutes of sleep and touched her sister's forehead. Still felt as hot as the surface of Momma's heating pad on "high." Dianne dangled her feet from the edge of the bed and steadied herself for the drop. She studied her toes for a moment—there were only splotches of red paint left at the center of each nail. She smiled at these ten tiny remnants of last weekend's sleepover at Aunt Gloria's house. The sooner she got through the week, the sooner she could get back to the haven of Aunt Gloria's motherly love.

Dianne's feet hit the wooden floor—a cool awakening. She made yet another trip past the empty living room, kicking empty plastic bags and carefully sidestepping discarded syringes. Smelled like the "funny" smoke that always made everyone laugh. She took a deep breath as she passed the living room. Try as she might, the smoke never made her laugh. Certainly didn't make her laugh at the moment, not with her little sister in the other room sleeping like a doll and burning like fire.

She couldn't have known.

She turned on the bathroom light, stepped up on the stool, and then placed one knee on the countertop. She wobbled a bit but caught herself by grabbing hold of the faucet. This was no time to be falling. She had to get the red medicine from the cabinet and give Shannon some more. Dianne was a big girl. Her momma had said so. She could take care of Shannon while her momma was gone.

"Sugarbee," Momma had authorized her, "you take care of things while me and Otis go out, okay?"

"When will you be back, Momma?" Dianne had asked. It wasn't the first time they'd left her to fend for herself and her little sister, Shannon. But each time they left, it seemed they were gone longer than before, and Dianne had to do things that she wasn't quite sure about. The last time they were left alone, Dianne went to the bathroom to run bathwater, and when she pulled back the shower curtain, a black, shiny rat looked up at her and bared his two front teeth in a high-pitched gnarl. Dianne and Shannon stayed in the fortress of their bedroom forever, it seemed. Shannon's diaper stank, but she was the lucky one. Dianne had to relieve herself in the pur-ple pail—her Easter basket.

"We won't be gone long this time," Joyce Ann lied currently. Dianne was used to the lies now. They came with the territory, but Dianne didn't care. Children really don't judge. They'll ac-cept you just as you are.

"Okay, Momma. But what if a rat comes out?"

"Otis killed that rat, I told you," Joyce Ann assured Dianne with all the frenzy of an addict craving a hit.

"But if another one comes out, do you want me to call Aunt Gloria?" Dianne asked, hoping that she could secure this one lifeline.

"No!" Joyce Ann stopped tying her shoes, grabbed Dianne's shoulders, and pulled her nose-to-nose. "You listen to me, Sug-arbee. Don't call your Aunt Gloria for nothin'! NOTHIN'! You hear? And if she calls here, you tell her I'm 'sleep. Don't you dare tell her that I left you here with Shannon. You do and I'll get Otis to tear you up! You hear?"

Otis pulled his head up from the pillow just long enough to give Dianne a glance. All he needed was the go-ahead from Joyce Ann and he would finally get the chance to beat that little whiny, skinny thing to a pulp. Every once in a while he got the chance to pop her, but for some reason Joyce Ann never would let him whip her like she needed. Between Joyce Ann and her sister, Gloria, Otis never had enough time to have his way with the girl. "And you better take good care of Shannon, too," he warned. "Don't let nothing happen to my *baby*." Not that he cared about his daughter. Just that he needed to lay claim on something. Truth be told, he wasn't even sure that Shannon was his.

Dianne didn't need that warning. She'd never let anything happen to Shannon. Shannon was the last twinkle of light in Dianne's life. Well, Shannon and Aunt Gloria. For the time being, she was down to Shannon.

That was two days ago.

The phone startled Dianne, and she fell to the floor despite herself. It had to be Aunt Gloria. Nobody else would call. Her momma's friends never called; they just came by.

Dianne left the bathroom and ran down the remainder of the hallway to the kitchen, where she jumped up and grabbed the phone from the receiver, all in one motion. She put on her best smile and answered, "Hello?"

"Hey, Sugarbee, this is your aunt Gloria. How are you?"

"I'm fine, Aunt Gloria. How are you?" Dianne used her most proper words.

"Well, things aren't so hot over here. Your cousin Regina got a real bad virus, the doctor says, so I've got to keep an eye on her. Otherwise, you know I would have been over to see my Sugarbee!"

A giggle escaped from somewhere deep down within Dianne. She always did like the way Aunt Gloria sang her nickname. *She wished that she could go to Aunt Gloria's house. Aunt Gloria would know what to do about Shannon sleeping all day and the fever that wouldn't go away. She would know how much of the red medicine to give Shannon. She could even go and get more, because the bottle that was full yesterday was now almost empty.*

"Is Joyce Ann there?"

Dianne crossed her fingers behind the nightgown she had been wearing since her mother left. "Yes, but she's sleeping right now."

"How long she been 'sleep?"

"Not long."

"Hmm. Is Otis there?" *Aunt Gloria clicked her cheek like his name had left a bad taste in her mouth.*

Dianne uncrossed her fingers. "No, he's gone."

"Well . . ." *Dianne could tell that her aunt Gloria was thinking. She held her breath and hoped that Aunt Gloria would* keep *thinking, come on over, and discover them here alone. It wouldn't be her fault if Aunt Gloria used her key to come in and check on them. But that didn't happen. Probably because she had just told a lie, the child figured.*

"I've got a good mind to come over there . . . let me see . . . Tell your momma that if Regina gets to feeling better, I'll be over first thing in the morning. If I have to take Regina in to the doctor, I'll be by later on tomorrow afternoon. Either way, I will be there tomorrow. Okay, Sugarbee?"

Dianne exhaled. "Okay. I'll tell her."

After a few attempts, Dianne finally managed to get the phone back on the hook. Though saddened by the fact that Aunt Gloria wouldn't be by today, Dianne took heart in knowing that tomorrow held promise. Tomorrow somebody would come by and save her. Save Shannon. So if they ran out of medicine tonight, that would be okay.

Dianne knew how to open the childproof bottle. She had watched her mother closely, in the way that children who are left to look after themselves often observe their part-time care-givers, knowing that sooner rather than later they'll have to perform those same actions alone. Dianne applied pressure with her palm and turned the cap to the left. It came off easily, now that she had done it so many times in the past two days. She tried to make sense of the letters on the bottle, sounding out the few words she could. If she were in the other reading group, she probably could have read those words. But Mrs. Coleman, her kindergarten teacher, had put Dianne with the rainbows instead of the butterflies. Everybody knew that the butterflies were smarter than the rainbows. "Sweetie, if you can make it to school a little more often, maybe you can move up to the but-terflies." How many times had Dianne gotten herself up, gotten dressed, and walked into her mother's room only to find Joyce Ann sprawled out on the bed, looking like the capital letter "X"?

And then she'd look over and see Shannon right next to her mother. Who would care for Shannon when she crawled out of bed looking for something to eat? What if she stuck her finger in an outlet? What if she was wearing that same diaper when Dianne got home from school? What if she cried until her eyes were red and puffy? Dianne couldn't go to school on those "X" days. She just couldn't. Maybe next year, in first grade, she would get to go to school more often.

Dianne rushed back to Shannon's side now, propped up Shannon's head in the crook of her elbow, and poured the last of the medicine down her sister's throat. "Swallow it, Shan-non," Dianne whispered desperately. "It will make you all better."

Shannon's eyes fluttered. Instinctively Dianne lifted one of her sister's eyelids, expecting Shannon to fight the movement and awaken with a cry. Instead, Dianne saw Shannon's eye-

ball slowly roll backward. Dianne dropped the empty bottle of cold medicine and shook her sister. "Shannon! Shannon! Wake up! Stop doing your eyes like that! Wake up!"

But Shannon wouldn't wake up. The color in Shannon's body was all gone except for a pinkish rash on her cheeks and arms. Dianne rushed to the counter and squeezed lotion into her hands to soothe the rash. That's what her mother would have done.

Dianne convinced herself to sleep that night, clutching to the hope that everything would be all right tomorrow, when Aunt Gloria came by. She prayed for her cousin Regina to get better.

The next morning, without even opening her eyes, Dianne placed her hand on Shannon's forehead. Cold. Clammy. Felt like plastic. Dianne, in her innocence, was relieved to know that her sister didn't have a fever anymore. And then she heard the front door open. Finally, relief.

Dianne jumped out of bed and ran to the front door, only it wasn't Aunt Gloria. It was her mother and Otis. What an odd homecoming, with everyone wearing exactly what they'd been wearing the last time they saw one another.

"Momma, Shannon is sick," Dianne spoke first.

"Did you give her medicine?" Joyce Ann asked.

"Yeah, I gave her the red medicine in the cabinet."

"That ain't for kids!" Otis shouted as he pushed Dianne aside and rushed toward the girls' bedroom.

Dianne's stomach churned as she waited for a word from Otis. He would tell her what an awful job she'd done, how Shannon needed to get a shot or how they needed to run out and get more medicine right away. But instead, Otis cried out, "She's dead! Joyce Ann, she's dead! Come here!"

Joyce Ann screamed a horrid, long shriek as she ran past Dianne. Sounded like someone had stabbed her in the heart.

Dianne's own heart tore, right down the center. The pain was almost tangible, a throbbing, drowning feeling. Dianne knew what death was. The next thing Dianne knew, she was latched onto Shannon's body, her arms and legs wrapped around the corpse, screaming unintelligible words, writhing in emotional anguish. She wanted to say, "I'm sorry! Come back!" but the words got all twisted on the way up the path from her heart to her mouth.

Having grown up near a slaughterhouse, Otis thought Dianne's jumbled words sounded like the torrential, wild squeal of pigs. That cry, forever etched in his mind, was the realization of final pain, of knowing that this was the end, that the end would be painful, and that there was not one single thing you could do to stop it.

The end was nearing for Otis, too. His grief was tempered only by the fact that this whole thing looked like a crime scene to him. He would have to suspend his pain—assuming that Shannon was his child—while he figured out what to do. "Get her off!" he screamed to Joyce Ann, who was really in no better position than Dianne. Her baby was dead.

"Get off! Crazy! You're gonna put bruises on her! Help me pull her off, Joyce Ann! Do you want to go to jail?" His train of thought registered with Joyce Ann immediately. As much as it pained her, she would have to stop and think. Think.

"Sugarbee, baby, let her go," Joyce Ann wailed. "Let her go, baby." Joyce Ann put her hand on Dianne's arm, and, like a desperate animal, Dianne bit into her mother's rough, ashen skin.

"Ow!" Joyce Ann jerked back her hand.

"Aaaah!" Dianne screamed and kicked when both adults, working in unison, managed to pry her from Shannon's body.

"You let go of her!" Otis wrestled Dianne away from the bed altogether, pinned her onto the floor, and screamed into

her wet face, "This is all your fault anyway! If it weren't for you, she wouldn't be dead!" Those words went straight from Otis's mouth to Dianne's, where she inhaled them deeply. The language began to ricochet in her tiny spirit. *My fault?* Still, Dianne held the air, those words, in her lungs. In an instant, Dianne looked over Otis's shoulder to Joyce Ann. Dianne's eyes pleaded for exoneration, permission to release the words Otis had spoken into her soul. A simple "No, it ain't her fault" or "Don't say that" would have done. But Joyce Ann simply lowered her eyes.

It must be true, then. It is my fault, *Dianne thought. Then she gulped down Otis's words. That is how the guilt came to live deep within her tiny spirit.*

When Otis let her go, Dianne did what any guilty child would do: She found a hiding place while the chaos around her escalated. There was quick, frantic talk amid yelling. "Hush up, Joyce Ann!" she heard. "Wait! Let me pull up the covers first," was whispered.

Then she heard her mother on the phone. "We need an ambulance! My baby's . . . she's not breathing!"

Dianne knew that she was in trouble when the ambulance came roaring down the street. Its flashing lights in the middle of a summer morning brought about misplaced memories of Christmas.

"Dianne, open up!" Joyce Ann bammed on the bathroom door. "Open this door now!"

Slowly Dianne unfurled from her foxhole between the toilet seat and the dirty-clothes hamper. With the slightest turn of the lock, Joyce Ann whisked through the door and knelt down to Dianne's level, grabbed her shoulders, and shook the child with every word. "Dianne, you keep your mouth shut, you hear? If they ask, you tell them that you got up in the middle of the night and gave your sister some medicine. You *slept in the bed with her while me and Otis slept in our bed, and when we all got up, she was dead. You hear, Dianne? You hear me?"*

The child's reply sounded more like a surrender. "Yes, ma'am, okay, okay, Momma."

When the police came, Dianne told them exactly what Joyce Ann told her to say. And she didn't even try to cross her fingers or her legs or her tongue this time. What was the harm in telling a lie after you'd already killed someone?

The invitation to Aunt Gloria's wedding had come in the mail just three weeks ago, and since that time Dianne's emotions had traveled up and down like an equally weighted seesaw. Her first thought was to do what she always did: send a gift and a note with a skittish explanation why she couldn't be there. A big deadline at work; she was just getting over the flu; she had to work double shifts because someone at work was sick.

But this time Aunt Gloria had followed the invitation with a call. "Hey, Sugarbee! How you doing?"

"Oh, I'm fine, Aunt Gloria. I got your invitation, but I won't be able to make it," Dianne's voice descended. "I'll be sure and send you a gift."

"I'd rather have you than a gift." Gloria stood her ground, looping her index finger through the phone cord. Her wedding day wouldn't be complete without Dianne.

"Well, it's just that . . . I have a huge project I'm working on at my job and—"

"Dianne, have I ever asked you for anything?" Gloria interrupted Dianne with a blow she had hoped she'd never have to deliver.

Dianne's jaw dropped, her stomach tightened, and her mind went blank. She didn't have an answer prepared for *that* one.

"Have I?" Gloria repeated.

"No, ma'am."

"I'm asking you to do this one thing for me, Sugarbee. Please come to my wedding. It means the world to me."

Dianne squeezed her eyes shut. She was a vacuum, taking in all the fear that constantly surrounded her. Fear, concentrated fear. In all the years she'd been living in Darson, no one had ever questioned her about the decision to move from Dentonville. Everyone understood that she needed to draw a line in the sand between the present and the past. "You don't know what you're asking."

"I do know what I'm asking. I'm asking you to come and be a part of this family again."

"I can't be a part of this family again."

"You can't stop being what you are, Dianne."

But Aunt Gloria didn't have to tell Dianne that. Dianne lived with who she was, all day every day. She was the little girl whose story unraveled in the Dentonville papers for weeks: "Parents Say Little Girl Was Dead When They Woke Up"; "Autopsy Reveals Child Died from Acute Meningitis"; "Investigation Results: Parents Charged for Leaving Children Home Alone"; "Charges Reduced to Child Endangerment—Nurse's License Expired, Testimony Inadmissible"; "Child Left with Sister's Corpse Will Be Taken In by Family Members." That was the public side of the case. The private headlines, however, read much differently in Dianne's mind: *Child Could Have Saved Sister If She'd Gotten Help Sooner; Girls' Mother Left and Never Looked Back.*

"So," Aunt Gloria said, snapping Dianne back to the present, "are you coming?"

Now a different set of headlines danced through Dianne's heart: *Aunt Provides Loving Home for Abandoned Child; Cousins Become Like Sisters to Girl Left with Corpse; Aunt Asks Child (Now Grown Up) to Come to Wedding as Token of Gratitude.*

"I'll be there."

Something within them both knew that after more than twenty years, it was time to stop running.

Chapter 1

*J*oyce Ann cursed the sunlight as it streamed through the slats in the blinds. Once again, God had ignored her prayer. He had kept her alive through the night. She pulled a pillow over her head and trapped the air in her lungs for a moment, wondering how long it would take to suffocate. Sometimes she felt like killing herself; other times she did not.

It wasn't *all* her fault. Some of it was, but not *all* of it. Pondering blame ushered thoughts of her sister, Gloria, and the money order—or rather, the absence of the money order. Joyce Ann tossed the pillow to the floor and sat up slowly. Her brain needed time to catch up with her body. She jumped, startled by movement on the mattress. She tried to replay the night before, but it was either too early or too late in the morning for her to think; her mind had pressed "rewind" without pushing "stop" first. Whoever the man next to her was, he sure slept soundly. Probably Greg, but it didn't matter. Men were like interchangeable paper dolls to Joyce Ann.

Joyce Ann scooted her behind to the edge of the mattress and then heaved herself up to a standing position. Maybe, if Gloria sent that money order, she could afford a decent box spring. That would be a couple of hundred dollars. Then the thought occurred to Joyce Ann: *do you know how much vodka you could buy with a couple of hundred dollars?* No, she wasn't going to spend good money on a box spring.

The room could have used a lot of things: a rug, sheets for the mattress, a lamp, clothes to decorate the closet. So far she'd done nothing more to add life to this dank, stuffy room than to bring in a bed on which to sleep (or repay debts), a table for divvying up drugs, and a trash can for straightening up when she had a mind to.

Joyce Ann shuffled across the stained carpet, grabbed her mailbox key, and walked barefoot past two buildings to the apartment complex's mail cage. It was early. The air was still light and promising, as if anything could happen today. Birds whistling, dew bathing the grass, and four little girls in a huddle, slapping hands and clapping to the tune of "Rockin' Robin" while they waited for the school bus. For as much mess as she had in her life, Joyce Ann did still appreciate the morning in all its blazing, annoying glory. She pulled her sweatshirt tighter around her torso and shivered as a breeze cut through the thinning fleece. Her hair flopped down against her cheeks with every step, reminding her of better days, when her hair was her best asset. Everyone always said she had "good" hair. With split ends, matted clumps, and graying roots, her hair was anything but good now. It was chaos, but that was fitting. A metaphor for her entire life.

Joyce Ann approached the red mail cage cautiously. She didn't want to walk up on something she shouldn't see or couldn't get out of. All manner of evil went on in that cage: drug deals, sex (consensual and nonconsensual), robbery. When she saw that the coast was clear, she unlocked the gate and made sure it clicked behind her. The concrete floor was littered with junk mail and newspaper. Quickly she put her key into the box, turned the lock, and pulled her mail from the slot. After getting a glimpse of the envelope from Gloria,

Joyce Ann happily skipped back to her apartment, making mental plans for the money her sister sent monthly.

Every once in a while Gloria would send a little less money, with a note explaining that she had an unexpected expense and that she'd double up the next month. She'd add, "I'll make some calls and see about getting you some sewing work on the side." Joyce Ann would smile inside to read those words, glad to know that she wasn't the only one struggling. Glad to know that Gloria wasn't really getting ahead. "Got a college degree and can't even afford to send money regular," Joyce Ann would laugh to herself. "Now, who's the stupid one? Who's the useless one?" Satisfied that Gloria wasn't too much better off than she, Joyce Ann would wait patiently, take a quick sewing job, and imagine that Gloria had taken a part-time job to catch up.

The only other time Gloria didn't send money was when she'd paid for Joyce Ann's care in one rehab or another. Joyce Ann had been in more step programs than a toddler learning to walk. Two steps forward, three steps back, then flat on your behind. But she humored Gloria every now and then for the chance to stay in the nicer rehabs. It might have cost Gloria an arm and a leg, but so far as Joyce Ann was concerned, Gloria owed every penny of it.

Greg met her at the doorway. "I'm out."

"Bye."

All the more money for Joyce Ann. After paying the all-inclusive rent and buying a few groceries, she could do what she wanted with the rest. Better yet, she might look through the paper and see if there was another all-bills-paid, first-month-free complex she could move to and skip out on her current lease. That would free up even more money. But to do that, she'd need to work for at least a few weeks to show income.

Joyce Ann tore through the envelope and found the money

order. It was wrapped in a piece of paper, as usual. And, though Joyce Ann hated to admit it, she was happy to see that her sister had written a note:

Joyce Ann,

This may be the last money order I'll be able to send you for a while. I'm getting married next month, and my husband and I will be joining our accounts. I'll send you money when I can. In the meanwhile, I'll see if I can get you some work.

Gloria

In disbelief, Joyce Ann read the note over again and again. "What you mean, you'll send money *when you can?* Get me some *work?*" Joyce Ann screamed. "Who does she think she is? She doesn't *deserve* to be happy, Miss Goody Two-shoes teacher!" The bare walls screamed back at her.

Suddenly, Joyce Ann wasn't so grateful anymore. How dare Gloria leave her out to dry! Again! Furious, Joyce Ann stuffed everything she owned into the wooden chest with wheels on the end. Gloria May Rucker-Jordan might have tried to dance around Dentonville like she was the belle of the ball, but she would never be rid of the bricks sewn into the hem of her gown. Joyce Ann would see to that.

Chapter 2

$\mathcal{W}$hite lines stitched the road beneath the bus window, lulling Dianne into a hypnotic trance. Each line drew her closer to the mosaic of her past—sharp, painful shards jutting into softer memories that she cherished. Were it not for the bad, the good might have sustained her. But the bad was too bad, and the good wasn't good enough to shield her from the nightmares that attacked her when she least expected them.

This morning she had taken a deep breath, blinked back the tears, and forced her feet to keep swinging out, one in front of the other. She went through the motions as though gliding on a moving sidewalk, the belt pulled by a higher Power she used to know well. Using her body as His glove, He guided her as she packed her bags, arrived at the bus station, and found a fourth-row window seat.

Driving would have been preferable, but she needed a new set of tires to make this trek. She might even have had the money for the tires if she hadn't spent so much of it buying men. Credit cards are no good once they're maxed.

She'd dressed conservatively for the occasion, wearing a pair of black slacks and a red V-neck with enough length and bulk to fold under at the waist, concealing the block of fat collecting at her midsection. Her feet were smooth and polished, with the nails painted a deep crimson that matched her blouse. A pair of black, strappy sandals added a few inches to her height and (she hoped) subtracted a few pounds from her plump frame. Big, brown, bouncy curls met with her shoulders to form a perfect frame around this face she'd put through all kinds of torture in preparation for this day. Exfoliating, tweez-ing, waxing, and pulling until every hair that was left stood in its rightful place, and every pore pulled its tightest to grant a faultless brown slate. Her final touches included diamond teardrop earrings and the latest designer fragrance, guaranteed to keep her smelling like a lady of elegance until well after five in the afternoon. Everything to give the appearance of normality or better, even if she wasn't feeling it.

Thank goodness for two-for-one bus fare. She had brought a man along to serve as a distractor—something to do if the memories threatened to press the sky down onto her head, as they often did when she sat still too long and left her mind to its own devices. Like now.

"Did you remember to turn off the iron?" she asked him, knowing that she had already double- and triple-checked to make sure the cord was unplugged.

"Yeah," James grunted, annoyed with Dianne's interruption. He had been admiring the woman attached to the pretty brown leg that protruded into the aisle two rows ahead. His eyes had traveled her whole body as she boarded the bus, and the journey had been a pleasant one from one end to the other. He was sure that he'd interpreted the woman's glance correctly and that she was interested. Now James hoped that he could slip her his phone number when the opportunity presented itself.

Dianne reached into her oversized drawstring purse and pulled out one of the *Essence* magazines she'd planted for such a time as this. It bloomed right there on her lap, with advertisements splashing across the pages. Red lipstick. Golden hair color. Lavender nail polish. A purposeful, entertaining bouquet to keep her mind off the menacing black milestones that lay ahead.

Her thoughts pacified, Dianne took a cleansing breath and let her gaze return to the window. That's when she read the sign that seemed to flash solely for her: "Dentonville 22." Twenty-two miles from the people who had given her the best definition of love yet. Twenty-two miles from the place where she'd first believed in Him.

Twenty-two miles from misery, too.

The last stretch had changed dramatically. Planned communities and home improvement stores packed on top of her old mental picture of Dentonville, making the town seem even more warped than before. When there was just dry earth to remember, the past fit the scenery. But now, with beautiful homes and shopping centers settling into the soil, Dentonville seemed to her a mansion built on top of a cemetery.

As the bus pulled into old downtown, she grasped what she could of the good. The candy store with the big sucker for a door handle. Tolbert's. The barbershop with its red-and-white-striped pole. But the pole wasn't moving anymore. It had just stopped one day, Dianne imagined. And everyone in the shop must have come out to stare at it, as though this rod were an extension of the earth's axis, and time stood still. Refused to budge because there had been a malfunction. Maybe the owner had even called to see about getting it repaired, but he couldn't because the parts didn't exist. Dianne decided then that the barbershop wasn't good or bad. Rather, it was reality.

"Oh, I think I left something in my seat," James announced after they stepped off the bus, just as he'd planned.

"I didn't see anything," Dianne assured him as they walked toward baggage claim.

"I . . . I think I'd better double-check," he insisted. He set off toward the bus, hoping that the woman with pretty legs would still be seated. He found her where he'd passed her, in the second row. The view from above her was just as inviting: a crucifix barely visible in the cranny between a set of breasts that defied gravity.

James tore his eyes from her beckoning chest long enough to introduce himself. "Hello. My name is James."

She licked her lips in a slow, purposeful circle, re-creating the lost shine of her cheap lip gloss. "Call me Mika."

"I'd like to call you *tomorrow,*" James said, sneaking a peek outside the window because (he smiled inside) a true player knows how to keep his eyes on two women at one time.

"Well, I don't mind. But what will your *girl* have to say about that?" She blinked seductively and cocked her chin to one side.

James clicked his inner cheek between his back teeth and dismissed the question with another one. "Do you see any rings on these fingers?" He waved his hands before the girl like a magician before saying "abracadabra."

They exchanged numbers, and James slithered back to Dianne as she waited near the baggage claim station. "Did you find what you left?" The tone in Dianne's voice scraped James up one side and down the other. She knew his game, he gathered, but he had already told Dianne in no uncertain terms that this relationship was completely open. Dianne had no problem with that. In fact, she had a sincere appreciation for the fact that James didn't hound her about a commitment, as some of the men in her little red book had been known to do.

Yet this blatant "macking" in her presence was downright dis-respectful, and she planned to cross his name off the standby list as soon as they returned from this trip.

Then again, James was good for a couple of reasons: he wasn't married, and he was usually available because he didn't keep a steady job. James's companionship might have cost her financially, but it was worth every penny if it meant she didn't have to be alone.

Dianne grabbed two of their three bags from the conveyor belt. James grabbed the lightest bag, and they walked toward the exit doors. The smell of fresh-baked bread went up through her nostrils and straight down to the pit of her empty stomach, drawing attention to the fact that she hadn't eaten since the night before. And even then, she'd only shuffled cold clumps of pasta around the plate in a game of mental musical chairs. The melody in her mind was like an old vinyl album playing a song that she should have been able to appreciate were it not for the crackle and the massive scratch that caused the chorus to replay itself over and over again.

She had opened a quick credit account at Target and bought gifts for them all. She had a gift for Regina's baby, of whom she'd only seen pictures. A set of his-and-hers towels for the newlyweds. Dianne didn't witness too much of what happened on the stomping grounds firsthand. She'd received invitations to her cousin Yolanda's graduation ceremonies for both her master's and doctorate degrees but only sent back gifts to stand in her place. She'd been invited to Regina's wedding but had called with her usual excuses about work and being busy with school. Anything to avoid coming back to Dentonville. She didn't have any trouble talking to her family, but seeing them was another story. Dianne counted it a miracle that she still kept in touch with them, given that packing up, leaving, and never looking back seemed to run in her bloodline.

Her original plan had been to come in the night before the wedding and leave immediately after the ceremony, with as little fanfare as possible. However, the bus schedule wouldn't accommodate her wishes. She'd have to stay a little longer, but maybe the extended trip would buy her another decade of distance.

Dianne preferred the distance of Darson, two hundred miles from the horrid memories. In Darson, Dianne could lay her eyes on fresh scenery. It was a fast, busy city that didn't slow down long enough to let her mind roam. There was always a movie to catch, a restaurant to try, an attraction to see, a new man to do. Not to mention the extra hours she could put in at work. If she kept her schedule full enough, she might plunge into bed, too exhausted for thoughts or dreams. She'd done a good job of staying away from Dentonville.

But Dianne couldn't sidestep Aunt Gloria. She loved her too much.

Chapter 3

*Y*olanda gave her house one last glance; arranging and rearranging the throw pillows on the couch that her sister had insisted she purchase. They seemed such nuisances, serving no practical function other than to saw on her nerves. For the second time now, she flipped on the bathroom light switch to make sure there was toilet paper on the roll. She smacked her lips and rushed in to realign the hand towels. Then she pivoted and pulled back the black shower curtain again, as though something might have had opportunity to grow in the tub since she scoured it an hour ago. She opened the closet door to make sure the towels were facing the right way: stripe on the right and facing her.

She went through the whole house this way—made sure labels were facing forward, drawers were flush, comforters lay flat. Her sister, Regina, used to tease her, "Girl, it takes you half an hour to clean up after you clean up."

Yolanda's appearance was the last thing to undergo scrutiny. Her tailored denim pantsuit was so heavily starched that it could have stood up on its own. There was only one cleaner who could do it the way she liked it. The red tank top was a perfect complement to the indigo of her suit, and she concluded the outfit with silver accessories and red mules. Not one for wearing much makeup, Yolanda had only to inspect her eyebrows and lip gloss this time around. She leaned in closer to the mirror and made sure that not so much as a millimeter had shot up through the undesirable follicles between her eyebrows. Yolanda had to keep her eye on that—that unibrow could get out of hand real quick. Aside from the brow, Yolanda couldn't alter what was left: light brown skin, almond-shaped eyes, nothing but naturally produced oils on her skin to keep that healthy glow.

Okay, now she could leave. Everything was perfect.

When she was satisfied that there was no more time left to clean, Yolanda made a full circle back to the living room and reached into her purse to check her cell phone for the fourth time, making quadruple-sure that it was powered. She didn't want to miss a call from Dianne en route to the bus station.

As Yolanda pulled the phone from its leather case, a business card fell out onto the floor, which was exactly where it naturally belonged. The card was from a man she had met at a gas station, of all places. He was a few inches taller than she was, wearing black slacks and a neatly starched shirt in a shade of mauve that only a man who's secure in himself can wear. He drove a white Camry, and Yolanda inspected it while he introduced himself. Older model, but not a spot or a wrinkle. Here was a man who knew how to "keep things up," as her great aunt Toe would say. Yolanda liked his crisp style, which was the only reason she accepted his card in the first place. But when he turned to go back to his vehicle, Yolanda noticed that he'd missed a belt loop. A whole belt loop. How does a grown man walk out of the house without checking himself from every angle? Simple: he doesn't pay attention to what cannot be seen. Socks probably had holes in 'em. Underwear, too.

Yolanda picked his card up off her freshly mopped floor, pushed her trash can's pedal, and tossed the card into the abyss.

Her phone rang—Dianne. It was time.

Though Yolanda spoke to Dianne off and on, she hadn't seen her cousin in years—wasn't even sure they'd recognize each other. In the eye of Yolanda's mind, Dianne was still in her early twenties.

Thankfully, Yolanda caught a glimpse of her cousin from afar. "Hey, girl," she said, realizing that she spoke only to herself since the window was still up. Kind of like elevator self-talk. She waved to Dianne from her car, though she wasn't quite sure that Dianne had seen her through the sun's glare on the tinted windows. Yolanda was late but just in time to avoid having to park in the lot and get out to look for her. The evening buses arrived with few passengers, even on weekends. She'd offered to buy Dianne a plane ticket, but Dianne had refused the offer. One look at the man beside Dianne explained her refusal.

Dianne had the same slight smile that Yolanda remembered. Her hair swayed with each step she took toward the curb. She'd put on a little weight but looked all the better for it. Yolanda and her older sister, Regina, used to tease Dianne about having a fat face. Finally, her body had caught up with her plump cheeks. She looked like a full-figured model, precisely proportioned to resemble a beefed-up skinny girl.

This john she had brought along walked with his hands in his pockets, leaning to one side, looking like Lenny-who-got-plenty from *Good Times*. Yolanda took a deep breath and told herself not to trip, that Dianne was a grown woman. If she wanted to keep fooling around with these weird men, that was her business. Dianne was still her cousin, her girl. And Yolanda blew a puff of air from her nose and put her judgment in check. She would respect Dianne's decisions.

Yolanda let down her window and called, "Hey, Dianne!" One of the benefits of living in a town with a population of nine thousand: you could act country in Dentonville. Dianne waved back and motioned for Yolanda to pull up a little closer. She got as close to them as possible, about twenty feet away, and then parked. The sensors chimed as Yolanda got out of the car to hug her estranged cousin.

"Aah! Hey, Yo-yo. Girl, look at you!" Dianne leaned back and looked her over from bottom to top.

"You ought to quit!" Yolanda hugged her again. Yolanda was happier to see Dianne than she thought she would be. Once upon a time they had been more like sisters. Yolanda took her turn, getting a good look at Dianne. "Girl, you look so good!"

She didn't accept the compliment. "Please, fat as I am? But look at you! What have you done to your hair?"

"I whacked it all off." Yolanda did a little pivot on the balls of her feet, stopping in midswing to give Dianne the profile of her tapered haircut. The bulk of her hair was brown, but she'd recently incorporated a bronze frost to accent her skin and light brown eyes.

Dianne ran her hand along the nape and gasped, "Aunt Gloria almost killed you, didn't she?"

"Girl, she cried for days. But you know how much I hate hair." Yolanda had been one of the first to jump on the bandwagon when the short, cropped styles made their debut. Maybe long hair was all that back in the day, but in Yolanda's experience, long hair was more trouble than it was worth.

"It makes you look so professional and powerful. I love it!" Dianne shrieked.

"Thank you." Yolanda smiled, her jaw muscles hurting from this unusually long set of push-ups. "I am so glad to see you. Momma's going to be so happy that you made it."

"Oh, Yo-yo, I'm sorry." Dianne stepped aside and introduced the man with her, "This is James. We're . . . together." She clasped her hands in front of her and waited for Yolanda's reaction.

Yolanda's face asked the question: *so what does that mean?*

"We're dating," Dianne lowered her head and whispered under her breath.

"Hi, James." Yolanda stepped forward a little to shake his hand. He didn't bother to fish his hand out of his pocket. Rather, he gave Yolanda that "what up?" gesture—you know, the one where you jerk your head back and tip your chin real quick? Yolanda just knew the next words out of his mouth were gonna be "What's your sign, baby?" But instead he said nothing, let his nod do the talking.

Dianne was a little embarrassed, and Yolanda was already suspicious, but this was Dianne's life, Dianne's choice. If she was happy with him, Yolanda would try her best to be civil to him, because if *anybody* deserved to be happy, it was Dianne.

"We'd better get going. The rehearsal dinner is in just a few hours," Yolanda said, leading the way back to her car. Dianne grabbed her purse and tugged the larger suitcase for a minute before Yolanda went over and helped her haul it to the trunk. James helped himself into the backseat of the car before Yolanda and Dianne even had that heavy suitcase patted down into the trunk. There was something wrong with the picture.

Yolanda had another self-talk: *All right, now, this is just what you've been praying about. Keep your mouth shut. Don't jump to conclusions. You don't have to put your two cents into everything, right or wrong. Just pray for him.*

Dianne jumped, ignoring the fact that her man had just proven himself a boy. Against every ounce of righteousness in her, Yolanda withheld commentary; overlooked it like a bad odor among strangers.

"Where's Regina?" Dianne asked Yolanda as they pulled from the curb and into traffic.

Yolanda shifted gears, looked behind her, and drove smoothly to the stoplight. "Oh, she'll be there. She's been so busy with the baby that I told her to stay at home and rest up for tonight and tomorrow. Actually, we already rehearsed because there was so much stuff that needed to be done. The timing was a little off. So, I guess this is a rehearsal dinner without the rehearsal."

"How old is the baby now?"

"He'll be four months old on the fifteenth. He is so cute, Dianne. He looks just like his daddy. I told Regina, all she did was carry that baby for Orlando."

"I'll bet you and Regina and Aunt Gloria are spoiling him rotten," Dianne guessed correctly.

"Oh, there is so much cute little stuff out. We can't help it."

"So what have you been doing with yourself?"

"Just working," Dianne sighed, "working every day."

"You still into computers?"

"Yeah, I'm still hanging in there. The market is a little tough right now, but I've seen worse in other fields, so I'm not complaining."

"Yeah, it's tough all over the country right about now," Yolanda agreed with her. "It's a blessing to be employed through all this mess."

Old downtown still had its charm, its brick-paved streets dividing rows of mom-and-pop businesses. The older ones still had cash registers with bells that rang every time the cash drawer opened. The newer shops and specialty stores boasted neon signs and state-of-the-art displays, though their edifices sang songs of decades gone. Old and new together.

Past the railroad tracks, the planned communities began their bombardment of advertisements: three-foot signs boasting maximum square footage next to minimum prices, with an asterisk. The fine print was illegible from the road. When Dallas got too busy, those who wanted to keep their jobs but lose the city sought out the quaint, small-town atmosphere of Dentonville. With the city flee-ers came city crimes and city taxes. But they also brought about conveniences and higher property values for the natives. Yolanda's mother's house had doubled in value, and the extra property she owned would bring in a nice piece of change, too, as soon as she found the right tenant.

Here, on the newly developed side of the tracks, came light gray streets and houses so close together that you could see into your neighbors' kitchen, if they were the kind who didn't put up curtains. And there were a lot of those in the new section of Dentonville.

Dianne and Yolanda chitchatted as much as was appropriate with James in the car, and then Yolanda made an effort to include him in the conversation. Whether Yolanda did so to confirm her suspicions or to give him a second chance, Dianne couldn't be sure.

"So, James, have you ever been to Dentonville?" Yolanda asked. The question itself was a joke. The only time visitors came to Dentonville was to shop at the new outlet mall—and it wasn't all that. Just a bunch of overpriced knockoffs.

"Aw he—" he stopped himself just shy of profanity. Rephrased his response. "Naw, I never even heard of Dentonville until now."

Suspicions confirmed.

"Ooh, James, look." Dianne tapped on her window. "There's that Nike outlet I told you about."

He perked up quickly, craning his neck to catch a preview of the store. "We gone have to check that out before we leave."

"How long do you plan to be in town?" Yolanda asked Dianne.

"We'll be here until Tuesday. I've got a few more days of vacation time I need to use up before November."

This led to Yolanda's next question. When she had thought that Dianne would come alone, the boarding arrangements were simple—Dianne would stay either with her or with Regina and Orlando. But with James here, things were questionable. "Where are you guys staying?"

"Well . . ." Dianne held her breath. "I was thinking maybe . . . we could stay with you."

"I really don't . . . We'll have to talk about it," Yolanda told her. This was a conversation better left between two women.

They drove back to Yolanda's house and got unwound for a little while before getting all wound up again for the dinner. Dianne took a shower in the hallway bathroom while Yolanda freshened up in the master bedroom. James parked himself on the sofa, took the remote in his hand, and commenced to flippin' through channels like a madman. Mind you, he didn't ask for permission to turn on the television, let alone change the channel from Lifetime. It took everything in Yolanda to keep from making a comment about his lack of home training.

Dianne knocked on Yolanda's bedroom door. "Can I come in?"

"Yeah," Yolanda called to her from the bathroom. Dianne came into the bathroom and stood beside Yolanda as she applied a fresh coat of lip gloss. In Dianne's eyes, the bright vanity lights made Yolanda look like a glamorous showgirl about to go onstage. Her eyes twinkled, her teeth glistened, and her skin glowed. In her youth, Yolanda hated the excess oil on her skin. But then again, in her late twenties, that oil was working to make her a living testament to the African-American adage "black don't crack."

"I used to watch you and Regina work magic with curling irons and makeup," Dianne said. "Even though I was the oldest, I wanted to be just like y'all." She squeezed behind Yolanda and made her way to the toilet seat. She sat on the stool and looked up at Yolanda the same way she had years before. She pushed her knees together and spread her feet apart, hiding her hands in her lap, just like she used to.

"Girl, please. Don't try to be like me. I'm not Jesus," Yolanda told her.

"Hmm. Aunt Gloria used to say that all the time."

"She was right, you know?"

"Yeah. I know." Dianne watched her a little longer, this time setting her elbow up on the counter and letting her chin rest on her hand.

For Yolanda, this moment of déjà vu, this easing back into old familiar roles was both comforting and menacing, somewhere between being in the spotlight and under the microscope.

"Yo-yo, about what you said earlier. You wanted to talk. About me and James and where we're going to stay." She slid into the topic carefully. "I mean . . . we're all adults here. It's not like we're kids, you know?"

Yolanda was hesitant, contemplating which part of her tongue she'd have to bite. She didn't want to come off like she was judging Dianne, because she truly wasn't. And Yolanda didn't want to sound like she was Dianne's mother, because

God knows Dianne really never had one. But Yolanda had her convictions. She had to answer to God for what went on under the roof He'd put over her head, even if Dianne wasn't her child.

"I know we weren't raised like this, but . . . like I said, we're grown. We all know about real life. So . . . is it okay if James and I stay here until Tuesday?"

"Dianne, you know I love you. And you know that I respect whatever decisions you make for yourself. But I also have to respect my house and myself. I can't let you two sleep together under this roof if you're not married."

Dianne laughed at herself and shook her head, then exhaled. "You haven't changed one bit, you know that?"

"I'll take that as a compliment. Besides, I just got this house built six months ago. I'm the only one who's lived here. This house is totally sex free. *I* haven't even had sex in here, so you know I'm not about to let somebody else be the first!"

"You got issues," Dianne teased, and stood, straightening out her pants with her hands.

Yolanda smiled back at her, looking down at her fat face like she used to back at Gloria's house. "Where's your phone book? I'm gonna call around and see about getting us a room somewhere."

"My phone books are at the top of my coat closet, right next to the front door," Yolanda directed her.

"Everything in its place, huh, Yo-yo?"

"You know it." Yolanda nodded.

Dianne hugged Yolanda one more time. "It's nice to know you're still the same, Yo-yo. Even if it means I won't have enough money to go shopping at the outlets while I'm in town!"

"Uh, you got a man in there." Yolanda pointed toward the living room.

"Please." Dianne rolled her eyes, looking as if she wanted to say something profane.

Yolanda didn't say anything, but Dianne knew that she'd let the cat out of the bag. Now, you have to understand. Gloria didn't have much to say when it came to men, because she didn't have one of her own. But rules number one, two, and three were: he must work. Yeah, they needed to be faithful and decent and respectful, but a sorry, lazy man was nothing but trouble from the get-go. Gloria got up on that soap box so often, the girls could mouth the sermon in their sleep. "That other stuff you can work on. You can teach a man how to treat you. But if he ain't got it in him to get his black behind out of bed every day and go to work, it's somethin' wrong with him. A real man ain't gonna sit up under you and feed off your breadcrumbs. You don't fool around with no man that don't want to work, 'cause his elevator ain't goin' all the way up!"

Dianne shrugged a little, avoiding Yolanda's eyes, and said, "He's in between jobs right now."

Yolanda reasoned within herself. *Okay, a man can actually be between jobs, Yolanda. It's when he has lost a job for whatever reason and he is about to get another one. That's called "in between jobs"; it does actually exist. There's been a lot of downsizing. Dot-coms have gone under. Lots of stuff has happened with the economy. Besides, this has nothing to do with you.* She left it at that because she didn't want to start sounding like her mother.

Dianne called from the kitchen as she searched through the phone book. "Which hotel is the closest to Richard's church?"

Yolanda rushed from her bedroom and stopped cold upon entering the living room. There was James, with his socked feet propped up on the edge of the table that Yolanda often used for dining. She could almost see the bacteria crawling from between the threads of cotton to the plate she might set down in another week or so. *I know he did not!* She didn't even take time to process the thought. "Get your feet off my table!"

James shot her a "who you think you talking to?" look, and Yolanda shot a "you" right back at him. He removed one foot in order to get his shoes, but let the other foot linger a little longer. By the time he'd finished putting on both shoes, Yolanda was back with the Clorox wipes, disinfecting the entire table as her guests looked on—James in annoyance, Dianne in embarrassment for both of them.

"I eat here sometimes," Yolanda huffed after she finished.

"Whatever." James flipped the channel.

Dianne called the first hotel in the phone book.

Chapter 4

*A*s much as Regina loved motherhood and Orlando Jr., there were days when she wished she could take it all back and return to the life she had lived before the baby. The whole "tote bag" routine was getting old, and Regina couldn't see how any woman in her right mind would go through childbirth or the dog-tired days of new maternity a second time, let alone a third.

Orlando thought it would be a great time to add to their small family. He was the third of five children raised in a loving biracial family where the house was always bursting at the seams with energy, music, and laughter—not to mention the complementing aromas of freshly made tortillas and fried chicken. "Baby, don't you want our kids to grow up close?"

"What kid-*s*? I'm not having any more kids." Regina's voice was chilly and stiff. She sucked in a deep breath and tried to snap the top button on a size ten checkered skirt that would have swallowed her before she got pregnant with Orlando Jr. She'd purchased a couple of new outfits for the occasion of her mother's rehearsal dinner, but neither of them seemed to fill the bill for tonight. It was painfully clear that she was getting bigger by the month. All the more reason to turn off the baby-making oven.

Orlando rolled over on his side to watch Regina try on a series of outfits that were still ten pounds out of her reach. Their master suite was the perfect aphrodisiac, with mirrors, candles, flowing draperies, and sexy little novelties that Regina picked up here and there to make their bedroom a love retreat. Little did he know that he'd picked the least appropriate time to talk to Regina about putting her body through nine months of alterations again. To him, she was beautiful. Though the outfits didn't fit the way they used to, she looked a whole lot better than some of his coworkers' wives. Besides, the best thing about Regina was her legs, and she was a long way from losing the slope that drove him crazy when she wore calf-length skirts—like the one she tried on now.

He smiled as he stuffed a satin throw pillow under his chin and took in the view. Regina stood, her bare feet flat on the carpet, facing their closet sliding door that doubled as a full-length mirror. Her long black hair flowed several inches down her back, a deep wave here and there. His wife was often mistaken for a teenager with her taut skin, bright eyes, and button nose. But once she opened her mouth, there was no mistaking her womanhood. She handled business.

This enigma was completely sexy to Orlando. Like her appearance, her personality had two sides. You rarely got what you saw. She could be ice-cold sometimes, but she could also thaw and melt and spread her love all over him when he pushed the right buttons.

"Baby, that looks good on you," Orlando hummed.

"Yeah, as long as the hook is hidden up under this top." Regina fussed and lifted the sleeveless knit tank so that Orlando could see the covert damage motherhood had done to her figure. "Do you see this?" She grabbed the flesh hanging over the rim of her skirt and pulled on it like a piece of bubble gum stuck to the bottom of a shoe. "This is what's left after having a baby. This fat ain't going nowhere, and I'm not about to add to it." Regina wondered sometimes how her husband's clear gray eyes could be so clouded.

"I think you're being overly concerned and selfish, Regina," Orlando ventured.

"Okay, how about if we just shave a big bald spot on the top of your head and let *you* go around looking like a middle-aged man? Deal?" she asked him, fully aware that losing his locks would be a devastating blow to Orlando.

Orlando forgot for a moment that he was talking to an attorney who just happened to be taking twelve months off to raise their son. "Regina, it's not that bad."

"But you agree that it *is* bad," she cornered him.

"It's not bad at all."

"Your words were 'it's not *that* bad.'"

"Please, Regina, I'm not about to play courtroom with you on this. I've told you for the past four months that you are a beautiful wife and the beautiful mother of our son, but I don't guess you're too thrilled about either predicament. Ay!" Orlando got up from the bed and walked out of their bedroom, leaving Regina to loathe her body in the mirror.

And loathe she did. Those minuscule changes in her appearance encircled her in a gay dance, taunting her the way the children at school used to when she was a child. She could hear them now: "Mirror, mirror, on the wall, who's the fattest of them all? Regina! Regina! Big fat Regina!" The teacher comes, her whistle signaling the end of their shift, and the tormentors scatter in different directions to make room for their replacements. The replacements came on the bus or into the lunchroom with blatant ridicule. There was more humiliation in the way the lunch ladies put a little less food on her plate.

Even at home there was no escape. Gloria's attempts to slim Regina down to Yolanda's and Dianne's size were undermined by Regina's late-night binges. Sometimes it didn't even matter that she would get a whipping in the morning for devouring an entire box of doughnuts. The high was worth the low because the low wouldn't be much worse than how she felt about herself for the other twenty-three hours in the day. The high, even if only for a minute, was paradise. Probably more joy than she deserved, she figured, but it was still all hers. A dozen powdered pieces of pleasure.

By the time Regina got to junior high school, she'd added a few more rolls to her torso but shed the shy and withdrawn aura. The pain turned to anger, and the anger built a wall. Regina decided that since she couldn't be beautiful, she'd be big and bold. She was loud and rude, her attitude a distraction from the body that she abhorred. She would gladly opt for hours in in-school suspension instead of the weigh-ins whenever it was time for the presidential fitness challenge. Time in the principal's office versus the humiliation of being picked last for a kickball team.

Truth was, however, Regina always had an undeniable natural beauty that couldn't be smothered beneath a million pounds. Her chocolate brown skin was faultless, a never-ending canvas that didn't need paint. Her eyebrows arched naturally, and that thing her eyelashes did was to die for—the way they bunched up on the lower lid so tightly that it looked as if she were wearing eyeliner, though she wasn't. Her lips pooched out just enough to accentuate the sultry line that movie stars pay thousands to create. Even on a bad day, Regina was more attractive than many of the smaller girls in her class. But she couldn't see that.

Because of her attitude, Regina almost lost her chance at her dream career as an attorney. Had it not been for a few big-girl-to-big-girl talks from Ms. Davey, an overweight African-American counselor at her high school, Regina would never have applied for all those scholarships that she was awarded. One thing led to another, and Regina was set for college. It was then that she realized, for all the names she'd ever been called, no one had ever called her "dumb."

Everything changed when Regina went to college. There, away from her small hometown of Dentonville, she met girls from every walk of life. Her roommate, a slender Latina with long brown hair and a personality that saw no size or color, was beautiful in Regina's eyes: five feet six, maybe 115 pounds soaking wet. Carlotta said she saw "fat" when she looked in the mirror, but somehow she didn't think Regina was all that fat. She did, however, concede that Regina could stand to lose a few pounds.

"Don't worry," Carlotta had said. "My dad's a doctor. I'll write you a prescription for Plathene; it's a weight-loss drug. I promise, you'll be thin by the end of the semester."

"You can do that?" Regina had asked in amazement, suspecting that what Carlotta suggested was probably a federal crime.

"How do you think I stay in shape? It certainly isn't because I like to eat right or exercise." Carlotta laughed and gave Regina a dismissive wave.

"I don't know about this, Carlotta. We could both end up in jail," Regina worried.

"I'll write it out to myself and give you the pills. If I get caught, my dad will hire a lawyer; they'll say I need counseling or something, and I'll go to rehab again for, what, a month?"

Regina knew that it might not be that simple, but Carlotta's welfare was the last thing on Regina's mind. If she could get her hands on those pills, her life would be changed forever. Regina agreed to the plan and all the tricks Carlotta taught her, including slathering on the vitamin E so that her skin would shrink right along with her body, and taking prenatal vitamins so that her body wouldn't give out. As a result of the strain she put her body through, her menstrual cycles were irregular to nonexistent (a bonus in Regina's eyes). She went from a size twenty to a size fourteen by December. Size eight by spring break. Head size from zero to one thousand by the end of the school year.

"Regina Jordan, is that you? You look so *good*!" people had said to her back in Dentonville. Everyone from church folk to the boys she'd had secret crushes on in high school seemed to notice her. Aside from her great-aunt Toe, who suggested on more than one occasion that Regina was "starting to look like she was on poppy seed and opium," Regina was received as new and improved. Strangers—what few there were in Dentonville—acknowledged her in the grocery store now instead of scanning her basket to see exactly what this fat girl was eating. She still had the same doughnuts, chips, and sodas in the basket, but that didn't matter anymore, because people looked at her *face,* and she was a part of the population now.

Carlotta inducted Regina into the clandestine world of weight management for those with no weight management skills. A dangerous recipe of binging here, fasting there, water pills, ephedrine-laced supplements, laxatives, an occasional purge, and working out to the point that they spent hours writhing from the painful tearing through their dehydrated muscles. Of those strategies, Regina came to favor fasting and diet pills. She could go a week on water and crackers, and she'd learned to use makeup to camouflage the dark circles that formed when her eyes threatened to unveil her secret. By the time she graduated from Smith-Preston, Regina had a bachelor's degree in criminology, but she was a master at matching the red line to the number 120 when she mounted the scale. Like clockwork, she lost three pounds every month in preparation for the three she would gain during PMS. Never, never would she let that hand go past 120. Granted, she would always be several pounds up from Carlotta due to the extra portion she carried on her backside, courtesy of genetics, but that was okay.

She crossed the line for the first time in her second month of pregnancy. Fear inched up her bones, and Regina could hardly breathe when she saw that red line to the right of her magic number. Her mind screamed, "What have I done?" But with Orlando taking such an active role in the pregnancy, and since she'd been on bed rest for the last ten weeks of the pregnancy under his watchful eye, Regina couldn't tiptoe around nutrition as she'd done for almost fifteen years. For the first time, someone actually prepared her food and watched her eat it. Regina knew that she'd beaten the odds by giving birth to a healthy baby, and, for what it's worth, she was thankful. She did have maternal instincts and a desire to give her baby every chance at survival, but old habits die hard.

Maybe, if the old tricks had worked again, she might have considered another baby. But her body wouldn't cooperate the same as it used to. It seemed to Regina that her metabolism had slowed down to zero while her appetite had gone into overdrive. Something had been thrown off with the pregnancy, and even with breast-feeding Orlando for a month, she still carried an extra twelve pounds. It might not have seemed like much to some, but life is different when you grow up fat, lose it all, and then become threatened by the fat again. Like being in prison, then having freedom, and then having someone refer to you by your number again. People don't think about numbers if they've never *been* a number. That number for Regina was her top weight of 229. In her mind, she wasn't 132 pounds; she was only 97 pounds from 229. Only 97 pounds from misery. And every day the red line bounced a little farther to the right, especially since she'd stopped breast-feeding.

Regina took one more look at the padding under her chin and the flab around her waist and decided that she was ugly and worthless and fat again. Then she promised herself that she would scrape the fat off her body one way or another.

Chapter 5

*Y*olanda blew her horn, and Regina came rushing out in a red sundress and jacket combination that hugged her in all the right places. Yolanda had always envied Regina for her shapely figure, and even now after giving birth Regina's body seemed to have more appeal than hers. Yolanda laughed to herself, thinking that even on her best day she'd never have a body like Regina's. And it would only get worse after having a baby—assuming that she'd meet the right man and get married, which was something that she wasn't holding her breath for.

"I like that dress," Yolanda said to her sister as she strapped on the seat belt.

Regina gave a grunt, but that was Regina. Everybody said she was mean, and Regina wore it like a badge. More than once Yolanda had suggested that Regina see a doctor about the mood swings, but Gloria fussed at Yolanda for bringing it up. "Just because you're a pharmacist doesn't mean you have to go around pushing drugs off on everybody. Some people are just sometimey, and your sister is one of them," their mother had said. Problem was, Yolanda didn't care to be around Regina during the sometimey times, and she was starting to wish, for the sake of her little nephew, that she hadn't listened to Gloria. A day like today should have been one of the good times, but Regina's attitude was stinking up the car.

"Put your seat belt on," Yolanda reminded her sister.

"Just go ahead and drive," was Regina's reply.

"I don't want to get a ticket—"

"Give me a break, okay? You are *not* going to get a ticket between here and the stop sign." It had always been Regina's pleasure to overthrow Yolanda's sense of order and watch her sister squirm when things weren't perfect.

Yolanda drove slowly until she heard the click, freeing her to ask the question she'd been holding since Regina came out of the house, without the carrier. "I thought you were going to bring the baby."

"Orlando will bring him later. Where's Dianne?"

"I dropped her off at her hotel so she could get checked in. She's our next stop."

"Why isn't she staying with you?"

"Well . . ." Yolanda pursed her lips and gave Regina a glance above the top of her glasses, replying tactfully. "She brought a guest."

"A man?"

Yolanda nodded, keeping her eyes on the road and re-minding herself to stay clear of judgment alley.

"Who is he?"

"Some guy. I don't know. Don't get me to lying."

"Yo-yo, you know what I mean. What *kind* of guy?" Regina probed her younger sister with all the expertise of an oldest child.

"His name is James." Yolanda's voice went up an octave in her attempt to refrain from spilling the beans about Dianne's friend, but it got harder and harder by the second. One more push and she would tip over.

"Is he crazy or what?" Regina shoved.

"He is *way* off, girl. No home training whatsoever," Yolanda spewed, took a deep breath, and closed the spout again. Regina leaned back, satisfied that the interrogation was successful. Dianne was still Dianne.

Regina got out and called Dianne from the house phone. They met in the lobby and exchanged smiles and hugs they'd both longed to give. "Girl, I've missed you." Regina shook her head.

"Don't start getting all sentimental on me now. I like my Reginas with bad attitudes."

"Shut up and come on."

"Now, *that's* the Regina I know," Dianne teased. They locked arms and walked to the car together.

A minute later the three yapped boisterously in Yolanda's car on the way to the rehearsal dinner at Macaroni Grill. It would be a twenty-mile trek, but to get a decent restaurant they had to get out of Dentonville. They talked about the time they cracked the watermelon trying to pick it up after Aunt Toe had specifically forbidden them to touch it. Dianne and Regina teamed up on Yolanda, insisting that it had been her idea to transport that thing from the floor to the counter in the first place. Then Yolanda brought up the time that Dianne tried to sign her own report card.

"And remember, the bad part was that Dianne thought an S was worse than an F," Regina howled and beat her hand on the seat.

"No, that's not the worst one," Dianne yelled. "You remember that time Aunt Toe got up there singing 'The Star-Spangled Banner' at church and she didn't even know half the words?"

Yolanda had to slow down to stay on the road as Dianne proceeded to mimic the blunder just as loud, as wrong, and as spirited as the day their great-aunt Toe was called upon to lend her anointed voice at the youth department's Independence Day tribute to the congregation's veterans. "If the rockets red hair! The bots bursting in there—oh, hallelujah—gave fruits to the whites, so now we all can share!"

"Whoo! Girl, stop!" Regina begged as she now beat the dashboard with her palm. "Stop!"

Dianne was breathless. She held her stomach, leaned back on the seat, and rolled her head on the headrest. She hadn't been this silly in a long time, and it felt good to be this free, her mind loosening the reins.

Yolanda's cell phone rang, and she answered it with laughter still in her voice. "Hello?"

"Yo-yo, where are y'all?" Gloria asked her daughter.

"We're on our way, Momma," she assured the bride-to-be. "You nervous, Momma?"

"No. What have I got to be nervous about? I'm coming up on sixty years old. I don't get nervous about much of anything anymore." Gloria's rapid rate of speech said otherwise, but Yolanda didn't want to argue with her.

"Okay, Momma, okay. Did the florist call you back?"

"Yeah. We've got all that taken care of. Everything is okay." She paused. "Yo-yo, you've got Dianne with you, right?"

"Yes, ma'am."

"Well, I just got word that Joyce Ann is in town," Gloria said.

"Oh." Yolanda's tone hushed the car.

Regina read her face and whispered, "What's the matter?"

"Nothing," Yolanda mouthed to her sister.

"Why?" Yolanda couldn't add any more to the question at the moment.

"I just know she's here." Gloria put a period at the end of

that line of questioning. "Aunt Toe talked to her this morning, said she's staying at the Holiday Inn on Main."

"Well, is that what you want?" Yolanda was fully prepared to uninvite her aunt Joyce Ann for the sake of her mother's special day.

"She's my sister. Can't do no harm in her coming."

"But, Momma, this is *your* day."

"She knows better," Gloria's voice swung high. "Believe it or not, Joyce Ann knows how to act. She'll be all right. But she's not the one I'm worried about—it's Dianne that I'm concerned with. How is she?"

"The same, I guess." Yolanda looked for the right words. Despite her sophisticated clothes and designer luggage, Yolanda wasn't sure that Dianne could keep herself composed around Joyce Ann.

Gloria continued, "Well, I didn't tell Joyce Ann about the rehearsal dinner tonight. I just told her I'd see her at the ceremony tomorrow afternoon. Let's pray about it. And talk to Dianne about it as soon as you get off this phone. I don't want her bumping into Joyce Ann around town."

"Yes, ma'am."

"Isn't she staying with you?"

"Um, she's gonna stay at a hotel."

"Why ain't she staying there with you?"

"Well, she brought a friend up with her, so they're gonna stay at a hotel."

Yolanda figured that Gloria must have been really nervous, because any other time she would have shoved that door right open. "All right, then, go ahead and tell her, Yo-yo. She needs to be prepared."

Yolanda held on to the phone after her mother hung up. Suddenly her heart was heavy. Why had Aunt Joyce Ann come to the wedding? She would ruin everything. No one had seen or heard from her in ages. True, she was family, but Yolanda preferred to pray for her at a distance. She loved her just like she loved everybody. But she did find it very hard to tolerate a woman who had abandoned her daughter at the worst possible point in the child's life. With the phone still in her hand, and nodding as though she were still having a conversation, Yolanda sent up a silent prayer.

Lord, I don't know why my aunt is here, and I don't know what she is thinking. But I ask that you would first remove the hard feelings that I have against her, because I don't want to be used by the devil this weekend. And I ask that you would help Dianne to get through this weekend with her head held high. I thank you again for sending my mother such a great person to spend the rest of her life with. Please don't let this weekend be a disaster. In Jesus' name I pray, Amen.

"What did she say?" Regina asked.

Somehow, Dianne already knew. "It's my mother, isn't it?"

"Yes."

"Take me back to the hotel," Dianne ordered.

"Dianne . . ." Regina tried to reason.

"I'm not playing, Yo-yo. I can't stay. Stop this car and turn around." Dianne's trembling voice betrayed her, and suddenly there sat the little skinny girl with toothpick legs whom everyone used to feel sorry for. Poor little Dianne, Joyce Ann's girl. The one that had to go live with Gloria and her girls after that god-awful incident.

Yolanda pulled into the parking lot of a gas station and stopped the car, hoping that she could persuade her dearest cousin to stay. She put the car in park and raised one knee onto the seat so that she could turn toward Dianne. Upon facing her, Yolanda could only take a deep breath and conquer her own tears. It always hurt to see Dianne so broken, so empty, that her body was nothing more than a chassis. Yolanda could only imagine how deep that pain had burrowed itself into Dianne's heart after all this time. "Dianne, you've come a long way to share this special time with us. Please don't leave. We want you here."

"Uh-uh." She sat with her arms crossed and her head turned to the side window as tears beat a familiar path up the crevices of her soul, then down their usual course on her cheeks.

"Dianne, it's not going to be the same without you. I mean, just a few minutes ago we were laughing and having a good time like we used to. We've missed you and we want you here. Besides, you haven't even seen my baby yet," Regina said.

"You don't understand." Dianne still couldn't look at them. "It took a lot for me to come back here and face these bad memories again. You two and Aunt Gloria and Aunt Toe are the only family I have, so I made myself do it. I figured I owed you guys that much. But if my mother is here"—she cried now, her shoulders sinking lower with every sob—"I just can't go. That's all there is to it."

"Dianne, you don't owe us anything. You're family," Yolanda told her. "We love you and we want you here to celebrate. Do I need to call my mom for you?"

"No, forget that." Regina folded her arms now and came up with a plan of her own. "If it comes down to a choice between Dianne coming to the wedding and Aunt Joyce Ann coming to the wedding, I'll see to it that Joyce Ann doesn't show up. Now, *that's* all there is to it."

"Look, I didn't come here to cause trouble, and I don't expect for you two or anybody else to understand. It's just too

hard. I can't do it. Take me back to the hotel." Dianne was re-
solved. She'd gone all the way up the roller coaster and all the
way down. Her appetite had vanished, and a headache came
in its place. *I knew this was a big mistake.*

"This is your home as far as I'm concerned." Regina rolled
her neck and repositioned her head, facing forward now. "If
there's anyone who ain't welcome, it's Aunt Joyce Ann, and
the more I think about it, the more I'm convinced that she is
not welcome to this wedding or anything pertaining to this
weekend's activities. Give me the phone, Yo-yo."

"No, we don't have to handle this tonight." Yolanda held
the phone in her hand still. "Aunt Joyce Ann doesn't know
about the rehearsal dinner, so she won't be there. Will you at
least come to the dinner, Dianne?"

Dianne sniffled and wiped her nose.

"Please." Yolanda gave Dianne a reassuring smile.

"Are you sure my mother doesn't know anything about
tonight?" Dianne asked.

"Positive."

"Who all is going to be there?"

Yolanda rattled off the list of invited groups, "Us, Orlando,
the baby, Aunt Toe, Momma, Richard, some of the members
of the church where he ministers, and a few of his relatives,
and some people Momma used to teach with. Not too many
people, I don't think."

Regina sighed. "I'm telling you, Dianne, if you need *me* to
handle this—"

"No, that's okay." Dianne's arms went limp and she blew
out a burden of air. "I'll do the rehearsal dinner, but that's it."

"It's gonna be okay, Dianne." Yolanda didn't know how
she knew this, but she had to say it in order to calm Dianne.
"Everybody is praying—it's gonna work out fine."

Dianne reminisced aloud, "Mmm. Aunt Gloria used to make us pray about everything."

"That's the only way to deal with *everything*," Yolanda said.

Dianne grinned a little. "I knew I'd been forgetting to do something."

Chapter 6

The tables were set with glasses, silverware, and glowing candles, creating an ambience of elegance. Later the room quickly filled with activity, and everyone let their hair down, cooing over the baby, exclaiming how good Dianne looked and how happy they were to see her again. Richard's natural and church family seemed to be having a family reunion of their own as well. Regina hadn't expected to see so many of his family members there.

Yolanda was dressed in a black pin-striped pantsuit, almost too professional for the occasion. Regina wished that her sister would show a little skin every now and then, but it was hard to get Yolanda out of her squeaky clean box. Gloria took the show that evening with a black, sleeveless slip dress. On a twenty-year-old the dress might have been simply appealing. But it was absolutely breathtaking on a woman who didn't just *have* it (as most twenty-year-olds do) but had managed to *keep* it well into her fifties.

Once they were all settled in, Richard thanked them for coming and sharing their joy. Just then Dianne noticed how handsome he was. He was a tall, bald-headed man with a thick and graying goatee. His rimless glasses were a contemporary accent to his aged tone. Dianne wished then that she knew her father. For as much time as she spent hating Joyce Ann, she didn't spend much time wondering about her father. Maybe he was as handsome as Richard. Maybe he towered over a roomful of people with his charisma and had the same booming, all-encompassing laugh as Richard. Maybe he was even a preacher. No, he couldn't be a preacher—not be a preacher and leave her like that.

Richard led them in a prayer of thanksgiving before the servers brought out their plates. Yolanda marveled at her mother's beauty, which always seemed to be enhanced when she was with Richard. Yolanda had never known how Gloria's whole face could warm up from the inside out when her love walked into the room. Yolanda saw it for the first time the night that Gloria introduced her and Regina to Richard, which was also the night he asked the girls for their mother's hand in marriage.

"Don't be askin' them—ask me!" Gloria had interrupted what would have otherwise been a tear-jerking moment.

Regina and Yolanda joked, *"Please* take her hand!"

Then Gloria had kissed him, right there in front of her daughters. Regina and Yolanda thought they would fall out of their chairs. They'd never seen their mother hold a man's hand, let alone kiss, before that night. They were aware that she'd gone out with men a few times (could have counted the number on one hand), but she never introduced them to any man she was seeing. She'd said she wouldn't do it unless she knew he was THE ONE.

Gloria was careful not to have men around her young, impressionable daughters. "Too much going on nowadays," Gloria had said once, many years ago, when Regina had asked her mother if she could meet the person she was going to the movies with. "I am a single mother with young daughters. I can't bring every Tom, Dick, and Harry around you."

"But Aunt Joyce Ann let me meet her boyfriend," Regina said with a mouthful of bread.

Gloria had abruptly ceased slicing the potatoes and asked Regina, her back still turned, "When?"

"Last time I spent the night over there with Dianne," Regina informed her. She was way too grown for her age. "His name is Michael. He has a dog."

"Did Michael spend the night over there, too?" Gloria held her voice steady, drawing out the entire story.

"Yes, ma'am. I think so." Regina smiled, hoping this would be the beginning of a new era when she would actually be able to meet the few male friends she suspected her mother had. Then she added, "The dog slept in the room with me and Dianne." Regina figured, if Gloria knew that Aunt Joyce Ann had introduced her man, maybe Gloria would follow suit. She could not have been more wrong.

Regina wasn't quite finished with that bread before Gloria was out that front door and headed down the street to Joyce Anne's place, the rental house. Now, it takes Gloria May and Joyce Ann Rucker to really demonstrate how to go tit for tat. They can go *at it*. That night the police got called out, and all the neighborhood was outside trying to see what was going on. People came out in rollers, house shoes, pajamas, and tattered robes. The neighborhood talked about it for days. Kept it going so until the pastor at church preached a sermon on brotherly love.

Aunt Toe said they had always fought like cats and dogs because Gloria was always trying to tell Joyce Ann what to do and Joyce Ann was always doing things to provoke Gloria. Whatever the problem was, they settled it that night, because Regina never went back to Joyce Ann's place again unless Gloria was with her. Up until the time Shannon died, Dianne came over to Regina's house all the time, but it would never again go the other way.

"Listen. Don't so much as borrow a cup of sugar from your Aunt Joyce Ann without me, you hear?" Gloria had threatened them.

"Why not?" Regina asked. She braced herself, unsure what had possessed her to question her mother. Fortunately, Gloria felt that Regina deserved to know as much as her vulnerable mind could handle. She knew that none of it made sense to the child. Regina idolized her Aunt Joyce Ann in all her beauty. Gloria had taught Regina that they were family, that blood was thicker than water, and that your family would always be there for you when the world turned its back on you. Now she had to explain why sometimes the rules need amendments.

"Your Aunt Joyce Ann isn't well right now. The devil's got hold of her mind. Just pray for her."

"And can we pray for Dianne, and baby Shannon in heaven, too?" Regina had asked.

"Yes, we can."

Then Gloria took Regina's hands and led her to that old familiar couch. There, they prayed for Joyce Ann, Dianne, and Shannon. Gloria's prayers turned to sobs, and Regina got the feeling that whatever was going on at Aunt Joyce Ann's house had to be serious. It was.

Things had gone downhill from there, and it seemed that Gloria was even more careful than before with the girls. They weren't even allowed to date until they were eighteen, and by then they were off to college, buried in books and higher education. Gloria herself was too busy worrying over the girls' well-being to bother with a love life of her own. This thing with Richard had just caught her off guard. That was the best she could figure. And, actually, there was nothing left to guard. The girls had moved out; the house was empty. Finally, she could think about what she wanted rather than concern herself with what it might cost the girls.

Gloria could live her life now.

Richard's oldest son made a toast, followed by Regina. She spoke for both daughters in wishing the best for her mother and Richard. They all gave three cheers and drank ginger ale to happiness. The night had gone well, complete with countless introductions, hugs and kisses, and even gifts from those who said they wouldn't be able to make the ceremony the next day.

Things would be a little different for Yolanda now that everyone was getting paired up. She was happy for them, but her Inner Child was a little green. Her mother and Regina, her two best friends, had new priorities in their lives. Regina was a new mother whose busy life left little room for shopping and late-night movies. And now her mother would be busy with her life as a newlywed. Up until tonight, as she watched her mother snuggle up to Richard, and Regina glow with pride as everyone talked about how cute her son was, Yolanda had not given much thought to the fact that she was the last single woman in her family. Well, there were always Dianne and Aunt Toe, though Aunt Toe was a widow who at least had known what it means to love and be in love.

Romantic love had always been an enigma for Yolanda, a catch-22. She was raised by a strong, single black woman of God. Gloria taught her that God was to always come first in her life. Yolanda learned very early that she did not need a man to survive and that while marriage was a wonderful institution ordained by God, she wasn't any less of a woman if she remained single.

The Jordan household was a woman's world—just Gloria

and the girls. The thought of having a man in the house was foreign to Yolanda. They never had the toilet seat problem or the remote control problem or the issue with gas. They were ladies. Their house was clean, stuff was orderly, and things didn't get messed up. In addition to teaching them how to cook, Gloria showed them how to change a flat tire, take out the trash, and call a decent plumber.

Yolanda didn't really have anything against men. She liked a good date every now and then, a night out, a dance. A good romance novel or a Lifetime movie when she had the time. Yolanda could enjoy a man's company without depending on it.

She had had a few boyfriends in high school. The problem was that she had zero tolerance for the stuff she saw going on back then: he-said-she-said, if-you-love-me-you-will, read-my-mind. She came very close to losing her virginity one night after homecoming. That next Monday the rumor was out that she'd "done it" with Byron. It's funny how people will believe a lie before they'll believe the truth. She thought things would be different in college, but they weren't. Same games, different faces.

It didn't help that she was also a neat-freak and something of a perfectionist. She liked her socks folded a certain way, her clothes arranged a certain way in her closet, and she wanted all the labels in her pantry facing forward—at all times. Yolanda didn't make any excuses for herself, though. She liked things done right. Gloria taught the girls that if you're not going to do it right, don't do it at all. Generally speaking, "right" meant "Yo-yo's way." But when you're single, that's okay. It was her house, her domain. It was all about order, minimal confusion. The coolness or reason.

Maybe that's why Yolanda became a pharmacist. In her field of work, precision was absolutely essential. Imprecision or incompleteness could mean the difference between life and death for someone. She liked using the instruments and gadgets that helped her fill a prescription right down to the milligram. She liked opening up the boxes from the pharmaceutical companies and meticulously logging in the lifesaving drugs. She checked and double-checked the prescriptions before turning them over to the assistants to dispense. She loved her career and knew that it was her true calling.

But still, she couldn't deny that she thought of love more often now. Maybe it was the mood, the atmosphere, that made her pull out life's measuring stick and evaluate herself. Yolanda watched, almost embarrassed, the secret smile that lingered between her mother and Richard for most of the evening. Truth was, she wanted to look in someone's eyes and smile like that someday. The stirring in her heart scared her, made her uneasy in her own skin.

Regina watched her mother—how, for once, she sat up on the pedestal and received all that was due her as the woman of the hour. She wanted to tell her how beautiful she was, how much her happiness meant, how much she'd always loved her. But Richard beat her to it. No one knew what he said, but it was all in the way that Gloria almost blushed when he put his nose to her ear and whispered. He would give her everything she needed now.

Regina fanned her eyes as she watched them do their courting—almost too private for this very public gathering, she thought. But no one else seemed to think twice, so she decided just to eat. When the servers brought out desserts, Regina tore into her chocolate cake and then had Orlando's piece as well. It would be her last night of bingeing, she swore to herself. Before setting her eyes on the food, she had thought that she could make it through this rehearsal dinner without blowing it. But it was too late now. She might as well see this binge on through, because starting tomorrow, she was fasting.

Dianne was busy stuffing her face, too. She kept her eyes on the entrance, her feet ready to scramble if Joyce Ann should come walking through that door. Dianne was occupied by that fear, and she searched the room for an outlet. She was pleasantly distracted when she heard a loud cheer from the Reed side of the room.

"Hey, DeAngelo, you made it!" one of the Reeds yelled out.

Dianne looked up and almost choked on her food. *Good Lord, who is that man?* He was light brown, dressed in black, and had beaucoups of muscles rippling under a formfitting shirt. Pants just loose enough, just tight enough, to indicate that the fineness didn't stop at his snugly cinched belt. *Mmm, mmm, mmm.* He couldn't be unattractive if he tried.

"I couldn't miss my favorite uncle's wedding," DeAngelo said, searching the room for Richard. His eyes stopped at Dianne for an instant and then continued their hunt.

"You ain't none of my nephew," Richard called out. The room roared with laughter as the man made his way to Richard. They hugged long enough for Dianne to deduce that they had a long history together, though they were many years apart in age.

Richard tapped his fork against his glass, calling the crowd to attention again. "Hey, everybody, listen up. For those of you who don't know him or don't remember him, this here is DeAngelo. He's Mattie's grandson. Mattie, raise your hand." A seasoned woman in African attire with trendy rhinestone glasses raised her hand. "Mattie is my . . . What are you, Mattie?"

"I'm your godmother, boy!" she laughed.

"Well, whatever. Everybody, say hello to DeAngelo."

"Hello, DeAngelo," the room spoke.

"Have you already made the toast?" he asked.

"Yeah, Bobby made it. But we've got time for another one."

The guests lifted their glasses once more. "To the man I've always known as Uncle Richard, the closest thing to a father I ever had. May God bless you and your lovely wife for years to come."

"Cheers!"

The last table made room for him, and the party went on, but Dianne's thoughts never left DeAngelo's table. He didn't have the kind of look that most women find attractive: the tall, dark, and handsome look. No, there was something more to him. The way he walked into the room and filled it with himself. The way he moved through the crowd. It wasn't just in his face or in his hair or in his clothes. It was in *him*. He was sexy from head to toe, and Dianne wanted a piece of that.

She followed him with her eyes when he excused himself to go to the restroom. After a minute or two she followed suit. Dianne caught him just before he left the restroom area, out of everyone's view.

"Hi." She smiled.

"Hello," he said in a friendly, passing kind of way.

"I'm Dianne." She put her hand out. He stopped, understanding that she wanted a moment of his time, and shook her hand.

"I'm DeAngelo," he said. "It's nice to meet you, Dianne."

"Do you live around here?" she asked as if she didn't already know.

"Oh, no. I'm living in Galveston now."

"Really? I'm in Darson!" She exaggerated her surprise. "About halfway between Dentonville and Galveston. Small world, huh?"

"Sure is," he said.

"So are you just in town for the wedding?" she asked.

"Yeah. I'll be leaving Sunday morning."

"Where are you staying tonight?"

"I'm a little north of town, in Farley."

"Oh, that's too bad," Dianne said, dangling the proposition.

He waited for a moment, looked as if he was thinking. Dianne licked her lips and smiled, hoping that she hadn't set herself up for disaster. DeAngelo had acknowledged God in his toast. But if there was one thing Dianne knew about the opposite sex, it was that no matter how holy a man was, he was a man before he was a man of God. Every last one of them had the primal urge to reproduce, whether or not they actually intended to. She was counting on that instinct to kick in. And the longer it took for him to respond, the more she knew that the messenger below the belt was talking to him.

"It doesn't have to be too bad." DeAngelo snapped up the bait.

At eleven that night, Dianne told James that she was going to spend the night with Yo-yo and left him with her Master-Card so that he wouldn't ask any questions. The cab dropped her off at DeAngelo's hotel, and he met her in the lobby as he said he would. They had a few wine coolers and laughed about Dentonville—how small it was, the fact that the post office actually closed at twelve for lunch. DeAngelo seemed like a nice enough person, certainly a better catch than James. Dianne thought for a moment that she might actually like to know DeAngelo. But she'd already blown that, seeing as she was in his hotel room on the same evening she had met him. She considered leaving, maybe just exchanging numbers, because he didn't seem like the type who would be upset if she changed her mind about the whole thing. No, she couldn't do that. She had come to this hotel for something very specific, and she wasn't leaving without it.

DeAngelo didn't know anything about Dianne or her past. He only knew that she was a desirable woman and that she found him attractive. To Dianne's surprise, DeAngelo was gentle and he actually wanted to make sure that she was pleased as well. But what she got out of it was much more than physical pleasure. It was a perverse, distorted kind of gratitude, because only in sex did Dianne actually feel as though someone found pleasure in her. For Dianne it wasn't about power or enjoyment or love. It was that look in his eyes, that smile on his face when it was all over. She lived for the moment when a man said, with or without words, "You *are* good for *something*." When DeAngelo's eyes rolled back into his head, the rim around the hole in her heart pulled in tight, as though a drawstring had been cinched. Even if it was only for a second, and even if it was only half closed, it felt better than the gaping absence she suffered ceaselessly.

Long after DeAngelo fell asleep, Dianne lay there looking around. The hotel room was generic, standard: a bed, a desk, a nightstand, a chair. She'd seen it all before, way too many times. This moment, after it was all over, was when she felt lonelier than ever. Every time, it crept up on her and drove her physically closer to the warm body that lay next to her in bed. Didn't matter who it was, so long as he was breathing.

Dianne was emotionally exhausted. So much had happened that day. Her feelings had traveled the whole gamut, and she wondered how much longer she would go on that way. How much longer before she could just have a normal, relaxing day—whatever *that* was? The only time Dianne felt sane was when she was working. She just wanted to be able to lie down, close her eyes, and see nothing.

But she never saw "nothing." She always saw the horrid scene playing on the movie screen inside her eyelids.

Chapter 7

They ripped and ran all Saturday morning. Dianne and Yolanda picked up the cake; Regina picked up the arches and everything else they'd rented. The three of them went to the church early, making sure that the flower arrangements were set in their rightful places, ready to receive the audience of family and friends. The videographer called to say that he was sending his assistant. The photographer was trippin' about his deposit, which Yolanda had already mailed and he'd already cashed. Regina told him that if he didn't get to the church by three, she'd sue him. He said he'd be there by two. Gloria called to say that her stockings had a run in them, so Regina made another trip to the drugstore for a pair of hose. It was a crazy day, typical of weddings.

Dianne and Yolanda picked up Aunt Toe on the way to Gloria's house. Aunt Toe was the last of the greats alive. When Great-grandmother Rucker left her bootleggin', whiskey-drinkin', wife-beatin' husband, she wound up in Dentonville with her daughters and all the money she'd sewn inside of her brassiere. Of all the girls, Hazeline (nicknamed "Toe" because she was born with six toes on both feet) was the prettiest girl in Dentonville. The younger generations had seen pictures of Aunt Toe in her prime, and she was breathtaking. She was the typical light-skinned, wavy-haired, and light-brown-eyed cotton-club beauty who could sing like Billie Holiday, not to mention that she was as smart as a whip and always had something to add to every conversation, whether her word was welcomed or not. Like her mother, Aunt Toe was too much woman for most men.

Since she'd been diagnosed with diabetes, the general family consensus was that Aunt Toe had lost a little of her mind. But the truth was, she had more sense than most. She'd seen nearly eighty years of the ups and downs of life, and she was tired now, but she knew that God wasn't quite ready to call her home. There was work to be done with her deceased sister's girls. Ruth's daughters, Gloria and Joyce Ann, had made a few messes that Aunt Toe wanted to see cleaned up. Aunt Toe couldn't blame it all on Gloria and Joyce Ann, though. Ruth had picked one bug-eyed fool of a daddy for them. He was nothing but a drunk old idiot with a death wish. Aunt Toe never liked him, especially not since he'd tried to kiss her behind the church house. Billy Neal talked a smooth game when he lied to Ruth and told her that he'd gotten that big bustin' knot when his horse kicked him in the head. Aunt Toe told Ruth the truth, but she wouldn't hear of it. She loved Billy and had decided that his farts didn't stink. "If it did happen," Ruth had said, "it was 'cause you tryin' to steal him from me!" Aunt Toe never could understand why Ruth was such a poor judge of men. And as rough as it was on Ruth, Aunt Toe thanked God for the day that Billy fell off the porch and broke his neck in a drunken stupor. Then, at least, Gloria and Joyce Ann wouldn't have to grow up watching their daddy make a fool out of their momma.

Maybe because Joyce Ann was the baby and never saw her daddy for who he was, maybe because Gloria May was the oldest and saw Ruth for who she was—for whatever reason,

Joyce Ann was the apple who didn't fall far from the tree, and
Gloria May was the apple who grew from the tippy-tip of the
farthest-reaching branch and built up enough momentum
swinging so that when she broke free, she tried to roll as far
from the tree as possible.

Dianne and Yolanda pulled up to their aunt's old, battered
frame house and blew the horn twice—not for Aunt Toe to
come running out, but to scare as many cats as they could
back under the porch. Aunt Toe insisted on leaving out food
for the neighborhood felines. Everyone in the family had tried
to get her to move out of that old house with all its old issues,
and the neighborhood with all its new troubles, but she
wouldn't hear of it.

Aunt Toe grew up with nothing, sharing one bedroom with
four sisters, two brothers, and a family of rodents that thrived
in their midst. Despite the number of times they smashed the
rats with makeshift brooms, the pests found their way back
through the cracks and nestled in the walls at night. It was the
country. Dentonville was a big city, as far as Aunt Toe was
concerned. She was from Craw Prairie, a town so far in the
woods that according to Aunt Toe, the state of Texas had to
pump sunshine in for them. Life in Dentonville had been good
to Aunt Toe. She'd met a man, the right man, who asked for
her hand in marriage.

Sixty-two years later she still lived in the home that she and
Albert Washington had bought with their hard-earned money,
and she would leave that house when she left this earth. The
house was surrounded by the same trees and flowers God
planted. Aunt Toe missed the country and insisted that they
keep many of those reminders about the home.

When the last of the timid cats was out of sight, Dianne and
Yolanda unhooked their seat belts and got out. They'd have to

deal with the confident ones that didn't budge at the warning signals.

"Mee-ow," one of them called to Yolanda. He was orange with white feet. He might have been cute if he hadn't been within ten feet of her with his scratchy claws digging into the wooden porch.

"Get back," she said, keeping her distance and hoping that he would keep his. The last thing she needed was to get all scratched up by one of Aunt Toe's wild felines.

"I'm coming," Aunt Toe called from beyond the door.

From blocks away, they heard someone approach Aunt Toe's street, spewing music with a heavy beat and vulgar lyrics—something about a woman's behind. That car was followed by another whose system wasn't quite as bumpin' but that was nonetheless part of the caravan. Somebody threw a beer bottle on Aunt Toe's lawn and burst into laughter.

"Ooh, hurry up, Aunt Toe," Dianne whispered, leaning her backside against Yolanda in what must have looked like a futile defense against a bunch of tired old cats and whoever might decide to do a drive-by that afternoon.

It took Aunt Toe a good three minutes to click-click all the dead bolts on her door. Finally it swung open, slapping against one of the humongous wheels of her wheelchair. Yolanda and Dianne rushed in, closing the door behind them just in time to shut out one of the bolder cats.

"Aunt Toe, when you gonna get these cats out of here?" Yolanda fussed for the umpteenth time, while folding over to hug her.

"Them cats ain't studyin' you." She pushed her aside and reached out for Dianne.

"Hey, Aunt Toe." Dianne planted a kiss on her cheek, purposely smelled the old woman's pearly skin, and took in the

breadth and width of the home, which had always repre-
sented neutral ground in her life. It had been so long.

"Oh, Jesus! Dianne! Oh, Dianne . . ." Aunt Toe held on to
her tightly now. "Girl, I ain't seen you in so long!"

"I know, Aunt Toe." Dianne stayed in her clutch until she
was released.

"Let me get a look at you." Aunt Toe rolled back a foot or
so and commanded Dianne to turn around. "Girl, you finally
got some meat on your bones. You married now?"

"Uh, no, ma'am," Dianne replied.

"Hmph. You sho' do look married to me, by the way your
hips spreadin'," she observed.

"Aunt Toe, did you take your medicine?" Yolanda asked
her.

"Yeah, I took it, but it don't make me blind." Aunt Toe
blinked at Yolanda repeatedly. "I know what I'm seein'. Dianne, you better start getting in before twelve, 'cause I'm
telling you, after midnight, ain't nothin' open but legs. You
hear me? Stop hanging out all hours of the night with these
good-for-nothing rascals, you hear?"

"Ooh, Aunt Toe, it is so nice to see you again. You haven't
changed a bit!" Dianne announced, ashamed that her great
aunt had called her out. "Not one bit."

"Well, I call it like I see it. I'm sure glad you're here, baby.
We've missed you," Aunt Toe carried on as if she hadn't come
near insulting Dianne.

Despite the scrutiny, Dianne wished she could stay a while
longer, go into that front bathroom and see if the jewelry box
still played "Fur Elise" when she opened it. "Now, this is your
jewelry box, but I'm gonna keep it here," Aunt Toe had told
her years ago. "You come over anytime you want to and listen to it, you hear?" As a child, Dianne had wondered why she
couldn't take it home, but she didn't question Aunt Toe. Then,

after Otis took the gold earrings Uncle Albert had given her, and sold them for drug money, she understood. Aunt Toe knew what she was doing.

Yolanda grabbed her keys and pointed to her watch, and the women filed out of the house one by one. Carefully they helped lift Aunt Toe into the front seat and strapped on the seat belt for her. Dianne rolled the wheelchair around to the trunk, and Yolanda collapsed the frame. Together they lifted the wheelchair and carefully placed it on top of the emergency blanket.

"Girl, Aunt Toe done read me by my hips," Dianne sniggered to Yolanda just before they closed the trunk.

"You know how she is," Yolanda reminded her.

"I know. Actually, I think I've kind of missed that."

Aunt Toe watched Dianne through the side-view mirrors. It pained her to see her great-niece going down the same road Joyce Ann had taken. She wondered what happened to the good old days, when you got married, moved out of your momma's house, and lost your virginity all in the same day. At the same time, Dianne laughed at Aunt Toe's simplicity. She gave Aunt Toe credit—maybe she was a virgin when she got married, but anybody can hold out till the ripe old age of eighteen, which was considered prime marrying age. After all, what else would she have to look forward to back then?

Yolanda backed out of the driveway and then stopped the car so that she could go back and put the locks on Aunt Toe's wobbly old gate. Aunt Toe insisted that the gate be locked at all times, as though it actually provided some impression of a barricade. *Thank you, Lord, for protecting her.* That's when she heard a cat's call, as shrill and as purposeful as any electronic alarm system. The bold, striped one had been watching their every move. He *was* the alarm system.

Dianne didn't waste any time getting Aunt Toe to talking when they got back into the car. "Aunt Toe, you still got twelve toes?"

"Sure do." She nodded. "Toes ain't never caused me a minute of trouble my whole life. And I ain't never fell once! You ask anybody. Ain't nobody ever seen me fall in almost eighty years!"

"Ooh, you eighty years old, Aunt Toe?" Dianne asked.

"Lord delay His coming and say the same, I sure will be eighty next year. I don't look it, do I?"

"No, Aunt Toe. You look good, girlfriend." Yolanda rolled her neck.

"I know, I know. This old red man from the civic center tryin' to court me."

"Why don't you like him, Aunt Toe? You're still young. We could be planning *your* wedding next," Dianne told her.

"Naw, chile, naw." Aunt Toe frowned. "I don't want no red man."

"But you're red."

"I don't like 'em red. I like 'em so black they look like they'll rub off on ya," she cackled. "Now, that's how I like 'em. Besides, that joker at the center got too many teeth missing in action."

Dianne fell over laughing on the seat next to her, holding her stomach.

"Aunt Toe," Yolanda asked her, "are you excited about the wedding?"

"Oh, yeah," she said, "your momma needs a man. I told her long time ago she needed a man. She ought to be about to burn up by now."

"Aunt Toe, what are you talking about?"

"You young folks know what I mean." She gave Yolanda an

all-knowing glance. "She's burnin' hot by now. That man better take him some Viagner. Help him, Lord Jesus!"

Dianne decided that she'd wait at Gloria's house during the wedding and reception. Despite the pleas of her family, she couldn't force herself to breathe the same air as Joyce Ann.

"You don't want me to take you back to the hotel?" Yolanda asked her.

"No. That's okay. I'll just wait here."

"Won't your friend miss you?" Gloria asked. She *had* caught the hesitation in Yolanda's voice when she explained that Dianne wasn't staying with her.

"He'll be okay," Dianne let it slip out.

"*He?*" Gloria asked. "You married?"

Dianne bit her bottom lip. "No, ma'am."

"Well, it ain't for me to say, but—"

"I'll say it." Aunt Toe went off on her rampage. "Shackin' up is wrong, and your Aunt Gloria taught you better. I don't care what the rest of the world do; that don't make it right."

The room was silent. Dianne could only say "Yes, ma'am" and swallow.

"Okay, let's get ready to go." Gloria hopped off the topic and sang, "It's my wedding day, everybody!"

At the church Regina went inside first to make sure Richard wouldn't see Gloria. Three generations of Rucker women took over the choir room and made it into a dressing room. Regina was the matron of honor, Yolanda the maid of honor. Aunt Toe took Ruth's place, giving Gloria away. Richard had a best man and a groomsman. It would be a simple ceremony with just the basics, at Gloria's request. That turned out to be a good thing because Yolanda didn't think she could take much more of Gloria's jitters.

The church was the perfect size for a second wedding, small enough to be conservative. Everyone knew that Gloria had been around the block. In fact, some of Richard's church members raised their eyebrows at the prospect of Minister Reed having a church wedding with a woman who was on her second walk down the aisle. "Don't seem right," they'd said. "The aisle is for untouched women," some of them had said to the pastor. But the pastor knew the truth. In years past, many of them had hoped to land Richard Reed themselves. Then, after they settled for other men, they had hoped that their daughters and nieces would catch him. Alas, Minister Reed always seemed so aloof, traveling the country on crusades, running off overseas doing mission trips. He was gone too much to keep a woman satisfied. Gloria Rucker, bless her heart—raised those three girls with no man—was a good enough woman for him. She had taught many of their children in school and served at a neighboring church. Surely she would transfer her membership (and her tithes) from Mt. Zion to Blessed Assurance Baptist Church congregation. They *tsk*-ed and frowned, but Gloria would do.

The choir room doubled as a dressing room for occasions such as this one. Regina, Yolanda, and Aunt Toe scrambled to get Gloria ready for the ceremony, but Gloria was less than amiable. "Oh, do you think I picked the right color?" She raised her eyebrows as she scrutinized her reflection in the full-length mirror on the wall. "I mean, maybe it's too close to white—I do have kids, you know."

"Aw, Momma, please," Regina assured her. "These days people on their third and fourth marriages get married in lily white."

"They ought to make 'em wear plaid," Aunt Toe interjected. "Don't make no sense what's going on in the world today. Other week, they said on the news the president's gonna make a law so folks who's shacking up can have a break on their taxes. Said they're saving the government money by not getting married. What you think about that, Gloria? I wouldn't be surprised if God strike us all dead!"

Gloria had seen the same newscast and realized that Aunt Toe had it all wrong. Gloria whispered to Yolanda, "Take Aunt Toe on into the sanctuary. I don't want her getting overheated in here."

Yolanda wheeled her great-aunt to the front row on the left side of the church and bade her to sit quietly until the ceremony began. When they were all dressed, Regina went out to find the photographer. He came and took a picture of them, all smiles. Gloria went back into the inner chamber of the choir room, a smaller room within a room, formerly an office, now reserved for breast-feeding, serious girdle-hoisting, and other intimate actions too big for a bathroom stall. She needed a last moment with herself before walking down that aisle.

Moments later there was another knock at the door. "I guess he wants to take a few more," Yolanda said, neglecting to ask before she swung open the door.

There stood Joyce Ann.

"Hello, everybody." She waved lightly and then clasped her hands together against the front of her paisley eighties-style ruffled-waist dress. The gesture was innocent enough, but her tone was bold. For a brief moment she was taken aback by her nieces. They weren't little girls anymore. They had grown up to be beautiful young women. She wondered if they looked anything like Dianne. She wondered if Shannon would have looked like them, too.

Joyce Ann was just as lovely as Regina remembered her. She looked a lot like the old pictures of Aunt Toe: tall, slender, with a natural beauty that wouldn't fade. She still had those dimples, as if time hadn't aged her one bit. Her eyes told a different story, though. It was there that Regina saw the woman who had left Dianne when Shannon died. "Hello," she said dryly.

"It's nice to see you two," Joyce Ann offered.

"I wish I could say the same." Yolanda surprised herself with these disrespectful words. She couldn't help it, though. The word mincer was turned off at the moment.

"Gloria, you in there?" Joyce Ann hollered past Regina.

"Joyce Ann?" Gloria stared at herself in the chamber's mirror. *Joyce Ann*. Gloria rushed to see her sister. Part of her thanked God for answering her prayer, for allowing Gloria to lay eyes on Joyce Ann again while the blood was still running warm in her little sister's veins. But the other part of her wondered just what Joyce Ann wanted. They hugged upon impact.

"Be careful, Momma." Regina pulled her mother back. "Don't let any of her makeup get on you."

"Gloria, I'm so glad to be here." Joyce Ann poured out her heart. That much was true. After all, she did love Gloria. Always had—maybe too much. "Oh, you make a lovely bride, Gloria." But within the same breath, she said, "We need to talk."

"Okay," Gloria moved aside, pointing Joyce Ann toward the inner room.

"Can't it wait?" Yolanda cut in. "We're in the middle of a wedding, Aunt Joyce Ann."

"No, it can't."

"It's okay." Gloria stepped between her daughters and her sister. "It's okay."

Gloria followed her sister to the room, barely big enough for two, and waited. Long ago they used to be this close all the time. Washing dishes, cleaning up, sneaking to wear lipstick. They had shared many secrets, spoken in such proximity that their very breaths intermingled. Now was no different.

"What do you want?" Gloria asked.

"I *don't* want to be kicked out of your life on account of some man." Joyce Ann crammed as much force into a whisper as possible.

"I never said I was kicking you out of my life. I'm getting married and I have to be careful now," Gloria said.

Joyce Ann looked into her sister's eyes and saw a pleading, same as before. But this time she wouldn't fall for it. "You can get married all you want to, but I will not let you leave me out in the cold again. Remember, I *know* you. We *do* have a history together."

"I'm well aware of that."

"I know how you use people and—"

"I never used you, Joyce Ann!"

"Well, it's mighty funny how you always come out on top with me standing right under your feet. Your life is always so great, and my life is nothing!" Joyce Ann struggled to keep her voice confined to the four walls. She was amazed at how carefully she still guarded Gloria's secrets.

"I can only take so much blame for your life, Joyce Ann. You made some bad choices on your own."

"I ain't the only one who made bad choices, but it seems like I'm the only one still payin' for mine. You walked away smellin' like a rose." Joyce Ann laughed and pulled both elbows. "Not a scratch on you."

"Believe me, I've got scratches. I've got wounds, slashes, gashes—I'm just doing my best to keep them from taking over my life." Gloria blinked rapidly. "And I *have* taken care of you—"

"Don't start that silly crying," Joyce Ann ordered.

"I'm not crying. I'm just trying to tell you that I have always done all I can to repay you for what you did for me." Gloria willed the tears to be still while she relieved herself of a load she'd been meaning to get off her chest for more than half her life now. "I know that I owe you. But it is *not* my responsibility to make sure you are happy."

"Not your responsibility? I tell you what *is* your responsibility. It *is* your responsibility to see to it that I'm taken care of. I took care of you; now you take care of me. If you don't, your husband's going to find out how much of a Rucker woman you really are," Joyce Ann promised.

Gloria eyed her sister and leaned into Joyce Ann's face. Years ago this was a mirror. "Don't threaten me. Don't you *ever* threaten me again. I'm not the one who got hooked on drugs."

"And I'm not the one with all the baby-daddy issues, either," Joyce Ann reminded her, wagging her head for emphasis. "Wonder if Richard knows *that*. Ain't he some kind of reverend, too? For somebody who's trying *not* to go into a marriage with secrets, I bet you ain't told him *that* one."

Gloria backed up. These were facts she'd hidden from herself as well. "What do you want from me, Joyce Ann?"

"I want a life."

"No, you want *my* life." Gloria shook her head.

"It's not easy being the black sheep of the family. Maybe I *do* want your life," Joyce Ann admitted, more to herself than to Gloria.

It was unreasonable, and they both knew it.

For as much trouble as Joyce Ann had always been, they were still sisters. Gloria knew that Joyce Ann loved her, even if Joyce Ann did forget this every now and then. "I'm going to go and get married now. Stay if you want to."

As Gloria turned, Joyce Ann grabbed her sister's arm. "Where's your blue?" Gloria was confused. "You know, something old, new, borrowed, blue."

"I've got the old and new," Gloria touched her earrings and necklace respectively, her breath still labored.

"Here." Joyce Ann unbuttoned her sleeve and slipped off a silver-faced, indigo-banded watch. "You've borrowed every-thing else; you might as well borrow my watch."

"Thank you." Gloria clipped her words as she took the watch and fastened it to her wrist. It was always like this be-tween them: love-hate.

"What about new?" Joyce Ann asked.

Gloria managed to loosen her lips a bit. "Time is always new."

"You do make a beautiful bride, Gloria. I meant that."

"So, you're staying for the ceremony?"

"I want my watch back."

Gloria formulated a makeshift plan in her head, one that would have to do until she figured things out. "You stay at the hotel until tomorrow. I'll bring it back to you then. Order room service and *do not* leave that room. Dianne is in town."

Joyce Ann held her throat as though the name choked her. "Dianne?"

"Yes, Dianne. She's so terrified at the thought of seeing you that she's not coming to the ceremony."

Joyce Ann shook her head and rocked it back once with a sinister laugh. "Guess I'll have to carry that blame to my grave, too?"

Gloria looked away from her sister. "Stay if you want to."

"What if I want to stay in Dentonville?" Joyce Ann proposed her plan as though she hadn't already settled on the idea of moving back to Dentonville. Everything she owned was in that hotel room on Main. Shame what she had to do with Billy for transportation, but he was the only one with a truck that might actually make it more than a hundred miles without breaking down on one of the lonely roads into this small town.

"I can't talk about this right now." Gloria massaged her throbbing head.

"Fine. Go on and get married like everything's okay."

"I will."

"And I'll be waiting for you when you get back from your little honeymoon." Joyce Ann left the room, her hands trembling as she pulled out a small package from her purse and practically threw it on the pew nearest the choir room door. She said to her nieces, "This is for your mother. Tell her that I said congratulations and best wishes." Joyce Ann let herself out.

Regina unfolded her arms and swaggered over to the pew. She scooped up the gift, mumbling, "It's the least you could do."

Gloria emerged from chambers wearing a strained expression. Her steps were quick and purposeful. She glanced down at the watch—Joyce Ann's watch—and announced that it was time for the wedding. "We ain't waitin' on nobody else. It's four o'clock straight up."

"See, I told you we shouldn't have let her in!" Regina fussed at her sister. "She got Momma all . . . distracted."

Yolanda agreed.

"Look, today is *my* day," Gloria said to calm them both. Then she grabbed her bouquet and announced, "Now, let's go have this wedding."

Chapter 8

*Y*olanda asked Dianne to come to church with her on Sunday morning, but she refused, saying that her man James wanted to get out and do some shopping with *her* money since they would be leaving that afternoon. She'd arranged for another cousin of theirs to take them back to the bus station so that Yolanda wouldn't have to miss the service.

"It has been too long since I've seen you," said Yolanda. "I know we talk every now and then, but I miss you, girl."

"I miss you, too. I miss everybody, actually." Dianne lowered her voice. "I'll call you next week." After she'd hung up with Yolanda, Dianne emptied her last load of apprehension. The sooner she could leave Dentonville, the better.

Yolanda's church, the Master's Tabernacle, was twenty miles out of the way. Traffic was hectic and parking was atrocious, but it was well worth the hassle. If there was one thing she loved about her church, it was the way the Spirit filled the massive building at every service. Whether it was with the praise dance, the choir, the youth-in-action Sunday programs, or (most frequently) the Word itself, she loved going to church and getting a Holy Ghost fill-up. There was so much power there, it was absolutely contagious. Regina and Orlando were members there, too, but without actually carpooling, there was no way they could expect to sit together. Just as well—Yolanda could always get a closer seat when she came alone.

The interior of the church reminded Yolanda of a stadium. During her first visit the spaciousness was disturbing. Having grown up in the small church where Gloria and Aunt Toe served in Dentonville, Yolanda was intimidated by the Master's Tabernacle. How on earth was she supposed to find God in a place like this, where you had to ride a shuttle to the sanctuary? She'd heard the pastor preaching on the radio and decided to give the church a visit, but never in her wildest dreams had she imagined that it would be like this. For all that overwhelmed her, there was something about the fact that everybody didn't know everybody that drew Yolanda to this place of worship. When the offering basket was passed anonymously through the crowds rather than having the offertory reduced to a fashion show, as it often was at the smaller Dentonville church, Yolanda quickly saw one of the benefits of worshipping with a larger body. For every positive in one church, there was a negative in the other, and vice versa. It finally came down to listening to the voice of God and changing her membership based on His direction. The Master's Tabernacle wasn't perfect, but it had been her church home for two years now.

When Pastor Rollins took his stand behind the podium, Yolanda's heart was ready to receive a word from the Lord. She didn't know why it always seemed that the preacher preached on exactly what she needed to hear. You know, when you've been going through something and you need some direction or confirmation about something and then you get in church and that's exactly what he or she is preaching about? She loved it when that happened. *You're right on time, Lord!*

The topic was "What's your Damascus Road?" Pastor Rollins started off by telling them how young elephants are trained for zoos or circuses or any kind of design that keeps them tame and under control.

"When an elephant is young, they take him and tie a rope or a chain around one of his back legs and anchor it to some sturdy, fixed object so that when he tries to move, he feels that yank on his hind leg. At that particular time in an elephant's life, he's relatively small and weak. And so he soon learns that when he feels that rope or that chain around his leg, he might as well be still, because he's not going anywhere; he's immobile at that point. How many of you have heard that elephants have good memories?"

"Amen," the congregation answered.

"Well, when that elephant matures and becomes an adult, his memory and his recollection are the very things that keep him subservient. At this point, the trainers and other persons working with this adult elephant know that the elephant is strong enough to break the rope they put on him, but guess what?"

A silence.

"The *elephant* doesn't know that."

There was a slight buzz in the building, clapping as some already saw where the pastor was going.

"That's right," the pastor informed them, "the elephant has been trained and conditioned to believe that when a rope is placed around his leg, he is frozen and unable to move. So all they have to do by the time he's an adult is just tie a rope around his leg and he'll be still. They don't even have to anchor it to anything. Because of what happened in the past, the elephant believes in his heart that he is powerless when he feels that restriction. Little does he know that there is *nothing* holding him back. Little does he know that even if there *was* something attached to the other end of the rope, he is strong enough and powerful enough as an adult to break whatever they tie to the other end!"

A few "Hallelujahs" and "Glorys" went out.

"Now, in the ninth chapter of Acts, we find Saul making a journey. Now, you have to understand who Saul was. He was a man who had persecuted the Lord's people for quite some time. Says here in verse one that Saul was handing out *murderous* threats. He had made up in his mind that this *Jesus* was not for him."

"Mmm-hmm," the congregation agreed.

"Now"—Pastor Rollins removed his glasses—"we all know what happened to Saul at this point. According to verses eight and nine of this same chapter, the power of God knocked him off his feet and rendered him blind."

"Well . . ." People swayed.

"There's a reaping and a sewing going on here, and that's nothing new. But what I want to point out today is the way that God delivered him from the chains of his past. God took Saul and turned him into a great preacher.

"Sometimes we have chains that we put on ourselves. Chains that our parents wore, and they got handed down to us. Chains that we didn't know we had on until we couldn't move anymore."

Yolanda nodded her head, though she wasn't quite sure why.

"Saul, who would later be known as Paul, did what many of us don't do: he started praying." The minister drove it home. "He prayed during his blind time, and God sent healing in a matter of days."

"You right," someone remarked.

"See, some of us have chains that God is willing and ready to break. Some of these chains we deserved; some we didn't.

Doesn't matter. They're on you, and you need them off! You've been there long enough. Some of you have been there long enough. It's time you got your healing and got out of Damascus and continued on with the work of the Lord. Don't sit there like those elephants.

"That chain that the devil used to have tied to your back leg is no longer tied to anything! Some of us are just like that grown elephant."

"Yes!" the audience rang out.

"We've been bought with a price. We've been set free. We've been redeemed, but the minute we feel Satan creeping up and trying to pull that fast one on us, we become immobilized. We don't even look down to examine the situation and see it for what the word of God says that it is. We don't even look down at our ankles to see what the rope is made of. Really, maybe it's just a thread. Maybe it's just a tiny little nothing that we could shake off in a second. Maybe it's just an illusion, like when you've worn glasses for so long you can feel them on your face even when you're not wearing them. So many of us think that just because that's the way it always was, that's the way it will always be. Momma didn't have, so that means I can't have. Daddy didn't try it, so that means I shouldn't. The last time I tried to do it, it didn't work out, so I'm not going to try again.

"When you begin to grow and mature in Christ, the things and circumstances around you change. You begin to look around and understand that even though it feels like the devil's got a hold on you, he really doesn't. It's just a rope!"

"Yes!"

"It's just a rope! It ain't tied to nothin'!"

"Yes!"

"It's just a rope! It ain't anchored to nothin'!"

"Yes!"

"And even if it *is* anchored to somethin', that somethin' ain't nothin' but a lie, and you got enough power by the Holy Ghost to break it!"

"Yes!"

"You got enough power to pull it all the way out of the ground! Say 'yeeeeeeah.' "

"Yeeeeeeah!" And they buzzed back into their seats. The saints were swaying their heads and making those serious faces.

Pastor continued, "And then some of us have people standing in the gap for us. We got grandmothers and fathers praying the ropes off of us, and the next thing we know, we go around *looking* for ropes to tie to our *own* legs. We, we, we just don't feel right unless we are bound in some way. Some of us have been tied down so long we don't know how to function *without* the rope around our legs. To me, that's the saddest elephant of all—the one who keeps the rope on himself for lack of knowledge. The one who has become so comfortable in his pain that life without pain does not seem like life at all. How many of you know it's uncomfortable to get out of your comfort zone, even if your comfort zone is uncomfortable?"

"Amen," the congregation agreed.

Yolanda took notes throughout the whole sermon, determined first to examine herself with the Scriptures. *Am I being an elephant about anything? Men, maybe, but I don't have to have a man to be a Christian.*

Then she thought about Dianne. She envisioned her cousin standing next to a flimsy wooden stick with the unattached chain around her leg, being whipped and tortured by someone so small she could have stepped on him if she wanted to, yet she stood there. Dianne received her torment because she believed she should. Quickly Yolanda pulled a "Just a Note" card from her Bible bag and wrote a note to Dianne that she'd mail later. Just the Scriptures and a hello would do.

Back home after church, Yolanda fixed herself some chicken Alfredo, watched a good Lifetime movie, and caught a nap before getting ready for her night shift at the pharmacy. The southward drive to work used to be a pleasant, uneventful one, but with the population boom near Dentonville came the construction. One-lane streets and temporary four-way stop signs were almost enough to make you want to scream.

Brookelynn, her coworker, was ready and waiting to leave when Yolanda arrived. Yolanda spoke briefly to Shelley, the assistant, who was also preparing to leave. After greeting them both, Yolanda took note of Brookelynn's makeup. Brookelynn was in her mid-thirties, straight out of the suburbs and very much out of place in Dentonville. Things were starting to look a little more like home for her, but she was still waiting for a movie theater. Brookelynn lived farther south of Dentonville, just on the outskirts of Dallas. It took her a good forty-five minutes to get to work, thus she always blew in and out of the pharmacy.

"Got a hot date, Brookelynn?" Yolanda teased her.

"I guess you could say that." She smiled. "I met him at church."

"You go, Missy."

"Pray for me, girl."

"You know I'm always praying for you," Yolanda said by way of reassurance.

Brookelynn gave Yolanda a quick hug. "Yolanda, sometimes I wonder where I'd be if I didn't have you praying for me." Though she and Yolanda were both Christians, sometimes it seemed to Brookelynn that she was way back at the starting line while Yolanda was sprinting on down the road.

"So, is *this one* the one or was the *last* one *the one?*"

"That last one doesn't count," Brookelynn laughed, charting her last few items on a ledger. "Turns out he was married."

"How did you find out?"

"I had one of those Internet research companies do a background check on him. He's been married for seven years; he has two kids and awful credit."

"You learned all that through the Internet? Legally?"

"Yes, it was *legal*. You'd be surprised what you can find out about *everybody* on the Internet. Save yourself two, maybe three months' worth of dating. It's worth every penny." Brookelynn took off her lab coat, revealing a formfitting black pantsuit. She pulled off the sturdy, flat Naturalizers and slid into a pair of excruciatingly stylish high heels. "How do I look?"

"You look great," Yolanda told her. Brookelynn's intense, long red hair surrounded her fair face and landed softly on her shoulders. She was model thin, with emerald green eyes that almost glowed when the light hit them a certain way. Despite their cultural differences, Yolanda and Brookelynn had a lot in common by way of profession and sense of humor, and they often compared life notes with each other. Brookelynn had been around Yolanda enough to know that Yolanda was a well of encouragement, and she asked Yolanda to pray for her or give her some sound advice about something—usually a man. They rarely had the opportunity to work together, but every once in a while one of them got wrapped up in paperwork and their hours overlapped at the pharmacy.

"I've been seeing him for a solid month now, and I think we're about to have that 'where is this relationship going?' talk. I can feel it coming on." She slowed down a bit.

Yolanda locked her purse in her drawer and squared her behind on a stool, giving Brookelynn her undivided attention. "Well, where do you think it's going?"

"I don't know." Brookelynn looked toward the ceiling as though the answer might fall from the sky. "I really like him, we have a lot in common, we have great conversations, and he's incredible in bed once he sets his mind to it. I just . . . I don't know. I'm not getting any younger, you know? And I'm getting tired of this whole dating game. I'm ready to settle down—get married, have a few kids, start going to church, join the PTA. But at the rate I'm going, I'll be pushing sixty by the time my kids finish high school."

"So what's wrong with being sixty when your kids finish high school?" Yolanda asked her anxious colleague. "A lot of women are waiting before having kids. It's not a crime, you know."

Brookelynn tilted her head. "I do not want to be *sixty* when my kids walk across the stage."

"You sound like a kid! Remember when you used to think thirty was old?" Yolanda reminded her. "And remember when you thought a hundred pounds was a lot?"

"These days a hundred pounds *is* a lot," she laughed. "Have you seen these magazine covers around here?"

"You're right about that," Yolanda agreed with her. "But the point is that you don't have to feel pressure to settle down, Brookelynn. Answer this question: what's the worst thing that could happen if you don't get married or have kids?"

Brookelynn crossed her arms and thought. Her eyes rolled to the right . . . back to the left. Then she said to Yolanda, "I could die alone."

"Is that really the worst thing that could happen?"

"Yeah, I think it is. If I don't ever get married or have kids, I could literally fall off the face of the earth and no one would miss me. My obituary would be in the paper with a little picture of me, and no one would cut it out and save it. I'd just be at the bottom of some bird cage getting pooped on." She

looked back down at Yolanda again. "I can live with being single. Honestly, I kind of like it. But I don't want to die and
leave nothing of me behind. I think that's what I'm afraid of."

"Hmm." Yolanda smiled. "The age-old quest for immortal-
ity."

"And the answer is . . . ?" Brookelynn asked. Then she
shook her head. "I shouldn't have asked. Let me guess—it's in
a closer relationship with Christ, right?"

"You know it." Yolanda laughed and put her hand on
Brookelynn's shoulder as a friendly gesture. "Your life's purpose isn't in a man. Yes, you can contribute to society by raising kids that are responsible, giving citizens—and that's no
small accomplishment, mind you. But your purpose, your calling in life, is looking for you. You can hear it calling your
name. You've got to answer to it or you'll never be satisfied
no matter what you do. And you'd better find out before you
get married, 'cause I don't want to be listening to you com-
plain in another year about how your husband isn't paying
enough attention to you or how your kids aren't fulfilling your
needs." She laughed with Brookelynn. "I'm serious. If it ain't
one thing, it's another. And that's the way it goes until you find
rest in Christ."

Miss Marva, the assistant for the night, came to relieve Shelley. Yolanda liked working with Miss Marva. They were sisters
in Christ, and sometimes, when it got really slow, they would
catch each other up on Sunday sermons. "Tell Brookelynn,
Miss Marva, the answer to all her problems is not a husband
and kids."

Miss Marva was a widow, but she'd been married for more
than twenty years before her husband passed. "Girl, please."
Miss Marva shoved Brookelynn out of her way. "That's the *last*
thing you need to add to your problems."

"Oh, Miss Marva, you don't miss having a man around?" Brookelynn asked her.

"Yeah, sometimes I miss the company," she admitted, "but I have no desire to get married again. I ain't got the time nor the energy to break another one in."

When the following Sunday morning rolled around, Yolanda found it very hard to hop out of bed. She prayed for extra strength to make it through the morning. She'd bargained away the next two weekends in order to get time off for Gloria's wedding, and the constant working was starting to zap her strength. Funny, though, how walking into the sanctuary, hearing the music, and feeling the spirit made Yolanda laugh at herself for even thinking of staying at home that morning.

Near the end of the service, Yolanda went to set up the hospitality room. Sister Willis and Brother Nichols helped her prepare for the visitors. After the benediction, the ushers showed the guests to the hospitality room. The workers said their hellos and "welcome to Master's Tabernacle" to hordes of people that morning.

Pastor Rollins came in and made a short speech, inviting the visitors to come again and consider membership. He also introduced the hospitality workers and thanked them for their service to the church. Then Pastor Rollins answered a few questions and told the visitors to be sure and read the information packet and call the office with any further questions they might have about membership, partnership, or any other aspect of the ministry. As the guests left they thanked the workers again for the refreshments and went on their way.

There was one guest in particular who was staring at Yolanda the whole time. She could never catch him in the act, but she knew he was watching her. Her suspicion was confirmed when he approached her just as she began clearing the table.

"Hello—Sister Jordan, is it?"

"Yes."

"Hi, my name is Kelan. We met in this room when I was a visitor several months ago. How are you?" He held out his hand.

So why are you back in here eating our cookies if you're not a first-time visitor, greedy? "Oh, I'm fine." She shook it. "How are you?"

"I'm blessed, blessed, blessed," he repeated the title of the Pastor's sermon.

"Same here." She smiled.

"Yolanda," he said, wasting no time, "I'd like to see you again."

Yolanda knew that worldly men came to church to find wholesome, sanctified women, but weren't they usually a bit more subtle about it? He looked like something straight off of MTV. She gave him a little credit—he had a nice, bright Crest smile. But then came the dreadlocks, shirttail out, ankle socks. Probably ashy. He was most definitely not her type.

"I'm at the church quite often." She tried to put it nicely.

"Oh . . ." He nodded politely. "I understand." He wished her a blessed day and excused himself.

No, he didn't try to get an attitude! She did a little instant replay in her mind: he said he wanted to see her. Her eyes ruthlessly brushed up and down his appearance, and basically told him he could see her at church just like everybody else. He said he understood, and walked away. In fact, he really hadn't been mean or rude. He just said he "understood" and left it at that.

For some reason, a bad feeling came over Yolanda, and she couldn't figure out quite why. All the way home from church, she thought about the encounter. She hadn't done anything wrong. She'd welcomed him to the church, but she did not owe him her phone number. The brother simply wasn't her type; she couldn't stomach dreadlocks. *People with dreadlocks look like they stink. All that hair all matted up like Shaggy D.A.* Still, the spirit had found her guilty of something.

Later she called Regina and Gloria to check up on them. Gloria and Richard were going out to eat. Regina and Orlando were about to take the baby over to his mother's house so they could go out to a movie. Everybody was busy doing family things.

Yolanda busied herself cleaning up the bathrooms (though they really weren't dirty), mopping the kitchen, and changing her linens before taking a nap. When she got up she did a little running around. She stopped at her favorite little mom-and-pop Italian restaurant and spent a good two hours reading the paper and consuming a dish of chicken Parmesan with spaghetti. Then she shopped for groceries and toiletries at the Super Wal-Mart. There she ran into one of her regular customers in the checkout line, and they talked for a few minutes. She asked Yolanda if headaches were a common side effect of the drug she was taking, and Yolanda told her that they were. She seemed relieved to know that she wasn't going out of her mind. Yolanda was glad to have been able to ease her worries. She thanked Yolanda and said she'd see her again the following month.

Yolanda knew that there was more to life than the day-to-day routine. She knew that her life had greater meaning and that she was meant to do her part in spreading the love of Christ across the globe. But sometimes, on days like this Sunday, she wondered if there would ever be anything else in her life. *Not necessarily a man or a family—maybe a dog. No, I'm not cleaning up after no dog. Maybe some huge project like writing the great American novel, starting a small business, anything to make my life feel more significant.* Then again, she thought, she *was* doing something helpful. She'd helped that lady at Wal-Mart. She helped people all the time when they had questions about what to give their children for a cough or lice. There was value in that.

Sometimes Yolanda wondered if she was the only person in the world who ever had such feelings. It seemed as if everybody else knew what they were doing. They were working on this or that, moving ahead, forging on. People like Brookelynn looked at Yolanda and said, "That Yolanda has really got it together!" Most of the time Yolanda felt that she had it together, through the power of God. But sometimes she just had the feeling that she was somehow falling behind or falling short— she wasn't sure which one.

Since the time that Yolanda had completed her degree and internship and become established as a pharmacist, there really wasn't anything else that she'd worked toward. She met with the Lord every night and learned more about what it meant to serve Him mind, body, and soul. And she was involved with making the guests at her church feel welcomed and comfortable in her Father's house. That was a job that needed to be done.

At times like those, when she thought too hard about her purpose, Yolanda's mind could go all the way back to her childhood, growing up without her father; her only images of him formed by snapshots and secondhand memories. She'd start wondering how her life would have been different, better, if her father had been there for her. She'd start wondering what would have happened if she had tried out for that play in the tenth grade. Would she have been a movie star making a bigger difference in the world?

Okay, she was on the way down to a "Yo-yo" rut (all puns

intended) so she did what she knew to do: slipped on the shoes, picked up her Bible and purse, and went back to church for the Sunday evening Bible study class.

Ironically, with the number of people meeting in small groups throughout the building, Kelan was in her group. She wasn't expecting him to smile at her, but he did anyway. It was a genuine, sincere smile. Yolanda didn't want to sit next to him, with the potential dread smell and all, but she didn't have a choice. When you're late, you've got to get in where you fit in. To make matters worse, her group leader broke them up into even smaller groups of four. And—wouldn't you know it?—Kelan was in that group, too.

"I guess it's hello again," he said.

"I guess so." Yolanda smiled wryly. She decided just to go with the flow.

The whole situation reminded her of the time the biology teacher put her with this weird punk-rocker boy to do the frog dissection. She gave them their frog, their tools, and the directions. One of the first things she told them was to be careful when cutting open the frog. Yolanda made a deal with the guy that if he did all the cutting, she'd read the directions, make the notes, and identify the organs. He agreed, grabbed the scalpel, and proceeded to live out his dreams. He opened it with a quick stabbing motion, destroying most of the organs in the process.

"What did you do that for?" Yolanda yelled at him, but not so loud as to cause Ms. Lanslin to approach their table.

"Yeah!" he hollered, holding his hands up in the air, exposing the wet spots and accompanying funk oozing from his armpits. "Yeah, dude!"

"Are you crazy? This is a major grade! You've ruined our frog!" Yolanda told him, reminding herself that this was the main reason she didn't like working with other people.

He laughed one of those little marijuana-induced laughs. "Man, I couldn't resist. I've been waiting all my life to do something like that!"

"You've been waiting all your life to stab a dead frog?" She got all in his face but to no avail. Ms. Lanslin had already said that she wasn't giving them another frog, and Yolanda knew she meant it. With no other choice, Yolanda waited for one of the other groups to finish and throw their frog organs in the trash; then she crawled over to the trash can, collected the discarded organs, and turned them in as the work of herself and her partner. She always did feel bad about that A.

Now, as she sat in her chair waiting for their group leader to give them their topic and scriptures, she wondered if this was going to be another one of those "frog" experiments, where Yolanda was doing all the work and the other poeple were just chilling. Maybe that was another reason she couldn't see herself paired up with anybody. She didn't like it when her reputation, at least partially, rested with someone else. *People are too unpredictable and unreliable.*

"Okay, this group can look up Isaiah sixty-four, verses five through seven. And here are the questions that I need you to be prepared to answer. You've got about fifteen or twenty minutes," the leader instructed them as they left their seats for a smaller meeting room down the hall.

Kelan took the initiative to start their small group in prayer. "Catch hands with the person next to you, please, and let's pray." Before Yolanda could position herself between the oldest man in the group and the other woman, Kelan grabbed her hand and made her his "next of seat." Try as she might, she couldn't keep her mind off the smoothness of his touch. With her eyes closed and her sense of touch in overdrive, Yolanda studied his hand almost well enough to identify his thumbprint, it seemed. There was something about his touch that distracted her so much, she almost missed the "in Jesus' name" cue for the "amen."

"Okay." Kelan sat down, and the group followed his lead. He read from the leader's notes. "Let's turn to verse six. All of us have become like one who is unclean, and all our righteous acts are like filthy rags; we all shrivel up like a leaf, and like the wind our sins sweep us away." He read like somebody with some sense.

They all sat there for a second, letting it sink in before starting the discussion.

"This passage was probably meant to humble us," the other sister in their group said. "But in some ways it makes me feel like I can never be good enough."

"I think, literally taken, it does sound like that," Kelan agreed, "but I think it also demonstrates the magnitude of God's righteousness."

"How so?" Yolanda found herself asking Kelan. *What else am I supposed to be doing for God? Is what I'm doing enough? And now to hear that it never will be enough isn't helping the situation any more. I need some help here.*

"I've come across this verse before, and I think the best way I have been able to make sense of it is to look at how this applies to us even now, after the death and resurrection of Christ. Ephesians two:eight"—he flipped through his Bible with ease and familiarity, glancing briefly at the headings, his hands slowing the fan of the pages in just the right spot— "reads, 'for it is by grace you have been saved, through faith— and this not from yourselves, it is the gift of God.' We know that our salvation is not tied to our good deeds or to our good works. All of who we are is wrapped up in Him.

"Really, is there anything we could actually *do* to pay for our lives? Is there anything *worth* our salvation—any amount of suffering, any amount of praying, any amount of money?"

The group members shook their heads no.

"Then if there is no way we could pay for it, there's no way on earth that we could earn our way into heaven. So, we don't do things to earn the reward God has for us; we don't witness or help others or give to win brownie points with God. Redeemed people *do* do those things, but they don't do those things to become redeemed. Our salvation is already assured," Kelan explained his interpretation.

"I think you're onto something," the other brother in the group added. "We are always going to be human beings in and of ourselves. The blood of Jesus, however, makes up the enormous difference."

Yolanda picked up the list of questions that they needed to be prepared to answer, and read question number one. "Well, that leads us to our first question. If what we do will never be good enough, why do anything at all?"

"I think that we are so much more empowered with the knowledge that our work is useless to God," Kelan said. "When we know that our own personal work is nothing to God, we can put ourselves aside and allow God to work through us."

"Precisely," the sister said. "I think I just had an 'aha!' moment." They all laughed with her. "When I make up my mind that I'm going to do something, most of the time I feel like I'm going to try and do this to secure favor in God's sight. And then, when it's all said and done, I feel like I've moved up. Maybe even like I'm better than other people."

Ouch! Yolanda decided to keep her mouth shut and listen. She just kept reading the questions and recording the answers, hoping they wouldn't ask her for her two cents' worth.

Kelan noticed and asked, "Sister Jordan, you've been pretty quiet. What's your take on this passage of Scripture?"

"I think I've always read it the same way she read it,"

Yolanda said, referring to the sister in the group. "I think I've even used it as an excuse sometimes—you know, saying things like 'I'm only human' to excuse myself. But after listening to the discussion and reading over the notes I made tonight, I think I'm coming away with two things. First, the fact that my self-claimed works are worthless is synonymous with the notion that my flesh is worthless. It tires easily, it gets me into trouble sometimes, it is frail, and it is our connection to Satan. As Christians, I think we're all okay with that, so the fact that the works we claim to be 'ours' are worthless should come as no surprise to us. Second, I feel so freed up now in knowing that when I allow God to work through me, I can't go wrong. There is no failure in God. This gives a whole new light to the old saying 'Let go and let God.' I mean, you don't have to make excuses for or to yourself when you know you're already covered. These Scriptures really bring that home."

"So you had an 'aha!' moment, too?" Kelan asked Yolanda, putting her on the spot.

"I think so."

And before the night was over, she had worked her way back onto his agenda. This time, she gave him her number.

Chapter 9

$\mathcal{I}$t was nice to be back in Darson again, if there was such a thing as "nice" in her life. Nice for Dianne wasn't a matter of things that are. Instead, nice was a matter of nots: *not* remembering, *not* feeling, *not* thinking too hard. As she unpacked her bags and sorted through her belongings, Dianne felt herself breathing again for the first time in several days. She was drained and could think of nothing better than a hot shower and slipping between the sheets.

The apartment was quiet. Still as a crooked picture. The management had stationed all the childless tenants in one section, and Dianne had paid an extra penny for what they called "peace and quiet." She had given a sarcastic laugh at the term when she heard it, but agreed to the slightly increased rent nonetheless.

If there were a monetary price to be paid for peace, she would have begged, borrowed, or stolen. Come to think of it, she *had* given everything already, including herself, in the pursuit. What else could she do? How can you *make* your mind listen? The million-dollar question. Everybody in Dentonville seemed to have the answer: pray, pray, pray. That was easy for them to say.

Regina and Yolanda always had it easy, so far as Dianne

could tell. Yeah, they had some things in common as far as fathers go, but even *that* wasn't quite the same. It was true that neither of them ever had a father. But there was a difference in their fatherlessness and Dianne's. *Their* father died in an accident. He didn't choose to leave their lives. Dianne's father, on the other hand, made the conscious decision to be absent from her life. What was it in a person that could allow him or her to just cut off (or refuse to establish) ties with their own flesh and blood? How do you just throw away what came from you? The question that plagued her most, however, was, why her? What was it about her that made people leave and take their love away, too?

That's why she wasn't like Regina and Yolanda. They also had a good mom, a good home, someone to provide for them, someone who always loved them, and somebody who was in their corner right or wrong. For the first four years of her life, Dianne thought she had that, but as it turned out, she really didn't. When the one person who is supposed to love you unconditionally doesn't give that love to you, then what do you have?

Aunt Gloria and Great-aunt Toe had tried their best to fill in the gap. When she really thought about it, Dianne was thankful that they'd taken her in rather than let her bounce around in the foster care system. That was the one good thing that had happened, but even *that* sounded crazy. *The best thing that ever happened to me was when my sister died and my momma lost custody of me, and my aunts raised me.* "That is pretty sad." Dianne managed a cynical laugh at the thought.

She was away from all that now. Safe in Darson—as safe as she could be within her mind. She braced herself for the nightmares. They were sure to come, since she'd stirred up the violent anthill of her memories. Maybe if she was dirt tired when she crawled into bed, she could escape them. But what if she couldn't? She'd merrily dropped James off at his momma's house after arriving in Darson. It was too late to call him back. For the record, she'd spent way too much money on him over the weekend, especially considering that he'd run up the phone bill talking all night. Probably to that woman on the bus. When Dianne got the bill at checkout, she asked James about the two conversations, both more than an hour long.

"I was talking to my homeboy," he'd lied.

Dianne had rolled her eyes and said under her breath, "What do two men have to talk about for two hours in the middle of the night?" But she couldn't question him. That wasn't their arrangement. He attended. She paid the fees.

As she finalized her unpacking efforts by hanging up the dress that she didn't get to wear to the wedding, Dianne dumped herself on the bed for a second. She could call Sean, but he worked the graveyard shift. He'd have to leave in another four hours. Charles was probably in Vegas with his gambling butt. He sure did know how to run through a sister's quarters. Elvin? No. She wasn't up for his porno flicks. Matter of fact, she wasn't dealing with Elvin anymore. Last time he came over, he got angry because she wouldn't perform some of the sex acts he'd seen on tape.

"I ain't no porn queen," Dianne had proclaimed.

"Well, you sure ain't the virgin Mary." A smile crept across his face, as if to say, who was she kidding?

"I have my limits. Besides, you don't have to be a virgin to be decent," she'd argued.

"I *know* you don't call yourself decent, booty-calling me two and three times a month." Elvin had sat up beside Dianne in bed and mimicked her, batting his eyelashes, taking on the voice of a southern belle. "I'm just having a bad dream. Could you come over? I'm scared and I don't want to be alone." He did that a little too well. Then he cracked up, falling onto Dianne as she lay in embarrassment and sadness.

Maybe other women were lying when they said they had bad dreams, but she wasn't. If he only knew how serious she was, that she really did want him there to shield her. Sex was only the mechanism she used to buy company, stay occupied, and appraise her remaining value.

Regina's eyes couldn't roll past her stomach. It was hideous. Atrocious. She'd been undone by the weekend's festivities. Butter cake, chocolate cake, honey mustard wings, chicken tenders, punch. Right down to the mints, it was all good. Now she was paying the price: 136.

Panic time.

Monday started off with an hour-long workout. Well, it was going to be an hour long, but Orlando Jr. started fussing after only two cranks of the baby swing. Regina stopped the aerobics tape after twenty minutes and decided she'd get back to it later tonight. She could *not* wake up tomorrow and be 136 again. The last time she weighed that much, she was . . . fat. Which is exactly what she thought herself to be this time at 136.

Regina tugged the baby from the swing and kissed him in rapid succession, telling him that everything was okay. She thought to herself that he was probably scared, never having seen his momma move like that. "It's okay, honey," she talked to him in the choppy song tone of baby talk. "Momma doesn't want to be a fat pig. You don't want a fat pig mommy, do you?" He smiled as though it didn't matter, but Regina figured she knew better. No one wants a fat pig around.

After getting the baby settled, Regina thought about fixing herself breakfast but abandoned the idea. No breakfast. Matter of fact, no lunch. Only dinner, and that would be the chicken she took out of the freezer to thaw. She'd eat only a chicken leg a day, she decided. A chicken leg and water. A chicken leg, crackers, and water. And the rest of those long-forgotten pre-natal vitamins.

Regina spent the better part of the morning running be-tween the baby and her computer. She spent some time on the Internet researching the latest cases, brushing up on the most recent decisions in family law. She read the interoffice e-mail and learned that the dress code would be strictly enforced. Apparently, some of the office personnel were dressing down for the hot weather, but policy didn't allow for modifications due to changes in climate. Accounting had a new associate. She was pictured wearing a formfitting red suit to die for. Probably a size four, Regina estimated.

Regina missed her work tremendously. She would miss the baby more, though. Before motherhood, she'd always joked about women who worried too much about their children. "Get a life," she and a coworker had laughed. Now she knew what moms went through in returning to work. The thought was disheartening. What would happen when he realized that his mommy was gone? Would he cry from the second she dropped him off until the moment she arrived at the babysit-ter's doorstep? She thought of the time she'd taken a long shower and emerged to find Orlando Jr.'s face a reddened ball of despair, his cheeks a shiny sheet of tears—his eyes so red they made *her* cry. "I'm here, baby; I'm here." She had com-forted him, calmed him with every ounce of maternal instinct in her, until he fell asleep cuddled against her chest, satisfied with her presence. What if he cried like that again when she went to work?

She couldn't take it.

All this worrying was making her hungry. Anxiety always went down well with a cinnamon roll. Or was it vice versa? Regina tried very hard to get her mind back on track with the research, but there *was* a box of cinnamon rolls in the pantry. Already made. She could see it clearly, the sugary icing hanging over the sides of the box. Maybe she'd add one little cinnamon roll to dinner. A piece of chicken, crackers, water, and a cinnamon roll.

Regina found a site for calculating calories and entered the contents of her planned dinner. She could swing it, no problem. Come to think of it, it didn't really matter *when* she ate the cinnamon roll. She could eat it now, if she wanted to. It had the same number of calories now as it would have at six in the evening. Maybe it was better to eat it in the morning— she'd read somewhere that you should eat most of your carbs in the morning. *Yeah, I'd better eat it now.*

Quickly she made her way to the kitchen with intentions to eat the cinnamon roll—get it over with so this thing wouldn't be teasing her all day. She uncoiled the white wire twisty and pulled the paper tray from its plastic bag. They were as beautiful as she remembered them. She took a knife from the drawer and cut one. It was small, so she pulled a bit more icing from the side of the tray—but only the icing from *that one* cinnamon roll.

Her heart started beating faster as she waited for the cinnamon roll to warm in the microwave—just enough to get the icing to run down the side of the moist breading by the time she sank her teeth into it. *Mmm.*

Regina was having second thoughts now about her life. She loved her job, but how could she be a great mom and a great attorney at the same time? Would her colleagues hold her in the same esteem as before? All that could wait. What she needed now was another cinnamon roll.

She ate the whole tray before noon.

Chapter 10

It took exactly thirty-four seconds for Kelan to walk from his truck to her doorstep and ring the doorbell. Yolanda knew because she'd started counting at 6:31 on the dot, which was the time he said he'd be there to pick her up. Thirty-four seconds late. Not a problem today, but what if he had been thirty-four seconds late for a job interview? The April 15 tax deadline? The birth of his child?

When the doorbell rang, she grabbed her purse, slung it over her shoulder, and all but pushed him out the doorway as she breezed past his hello.

"We're gonna be late," she said over her shoulder on the way to the passenger's side of his truck.

He stood in her doorway for a second, wondering what had occurred between himself and the beautiful woman who had just wrapped a tantalizing scarf of perfume around him. Her backside swayed—no, "shimmied" was a better word—in that blue skirt as she pranced double-time in the strapless heels. It was supposed to be her professional power walk, but that was not quite what Kelan gathered. "Sexy" was more like it.

He walked to her side of the truck and opened the door. Without a word, she stepped onto the running board, positioned herself in the seat, and clicked the seat belt. "And how are you this evening, Yolanda?" he asked as he placed both hands against the frame of her door. It was one of the few times he actually wanted an answer to that question.

She looked over at his figure. His chest peeked at her between two of his buttons. She hadn't considered him physically beyond those dreads until this moment. Strong jawline, rugged manly skin, eyebrows that just grew where they grew. Nothing she recognized from her woman's world of waxing and shaving.

Finally, she answered curtly, "I'm fine."

"Are you sure? I mean, do you want to do this another time?" he double-checked.

She could very easily have challenged him—"What do you mean, 'do I want to do this another time?'"—then they could have had words and she could have gone back into her nice, safe house with its aligned rows of canned goods. Nothing ventured. But that would be downright mean, like Regina. And what would that say of her hospitality ministry—that she could be nice at church but mean outside the Lord's house?

"No, tonight is fine."

He got into the car and sprayed some jazz through the speakers to clear the air. Yolanda listened as Miles Davis played tunes she'd heard more than once at Aunt Toe's house. What would Aunt Toe think of her now? She'd probably smile, say that things were looking up for Yolanda.

She could accept that. But when it came to a man, her expectations were . . . Well, she couldn't quite say what they were. He'd have to be outstanding, that was for sure. No half-stepping. Say what you mean; mean what you say. Be straightforward because if there was one thing Yolanda didn't have time for, it was games. Worse, she didn't know how to play them and was sure to lose. Like an inexperienced spades player, she knew the objective and the basic rules, but she didn't know exactly how to bid, watch the board, or read her partner, always confusing the high joker with the low one. She was sorely inept, and she hated feeling inadequate. Imperfect.

"So, do you enjoy jazz?" Kelan broke ice that he hadn't expected to have to chisel tonight.

"I don't listen to much music," she said.

"Well, your foot is sure tapping like you know all about Miles Davis," he remarked.

Yolanda seized control of her disloyal foot and crossed her arms over her chest. "My aunt likes this music."

"You don't have to stop feeling it on account of me. That's what art is all about." He tried his best first-day-of-class spiel. "Art is universal, transcends boundaries."

"*Math* is universal." She rolled her eyes and looked out the window. *How dare he call* art *universal.*

"Math might be universal, but you must have prior knowledge to fully process and understand it—unlike art. You can listen to a song, look at a picture, or see a dance and be able to appreciate it in your own way without a formula." He argued his profession. A smirk spread across his face as he realized that this was the first time in a long time that he'd been so intrigued by a woman.

"That's because art is subjective. Everyone has their own interpretation. At least in the exact science of math, we can prove that the answer is five," she said. These artsy types got on her nerves. But this was a good nerve-getting-on. Kelan was quick and smart. Just as he'd done in Bible study, he matched her wits with his own and challenged her to think. Maybe that was one of his artsy tricks. If so, she had fallen for it.

"Are you always this temperamental?" he tested her.

"Are you always this rude?"

"I could ask you that question, too." He threw it back at Yolanda.

"Look, Kelan. I don't have time for games, okay?" She laid down the law Gloria May Rucker style.

"What makes you think I have time for games any more than you do?" He shook his head. This was turning into a questionable date. "From what I can see, you're the one with all the games, not me."

"How did you come to the conclusion that *I'm* playing games?" Yolanda pressed one hand against her thumping chest.

"You meet me at church with a smile on your face, then turn me down. Later that night, you work your way into my small group—"

"You think I *tried* to get in your group?" She looked at him with a grin, her chin tucked into her neck now.

"Well, actually, I worked my way into your group," he confessed.

Yolanda laughed with amusement, flattered that he'd pulled the strings in his grasp to spend time with her in Bible study. Showed ambition. "Go on." She unfolded her arms now.

"When I called you and asked you out, it was all good. But when I get to your door, you've got an attitude—but you say you're fine and you want to continue with our plans for the evening. It's like you want me to read your mind, or something. Now, if *that* ain't playing games, I don't know what is."

Kelan had called her out, and she wasn't quite sure how to respond. If ever she wanted someone who didn't mince words, she'd found him. Actually, it was more like she'd met her match. They could be good friends, she figured. He could give her an honest opinion about things, not watered down with flattery, flowery language. She could give him a female ear, a woman's perspective. It might work.

Shame it had come down to this: resorting to male companionship. But with her mother's recent nuptials and altered priorities, what other choice did she have? Regina was a newlywed with a newborn. Brookelynn was on another wavelength. Miss Marva was from another generation. Dianne was a couple of hundred miles away. It just might work with Kelan.

"Okay," Yolanda surrendered finally. "If you really want to know, I was a bit upset because you were late."

"Oh, this will be interesting. How late was I?"

"Several seconds."

He looked her upside the head. "Are you serious?"

"Yes." She gave him the look of "duh."

"You have to get out more, Yolanda. You need a life." He wagged his index finger toward her.

"And I suppose you're gonna show me how to get that life, huh?" she quizzed him, trying her best to keep that pesky smile from wrapping around her face. He was flirting, and the interior of the truck had suddenly been charged with unmistakable boy-meets-girl electricity—her perfume, his cologne, their conversation.

"It takes two," he proposed.

"Well," she hesitated, "let's just see how this evening goes."

Yolanda tried her best to keep the guard up all night. She talked to him indirectly, never looking into his solid black eyes—afraid of what might happen if she did. Would he know that she liked him and hoped like crazy that he'd call her again? Worse, would he take advantage of her feelings? Better to be safe and keep that brick wall in place.

At the mall, they caught a movie and ate dinner. Kelan was

polite, kept his distance. Yolanda asked him if he'd mind going with her to Folman's to look for a white blouse. "I'm not that crazy about wearing white, but I need another one for the hospitality committee."

As Kelan waited for Yolanda outside the dressing room, he noticed that he was the only man in the ladies' wear department. At least she hadn't asked him to hold her purse.

Yolanda already knew which blouse she wanted, but she'd picked two others just to feel out Kelan's fashion sense and truthfulness. The other blouses were ridiculous, and he *had* to tell her so.

When she came out wearing a blouse that made her look like a snowwoman and asked, "What do you think of this one?" Kelan couldn't find the words in all his artistic vocabulary to describe that blouse.

"It's . . . I think . . ." He got the benefit of reading Yolanda's face and realized that it was a test. "What did they *feed* that thing?" They both laughed at the hideous blouse with its bulging sides and gathered waistband. Maybe on some runway in Paris the style had been the talk of the town. But the buyers at Folman's had purchased an awful replica, hence the rack full of discounted blouses that probably wouldn't budge by the season's end.

After Yolanda purchased her blouse they took a scenic route through the mall. Kelan coaxed her into a quaint art gallery, where he gave her little-known tidbits about artists and their works. He taught English at Dentonville County Community College and knew a great deal about the visual arts. He was on top of his game, and Yolanda soaked up his expertise as fast as it flowed from him.

They stopped at a few more shops that Yolanda had only casually noticed before: the music store, a ceramic store, and a store with Texas memorabilia. Venues that she had never given a second thought suddenly gained appeal with Kelan's knowledge.

One of their last stops was a store full of figurines and other collectibles. "This is cute. What's it used for?" she asked about an inexpensive, oddly shaped ceramic boot.

"It's for decoration," he said as he examined it.

"It has no function?"

"None other than to make the setting more appealing. Some things don't have functions—they just *are*. They make the space you're in feel better," he explained. "That's the function."

"Mmm," Yolanda groaned, and placed the useless boot back on the shelf.

Kelan picked up the discarded piece and asked her, "Do you like it?"

"Yeah." Yolanda shrugged. "It's okay, I guess."

"Then you should have it," he said as he quickly approached the counter and pulled out his wallet.

"Kelan, I don't need that thing," Yolanda protested as she followed him to the counter, but he wouldn't respond until the transaction was complete.

"I know you don't *need* it. But you liked it; you admired it; it caught your eye; it spoke to you," he concluded.

"I wouldn't say all *that*."

"Well, maybe not now. Take it home, find a place for it, and just let it sit there. You'll get it," he said as he transferred ownership of the boot.

She didn't have the heart to tell him that the boot was just one more thing she'd have to dust.

On their way out of the mall, Yolanda heard her nickname as loud as if she'd been paged on a PA system. "Yolanda! Hey! Yo-Yo!" She was mortified. There was Joyce Ann, running through the mall like a madwoman, head bent down low, cardigan swishing behind with her speed. *Why is she still in Dentonville?* "Yo-yo!" Twenty feet behind her was Gloria, trying her best to speed-walk and catch up with Joyce Ann before security was summoned.

Kelan took his cue from Yolanda and stopped to wait. "Who's Yo-yo?" he asked.

"*I'm* Yo-yo."

"Yo-yo . . ." Joyce Ann finally reached them, panting. "I thought that was you."

Kelan stood in awe of this woman's speed.

"Hello, Aunt Joyce Ann. What are you doing here?"

"Just out here with Gloria," she said, and turned as though she expected to see Gloria right behind her. "Come on, Gloria!" she called clear across four stores.

Gloria finally made it to the resting spot, and Yolanda introduced them both to Kelan. Kelan shook their hands in bewilderment, pulling his dreads back in thought.

"Well, we were just leaving." Yolanda kept the encounter as brief as possible, but she did want answers from her mother. She looked Gloria in the eyes and said, "I'll call you later tonight." Yolanda wanted to know why Joyce Ann was still in Dentonville, where she was staying, why she was running through the mall like a madwoman probably high on something or other. Most of all, she wanted to know why her mother was acting as if there was nothing wrong with the picture. But now wasn't the time to press for the answers, not with Kelan around.

Graciously Kelan refrained from asking Yolanda about Joyce Ann. He only clarified, "You're Yo-yo?" To which she could only reply with a nod. The "best foot" was over. He knew she had some crazy peoples now. She might as well give him a window in the brick wall.

Chapter 11

*Y*olanda found herself searching for Kelan, though she knew she probably couldn't spot him in such a dense crowd. Still, she looked for him when she should have been listening to the announcements so that she could govern herself accordingly. Her eyes swept the congregation and crossed hundreds of members she had personally welcomed to the church in the hospitality room following Sunday services. Most of the time they recognized her before she recognized them—funny how far-reaching a warm smile and a cup of juice could be.

Even after the service she held up hopes of bumping into him in the corridor or maybe the parking lot. Since their date, they hadn't done anything more than talk on the phone, but Yolanda longed for those moments. She didn't really *like* like Kelan, she told herself, but she enjoyed his company and conversation, not to mention the way that ceramic boot seemed to wink at her every time she passed the kitchen counter.

As she exited from the church foyer she gave up all hopes of locating Kelan and reluctantly joined the small crowd gathering near the west doors, awaiting shuttles to the parking lots. She spotted Regina and Orlando in the huddle and inched her way toward them.

"Hey." Regina hugged her.

Yolanda took in her sister's scent, well aware that it had to be one of the latest fragrances at Nordstrom's or Neiman's. Then she took Orlando Jr. from his proud father and kissed the butterball baby on his chubby brown forehead, smelling the tender scent of baby lotion. "I'm sorry, Orlando, but my nephew is looking more and more like Regina every day. Look at these fat little cheeks!"

Yolanda didn't mean to insinuate that Regina had a fat face, but Regina took the observation as proof that the world knew that she was fat again. Despite her efforts to lose weight the past couple of weeks, the red line betrayed her daily. She'd even purchased a new scale, thinking that her old judge was too old to render a just verdict. The new scale was worse—she couldn't get a lower reading by standing on one foot or leaning slightly forward, as she had done in the past.

No, this scale was acutely torturous, causing great gnashing of the teeth every morning. First she rushed to the scale, as though she could beat the fat in a race to the platform. The initial weigh-in might be the worst. She used the restroom and weighed herself again. Little change, if any. She brushed her teeth and weighed. No change. Then she did twenty-five jumping jacks and ten push-ups, silently so as not to wake the baby. The change, if any, was never in her favor. To put herself out of her misery, she drank a glass of water. With the water, she was certain that she'd already seen her lowest reading of the day. The entire procedure took no less than ten minutes.

After her mother's wedding reception Regina had given up on fasting and decided that the best thing to do was get in touch with Carlotta and get more of those pills. That didn't go over well, because in her search on the Internet for Carlotta and for the brand name of the pill, she learned that it had been banned from the U.S. market. *Great, now I've got to fly to Mexico.* It wasn't a bad idea. After all, Orlando did have some family in Mexico. But he'd never let her out of his sight long enough to get her hands on those pills. In desperation, she turned to her own version of over-the-counter weight loss: fat-blockers and metabolic enhancers combined, taken half an hour before eating. Her stomach cramped as though someone were wringing it like a wet towel, but it appeared that she'd endured all that pain for nothing. Regina was convinced now that Yolanda saw the pudge, too.

The shuttle pulled under the canopy and was filled before they had the chance to get on. The sea of heads and shoulders in front of them seemed to have moved only a few inches. "How far are you parked?" Regina asked.

"Row G."

"I think we're on I. Let's just walk." Regina started walking before anyone could object. She walked quickly, intending to burn a calorie a step. Yolanda admired her sister's perfectly formed legs and wished for the millionth time that she'd been blessed with such muscular definition. Never in a thousand lifetimes could she hope to do justice to a skirt and heels the way Regina did.

"I don't know how you stay so little," Regina commented/fussed at Yolanda as they approached Yolanda's car. "You *don't* exercise."

"I'm younger than you," Yolanda teased her.

"You keep on thinking that." Regina ground her teeth, staying one step ahead of Yolanda. "You just wait until you have a baby, Yo-yo. Then you'll see how hard it is."

Yolanda heard the edge in Regina's voice and wondered what had brought about this change in attitude. She looked to Orlando for a hint, but he just shrugged his shoulders and shook his head as if to say, "Your guess is as good as mine."

Yolanda caught up at her car and gave the baby back to her sister. "Well, I don't know why you're so touchy, but I think you look great. I think you're a role model for new mothers."

"A *roll* model, maybe." Regina thumped her stomach and couldn't help but laugh at her own joke.

"Bye, girl." Yolanda hugged her again, then fumbled through her purse, looking for her keys. She unlocked the door, but Regina placed her hand on the driver's door, securing Yolanda's complete attention.

Regina motioned to Orlando to go ahead to their SUV with the baby.

"Yo-yo," Regina changed the subject, "Aunt Joyce Ann is moving back into Momma's rent house."

"What?"

"She's moving back to Dentonville, and she asked Momma if she could move into the rent house while she gets back on her feet." Regina waited for her sister's reaction. The wind caught Regina's bangs and blew them away from her distressed forehead.

Yolanda didn't know what to think of Joyce Ann's return. It wasn't as if they were kids. They were all adults, and what Joyce Ann did was none of her business. On the other hand, Joyce Ann's elevator didn't go all the way up anymore—hadn't seen the top floors in a long time. "And Momma agreed?" Yolanda asked.

"Yeah." Regina nodded. "She had me draw up the lease and everything. Now, call me crazy, but I think Joyce Ann is smokin' something. And the way Momma's acting, she's got some kind of contact high, because she can't seem to say no to Aunt Joyce Ann—like Aunt Joyce Ann has some kind of hold on her."

"Well, it's Momma's house," Yolanda recognized. "I guess if

she wants to rent it out to Aunt Joyce Ann, that's her business."

Regina looked away from Yolanda, toward Orlando and the baby. "It's just hard for me. I don't understand how somebody could just walk away from their child and never look back."

"Maybe she's looking back now."

"I guess I'm more worried about Dianne than anything else." Regina folded her arms across her chest. "She's been on my mind lately. I've tried to call her a few times since the wedding, but I couldn't get her. And she never returns my calls. I've been praying for her ever since that night. I still think we should have escorted Joyce Ann's butt right out of the sanctuary."

"It's a *sanctuary*, Regina. It's open to the public." Yolanda smacked her lips and sighed. "You know, we do have to forgive her."

"She needs to—"

"No, Regina, you know that's not how it works," Yolanda reminded her. "Forgiveness is not contingent upon what someone else does or doesn't do."

"I am so sick of these wings sticking out of your back. Here, turn around. Let me snap these suckers off." Regina's smile made the day even brighter. There was something about her big sister that always made Yolanda look up to Regina. Regina could be rude and abrupt; to be graced with her stunning smile was a reward in itself.

"I'll call you later if we don't stay at my mother-in-law's house too long."

"I've got to work tonight."

"I guess I'll call you later this week, then."

Yolanda hugged her sister again, thinking that Regina was lucky to have different people to see on Sunday afternoons. "Y'all gonna stop by Momma's house?"

"No, I don't think we'll have time." Regina looked at her watch. "You going by there?"

"Yeah. I'm gonna go home and change first."

"Okay." She backed away. "Tell Momma I said hi. I'll see you."

"Bye."

Halfway to her mother's house, Yolanda's cell phone blared its tune. "Hello," she answered.

"Hi." Kelan made no attempt to hide the smile in his voice.

"Hey, what's up?"

"Nothing." She could almost hear his dimples punching into his face. "Did you enjoy the service today?"

"It was just what I needed," she sighed. "Pastor really hit home today—some of us have some *serious* spiritual house-cleaning to do."

"You're right about that," he concurred. "Hey, have you eaten yet?"

"No," she replied, "but I'm on my way to my mom's house—well, I should say, my mom and stepdad's house—to eat." Acknowledging Richard tasted like bad medicine.

"Oh." his voice fell. "All right, then. You working this evening?"

"Yeah." Her voice fell, too. *No Kelan.* It occurred to her, at the corner of Jake and Windfall Court, that she'd invited friends to her mother's house before. *Why not Kelan?* "Kelan, would you like to eat dinner with me at my mother's house?"

"I don't want to impose," he kindly declined.

"Kelan, you know you hungry."

"You know you right," he laughed. "Give me directions."

At Gloria's house, Yolanda asked her mother to make another setting at the table. "I invited one of my friends from church."

"Oh, good," she sang. "We've got plenty."

"Baby, hand me a fork," Gloria said. Yolanda reached for the drawer but quickly realized that she wasn't "baby"—"baby" was Richard. He already had the fork in hand. Seeing him in the kitchen with her mother was . . . It just didn't seem right, even though Yolanda knew it was. Gloria had eased herself into wifehood as if it were second nature. Yolanda watched them move about, flowing smoothly in and out of each other's path, passing utensils, tasting sauces, and stealing knowing glances. She'd never been so happy for her mother, but Yolanda felt completely out of place in the home that used to be hers.

Aunt Toe rolled her chair into the kitchen.

"Aunt Toe, what are you doing in here?" Gloria asked her.

"I know my way around a kitchen," she snapped back. "I'm the one taught *you* how to cook."

"Aunt Toe, you ready to get in here and teach these young gals a lesson?" Richard asked her.

"Don't get her started," Gloria warned him softly.

"Yeah, but I'm still learning. You got any uncles? Brothers?" she asked Richard. "I could use a classmate."

"Aunt Toe, did you take your medicine?" Gloria asked her.

"Aw, gal, y'all act like insulin is supposed to zip my mouth shut," she said. "Ain't nothin' wrong with me. I just asked the man a question."

"Aunt Toe, what you gonna do with a man?" Yolanda joked.

"Same thing you'd do with him," she winked at Yolanda. "You know, Sarah was ninety-five when she gave birth to—"

"Aunt Toe, I'm gonna push you back in the living room." Gloria wiped her hands on her apron and twirled Aunt Toe around, though Aunt Toe showed her objection by letting her feet drag on the floor. "We got company coming, Aunt Toe. I don't want to hear any more talk about you and a boyfriend, okay?"

"All right," Aunt Toe agreed. "All right. I was just foolin' with you, Gloria. You take everything so serious all the time."

"Life *is* serious," Gloria sang.

"Yeah, it's serious, but it ain't no sin in laughing every once in a while."

"I guess you're right. And you certainly do make us laugh." Gloria locked Aunt Toe's wheelchair in place and kissed her lightly on the forehead before heading back to the kitchen.

Kelan's knock on the door surprised Aunt Toe. "Gloria!" She alarmed them all. "Gloria! It's a man at the door!"

"A man?" Gloria questioned.

"Remember," Yolanda said, "I told you, one of my friends from church was coming by for dinner."

"Well, you didn't say it was a *man*, missy," Gloria pinched Yolanda's shoulder and gave her daughter one of those smiles she usually reserved for women her own age.

"I said it was a *friend*," Yolanda repeated, embarrassed at the exchange. Especially with Richard there. She took off her apron and went to the front door.

Kelan was his usual old goofy self, waving at her through the screen door.

"Hi," she said, taking the brown hook out of the little ring that barely held the screen door shut. It was one of those by-gone things that made an old house a home—well, what used to be her home.

She fought the door back with her hand, making sure that the springs didn't slap him on the backside. His dreads were pulled back, held in place by a black rubber band. He balanced a cake on his right hand, though she hadn't asked him to bring anything. Yolanda could smell the fresh butter through the foil. On his way in, he took the liberty to greet Yolanda by brushing his lips against her cheek. It seemed only natural that he should do it, coming to a friend's house for dinner. It was an innocent gesture, but it felt more significant to Yolanda.

Aunt Toe's face lit up when Yolanda introduced her to Kelan. *Oh, Lord, please don't let Aunt Toe get to talking.*

"It's nice to meet you." Kelan bent down to hug Aunt Toe.

Gloria and Richard came into the living room next. Yolanda really hadn't thought about how she should introduce Richard. "Kelan, this is my mother. And . . . this is . . . Richard," she fumbled through.

"It's nice to meet you both," Kelan said, then offered the dessert to Gloria.

"I hope you all like pound cake."

"Oh, yes. This sure smells good." Gloria relieved him of the cake. "Have a seat, Kelan. We're almost finished in the kitchen."

"If you don't mind, I'd like to use your restroom."

"Oh, sure," Gloria said gracefully, "Yo-yo can show you where it is." Aunt Toe almost broke her neck watching the two of them walk down the hallway.

Yolanda whispered as they neared the restroom. "I guess you've got homemade pound cakes just lying around your house?"

"A man can make a cake for Sunday dinner," he smiled. "I'm single, but I still have to eat."

"All I brought was Kool-Aid." Yolanda stamped softly. "You're making me look bad."

"You could never look bad," he flirted, backing into the bathroom doorway.

Spying on Yolanda, Aunt Toe leaned so far over in her chair that she almost fell out. She caught herself and then called, "Yo-yo-o-o!" as if the girl were outside playing after the street lights came on. "You come out that bathroom with that boy!"

"Oop!" Yolanda put her hand over her mouth, a flush of embarrassment crossing her face. Kelan slammed the door shut.

Minutes later he joined them at the dinner table, his lips threatening to give way to mad laughter during grace. Gloria kept food on Aunt Toe's plate so that her mouth would stay busy chewing.

"So, Kelan," Richard asked, "what do you do?"

"I'm an assistant professor at Dentonville Community College. I teach English, and I also dabble a little in art."

This whole thing—eating with her family, watching out for Aunt Toe, Richard interviewing Kelan—it was odd. It made Yolanda feel like . . . like a teenager bringing home a date. It wasn't a date. It was Kelan, for goodness' sake. *So why am I making such a big fuss over it?*

"Oh, I love art." Gloria touched Richard's hand and added, "Richard's always getting me things at the starving-artists exhibits in Dallas. Do you sell at those?"

"No, ma'am." Kelan shook his head. "Not yet."

"Well, when you get ready to sell, let me know," Richard said. "I've got some friends around the city with connections. If you're pretty good, I'll bet we could get your work in front of the right people."

"Thanks, Richard. That would be great. We'll have to talk more."

"Sure thing."

Kelan's leg came to rest against Yolanda's knee during the course of the dinner. She almost jumped the moment his slacks swept her skin, yet she doubted he even knew that he was touching her. Who could have known she'd get such a kick out of their contact? Simple . . . innocent.

"Kelan?" It was Gloria's turn. "Yo-yo says you both attend the same church."

"Yes, ma'am," he mumbled, swallowing his food so that he could continue. "I met Yolanda on my first visit."

"How nice." Gloria smiled at Yolanda. "And are you enjoying the church?"

Kelan dabbed the corners of his mouth with his napkin. "Immensely. I've learned so much in the short time I've been a member."

"Where did you worship before?"

"At First United."

"First United?" Aunt Toe asked.

"Yes, ma'am."

"How you get from First United to the Master's Tabernacle?"

"The Word," he laughed, eager to tell her. "The unadulterated Word. A colleague of mine invited me to the Master's Tabernacle for a men's conference. I got more out of that weekend than I got in almost thirty years at my old church. I knew I needed to get someplace where my soul could be fed—quickly. Initially, I thought the Master's Tabernacle was too large for me. But when I met people like Yolanda and the other brothers and sisters in the Sunday night Bible study class, I really got into it. I prayed about it, and here I am."

"Hmm," Aunt Toe thought. "I like First United. They got the best garage sales. I got a purse for a quarter one time. Nice, fancy purse. Had two zippers on it—one across the top and one right there in the front for your knickknacks."

"What color was it?" Kelan indulged her.

"Red with a silver buckle, only the buckle wasn't real," Aunt Toe replied. "They just put that on there to fool the pickpockets."

After they finished dessert, Richard invited Kelan to stay and watch ESPN, but Kelan declined. "I've got to get on back home."

"Well, we certainly enjoyed you," Gloria said.

"Thanks for having me. The food was great." He gave Gloria a light hug, then reached to her left to shake Richard's hand.

Yolanda walked outside to Kelan's car with him. Finally, it was just the two of them. She was relieved that the show was over. It was all too Cleaver-ish.

"You sure were quiet," he remarked.

She looked down at the ground and shoved her hands into the front pockets of her denim skirt. *Why am I acting like this?* "I'm just tired, I guess. I had a long weekend."

He let it go. "Well, I hope you get some rest after tonight's shift. Sleep all day tomorrow if you have to."

"I will," she said. "So don't be calling me and waking me up on your lunch break."

"I'll remember that," he laughed. "Your aunt is too funny."

"I know," Yolanda apologized. "That's my aunt Toe."

"I like her."

"She's something else," Yolanda agreed with a slow nod. "I'll call you tomorrow as soon as I get up."

"Okay," he said, leaning forward and hugging her.

Yolanda watched Kelan get into his truck and secure himself with the seat belt before waving good-bye once again. Pull those dreads back into a neat ponytail and Kelan was strikingly handsome. His full lips were sometimes distracting, calling her attention to their form and line. He had a kind of boyish handsomeness that he'd probably had since he was an infant. *I'll bet Kelan was a cute baby.* Yet his body told the story. Kelan was far from childhood. When he hugged her, she'd felt the muscles beneath his cotton shirt. Strong, solid. She liked that he didn't flaunt his body for everyone to see. *Maybe he's saving it.* Yolanda went back into the house and watched as his truck disappeared from view.

"Yo-yo-o-o!" Aunt Toe screamed, though she was only a few inches behind Yolanda.

"Yes, ma'am." Yolanda turned and nearly fell over the wheelchair.

"Didn't you hear your momma calling you?"

"No, Aunt Toe, I didn't."

"Too busy thinkin' 'bout that man," she snickered. "He's a nice-looking one, even if he do have those nappy strings on his head."

"They're called dreadlocks, Aunt Toe," Yolanda laughed at her, sidestepping the wheelchair and heading to the kitchen. Aunt Toe rolled in behind her.

"Grab a drying towel," Gloria ordered.

Yolanda pulled a towel from the drawer next to the oven and joined Gloria at the sink.

"He seems nice," Gloria said, opening the conversation.

"He is. We're just friends."

"I didn't say anything." Gloria drew back, sticking her lips out all the while. "I didn't say a word."

"Well, I will," Aunt Toe started in on Yolanda. "You're thirty-something, you ain't got no man, and you ain't got no kids. It ain't natural goin' around like this. Everybody tryin' to be like that Oprah Winfrey—makin' all that money and ain't got nobody to share it with. It ain't natural, I tell ya. It ain't the way God intended it to be. Now, I said it. I said what I got to say."

"Thank you, Aunt Toe," Yolanda overenunciated, annoyed with her great-aunt. Yolanda had pondered those thoughts already, but she refused to be pressured into marrying or having kids just because it was the way of Aunt Toe's generation.

"It would be different if you was a widow," she went on, "but you ain't. Your sister's married. Your momma's married. What you waitin' on—Jesus to come back?"

"Aunt Toe, I'm waiting on a word from the Lord, okay? Is that all right with you?"

Yolanda put a little too much sass in her voice for Aunt Toe.

"Don't you talk back to me! I don't want to have to pop up out this wheelchair like Lazarus coming up from the dead!"

Yolanda hung her head in silent laughter. "I'm sorry, Aunt Toe. I didn't mean to raise my voice at you."

"You *better* say you're sorry." She swung her finger at Yolanda with conviction. "That man done made you lose your mind, I see."

"Aunt Toe," Gloria intervened, "I'm gonna take you in here with Richard, okay?"

"Mmm-hmm," Aunt Toe moaned on her way out.

With Aunt Toe out of the kitchen, Gloria apologized. "You know she's just looking out for you, don't you?"

"Yes, I know," Yolanda laughed. "I know that's all they had to look forward to back then."

"Well, it's not just that." Gloria shook her head. "Aunt Toe couldn't have children. She can't understand why any woman in her right mind wouldn't get married and give birth, given the opportunity. Everybody has their thing, you know."

"Hmm. I never knew she couldn't have kids."

"So, you and Kelan are friends?" Gloria switched gears.

"Yes." Yolanda tried to hide her smile. "We have been talking on the phone and we've gone out. He loves the Lord. He's a great listener and he's . . . he's a pretty good friend. I think that's what I like about him the most."

"Well, next to a man that loves the Lord, a friendship is the most important thing," Gloria advised her daughter. "If all of that is in line, there's not too much else you have to worry about."

"I don't know," Yolanda told her. "I'm in no hurry whatsoever to settle down. I just want to live my life with as little disruption as possible."

"Sounds like you don't want to live," Gloria huffed. "You know, you can't go through your whole life pushing people away because they might alter your plan or mess up your perfect little world."

She should talk! "You did."

Gloria's hands went still in the dishwater. "And I was wrong."

"What do you mean, you were wrong? You raised me and Regina and Dianne; you taught us to live by the Word, gave us a respect for education, kept us fed and clothed—we never wanted for anything," Yolanda raved. "How do you figure you were wrong?"

"Because I put *my* life on hold for twenty-something years," Gloria admitted. She lifted her hands from the water, dried them on her apron, and faced her youngest child. "When your father died, I spent a good three or four weeks living in chaos. Angry, frustrated, crazy. I ran as far away from God as I could. It was all I could do to get back in church and lay out on the altar—I was a wreck. I don't know what would have happened to me if it hadn't been for the prayers of the saints.

"After that bout with my mind, I made the conscious decision to do everything within my power to keep from ever having to go through that kind of pain again. I wanted complete control over everything—I kept the house spotless, I scrimped and saved every penny I had, I planned everything for you girls down to the last detail because I didn't want any more surprises in my life. God was faithful and blessed those plans because He knew I couldn't bear anything else happening. We made it—not because I was so perfect but because God is faithful."

She turned back toward the sink and continued washing

the dishes, talking as though she were reading a story. "I met Richard fifteen years ago at a revival in Dallas. He asked me for a date then, but I didn't accept his invitation. I knew that I'd prayed and asked God to send me a man who would be a loving husband for me and a good father to you and Regina, but when God sent him I was too afraid that my life would be torn apart again. So I let him go. And now, many lonely years later, we're together again. I don't have many regrets in my life, Yo-yo, but I do regret that I didn't say yes to Richard that night at the revival."

"So you've known him all this time?"

"I can't say that I've known him. I put him away in a corner of my mind."

"And he stayed there?"

"Yes, I guess he did." She laughed to herself. "He threw himself into full-time ministry, missions, volunteering, and helping his immediate family."

"That's a wonderful story, Mother," Yolanda sighed, realizing now that her mother had held Richard in her heart all these years but denied her feelings in order to maintain balance for the girls.

"So, now that I've poured my heart out to you, you still claiming to be *friends* with Kelan?" Gloria flicked soapsuds at Yolanda's face.

"That's my story and I'm sticking to it." Yolanda returned the playful gesture and savored this moment in her mother's presence without Richard. Regina, Gloria, and Yolanda had worked at that sink countless times over the years doing the dishes. Now there was a man sitting on the lounge chair with his feet propped up on the coffee table watching ESPN in the next room. Things were different . . . out of order, somehow.

"Momma," Yolanda asked as she finished drying the last

few items, "Regina told me that you're letting Aunt Joyce Ann move back into your rent house."

"Regina's got a big mouth." Gloria scrubbed. "But it's true. Joyce Ann is moving in first thing tomorrow morning."

"When were you going to let me know?"

"You plannin' on payin' the rent for her?" she came back.

"No, ma'am." Yolanda softened. "I was just wondering if she's moving back for good. I mean, does she have herself together now?"

"I can't be sure." Gloria avoided her daughter's eyes. "She just asked me if she could move in, and I told her she could. She's paying half rent right now, but it's better than no rent, which is what I've had since before Richard and I got married."

"I thought you were going to sell the house."

"We were thinking about it, but I guess God had other plans for it." She chuckled a bit.

"This isn't funny." Yolanda shocked herself with the sharpness in her voice. "If Aunt Joyce Ann isn't in her right mind, she's liable to do anything. I think she ought to go to a rehab or something."

"For your information, she's already been to rehab." Gloria threw her hands to her hips. Aunt Toe's wheelchair creaked across the slightly elevated divider between the living room and the kitchen. "Joyce Ann has a right to God's mercy just like every other person on the planet. You think we've all been perfect? Huh? Some of us have done things that we'd sooner jump off a cliff than have everybody know what we did.

"Your aunt Joyce Ann has been through the worst pain known to womankind. She lost a child, Yo-yo. Worse than that, she watched her child die right in her own home, in her own care. You can't even measure that kind of pain. I imagine it's enough to make anybody go crazy, but for the grace of God."

Aunt Toe rolled onto Yolanda's foot, letting the weight of her body and her wheelchair rest on Yolanda's tiniest toe. "Ow, Aunt Toe! You're on my foot."

"I *mean* to be on your foot," Aunt Toe said as she held her wheels in place. "You don't forget what your mother said, you hear? Joyce Ann is family. She belongs with us." She rolled herself off, but not before Yolanda was sure that her great aunt had left a bruise.

Chapter 12

*A*s her latest fling showered, Dianne watched his figure through the clear glass shower door. Trey's body was a perfect poem waiting to be written. Not a scratch, not a stretch mark, not a bump on it, okay? He didn't even have the mark on his arm that everyone else had from those horrid childhood booster shots. Flawless. Trey was liquid-smooth yellow skin from top to bottom and every place in between, with a booty that could shelter you from the rain.

She wondered what it would be like to go places with him—to walk around holding hands, talking, laughing with him before he tried his darnedest to please her with that twinkle of a thing he had the nerve to call "the rocket." Bless his heart, he did try. But Dianne dared not tell him what she wanted in bed—he might not like that. He might get angry and hit her, like one of her past bed partners.

Well, maybe not. Trey seemed like a nice enough guy. She'd seen him smile a few times but never directly at her. Dianne wondered what it would be like to actually have a relationship with Trey. After all, they couldn't go on this way indefinitely. Sooner or later one of them would get seriously involved with someone else—assuming that he wasn't already.

But who was she kidding? She couldn't push "rewind" and

play it all over again. Furthermore, he really didn't have any-thing to bring to the table financially. He was far better-looking than smart, and he had a lot of baby-mommas. The best thing about Trey, and all the other men, was the fact that he was an available warm body. Sometimes he stayed all night. Tonight, however, would not be one of those nights.

"I've got to be at work early tomorrow," he said as he zipped his pants.

"Yeah, me, too," Dianne lied. Trey accompanied her in the wham-bam-thank-you-ma'am waltz. They both knew the rou-tine.

"Well," she said, pushing back the comforter and sheets and pulling her T-shirt down in a moment of unnecessary modesty, "I'll see you later?"

"Yeah," he agreed, slipping into his shoes. "I'll call you."

Dianne walked him to the front door of her one-bedroom apartment. A kiss would have been nice, but it wasn't essen-tial. She liked Trey, but he was just another man she knew. Another person to whom she'd given a piece of her. As she locked the dead bolts behind him, she wondered, *How many more of these pieces do I have left to give away?* The trip home to Dentonville had jolted her sense of morality. Actually, this uneventful tryst with Trey might have been more a matter of her mental wandering than his lack of performance.

She knew better. Aunt Gloria had taught her better. But that didn't help when her sheets were freezing cold.

Dianne had been reminded of the fact that she needed to get serious about God. But facing God would mean facing herself and facing her past, and she just wasn't ready for all that. She figured there was too much that couldn't be changed. There was too much that she'd done wrong. And it was far too late for her to reconcile with her ghosts, namely, Joyce Ann. Yet, in the weeks since she'd come back from Dentonville, she found herself praying, almost involuntarily, and piddling around with the thought that He might actually be listening to her.

She stood with her back against the door and let her head hit the wood with a soft, deliberate thud. As she did, her eyes landed on the clock: 1:42. She laughed as she thought of what Aunt Toe had told her. "Yeah, Aunt Toe, you were right about what happens after midnight." She retired to her bedroom and flicked the television on to *Nick at Nite,* turning up the volume so that Gilligan could rescue her if the nightmare came back again in the next four hours.

Eight hours later she was named the information systems analyst for the month of August. She got a reserved parking space near the main entrance, a certificate, and the first slice of the cake that her coworkers later devoured to celebrate her recognition.

"Dianne," her boss, Marguerite, read from a piece of paper as the rest of her team stood assembled in the small conference room, "this month couldn't have been nearly as productive without your contribution to Palljen Technologies. We want you to know that we appreciate your sound skills, sound practices, and sound thinking." Gwen, one of the few African-American women with the company, gave Dianne a secret sisterly pat on the back as Dianne made her way to the cake. The room was decorated with the pathetic arrangement of streamers and confetti—about all that could be expected from a bunch of computer personalities. It was a nice gesture.

Dianne stood before her coworkers as they applauded. The whole time she felt like pulling a poor-little-rich-girl routine: running to the bathroom and locking herself in for a good cry. All these people applauding her for her "soundness." Little did they know how unsound she felt inside. Yes, she was good at what she did. Dianne knew the company's systems and operations backward and forward. Her mind could work wonders with computers, but that same mind malfunctioned in the important areas of her life.

She yanked her office smile into place and held the tears at bay. "Thanks, everyone."

After the short-lived celebration, they all turned on their headsets and returned to their respective work areas. Bruce, a brilliant but egotistical short man with a sarcastic answer for everything, caught up with Dianne and tapped her on the shoulder. "Congratulations, Dianne. I'd kill to get your parking spot." The smirk on his face told her that he meant to belittle her recognition. If Bruce hadn't been so knowledgeable, she would have told him exactly where to go. Problem was, Dianne respected his technological advice and collaborated with him often. No need to mess up a decent work relationship.

"Maybe next time." She winked at him. *Ooh, if I could just pass him up one time in the parking lot on the way to my new parking spot!*

During the lunch hour Dianne felt obligated to sit with her coworkers since they'd all been so gracious during her morning spotlight. The twelve o'clock news shot across the TV screen in the break room: a man killed his wife after forty years of marriage, two kids got arrested for throwing things off a bridge, and a little girl was missing. Dianne wondered if, compared to her life, the people on television had bigger problems than she did.

Genevieve, the oldest and by far the largest woman in IT, was first to strike up the age-old woe-is-my-body conversation at the table. "I don't know what possessed me to have kids. I knew my behind was big before I got pregnant—I don't know what I was thinking."

"I don't have any kids, and I'm putting on weight. What's my excuse?" Dianne joked. Dianne wasn't close to any of her

coworkers, but she figured any group of women could get together and rattle off a list of grievances about their bodies.

"Well, at least you didn't grow up fat." Gwen shook her
head while biting into a half-baked potato.

"You were fat?" Genevieve asked in amazement.

"I was fat until about four years ago. I had a gastric bypass
and lost almost a hundred pounds. But my self-image is still
the same. It's like, in my mind, I'm still overweight and undesirable and all this other crap. I've turned into a total slut—
weekend after weekend of great meaningless sex," she
laughed halfheartedly. "I'm seeing a shrink now," she admitted, carrying on as though she'd just announced that she was
seeing a movie.

It had never occurred to Dianne that she might actually
know someone who had seen a psychologist, let alone that
the person would be black. She was careful not to gaze into
Gwen's eyes. Maybe Gwen knew—as in, it takes one to know
one. Dianne excused herself only half an hour into the lunch
hour, smiling at their comments that she was a workaholic.
But she called Gwen later.

It took some convincing and a promise to accompany Dianne to the psychologist, but Gwen had done it. Dianne sat in
the waiting room, noting that it looked exactly the way Dianne
had pictured a shrink's office: exactly the opposite of crazy.
All those nice, calming pictures were enough to make her
want to run out of there. What was the point? Every patient in
there was so far away from peace and serenity that the office
probably only made them painfully aware of the distance between themselves and any semblance of normality.

Gwen placed her hand on Dianne's knee to stop the
bouncing. "You're going to be okay, girl. It's just the first visit."

Dianne rolled her eyes at Gwen. That was easy for her to

say. She wasn't the one who stayed up in bed, too afraid to close her eyes at night, like somebody in a Freddie Krueger movie. Dianne was crankier than usual that morning—assuredly because of her dire need for rest on top of the fact that she was sitting in a psychologist's office like a regular wacko. And it was all Joyce Ann's fault.

Drops of condensation from the steam of the anger boiling within Dianne's soul collected behind her eyelids and then fell from her eyes. She swiped at them quickly, turning her head from Gwen's view.

"Dianne, I know this is hard, but you can do it. Dr. Tilley is a good psychologist who's also a Christian, remember? She knows how to help you professionally and spiritually. I promise you, you won't be sorry." Gwen gave Dianne's hand one final squeeze before letting go of her completely. "I'll see you when you're finished."

Dr. Tilley was just as open and inviting as Gwen had said she'd be. Her cocoa skin caught light on all the right slopes, her smile taking center stage beneath lips with just enough gloss to keep the chap away. She was naturally beautiful, the kind of woman who woke up gorgeous every single day of her life. She could have been anything she wanted to be: a model, a rich man's wife, the *Jet* beauty of the month, a stuck-up snob. Yet, for all her good looks and education, she wasn't the least bit arrogant. Dr. Tilley had a humble servant's spirit about her. Dianne liked her already.

"Dianne," she began. "I'm sure Gwen told you, I am a psychologist and a Christian as well. I don't force my beliefs on my patients, but I know Gwen well enough and I've heard enough about you to take for granted that you don't object to prayer before sessions."

Gwen had taken a lot for granted, but Dianne's response fell right in line with the plan. "I welcome the idea."

"Very well, then. Shall we pray?" They bowed their heads as Dr. Tilley prayed for guidance and wisdom in helping Dianne dwell in the peace God promised His children. In Dr. Tilley's prayer, Dianne found the glimmer of hope she needed to open herself up to the fullness of life's possibilities. It wasn't enough hope to light up a Christmas tree, but it was *something*.

Chapter 13

Finally, she'd found something that worked, at least marginally. The laxatives and metabolic enhancers had stopped the scale at 139, and Regina could take a little breath long enough to figure out plan B. With Plathene off the market and her appetite too powerful a force to combat, she'd have to come up with something else. She didn't weigh enough for a gastric bypass, and she was too busy to fool with some group approach to weight loss. It occurred to her that she might need to take this whole weight thing to the Lord in prayer. That, she realized, would leave her at the mercy of God's timing, and He's got all the time in the world. If she went through Him, it might take years to get this thing right.

With the way the past months had flown by, it wouldn't be long before she had to return to the office. She was determined to return to work in the tailored suits she'd worn before Orlando Jr. No secretary or paralegal at the law firm of McGruder & Lawson was going to out-skinny attorney Regina Hernandez. She would see to it that Fat Regina stayed dead at all costs. It was only a matter of time before she uncovered the magic shortcut.

"Mmm," Orlando hummed, snuggling up behind her naked body as she finished her self-evaluation routine following her morning shower. He missed the old Regina, but not because she'd been thinner. Truthfully, he liked the fuller curve of her behind and how these new, round hips felt in his grip. What he missed most about his wife of five years was her zest for sex and how she used to love it as much as he. Lately her libido had been pushing the snooze button, putting him off until the last possible minute, when he brought up the fact that they hadn't been intimate for a week or so. Then she'd roll over with that go-ahead-and-do-it attitude, as if she was doing him a favor.

Alas, he told her what she wanted to hear in hopes that she would make him late for work. "I can tell you're losing weight."

"Can you?" she raised her arm and ran her nails along the back of his neck. *There,* she thought as she focused on her body's reflection. *If I could just get my waist to look the way it does when I raise my arms.*

Orlando kissed his wife behind her ear and along her shoulders, from left to right. Slowly, intently. With each kiss, he hoped to implant the idea that she was beautiful just the way she was right now. He walked his fingers down her spine, savoring every inch of her body. Regina's mind, however, was fast at work computing the number of hours she'd have to wait until she could take her next laxative.

It was risky, she knew, but to feel half as sexy and as powerful as she did now was worth it because there were *definite* drawbacks to being fat and unattractive. Six weeks after giving birth, when she'd weighed 147, Regina couldn't muster up an ounce of sexy. When Orlando caressed her body, she didn't feel the tingle of his touch. She could only calculate the extra half-second it took for his hand to cross her thighs. During their lovemaking, she couldn't hear his confessions of love. She only heard the disgusting clap of her new gut against his washboard stomach at the height of his satisfaction—a sound that completely destroyed any hope of pleasure for her.

"Don't you hear that sound when we're doing it?" she'd asked Orlando one night in total darkness.

"No," he said matter-of-factly.

"How can you *not* hear it?" Regina cross-examined him.

"Regina, I just don't hear it, okay?"

"I don't understand how you can't hear *that* sound, but you can hear your cell phone a mile away." She dragged the argument to another domain, referring to Orlando's speedy response to calls on his business line.

She couldn't imagine what Orlando's problem was and how he could fail to notice what was so obvious to her; a sound that reverberated through her head for hours after Orlando turned off the night-light. Another night of feigned ecstasy, going through the motions so as not to alarm Orlando and get him to digging beneath the surface, as he surely would. He adored Regina, worshipped the ground she walked on. Most of the time that was great. Other times he got on her last nerve being so concerned about everything. Besides, she told herself, she wouldn't have to fake it much longer. Once she got back on the path, she'd make up for lost time.

With the scale stopped and the promise of weight loss on the way, there would be no faking this morning's quickie. Regina took her favorite position beneath Orlando, closed her eyes, and fantasized, something she could do now that she was soon to be on her way back down the scale. She saw herself skinny again. Skinny. So skinny, in fact, that she could wear her college clothes again. No, maybe she could do better. Junior sizes—*that's* the kind of skinny she wanted to be. She squeezed her eyelids together in anticipation of the moment, now matching Orlando's movements with her own, concentrating on pleasure.

And then there was reality. *Clap. Clap. Clap.* Great flaps of pendulous, quivering flesh. *No!* Regina's mind screamed every expletive she could think of, but it was like being snatched out of a wonderful dream by a telephone's piercing ring. Try, wish, cry as you might, you couldn't just jump back in where you left off.

Aunt Toe rolled around her house straightening up what she could before Regina and Yolanda came over to do the heavy-duty cleaning. She hummed her favorite gospel hymns, ignoring conditions that might raise an eyebrow or two at the Department of Housing. The antique heater had no cover, the wooden floors had weak spots, the outlets (what few there were) were all jammed with extension cords to compensate for the fact that, when the house was built, there weren't many things running on electricity. No central air-conditioning, only wall units to aid her in staying "comfortable." Against her wishes (and sometimes while Aunt Toe was out with her senior friends), Yolanda, Regina, and Gloria managed to sneak in a handyman to fix up this or that.

Aunt Toe laughed at them. Little did they know, she'd lived through many a day without all these modern conveniences. She'd lived with dirt floors, outhouses, and a whole slew of other circumstances that young folks today couldn't imagine in their wildest dreams. The present condition of her house was a hundred times better than the shack she grew up in, so Aunt Toe was not about to leave her house, no matter how much Gloria and the girls pressed her on the issue. They'd understand, years from now, when their own grandchildren declared, "Grandma, we can't possibly let you live in this house without an Internet connection!"

Aunt Toe had seen too many of her friends sell their homes at their family members' request, trusting their good intentions and promises to take care of their elderly relatives. Maybe the children promised to set up a room for Big Momma in their new suburban home, or rent a house not far from them, or put her up in a fancy hotel-ish retirement community. Then came life—divorces, job losses, transfers, illnesses, and other unexpected changes in financial or social status. Next thing you knew, Big Momma was in a cheap, nasty old-folks' home, thinking of how she could just kick herself in the behind for selling her house. No, Aunt Toe wasn't about to leave the security of her property so she could end up in a nursing home, chewing on her tongue all day.

Besides, she had memories in this house. Memories were music to her soul—some were gospel: uplifting and hopeful. Others were the blues: sad and painful. But she could *feel* them all through the house, singing the tunes of her life. If she left, she might never hear the music again.

The cats meowed, and Aunt Toe grabbed the metal railing of her wheelchair to let the cleaning crew in. Yolanda, with her scary self, was backed up against the door. Aunt Toe smiled and let the child in.

"Hey, Aunt Toe." Yolanda quickly closed the door behind herself.

"I keep tellin' you, those cats ain't studyin' you," Aunt Toe reminded her.

"All I know is, the day one of them scratches me, I'm calling the Humane Society," Yolanda warned.

"Naw, you ain't. Those cats keep the rats and squirrels away. I'd rather have cats on my porch than rats in my house."

"*I'd* rather have you come live with me," Yolanda offered, knowing that she was wasting her breath. For the life of her, she couldn't figure out why anybody in their right mind would want to stay in that old scrap of a house when they didn't have to.

"Then what am I supposed to do when you get married to what's-his-name?" Aunt Toe teased.

"Who said I was getting married to *anybody*?"

"You ain't *funny*, is you?" Aunt Toe's eyes probed for Yolanda's reaction.

"Aunt Toe . . ." Yolanda started to get up on her soapbox but decided not to. That was the way it was in Aunt Toe's day. No sense in getting all puffed up over something that wasn't going to change. "Oh, Aunt Toe, sometimes I don't know what I'm gonna do with you."

Regina's car made the gravel hum as she pulled up behind Yolanda's late-model Toyota Camry. Cleaning up at Aunt Toe's was not what she'd call great Friday evening plans, but it was better than nothing. She could get out of the house and talk to adults for a change while Orlando bonded with their son at home.

She walked toward the door, eyeing those cats as if she were a cat herself, with her back arched and ready to strike at any one of them if they weren't careful. After the morning she'd had, she was ready for a good fight. "Get back!" she fussed. They all scattered, even the one that was usually stubborn. Regina bounced on the balls of her feet while she waited for someone to come to the door. *What's taking them so long?*

"Yo-yo! Aunt Toe!"

"Hold your horses, gal," Aunt Toe snapped at her.

Regina pressed her palm against her forehead, willing her tongue to be still. Under normal circumstances, she realized, she wouldn't have been so irritated. It was *always* like this at Aunt Toe's. Both she and Yolanda had been meaning to get a copy of the key from Gloria, but it was one of those things that got put on the back burner despite the fact that *not* doing it would lead to future inconveniences.

Just as Aunt Toe opened the door, Regina's stomach cramped up. The sharp pain, like an ice pick hooked up to an electric toothbrush, shot through her, almost taking her breath away. She grabbed her midsection and doubled over in pain, mentally repeating the mantra that she called on when the spasms hit: *No pain, no gain! No pain, no gain!* Aunt Toe fumbled with the locks just long enough for Regina to regain her erect posture but not her composure.

"You okay, Regina?"

"Yes, ma'am," she said through clenched teeth.

"You don't *look* all right."

"I just need to go to the bathroom." Regina pressed past her great-aunt and locked herself inside the matchbox of a restroom. The laxatives did their job, but Regina stayed on the toilet seat for another fifteen minutes, recovering from the sudden plunge into pain.

"What's she doin' in there?" Aunt Toe asked Yolanda, as if she would know.

"I don't know. Probably farting up a storm," Yolanda laughed with Aunt Toe.

"Well," Aunt Toe joked, "if you can't fart in a bathroom, where can you fart?"

Yolanda continued looking through the mail that Aunt Toe had saved for further scrutiny. Regina would go through technical notices; Yolanda went through everything else. "Ooh, look, you might have won a million dollars!" Yolanda announced with mock excitement, waving the brown envelope in front of Aunt Toe's face.

"Get that thing on out of here." Aunt Toe pushed Yolanda's hand.

"Think of all the good you could do with a million dollars," Yolanda said.

"I'd get myself a shotgun so those old buzzards at the senior center would leave me alone," she fussed.

"Aunt Toe!" Yolanda scolded. "You would never shoot anyone."

"Don't have to shoot. Just havin' 'em look down the barrel ought to be enough." She laughed at herself now.

"You really ought to stop pushing those men away."

"You should talk." Aunt Toe threw a line, but Yolanda wasn't biting.

Regina tried to appear settled as she finally came out of the bathroom, but dishevelment was written in the folds between her eyebrows and the tight creases of her lips. "What?" she finally asked them.

"Regina, when something's wrong, you need to let somebody know." Aunt Toe wasn't so much asking as telling Regina that she already sensed something.

"You look tired, Regina," Yolanda did her best to describe the look on her sister's face. "Like maybe you're not getting enough rest."

"Hello! I have a five-month-old. How much rest do you think the mother of a five-month-old gets?" Regina laughed, trying to quell their inquiries with humor.

Yolanda went into pharmacist mode. "No, it's not just that. Your eyes are sunken and your skin looks dry, which is not at all like the Rucker women. Are you drinking enough water?"

"Yes, I drink water. I don't know why y'all just have to find something to worry about." If laughter didn't work, maybe getting an attitude would. Everybody already knew that Regina was sometimey. It didn't hurt to reiterate that theory every once in a while, and she would have no trouble mustering up an attitude after the morning's frustrations in bed with Orlando. Twelve hours later Regina was still angry with her body's betrayal.

"I'll look it up tomorrow on the doctors' diagnosis website. Maybe then I can get an idea. Are you having any other symptoms?" Yolanda had gone so far as writing on the back of a discarded envelope.

"I don't have any symptoms, Yo-yo. I'm fine. Neither one of you has given birth, so you can't possibly understand what I'm going through, okay?"

Aunt Toe had had just about enough of this sassing, and needless to say, Regina was getting mighty close to rippin' her panties with that reference to childbirth. "You ain't got to have no baby to be able to see when somebody ain't takin' care of theyself! Now, I'm telling you, you are sick—or something. You don't look like yourself, and you ought to be glad Yo-yo can help you figure out what the problem is. Everybody don't have a real live pharmacist in the family who can understand all these different sicknesses and diseases that you young folk keep coming up with!"

"They're mutations, Aunt Toe." Yolanda managed to ease the tension with a chuckle.

"I don't give a fat rat what you call it; we didn't *have* it back then."

Regina got busy cleaning.

Chapter 14

Kelan was fast becoming Yolanda's "Sunday night friend." They often went for a bite to eat after Sunday evening Bible study class. Sometimes they'd continue discussing the topics covered during Bible study. It was amazing how much the Bible could be debated and reviewed. Yolanda already knew that, of course, but it was nice to have someone to go back and forth with debate.

Slowly Kelan had carved himself a niche in her life. A midday phone call here, a door held open there. Yolanda could get used to this. He did have to talk to her now and then about the difference between being a realist and a pessimist—a fine line that Yolanda walked. And she threatened to block his e-mail address if he didn't quit with the mass forwarding. He had it bad about forwarding every little joke, picture, and friendly message he got. "Could you be a bit more discriminating?" she'd commanded, but then softened her request with an explanation after seeing a scowl creep across his countenance. "Sending out all these mass e-mails is like crying wolf. I don't know when you have something really important to say. Besides that, everybody you sent it to then has my e-mail address, and they put me on their mass-forwarding list, too. Pretty soon, I'm on the pervert list, getting all kinds of e-mail about X-rated videos and penile implants."

They were both learning how to slide into each other.

In Yolanda's eyes they had that platonic thing working. He talked to her about a few ladies he was interested in and she talked to him about . . . well, no one in particular. Every once in a while, she made up something or other about a potential love interest, so that Kelan wouldn't think he was the only item on her agenda.

At one of their usual dinners out, Kelan and Yolanda sat so close they might have been mistaken for a couple. Their waitress that evening was their usual server, a single mom with two school-age children who often sat in a booth and colored as their mother worked. Kelan always tipped her well. After ordering drinks, Yolanda reached into her purse to turn off her cell phone. It was their time to talk, her time to feel that little tingle in her mind, even if Kelan did have Carla, his newest prospect, on the brain.

"So you think I should date Carla?" he asked.

"I think Carla is great for you. She's down to earth; she's realistic. That's what you need in your life, Kelan," Yolanda surmised in a big sister's tone.

"Yeah, but she's moving to Colorado with her job in a few months," he said.

Yolanda encouraged him. "I think you two could work it out. I mean, you stay pretty busy with teaching and with your art—it's not like you see her every day as it is. You could at least try it out."

Kelan explained, "If I'm gonna be in a relationship, I want to see that person on a regular basis. I want to talk to her; I want to be able to have lunch with her, you know? All the stuff that usually happens when a man and a woman are dating exclusively. This business of 'catch me if you can' is not for me."

"You know this is strange, don't you?" Yolanda laughed.

"What?"

"Here I am, the woman, telling you to lighten up on the relationship and stop trying to be so tied up in it, and you're the man, telling me that you want it all. Role reversal, don't you think?"

"I wouldn't say that," he disagreed with her. Their waitress placed a family serving of catfish between the two of them. They said grace and dove into it. "It's really not about roles. It's about desires and what we want out of a relationship. I find that often I want more out of a relationship than the woman does."

"Stop right there," she interrupted him. "If that's happening over and over again, maybe you should think about it."

"I don't see what there is to think about. I want a commitment; she doesn't."

"Most women want a commitment at some point, Kelan, but not at the beginning." Yolanda wanted to be tactful with Kelan; after all, he was her friend. "Take Shayna, for example. You knew her for, what, two months?"

"Yes."

"And you gave her a necklace for her birthday."

"It was a token of the feelings I had for her."

"It was a big mistake!"

"So, what are you saying? Is there a time minimum before you give a necklace?" he asked with a fake grin.

"No, there is not a time minimum per se, but if the relationship itself is still pretty casual in nature, you don't give a commitment kind of gift. That can put a lot of pressure on a woman," she explained. "Some of us were taught not to accept expensive gifts from men because men always want something in return—hint, hint."

"I wasn't expecting sex from her. I told her straight up front that I was a Christian and that I was abstinent. I never gave her any reason to think that sex was the issue," he argued. "Besides, it wasn't a casual relationship."

"Not to you"—she pointed her finger at him—"but maybe it was still casual to her.

"Kelan, no offense, my brother, but how long have you been dating? I mean, you are so smart and you know so much about the Bible and you interpret all these scriptures with such insight; how is it that you seem to know so little about relationships?"

"You want to know the truth?" he laughed.

"Naw, tell me a lie."

"Here it goes. I grew up fat, and—"

"For real?" She smiled but quickly erased it when she saw that Kelan was serious.

"Well, I was. I was pretty chubby from the time I was a toddler until my sophomore year in high school. I had some girls who were friends, but everybody just knew me as the fat boy who was still cool. During my sophomore year, I grew almost five inches, and suddenly I wasn't so chubby anymore. But by that time most of my friends were already talking to their second baby's momma, and I hadn't even gone out on a date. So there I was in the eleventh grade, still hanging up in people's faces—playing tricks on the phone and stuff that I should have been doing in middle school. I think I've been playing catch-up ever since. It's not so bad now that I'm an adult. I understand that people have to play these games. They have to unlearn some things and learn themselves the way I did as a lonely child. We all get our turn."

"Aw," Yolanda said, "that sounds like something straight out of a teen magazine." She thought of her own sister and wondered if the years as an obese child had affected Regina's adult life.

"I wish it weren't true," he said, "but my theory proves it-self over and over again; like when I introduced myself to you at church and you dissed me."

"What!" Yolanda rushed to swallow her food and protest.

"Oh, don't even try it. You *know* you dissed me." He shook his head, bringing his hand to his chin and resting an elbow on the table. He watched Yolanda attempt to squirm out of what they both knew was true.

Yolanda moved her mouth in vain, like a fish on land gap-ing for air. She stuttered and gestured herself into a corner. *Oh, just admit it already.* "Okay, I dissed you, but it wasn't be-cause you were a chubby child."

"Go on."

"I dissed you because of the dreads and because . . . you just seem like the artsy type. Mind you, I was right about the artsy stuff. You *do* paint." She went down swinging.

"So what if I have dreads and I like to paint?"

"You have to admit, there aren't many brothers out there who stop in a store full of Texas memorabilia, let alone *buy* something. That's different."

"Different is bad?"

She told him, "Different is different. Different takes the long route, makes things harder than they have to be. Different is challenging. I just don't think the average woman is up for a challenge all the time."

"I'm not looking for the average woman. Does the average woman want the average man?"

"No."

"Then maybe different is better." He had a point.

"Different is difficult."

"Difficulty brings about a change."

"Difficulty brings about frustration, unnecessary explaining to do, stuff like that."

"You are so fastidious, you know?" He stared at her for a moment. He wondered if she knew how difficult *she* was being. And how much he liked it.

"What?" she asked him.

"What would happen if everything in your world wasn't perfect?"

"It's not perfect," she said to him. Little did he know that she'd been battling her feelings about him for several weeks now. "I have issues just like everybody else. I ask God to help me with them. He is faithful, and I go on."

"I'm talking about the things you have reasonable control over. What if all the little things weren't exactly in the right order?" he rephrased the question.

"The little things like what?"

"Let me take a wild guess. Are all of your videotapes arranged alphabetically?" he asked.

"As a matter of fact, they are," she said proudly, sitting straight up.

"What would happen if they weren't?"

"I would put them back in the right order."

"What would happen if you couldn't?"

"I'd pay somebody else to do it for me."

"Could you rest knowing that the movies in your . . . armoire, I'm guessing, weren't in there the right way?"

"Yes, but it would bother me every time I went to look for a movie and couldn't find it. I like order, Kelan. I guess that's where you and I just don't see eye to eye. I mean, let's start with your vehicle." She turned the tables.

"What's wrong with my truck?"

"I parked right next to you, and I took a look inside your truck. You've got newspapers all in the front seat, and you've got a coffee mug in the holder that you've probably had in there since you were on your way to church this morning. It's an overall junky vehicle, Kelan. You need to vacuum that thing out."

He leaned back and gave her a smirk. "You've been spying on me."

"I have not been spying on you," she said.

"Mmm." He gave her that "yeah, right" look.

They decided to stop by Bruno's Ice Cream for dessert after dinner. Kelan had a banana split, and Yolanda ordered a double-dip hot caramel sundae with nuts and whipped cream. Yolanda wasn't really all that hungry, but she needed an excuse to stay with Kelan a little longer. There was something about him that irked her and drew her at the same time.

Regina beat herself up all the way to Bruno's; her eyes were faucets for her soul. She'd left Orlando Jr. with his father and dashed off to run a few errands. Once she was out of the house, the ice cream was calling her, and she couldn't stop herself from making this last stop. She knew that she would have to pay for it tomorrow when she stepped on the scale, but some foods seemed to have a spell over her, especially when things weren't going her way—the scale being one of those things.

In addition, she'd stopped by Gloria's house and seen Joyce Ann lounging on the couch watching television. Joyce Ann reeked of a nauseating combination: dirt mixed with hair grease on her scalp. Regina could almost taste the stench in her mouth. She put her finger to her nose to keep from vomiting and kept out of smelling distance, racing straight to the kitchen to drop off pictures of Orlando Jr.

"You could *speak* to your aunt, you know," Gloria fussed quietly as Regina pulled the pictures from her purse.

"She could speak to her *daughter*, too," Regina said.

Gloria turned from her pantry to give Regina a nonverbal

chastisement but stopped when she noticed her daughter's pallid complexion. Her skin, usually a lively, earthy brown, was dull and drained. Not to mention how brittle her hair looked, pulled back into a stiff ponytail. Gloria remembered the hard days after the death of her husband. Then, nine months later, she'd been almost run into the ground with caring for a newborn and a kindergartner at the same time. Even though Regina only had this one baby and although Orlando did everything he could to help, Gloria empathized with Regina. No matter how much help a woman got, motherhood could still be overwhelming. "Regina, you've got to start taking better care of yourself. I know it's hard with a baby, but don't let yourself go. You hear? A pair of earrings and a dash of lipstick go a long way. And it wouldn't hurt if you did a few sit-ups every now and then to help out with your waistline."

The things people say. Regina left before Gloria had the chance to take those words back.

Little did Gloria know, Regina was doing everything she could to keep from letting herself go. Water pills were in the routine now. If Regina wasn't busy peeing, she was busy emptying her bowels several times a day, all in between the never-ending task of caring for the baby and searching the Web to keep abreast of the latest news in her field. Then there was Orlando, always wanting sex. She wanted to want sex, but the extra pounds had smothered her libido.

Only ice cream could help her out of this mess; give her a quick fix the same way it used to years and years ago. When everything else caved in, Regina could always depend on food to be there. It didn't lecture her. It wasn't judgmental. It was simply there for the relief of discomfort. If she could just lose herself in the sweetness, the crunchiness, or the saltiness of her favorite snacks, there would be that instant of satisfaction. Who cared about the other twenty-three hours and forty-five minutes of the day that she would regret the binge? This fifteen minutes was life, even if it was death. As much as she didn't want to go back to the old way, she still found herself scrambling into Bruno's Ice Cream shop like a thief in the night.

Regina's heart quickened its pace as she anticipated this moment of gratification. Her fixation was so strong that she breezed past Yolanda at Bruno's.

"Hey, Regina!" Yolanda called to her sister.

"Oh, hey, Yo-yo." Regina stopped in her tracks and twitched a bit, eyeing the stranger sitting next to her sister.

"Kelan, this is my sister, Regina. Regina, this is my friend Kelan." Yolanda introduced them, hoping that Regina wouldn't say anything embarrassing. It was, after all, the first time in a long time that Regina had seen Yolanda with a man.

"It's nice to meet you." She shook Kelan's hand, and he sat back down.

Yolanda noticed the redness in her sister's eyes and asked Kelan to excuse them while they stepped down a few booths. "What's wrong?"

"It's . . . it's really nothing."

"I lived in the same room with you, Regina. I know when something's wrong with you. You were acting funny at Aunt Toe's house a few weeks ago, too. Now, I'm not going to take 'nothing' for an answer. What is the problem?" Yolanda insisted by crossing her arms.

"I just . . . I guess I'm going through postpartum blues. Everything is going wrong. I feel so ugly and fat." Regina buried her face in her sister's shoulder, and Yolanda held her while she broke down and cried.

The stern expression on Yolanda's face melted as she discounted her sister's condition. "Hey, listen, it's okay. Lots of women go through this. You're gonna be okay when it's all over. I promise." Yolanda pulled her sister off her shoulder and faced her head-on. "If it gets too bad, you need to talk to your doctor. Have you prayed about this?"

Regina looked down at the floor.

"Well, there's no time like the present." Yolanda grabbed Regina's hands and led her in a quick word of prayer, thanking God for her sister, her nephew, and the life ahead for their family. She asked God to give her sister strength in the midst of this time of emotional adjustment. But as for the fat part, Yolanda didn't know what to pray, so she simply asked for wisdom and guidance. As far as she could tell, Regina's weight should not have been an issue for her. This fat and ugly thing was simply a figment of Regina's postpartum imagination.

Regina dried her face, squared her shoulders, and threw her head back. "Well, I guess I'll get my ice cream and go on home."

"You sure?"

"Yeah," Regina laughed at herself, "I'll be okay."

But the headache started just as she pulled out of the parking lot. And the pain in her abdomen was no longer an ice pick but a jackhammer. It battered her with such force that she had no choice but to grab her stomach with one hand, causing her to swerve out of her lane, off the road, and into a light pole.

Chapter 15

It wasn't like Regina to stay gone so late in the evening. Despite her recent distancing from him sexually, she was a good mother to their son. With only one bottle of formula left in the refrigerator, she couldn't have planned to be gone this long. He called her cell phone, and terror shot through him as he listened first to his wife's moans and then a barrage of male voices. When he couldn't make out what they were saying, Orlando yelled loud enough for someone to put phone to ear and answer the questions that were half-forming in his head.

"Hello! Hello!"

He heard Regina ask someone to talk on her behalf. "Hello, this is Officer Collins."

It was worse than he thought. He clutched his crying son closer to his chest. "This is Orlando Hernandez. I'm trying to reach my wife, Regina Hernandez."

"Mr. Hernandez, there's been an accident."

"Is my wife okay?"

"Yes, I believe she's going to be fine. She's with paramedics now, and I expect that they'll transport her to Central Hospital in a matter of minutes. Can you meet us there?"

"May I speak to her?" Orlando threw his head back and began praying.

"Hello?" Regina's voice creaked with emotion.

"Baby, are you okay?"

"I'm sorry," she apologized profusely. "I'm so sorry, Orlando."

"What are you talking about, Regina? You had an accident; it's not your fault." He couldn't comprehend why his wife would feel guilty about a car wreck.

"I'm sorry . . ." Regina's voice trailed off as Officer Collins took the phone from her trembling hands.

"Mr. Hernandez, the ambulance is leaving now. We'll meet you at the hospital."

"I'm on my way."

Orlando called Yolanda and Gloria and then his sister, Angelica. Angelica agreed to keep the baby through the night so that he could meet his wife's family at the emergency room.

Gloria hopped out of bed and turned on the main light in the bedroom she now shared with Richard.

"Where . . . What are you doing?" he asked, rubbing his eyes to get them focused.

"Regina's had an accident. I'm going to the hospital."

Instantly, Richard threw back the down comforter and slid his feet into his brown leather slippers.

Gloria stopped in the middle of hoisting her jeans up her slender thighs. "Oh, you don't have to go, honey. Orlando talked to her, so I'm thinking she's not too bad off." She resumed with the pants, zipped them.

"Well, I'd really like to be there. Besides, I don't want you out driving alone at this time of night."

"Yo-yo is on her way to pick me up." Gloria thought she'd adequately addressed his concern. She didn't bother to look up, or she would have seen the confusion written on Richard's face. He'd married into a fully functioning family of women. When they did this thing they did so well—worked everything out without the men—he felt alienated.

"Well, call me when you know something," he said, reluctantly yielding to his wife's insistence. This probably wasn't the time to elbow his way in. He followed Gloria around the house, helping her make sure she didn't forget anything.

When she was fully dressed, Gloria grabbed her husband's face and kissed him square on the lips and said, "Richard, thanks for being so supportive."

Is this her idea of support? "I'll be along in a little while." He needed to show her what support was.

"You don't have to do that." Super-Gloria refused help.

"I *want* to," Richard insisted. "I'm a part of this family now."

Gloria paused for just a moment, realizing Richard's place in all of this. She then called Yolanda on her cell phone, telling her daughter to go on to the hospital. "I'm coming with Richard." It sounded funny, but it was right.

Officer Collins met them all in the emergency waiting room and explained what he knew already about the accident. "It appears that this was simply a matter of overcorrection, where a driver crosses a line and then tries to compensate by steering in the opposite direction. Since we can't factor in weather conditions or slick roads, I can only say that it was a matter of driver miscalculation. I . . . just want you to know that it's standard procedure to do a blood test and check for alcohol in situations like these. Does anyone know where she was tonight?"

"I just saw her a few hours ago at Bruno's. She was just fine then," Yolanda offered.

"My wife doesn't drink." Orlando defended his love.

"It's just standard procedure, sir," Officer Collins repeated. "She's a lucky woman—that car took quite a beating."

"God is good," Yolanda said.

"Yes, He is," Officer Collins agreed.

One at a time, doctors allowed them to see Regina. Orlando was the first to see her. He hugged his wife and asked her if she was in any pain.

"Just my head."

"Baby, I'm so glad you're okay. I don't know what I'd do without you."

Regina wanted to melt into his arms and receive his shower of kisses, but he didn't know everything. She didn't deserve his kisses just now.

Gloria thought she would faint at the sight of the blood seeping through the bandages around her daughter's head. "Regina." She hugged her and asked, "Are you okay?"

"Momma, it was . . . it's all my fault." Regina tried to tell her mother the dreadful truth about the accident.

"Oh, that's nonsense, honey." Gloria rubbed Regina's arm and hushed her delirium. Never mind that she couldn't imagine how on earth her daughter had managed to skid into a pole on a perfectly clear night. "Accidents happen. I'll take care of the baby tomorrow; don't you worry about anything."

Yolanda took her turn with Regina, offering a prayer and humor. "Girl, I just saw you a little while ago; now here you are laid up in a hospital bed!"

Regina's eyes filled with grief and anguish. Lifting her eyes was like lifting fifty-pound weights; it was too hard. *How could I have been so stupid?* Her sniffling led to an outpouring of tears that she couldn't hold back any longer. It was a rare moment for the sisters, Regina opening up like this. But when it happened every once in a blue moon, Yolanda knew that her sister was in dire need of help.

"Regina, what is it?" Yolanda rolled over on a round stool and faced her sister head-on, meaning that she was not leaving that room without the truth.

"I just don't want to be fat again," Regina cried. "I can't go back to that life."

What does that have to do with the car accident? "Okay, Regina, start at the beginning."

"I had to do something to keep the weight from coming back, so I started taking pills—"

"What kinds of pills, Regina?" Yolanda's mind ran through the number of weight-loss pills on the market and their possible side effects, but incoherency was nowhere on the list.

"I took laxatives and a metabolism pill, and water pills. I kept getting headaches and stomach cramps, so I took ibuprofen every so often to ease the pain. It just got out of control." Regina's breath was short, but with this confession she was lighter already.

Yolanda sighed and looked up at the ceiling, sending up a silent thank you for sparing her sister. The accident had probably saved Regina's life, because under the veil of the "baby blues" this problem might have gone undetected for months. "But Regina, you're *not* fat."

"Yes, I am, Yo-yo. I wish everybody would stop *lying* to me—you and Orlando in particular." She looked away from her sister, angry that Yo-yo would patronize her during one of the worst hours of her life.

Yolanda looked at her sister, and for the first time she realized that Regina was serious. "How . . . when did you decide that you were fat?"

"I can see it in the mirror." Regina bit into her sister, wondering if she'd done the right thing by talking about the block of fat she saw in the mirror. It *was* there. It existed! Why was she the only one who could see it?

"I don't know what to say about you being fat. I'm just glad you're okay right now." Yolanda gave up trying to convince her sister that she wasn't fat. From her updates at conferences and other professional venues, she knew that she was fighting a losing verbal battle. She'd recommend professional help as soon as Regina got out of the hospital. "Let's just worry about one thing at a time."

As Yolanda rose to her feet, Regina clamped her hand on her sister's arm. "Promise me you won't tell anyone."

"Regina, I can't promise you that." Yolanda shook her head, knowing that she couldn't—wouldn't trade her sister's life for her trust. Regina was playing with fire, and Yolanda wasn't about to hide her matches. "This thing is bigger than you and me put together."

"Please, Yo-yo. I can get better; I know I can. I just need some time."

Yolanda kissed her sister on the cheek, and Regina released her grip in the warmth of sisterly love. "You *will* get better, that's for sure."

Regina watched as she pulled back the wall of white curtains and walked out of the makeshift room. It was only a matter of time before Yo-yo told her mother and Orlando, and everyone found out that she had gone mad. Well, they could think whatever they wanted. They hadn't lived through the torment of her childhood and would never understand the humiliation of being relegated to the choir in the fifth-grade Christmas play because she couldn't fit into any of the little costumes. She hadn't even shown Gloria the flyer announcing the play.

Every time Regina thought about praying, the consideration

was immediately seized by the far-reaching grip of her past. What should have stayed in the recesses of her mind transcended time, extending from the fat years to the thin, and pulled her back under its influence. Submerged, she saw the real Regina: a fat girl who had sucked in her gut only for a little while—just long enough to pull in a man and have a baby.

Baby . . . baby. She thought of her son and what kind of mother she was to him. When she looked into his bubbling face, she saw a reflection of her husband's virtues. Love. Patience. Joy. Everything she'd ever wanted in a man. They didn't deserve this turmoil in their lives. She would not put her son through this. Divine motherly instinct came to the forefront and guided her thoughts now. Somewhere, deep down inside, Regina knew that she had to grab on to faith and pull herself out of this rut. She had to get a hold of herself, get a hold on this thing—fight it. But Yo-yo had said that it was bigger than both of them. Again she thought of praying. And before the past could dunk her, she gasped and called for help.

God, I know I've done wrong. I'm sorry. Please forgive me for the way I've abused my body. I can't do this anymore. I don't know what the solution is. I don't . . . I don't even know what to pray right now. I'm just asking you to come in and . . . do . . . something . . .

The more she prayed, the more frustrated she became. This was one of those situations that plop down in your lap and say, "deal with me." She couldn't recall a time in her life when she hadn't been dealing with it in some way or another, but everything was different now. When she was younger she would pray hard to be skinny. And when she had found Plathene, she thought it was the answer to her prayers. Love and happiness followed as she quelled the fear of rejection and isolation through her twenties and early thirties. Now what would she pray for? Another drug? A miracle diet? A fast-acting, fat-burning potion? No, He probably wouldn't grant her that. None of that sounded like His m.o. If she remembered her Bible stories correctly, there was always something a little peculiar about how God delivered His people. She surrendered.

Lord, I don't know how you're gonna fix this mess, but I give it to you. Amen.

In the waiting room, Dr. Anderson informed the family that Regina's blood work confirmed that she hadn't been drinking. This came as no surprise to the family, but they felt better now that the cloud of suspicion had been officially removed. Yolanda fidgeted in her seat, wondering when she should break the news.

Chapter 16

$\mathcal{D}$r. Tilley had suggested that Dianne give some serious thought to finding her purpose in life. Easier said than done. *Of all the great things God called people to do—part the Red Sea, build an ark, kill giants, and make dry bones live again—what on earth would He want with me?*

"There's something that you do that no one on this earth can do quite the way you do, Dianne. It's a gift—an intrinsic talent that He gave you to glorify Him. Maybe it's something you've never tried; maybe it's something you do in your spare time. Whatever it is, it's probably bigger than you, and you'll need Him to make it come to pass," she explained. "What is it that you do that you'd probably do even if you never got paid a penny for it?"

Dianne thought, and her mind traveled to a time long ago. Once, in fourth grade, her teacher had praised her for a poem she'd written. "This is beautiful, Dianne," Mrs. Ripley had said, giving her a great big hug. "I'd like for you to read this at the PTA meeting next week. Do you think you could do that?"

Dianne had shrugged, proud to be chosen but terrified at the thought of getting up before a roomful of people and reading her poem about how butterflies change with time. Dianne didn't want to read the poem, but Mrs. Ripley sent that blasted undecipherable cursive note home and Aunt Gloria made such a big deal out of it—how could she *not* read the poem?

Aunt Gloria had bought Dianne a blue sailor dress, a pair of Buster Brown shoes, and long white socks that came up to her knees for the occasion. She'd even given Dianne that coveted zigzag part between her two pony tails so that when she bent her head down to read the poem, the nearly all-white audience would know that someone had taken extra special care in preparing this little bussed black girl for the evening.

With her family in the front row, Dianne took a deep breath and read "Butterfly Time." Gloria was the first to hop out of her seat, leading the standing ovation that followed Dianne's reading. Truthfully, that was the last time Dianne could remember really feeling good about herself. She pulled out her poetry journal every now and then, but it was not for the public's eye. Besides, her writing was so dreadful that she might cause her readers to become depressed. No sense in making everybody miserable.

"Do you have any ideas?" Dr. Tilley asked. She believed and prayed that Dianne would get a revelation. More than anything, she wanted to see Dianne freed from the shackles of her mind.

"Well . . ." Dianne switched positions on what she now referred to as the thinking couch. "There was a time when I liked to write poetry."

Dr. Tilley pounced on the opportunity. "Writing is very therapeutic, Dianne. It's one of the best ways to get your feelings out there and hear from heaven as well. Why don't you try writing a couple of poems before the next session? They don't have to be anything fancy. Just whatever comes to your mind."

With her doctor cheering in her corner, Dianne wrote several poems over the next few weeks. Dr. Tilley had one of them, entitled "Off the Edge of the World," matted, framed, and hung in her office with a little copyright symbol and Dianne's name. It was clear to Dr. Tilley that the lucid truth of Dianne's poetry expressed what other victims could not put into words. "I can't tell you how many people will read this and know that they have come to the right place to seek healing. Your writing can really be a blessing to others, you know?"

With Dr. Tilley's prayers and encouragement, Dianne embarked on a literary path to healing. She even worked up the nerve to sign up for poetry reading at an eccentric local bookstore. The lights were dimmed; candles and incense burned throughout the small store. The audience literally gathered at her feet, sitting Indian-style on little carpet squares. It was quaint and comfortable, and Dianne felt right at home with a group of people who heard the beats from that different drum. With time, they might discover how to sway and flow with it despite the unconventional tempo.

"This is a poem that I wrote for a very speical relative of mine who couldn't be in the audience tonight. Her name is Yolanda—we call her Yo-yo. It's called 'Sister I Lost, Sister I Found.'" Dianne had a copy of the poem in her pocket, but she didn't need it. The lines were written on her heart. She closed her eyes and assigned her voice to the poem. The words flew out of her like a flock of doves that had been waiting patiently to use their wings at the sound of the cage door creaking open.

Sister I Lost, Sister I Found

When I lost her, I lost me.
Even the chamber that once held me

Disappeared.
Then appeared another circle—
Another sphere. And the both of you.
Opening the door, filling me
With You and Him.
He loved me through you,
Sister I Found.

The reading was over before it started. And when she bowed her head and heard the praise of the audience, Dianne knew. She just knew. Suddenly it all made sense. All the pain and trauma she'd been through—every experience she'd ever had in her life—had formed her into the woman she was at that very moment. Every situation had worked together for her good, just as Aunt Gloria had always told her. Just as God promised in His Word. He really did love her, and He always had. She just couldn't see it until that night.

After the final reading, Dianne bought a few books and walked back to her car, still on cloud nine. The night air seemed to soothe her, and she breathed deeply to take in its effect. She remembered the times her mother woke her and told her to take Shannon outside so that she could get some night air and stop all that wheezing. With sand still in her eyes, Dianne would pick up her raspy sister, stopping every few steps to readjust Shannon's butt on her bony hip, and go out to the patio in the middle of the night for this very air.

Dianne felt bitterness creeping up to her otherwise pleasant mood and decided that she'd hum a tune to keep her mind clear. She smiled, thinking of how Aunt Toe always seemed to be humming some gospel tune or other for no reason at all. Maybe she did it to keep her mind settled, too.

"Say, wait up," a male voice called to Dianne just as she reached her car.

She stopped and waited for her suitor to delineate himself from the thinning crowd. He trotted to the side of her car and then slowed down so as not to appear too eager. He'd obviously been drawn by the old low-self-esteem magnet that she still wore on her forehead. "Say, girl, how you learned-ed to read like that?" He hadn't heard Dianne's poem, only saw her through the glass windows and hung around near the store long enough to catch her on the way out.

"I went to school." She gave a sly smile.

"You got to call me some time." He got straight to the point. The shiny crests of his finger waves glistened in the moonlight.

"Sure." She watched herself this time, though. As good as she felt, she didn't necessarily need a man in her bed tonight.

She watched him as he flipped through his wallet for something that would have his phone number on it, she assumed. In the process, she noticed that he had several pictures of an adorable little boy.

"Is that your son?" she asked.

"Yeah. I see him when I can," he said, revealing himself.

A surge of irritation charged through her. "Well, if you find it difficult to make time for your son, you certainly don't have time for me. Good-bye." With that, she stepped into her car and revved up the engine. He hopped back on the curb in time to save his foot.

Dianne laughed at herself all the way home. It was an empowering thing, she thought, to be able to pick and choose what and whom she allowed in her life.

Chapter 17

*A*t the hospital, Yolanda thought it best to keep her mouth shut, at least for the time being. It had been a long night, and emotions had everyone on edge. She needed a few hours' rest, followed by a stiff cup of coffee, before starting her shift at the pharmacy in five hours. She hated going to work exhausted. One heavy-eyed mistake in filling a prescription could cost a patient's life and Yolanda's credentials. She decided to call Brookelynn and see if she'd work the first part of her shift. After all, Brookelynn owed Yolanda many a morning-hangover favor.

So long as the job got done, Brookelynn and Yolanda had the flexibility to pinch-hit for each other when necessary. The owner of the franchised store was an easygoing man who was too busy enjoying his golden years to micromanage the business anymore. He didn't have to; he hired good people. He'd known the Rucker family for a long time, and any daughter of the saint' who had rescued that poor child who cradled her dead baby sister for a week (he'd heard) was someone he wanted at the helm in his pharmacy. Perhaps that was one of the reasons Yolanda had decided to stay in Dentonville, where people still held family connections in high esteem.

"I've got to go make a phone call," Yolanda announced as she made her way to the guest phone at the nurses' station.

"Call Aunt Toe and Joyce Ann," Gloria instructed her.

I ain't calling no Aunt Joyce Ann. "Mmm," Yolanda murmured.

Orlanda joined his wife at her bedside and promised her the moon if she'd just stop crying.

Yolanda had a good prayer, a refreshing slumber, and then bounded in to work at a little after one in the afternoon. "It's been wild around here today. Dr. Hamilton's on a rampage again because we're out of Coumadin," Brookelynn said as she printed out a label for a pill bottle. "He wants you to call him."

"Why me?"

"I guess because I wasn't giving him the answer he wanted to hear."

"Whatever," Yolanda sighed. "Thanks for coming in for me."

"Is your sister going to be okay?"

"I'm sure she will be," Yolanda said, touched by Brookelynn's concern. "Just pray for us."

"Oh, and your boyfriend called," Brookelynn teased.

"He is not my boyfriend. He is my friend," Yolanda said.

"Whatever you say, Yolanda." Brookelynn watched Yolanda out of the corner of her eye. She didn't care what Yolanda said; there was something between her and Kelan, as evidenced by the spark in Yolanda's eye when she talked with him.

"Can't a woman have a male friend?"

"Yes, a woman can have a friend. But Kelan is *not* just your friend," Brookelynn argued.

"And how do you know so much?" Yolanda asked, stopping long enough to humor her coworker.

"It's in the way your lips curve toward a smile when you talk about him. It's in the way you cradle the phone in the nook of your neck when he calls. Believe me, I know these things." Brookelynn spoke the truth.

Yolanda glared at her, unable to find the words for a rebuttal. "Whatever."

"Well, if you don't want him, I'd love to introduce him to my little sister. She's into art. I'm sure that she and Kelan would hit it off great."

Involuntarily Yolanda's left eyebrow shot up and her lips thrust forward.

"Gotcha." Brookelynn winked at her. "I'll see you tomorrow."

Yolanda wondered if everybody else sensed this . . . this chemistry between her and Kelan. If Brookelynn knew it from just their phone conversations, Yolanda was sure that her family could tell from the interactions at Sunday dinners. The whole thing was extremely uncomfortable. She shook her head and forced her mind to get back on work.

Yolanda made herself a note to call Dr. Hamilton and held it off until she could carve out a good ten minutes to talk to him. She was in no way fond of Dr. Hamilton and had been tempted to light a candle when he announced his retirement seven months ago. Dr. Hamilton was a mean old something and he wasn't even a good doctor, but he had been in the town long before the McDonald's, and he was still revered in the community. Back when Dr. Hamilton was in his prime, he had done just about everything from setting broken bones to delivering babies. Shortly before he retired, Yolanda had a big run-in with him regarding a seven-year-old patient who had undergone a circumcision. The child's prescription for pain medicine had run out, and the mother pleaded with Yolanda to call Dr. Hamilton and see about getting a refill. She called his back line while the mother waited in one of the chairs just beyond the pharmacy counter, rocking back and forth as though she could feel her son's pain.

"Tell her to give him Tylenol," Dr. Hamilton bickered.

"But, Dr. Hamilton, the child is still in tremendous pain." Yolanda tried to convey the same sense of desperation the child's mother had communicated through the overflowing tears in her eyes. Yolanda wasn't in the habit of questioning doctors, but to the degree that drugs were able to relieve pain without establishing a habit or causing detrimental side effects, she pushed for them.

"Did you hear what I said? He'll be fine. His parents are crazy. They should have circumcised him at birth."

"Dr. Hamilton, that is irrelevant. This isn't about your own personal beliefs."

"The boy will be fine in a couple of days. I'm not ordering any more meds for him unless there's sign of infection."

The Gloria in her came out as she said to him, "How about we snip a piece off of your peter, Dr. Hamilton, and then give *you* a couple of Tylenol afterward?"

Yolanda heard him wince from the sound of how painful that must be. He hesitated. "One more day's worth—that's it."

Since then, Dr. Hamilton seemed to be under the impression that if he wanted something done at that pharmacy, he needed to talk to that brazen pharmacist by the name of Jordan. Yolanda called him and let him know that the next day's incoming shipment would include Coumadin. He fussed a little, but Yolanda was used to dealing with his type. If Yolanda could deal with Aunt Toe, she could deal with anybody.

As she hung up the phone with Dr. Hamilton and trashed the yellow reminder note, Yolanda wondered if her own father would have been like Dr. Hamilton. She wondered, too, how he would have handled the situation with Regina. Would this morning have been different with a patriarch in the picture? Would he have been an overbearing chauvinist, or would he have provided a brawny shoulder to cry on? Would she and Gloria have been carrying on like a couple of weak, whiny wimps because there was a bossy male present to assume the "strong" role? God forbid.

Yolanda searched the medical encyclopedias at work between prescriptions to learn more about her sister's situation from a medical standpoint. When she put two and two together, she realized that Regina had been suffering from an eating disorder for the better part of her life. Secretive eating, mood swings, self-degrading comments, mood swings, eating large amounts of food with no apparent weight gain, mood swings—everything made sense now. She'd seen Regina eat like crazy when she came home for the holidays in college, but she never gained an ounce. Not once could Yolanda remember ever having seen Regina exercise. Never mind the times in grade school when she'd found dozens of candy wrappers in the trashcan. Everybody knew that Regina ate a lot—she always had. But no one had a clue as to how she managed to get all that weight off in college and keep it off as an adult. Until now.

Yolanda went straight to Regina's house after getting off work. The doctors had agreed to release Regina with notes about seeing another physician soon. Regina, however, was still sulking and refused to lighten up despite the delightful bouquet Yolanda picked up at the drugstore. "Thank you," Regina mumbled dutifully as Yolanda set them on the windowsill and hoped that the sad air wouldn't kill them.

Yolanda sat on the love seat across from her sister, resisting the urge to pull the curtains and lighten the room. Orlando's family was keeping the baby so that Regina could recover in peace, but this place wasn't peaceful. It was depressing.

"How's your head?"

"As good as it can be with twenty-three stitches and a few bruises," she said sarcastically, raising one eyebrow and then lowering it with the pain that shot through her forehead.

Regina turned her throbbing head and focused on the flowers. A single tear rolled from the corner of her eye and disappeared in her hairline. If she could click a mental switch and turn off the voices of ridicule in her head, she would. But it was not that easy. Regina hadn't asked for any of this. Not once had she fantasized, *Hm, I wish I could be fat, then get skinny, then have a baby, then have a wreck while trying to get skinny again. That's what I want to do when I grow up!*

Yolanda gave up her cheerleading efforts and decided to leave Regina alone. When she got like this, there was no coaxing her out of it. Yolanda exhaled noisily and stood, slinging her purse over her shoulder and approaching Regina's bedside. "I'll see you tomorrow, sis."

Regina said her good-byes faintly, her eyes still set on the bouquet. She had no intention of keeping that thing alive.

Yolanda took a deep cleansing breath. She'd hoped to be able to introduce the idea of seeking professional help about the eating disorder today, but Regina's attitude threw the plan way off. Yolanda wondered if there would ever be a good time to talk to Regina about the help she needed. Probably not. Still, *something* had to be discussed.

It wasn't like Yolanda to call anyone for advice about her problems, least of all a man. But she'd come to value Kelan's perspective on things. He viewed things through a different lens and often brought spiritual insight that Yolanda hadn't considered. Yolanda liked bouncing her ideas off him. She was hardly in the car before she called on his friendly voice.

"Hey, what's up?" he screamed over his classical music.

"Turn that down!" Yolanda screamed back, wondering how on earth Kelan managed to put bass in Mozart.

"Hold on."

She waited while he adjusted the volume.

"What's up?"

"Nothing much. I'm pulling out of my sister's driveway."

"How is she?"

"Not good."

"So, what happened?" he pushed Yolanda, knowing that they'd set a deadline for this talk.

"She's still depressed. I guess I was hoping to catch her in a good mood to tell her that she needs help. That's crazy, huh?"

"Well, I don't know that there will ever be a good time to inform someone that they need to see a psychologist. Probably a dietician, too—you know, a team of people to help her through this." Kelan was firm in his suggestions.

"I know, you're right." Yolanda gave into his suggestions easily. In fact, she alarmed herself with how effortlessly she relented. She gave him credit for that, however. Kelan posed no threat to her independence. He had his *other* little female friends, and he gave Yolanda space to be herself.

Yolanda was warmed by Kelan's level of concern for her family. Likewise, he was flattered by Yolanda's obvious distress over his love life. He wished he could tell her how much he wanted *her* as part of his love life, but doing so would push her away. He'd listened enough to know that Yolanda was afraid. For the moment, he'd settled for friendship and Sunday dinners at Gloria's.

Chapter 18

$\mathcal{G}$irl, I'll be praying," Dianne told Yolanda as they finished up their telephone conversation.

Yolanda had to tell *somebody* in the family about Regina, and since Dianne was the most distant relative, she would do. "Prayer is what we need right now." Yolanda nodded as though Dianne could see her. She never thought she'd see the day that Dianne was praying for them instead of vice versa.

"I could ask Dr. Tilley if she has any associates near Dentonville," Dianne proposed. It was their little secret that Dianne was seeing a psychologist, maybe more at Yolanda's insistence than Dianne's. "*Anyone* that she recommends will be worth seeing."

"That's a good idea," Yolanda agreed. "It'll be a hard sell with Regina, though."

Dianne called upon her newfound wisdom and volunteered to come to Dentonville and accompany Regina to the psychologist, as Gwen had done for her. "It means a lot when someone who's been in your shoes steps in and takes your hand." Even as she said the words, she remembered how Yoyo had taken her hand years ago and led her to the altar to give her life to Christ. They shared a fatherlessness that only a daughter's aching heart could feel.

"I'll call and ask her"—Yolanda blew the words out of her mouth like smoke from a cigarette—"but I don't think it'll do much. If anything, she'll probably be angry that I told you."

"Well, people who need help are always getting angry about something or another. That's nothing new. It's all in how we approach her."

"Easier said than done." Yolanda felt helpless, and she hated it. She was a pharmacist, for crying out loud, but it certainly wasn't doing her any good now.

"I'll ask Dr. Tilley. She'll know," Dianne offered. "Tell everybody I said hello. I'll call you later this week. Bye."

The list of *everybody* passed quickly through Dianne's mind. Everybody, if Yo-yo took her literally, would include Joyce Ann. *Everybody except my mother*, she should have said. On second thought, Joyce Ann didn't deserve that title. A mother is someone who's there for you, thick and thin, and a mother doesn't make thin thinner by renouncing her own flesh and blood for a man. *How do you just turn your back and walk away from your child? What did I do to deserve that?* No, that woman didn't deserve to be called a mother, as far as Dianne was concerned. And since she was the only child left, it was her prerogative to revoke the title of "mother" from the person who'd given her little more than a womb to kick in. *From now on, she's Joyce Ann to me.*

Dianne grabbed her poetry journal and headed off to meet with her writing group, which consisted of other writers she had met at poetry night. Joining a group that met once weekly was a big investment that turned out to yield a great deal of interest. She could hardly wait to gather at the members' homes on Saturday night to listen, learn, and share. Somehow, the group that started under the premise of female poets gathering to discuss their writings turned out to be a divine assembly of women who honored God in their writing.

Keisha, though the youngest, was the undeclared leader of the group. Her natural Afro and gold hoop earrings lent her the appearance of wisdom, which she quickly affirmed when she opened her mouth to speak. She had been the first to make the observation at their second meeting. "I might be reading too far into this, but I think this is a Christian poetry club, if you ask me."

"I was thinking the same thing, my sister," Juanita chimed in. Dianne felt the hairs on her arms stand at attention. *He's still thinking about me.* Since that time, they'd opened and closed each meeting with praise and prayer.

Dianne pulled the belt on her camel suede jacket tighter and tucked her hands under her armpits as she waited for Juanita to open the door. Winter's early arrival had caught her off guard, with much of her winter clothing still packed away in large plastic bins. This jacket, her only hope, might as well have been a sheet, because the wind was cutting through cowhide, kicking behinds and taking names later that night.

Juanita finally appeared through the beveled glass and opened the door just wide enough to let Dianne in. "Ooh! That's a strong gust!"

"Who are you tellin'?" Dianne rubbed her hands together for warmth.

Juanita's home smelled of pumpkin and cinnamon—a treat in the oven, Dianne supposed. It was just like her to have hot food available. In the gathering room, Keisha and Dianne lounged on plush sink-down sofas with their shoes arranged neatly by the fireplace. Overhead, the sound of Juanita's two sons trampling about their bedroom added to the simple charm of her home. Neither of the guests cared about the boys making life's noises, but Juanita propped one fluffy pink house shoe on the bottom step and called upstairs, telling them to pipe down or go to bed.

Keisha laughed, "Girl, is that your solution to everything—go to bed?"

"Sure is." Juanita rolled her eyes and gave a few comical examples of how she'd remedied many a problem by simply sending the boys to bed for everything from turning the television up too loud to burning toast.

Following their worship and prayer, Dianne read first:

"I am five fingers—one for each sense.
To see, touch, taste, hear, and take in the fragrance of
*   existence.*
I am, then, a glove.
And You are the hand that fills me.
Move me by Your power.
Let me do, let me work, let me BE
The hand that does Your Will
In Every Sense."

Gloria piled baked chicken, corn, and greens on the plastic plate she would carry down the street to Joyce Ann. It had been like this 90 percent of the time: Gloria picking up the pieces of Joyce Ann's life, trying to keep her little sister in line. Their mother, Ruth Neal, passed that responsibility to Gloria long ago. The "mother hen" in Gloria quickly assumed the maternal role with Joyce Ann, to the extent that Joyce Ann would allow it. She could be as stubborn as a mule, though, and buck up to Gloria when she got a mind to. "You ain't my momma!" she had spat out when, as teenagers, they argued nearly every morning about what Joyce Ann should wear to school.

"I might as well be!" Gloria had shouted back, angry with both her mother and her sister.

Ruth was nowhere to be found, so Gloria would call Aunt Toe for support. Aunt Toe did her best to intervene, but she was busy caring for her ailing husband and was in no position to come over there and straighten out Joyce Ann.

The task of getting Joyce Ann on the straight and narrow had proven to be an exhausting effort. Over the years, unbeknownst to her family, Gloria had bailed Joyce Ann out of jail more times than she could remember. As much as she hated her sister's lifestyle, Gloria breathed a sigh of relief every time the phone rang at two a.m. and the caller was an operator asking her to accept a collect phone call from jail, rather than a coroner calling her to come and identify Joyce Ann's body. Gloria was a regular at the grocery store's Western Union counter, wiring money all over Texas to cover her sister's petty antics. She'd had Joyce Ann admitted to four rehab centers over the past seventeen years, and lately she seemed to be settling down a bit.

Everyone else in their small family had given up on Joyce Ann. Even Aunt Toe had called Gloria once to tell her that she might as well let Joyce Ann fall flat on her face, flat into the capable hands of God. Gloria couldn't do that, not after how close she herself had come to rock bottom in the weeks following Willie's death. Other people went back to work, back to church, back to life after they sealed the casket and lowered her Willie into the dispassionate earth. It was Joyce Ann who had come to Gloria's rescue when the rest of the world went about its business.

She'd spoon-fed Gloria, bathed her when she couldn't rally strength to lift her sorrow-leadened arms. Joyce Ann had cooked for her, brushed her hair, tended to Regina when Gloria's heart was totaled with grief. Gloria was doing good just to get out of bed some days.

Weeks later, when Gloria had found enough strength at least to go through life's motions, it was Joyce Ann who had helped Gloria fold and pack her bedding rather than wash it, because Gloria couldn't bear to extract Willie's scent from the tattered old bedspread, now priceless. Carefully she and Joyce Ann had folded the sheets with the meticulous reverence of soldiers folding the American flag.

Gloria would never forget that.

Returning Joyce Ann's kindness had come with a price tag. Bail wasn't cheap; neither were counselors, mental health clinics, or drug rehab centers. Gloria never could figure out exactly which one Joyce Ann needed, so she just kept paying the bills as best as she could for as long as she could. Had it not been for Willie's life insurance and the generous provisions he had made before his untimely death, none of this would have been possible. He was a good man. Gloria thanked God every day that Willie had signed up for every possible savings and benefit plan Grayson Steele offered, leaving her and the girls in a position to live comfortably—not rich, but comfortable. With her earnings as a teacher covering most of the bills, Gloria had money to spare.

But now that she was married, Gloria had to make some changes. Richard wanted to do things the traditional way: one checking account. He didn't mind that Gloria kept her own savings—his own mother told his sisters to keep a little of their own money set aside "just in case." He did, however, want to sit down and reconcile their joint checking account every once in a while. Hundreds of dollars missing here and there wouldn't go over well.

Gloria would have to make the best of this current arrangement with Joyce Ann, try to get her to stay as long as possible. Keep Joyce Ann under her watch. She was back on some kind of drug, that was for sure. But maybe this time, with Gloria standing over her, Joyce Ann could stay long enough to kick her old habits for good.

Gloria laughed at herself, though. Joyce Ann couldn't stand to be in one place too long. Her oxygen dwindled under obligation. When she could make her way to the bathroom in the middle of the night without bumping into anything, she knew that it was time to leave.

Gloria's offer to provide steady shelter had come as an ultimatum: either move back to Dentonville and stay in the rent house, or face life without her sister's boundless support. "I'm getting married next month, Joyce Ann. I can't be running behind you anymore," she'd said.

Joyce Ann *tsk*-ed and fingered the pay phone's coin return box. "I thought *I'd* won the prize for pushing my family aside for a *man*." She always did know how to push Gloria's buttons. Problem was, she could never be sure which button she'd pushed. She was going for the "guilt" key but landed on "irritation."

"You know what, Joyce Ann? I'm fifty-eight years old. It's time for me to live my life. Now, if you want my help in getting back on your feet, you're gonna have to move back to Dentonville. It wouldn't hurt for you to sit down somewhere. We're both getting too old for this."

Joyce Ann, though, knew she couldn't live down the street from her big sister for too long. Worse was the thought of permanently moving back into the rent house. From the moment she dropped her sack at the doorstep, the house stoned Joyce Ann, pummeled her with questions, persecuted her incessantly. *Your baby died because of you—how could you let that happen? And what about Sugarbee? You threw her away like trash! You don't deserve to breathe.*

In the weeks since moving back into that house, Joyce Ann had succumbed to its mental torture. When she'd lived in the housing projects or with her temporary suitors, she'd been able to run from these accusations. But now, in the very space where Shannon had gasped her last breaths, Joyce Ann crouched in the darkness and awaited her sentencing. Part of that sentencing included drugs. A long torturous execution of the death penalty. The kind she felt she deserved.

With the help of marijuana, Joyce Ann was losing the remainder of her sanity.

Chapter 19

$\mathcal{J}$oyce Ann never went to church, but she always came to the dinner. This Sunday she arrived wearing an outfit that would have made the devil ashamed. With her belly button winking, her breasts clapping up and down in an under-size halter top, and the bottom two inches of her behind spilling out of her skirt, she wiggled up to the porch, attempting to make a grand hoochie-style entrance at Gloria's house. This outfit was one that always got the men's attention when she wore it, and she was sure that both Richard and Yo-yo's little boyfriend wouldn't be able to keep their eyes off her. They were, after all, living, breathing, sighted men. But they were only pawns in Joyce Anne's plan to move on. Maybe if she could have a big falling-out, leaving would be easier and the bridges wouldn't be totally disintegrated, because years later they could all reason that it takes two to tango.

"What in the world you got on?" Aunt Toe confronted her at the doorway, blocking the entrance with her wheelchair.

"Clothes." If she could just make it to the kitchen . . .

Aunt Toe gazed at her, from the hideous blonde wig to the run-down open-toed red pumps. "Looks like you got on naked with a few raggedy patches tacked on. Got your stom-

ach hanging all out between your clothes like a can of ex-
ploded biscuits."

Gloria entered the living room and gasped at her sister's
bold outfit, moving Aunt Toe aside and shoving Joyce Ann
back out onto the porch. She would handle it from here. "You
are not coming in here dressed like that."

"You can't tell me what to wear."

"I can tell you what you will *not* wear in *my* house," Gloria insisted. She was prepared to send Joyce Ann packing with
a foil-covered plate if she wanted to have one of her spells.

"Ooh!" Joyce Ann huffed and puffed all the way back down
the street. A carful of youngsters rolled by and whistled at her
pathetic attempt to look sexy in her seventies disco attire. She
gave them the finger, and they laughed at her senseless gesture.

Back in the house, the phone rang, and Yolanda answered.
"Hey, everybody, it's Dianne!" she announced.

Dianne wasn't too happy about Yo-yo's announcement.
She assumed that Joyce Ann was there, too. "Girl, you ain't got
to tell the world. I just called to see how Regina was doing."

"She's still Regina," Yolanda explained.

"I'll take that to mean that she's still moping around."

"Pretty much. We're all getting ready to sit down for dinner."

Though Dianne couldn't be there, it wouldn't hurt to imagine. "What did Aunt Gloria make?"

"She cooked a ham, some black-eyed peas, cabbage, and
cheese rolls." Yolanda let the words slide off her tongue with
every intent to entice Dianne into making a trip back to Dentonville. Since they'd begun talking regularly, Yolanda missed
Dianne. She wanted her back in the family so maybe she
wouldn't have to run to Kelan so often.

Dianne could almost smell the food, hundreds of miles
away. Now that her weekend plans didn't include a leech, she

had time to think about her life's direction. She was thankful for the writing group, but they couldn't replace the kinfolk who'd loved her from the day she was born. "Mmm, I'd give anything to be there right now."

"The door is always open," Yolanda said loud enough for Gloria to hear. "Here, talk to my momma."

Yolanda passed the phone to Gloria, who had come back into the kitchen mumbling unintelligibly. She tried hard to swing her attitude back the other way for Dianne's sake, but Joyce Ann had rubbed her the wrong way. "Hey, Sugarbee."

"Hey, Aunt Gloria, how's everything."

"Everything's fine, fine. You know, I wish you'd join us for all this good cookin' I do on Sundays," she hinted.

"I sure do miss your cookin', Aunt Gloria."

"Well, if you'd move back home, you wouldn't have to miss it anymore."

Is this a conspiracy? "Aunt Gloria, you know I can't move back to Dentonville. I've built a life in Darson."

Gloria held the phone from her face and passed the buck. "Aunt Toe, come talk some sense into your great-niece."

Dianne looked up toward the sky and prepared herself for a heaping helping of Aunt Toe. "Dianne?"

"Uh-huh." Aunt Toe sucked her teeth. She didn't doubt that Dianne could survive on her own. She'd come from a line of strong women who weren't afraid to get out there and do their own thing. What she did doubt, however, was that Dianne was surrounded by love. It was a mean, cold world out there, and the more loving people you had to hold on to, the better. Maybe Dianne could find love out there on her own, but it would be hard to do if she couldn't love herself and her own people first.

"What's that 'uh-huh' all about?" Dianne asked.

"You got any friends in Darson?"

Dianne thought of the bond forming between herself and the women in the poetry group. "Yes, Aunt Toe, as a matter of fact, I do."

"Men?"

The nerve! "No, no men," Dianne laughed. "I've been coming in before midnight."

Aunt Toe gave a laugh of her own and thanked the Lord that at least Dianne had the good sense to quit while she was ahead, before she brought a baby and a knucklehead daddy into all this mess. It was one thing to be in a mess, another thing to bring somebody else into it. "Well, we sure miss you, Dianne. I've always told you that. I'm glad you're calling more often now. Maybe we can talk you back to Dentonville."

Enough already. "Aunt Toe, I'm perfectly fine right where I am."

"I'm sure you are, baby, and I'm sure you've got some decent friends in your new town. But just remember that we love you, too. I mean, *really* love you. And I think that folks ought to spend their lives with the people who love them most." Aunt Toe began her lecture just as the family gathered around the table. They caught the tail end of the sermon. "Now, maybe it ain't the most exciting life, but things start getting real clear in your old age. I'm telling you, Dianne, the people who really love you are the ones who would bend over and wipe your behind for you if you couldn't."

"Preach, Aunt Toe!" Kelan pumped her up.

"Lord knows I'm telling the truth!"

"Okaaaay, we get the picture." Gloria grabbed the phone from Aunt Toe and whispered to Dianne, "Hurry up and get yourself back to here, gal. At least for another visit."

Dianne was still trying to retrieve her jaw.

"You hear me?" Gloria asked.

"Yes, ma'am. I hear you."

Richard could hardly say grace for laughing at Aunt Toe.

After dinner, Kelan and Yolanda excused themselves to go to the African-American Museum in Dallas. He'd told her so much about the collections and displays that she practically begged him to take her there. "Are you asking me for a date?" he'd taunted her one evening as he drove her home following Bible study.

Yolanda threw daggers at him with her eyes.

"Oh-oh." Kelan had jumped back away from the dashboard. "Dang, girl, you sure do know how to give a brother the evil eye. But that's what I like about you."

"I am not asking you for a date, because I do not intend to infringe on your relationship with Paulette," Yolanda had alleged in her most proper tone.

"Paulette and I are taking it slow, remember?" Kelan had reminded her.

That was weeks ago, but now as they buckled themselves into Kelan's freshly vacuumed truck, Yolanda didn't know exactly what to think of all this. Having dinner at her mother's house after church, Kelan fraternizing with her family, and heading off to a museum together? If she wasn't careful, someone might mistake them for a couple. "Kelan, what does Paulette think of all this hanging out we do together?"

"Is that what you call it—hanging out?"

"Yeah." Yolanda bobbed her head up and down.

"Well, for your information, she's not sure that she wants to see me anymore."

"Why?" Yolanda felt a spark of joy but shoved it behind a look of astonishment.

"One guess." Kelan looked at her for a second and then set his eyes back on the road again.

"Me? What do *I* have to do with it?"

"Yolanda, I don't think we're fooling anybody with this

whole 'we're just friends' routine." Kelan merged with traffic on southbound I-35, beginning their lengthy trek into the city. He'd found the perfect time to have this heart-to-heart with the woman he'd grown to hold dear.

Yolanda nervously shoved her hands beneath her thighs. She was trapped. "I *am* your friend, Kelan."

"I agree that we are friends. But the fact of the matter is, I'm a man and you're a woman. I see you as more than a friend, Yolanda," he confessed.

Yolanda didn't appreciate being put on the spot. Was it her problem that he wanted more than a friendship? Okay, she did like him for more than a friend, too, but wouldn't that change things if she admitted it? What if he wanted to be around her all the time? What if she lost her identity in him?

"Well?"

"I need some time to think."

"That's fair." He nodded, keeping his eyes on the road. "May I ask what you need to think about?"

"I need to think about whether or not I'm ready to go down this road."

"What road?"

"The whole *man* road."

"Oh, I'm a *road* now," he laughed.

"I don't think it's funny, Kelan. I really do have to think about this."

"Would it help if I said that you're on my mind all the time?" he asked.

No. Yolanda was beginning to think that this museum trip was the worst idea she'd had in a long time.

"What are you asking of me?" she wanted to know.

"I'm just asking you to be real with me. You can't convince me that you don't feel the attraction between us." He gave her a suggestive glance.

The very declaration of their magnetism, not to mention the look he gave, turned her stomach upside down. Now she knew that Kelan felt it, too. His presence summoned the giddy girl within her and created a new level of vulnerability. She was, to some degree, willing to trade safety for the way he made her feel. "Okay, I'll admit to that." She kept her eyes straight ahead and pulled her hands from beneath her thighs, placed them flat beside her.

Kelan slid his fingers across the center of the truck and touched Yolanda's hand. She drew in a sharp breath and held it, paralyzed by the pleasant sensation of his manly skin against hers. Electricity flickered inside her like fireflies lighting a pitch black night. He gave her hand a squeeze and put both hands on the steering wheel in order to switch lanes.

She exhaled.

Chapter 20

As a favor to Orlando, Yolanda stopped by Regina's on her way to work Monday morning. She answered the door in a pair of cotton pajamas and slippers. *So* not Regina.

"How you doing?" Yolanda tried.

"Just like I look." Regina moved aside so her sister could enter.

Yolanda spotted the flowers she'd given to her sister only days ago. They were withering faster than they should. It was obvious that Regina had made no effort to keep them in bloom.

It was the little things Regina did, like this, that pinched Yolanda's feelings the most. *What would it hurt for her to be nice?* Yolanda forgot all about Regina's body issue and let the Gloria in her loose. "I see how much you cared about the flowers I got you."

"I never asked you to bring me flowers," Regina said. What she meant in her heart was that she didn't *deserve* any flowers.

"You know what? There's a lot that you haven't *asked* me to do, but I did it for you because I care about you—obviously more than you care about yourself. What is your problem anyway? You are *not* fat, Regina. Now, if you want to sit up and convince yourself that you're fat, let that be on you. But don't take it out on the rest of us, okay? Think about someone other than yourself for once."

Regina willingly received the verbal assault. Just another set of words to beat her down, this time coming from her sister rather than from her own head. Same thing, and it only confirmed that she was indeed a bad person.

"I get so sick of you sometimes."

"Yeah, well join the club. I'm sick of me, too," Regina muttered.

"What did you say?" Yolanda yelled at her sister, commanding Regina to repeat herself.

"I said I'm sick of me, too!" Regina screamed violently.

Yolanda squeezed her eyes shut and pressed her fingers against her temples. Of all the things she should have done, screaming at Regina was near or at the bottom of the list. As a professional, she knew that the last thing Regina needed was someone fussing at her for having an illness. But as a sister, from the outside looking in, she found it frustrating to see Regina go through what appeared to be voluntary torture. *Why can't she just change her mind?*

It was too late to take the words back. Yolanda had blown her fuse, let out the steam; whatever it was that she'd heard Gloria call it, Yolanda had done it. "I'm sorry," she offered.

"Just leave. There's nothing for you to be sorry about. I'm the one with the problem."

"I—" Yolanda tried to backpedal.

"Just leave."

Yolanda left her sister's house and drove on to work with regret in the passenger's seat. *I really did it this time.*

"What's wrong?" Brookelynn inquired before Yolanda even had a chance to take off her coat. She slung it on a stool and did her best to answer the question without going into another full-fledged crying episode—head jerking back and forth, huffing between sobs as she had done all the way from the hospital to the pharmacy.

After a few moments, she gathered up enough composure to speak. "I screamed at Regina today for having an eating disorder."

"Oh, Yolanda, she knows you didn't mean it." Brookelynn hugged her, and the smell of Pantene shampoo filled Yolanda's nostrils.

"I *did* mean it, though," Yolanda cried behind the veil of Brookelynn's hair. "I meant every word of it. I'm just sorry I *said* it. That's not what she needs to hear right now."

"Hey, we all make mistakes."

Yolanda slammed her fist on the counter. "I know, but I *hate* it when I mess up."

Kelan met Yolanda at their usual table in the coffeehouse after work on Monday. She was still dressed in her light clothing, Kelan in his jeans and suit coat. Yolanda was determined to tiptoe around Kelan's confessed attraction; he was equally set on getting to the bottom of things with her. Well, maybe not the bottom. After all, he had been known to test the waters with both feet. This relationship with Yolanda was turning out to be an eye-opener. But the way she treaded so lightly annoyed him. What else did he have to do to win her?

Kelan looked at her, rolled his tongue along his teeth, and ventured deeper. Whether or not Yolanda knew it, Kelan did pray for her. He loved her already, even if it wasn't requited just yet. "Yolanda, I've been watching you for the past couple of months. I see how you react when I start talking about the possibility of you being with a man, and I have come to believe that you are afraid."

"Afraid of what? *You're* a man." She tried to dodge his insinuation, taking a big, nervous, throat-scorching gulp of coffee. "I'm here with you, ain't I?" That swig was so hot, it was all she could do to keep from crying again.

"Yeah, I'm a man, but this is not a declared romantic relationship. You're beautiful; you're single; you're smart—I've seen the way guys look at you when we're together. I'm starting to think that you hang with me so that men *won't* approach you." He waited for her to deny what they both knew to be true. "Tell me, do you ever go any place where a man might approach you?"

"I go to church; I go to work; I go to the grocery store." She eyed him.

"And what do you do when men approach you? Do you give them the same cold shoulder you gave me when we first met?"

"Why do you have to keep bringing that up?" She gave a simple smile, hoping to throw him off, but it wasn't working.

"No, answer the question. How do you respond when men approach you?"

"How am I supposed to respond?"

"See, this is the thing I'm talking about. Your attitude toward men—it stinks."

"*My* attitude stinks?" She pressed her back against the chair and brought her hand to her chest.

"It's *foul*, Yolanda."

"Kelan, I'm tired," was all she could say. "Could we please not talk about this today?" They drank coffee and read for a few more minutes; then Yolanda gathered her things and left. Kelan could finish up his coffee alone. All the way home she thought about Kelan's accusations. He'd rubbed her the wrong way, that was for sure. *Who does he think he is?* Yolanda bounced in her seat as she waited for the traffic light to change. After a long day at work, this situation with Regina, and Kelan's harsh words, her patience was paper thin. She threw her head back on the headrest in frustration after waiting another thirty seconds. *What a day, what a day, what a day!* She felt the beginnings of a headache; the twinge lodged between her eyes. Yolanda rarely suffered headaches, so she didn't carry pain relief around with her. "Maybe I need to start," she said out loud.

"No, I take that back," she said after giving it a second thought. She'd made it nearly thirty years without lugging medicine around with her, and she wasn't about to take up that habit now. She popped in her Fred Williams's *Dwelling Place* CD and opted to praise her way out of this frame of mind. With her attentions focused on thanking God for all that had gone right, rather than sulking about the problems in her life, Yolanda was open to revisiting Kelan's words with some level of objectivity. She laughed at herself, thinking, "Okay, maybe he was a little right."

Once at home, she hung her keys on the designated hook, popped out of her shoes, and ran bathwater right away. After bathing and devotional time, she checked her messages. There was one from Orlando, saying that he wanted to ask Yolanda a few questions. The second one was from Kelan, as she figured it would be. He simply called for a truce, offering a partial apology. "I apologize for my word choice," he said, "but I do think that you should consider the message I was trying to convey. Call me when you get in, okay? Bye."

Nope. You've got a little silent treatment coming to you, my brother.

Yolanda returned Orlando's call first, asking him to read the questionable statements. He talked under his breath as he scanned the documents. "Height five-six . . . blood type B . . . African-American . . ." Finally, he read the troubling statement regarding his wife's condition. "What's this body dysmorphic disorder?"

"It's . . . like . . ." Yolanda stumbled through the words. "Kind of like an eating problem."

Orlando wanted the whole truth where his wife was concerned, and Yolanda was glad to have him drag it out of her. This was one time that she was glad to spill all of the beans. "She thinks she's fat but she's not. When Regina looks in the mirror, the image that she sees is much bigger than what she is in reality."

"Isn't this just a part of postpartum depression? I mean, I've heard that can last for quite some time."

"Well, if she really thinks that she's fat—and she obviously does—that's not going to change in another couple of months."

Orlando respected his sister-in-law's opinion, both professionally and personally, but if there was one thing he had learned in observing his mother and her sisters, it was that women stuck together, right or wrong. "Okay. I'll talk to her about it tonight and we'll get something set up."

"Tonight?" Yolanda asked. Regina's wrath so soon?

"Yes. Tonight."

Orlando put the phone on the receiver and took a deep breath. He wasn't afraid of Regina, but he didn't like arguing with her. Somehow she always twisted his words and left him twenty leagues below wondering which way was up. That came with the territory of marrying an attorney, he knew, but that knowledge didn't make him feel any better. As much as he hated what was about to happen, there was no way around it. His wife and his entire family were in danger, and he was not going to sit by and watch this eating problem tear *this* Hernandez family apart.

He sat at the foot of their bed and looked into her swollen eyes. "Regina, we need to talk."

"I'm listening."

"I'm going to schedule you an appointment for counseling."

She cocked her head and calmly stated, "For the record, have you been talking to Yolanda?"

"I am *not* going there with you." Orlando stood his ground, his eyes fixed on hers, not a break in his stern face. They battled it out, fussing and arguing until Regina finally kicked him out of the bedroom. He'd hoped to cuddle his wife tonight in the comfort of their bedroom, with their son sleeping quietly in the next room. Instead, Orlando curled up on the couch with a blanket and a flat pillow. Regina was angrier than he'd ever seen her, but he'd meant what he said about her getting into therapy, whether they were living under the same roof or not.

Chapter 21

Dianne put the finishing touches on the guest bedroom in preparation for Yo-yo and Aunt Toe's arrival. It had been easy getting those two there. With Gloria spending her first Christmas with Richard, Regina spending Christmas in New Mexico with some of Orlando's family, and Yolanda needing a break from Kelan, Dianne easily managed to get them to leave Dentonville for Christmas. Country folks never want to leave their safe little worlds. Maybe if they saw that she had a life in Darson, they wouldn't pester her so much about moving home. In her heart, Dianne determined that she couldn't move back home again as long as Joyce Ann was living and breathing in Dentonville. The best thing she could do was bring a piece of Dentonville to Darson for the holiday.

Dianne hoped like crazy that the plan wouldn't backfire, leaving her with even more longings for the company of her family than before. She couldn't think about that now, though. They were at the door.

"Merry Christmas!" Dianne welcomed them into her modestly furnished apartment.

"Merry Christmas to you, too, Dianne." Aunt Toe reached up to hug her great-niece. That girl was looking more and more like Joyce Ann every day. *Shame they don't even talk.*

Yolanda pushed Aunt Toe past the entrance and then stopped for a hug. "Merry Christmas, girl."

Aunt Toe took it from there, rolling through the widened paths Dianne created in anticipation of their overnight stay. She might as well have pulled out her old white ushering gloves, the way her eyes roved the premises. Dianne and Yolanda stood in the kitchen and watched Aunt Toe as she broke all the rules of home training and inspected what she could from the seat of her wheelchair. She respected Dianne's privacy enough to leave the closed doors alone, but Dianne knew that she'd have to open up her master bedroom to Aunt Toe sooner or later because that bathroom was the only one with an entrance wide enough for the wheelchair.

"How was the drive?" Dianne asked Yolanda.

"Girl, she fussed the whole time," Yolanda replied, performing her best ventriloquist act.

"I owe you one."

"You owe me a million." They shared a private laugh and spoke in their normal tones as Aunt Toe turned up the volume on the television.

"You want some hot chocolate, Aunt Toe?" Dianne yelled over the blaring volume.

"Yeah, baby, that would be fine."

Dianne filled a kettle of water on the stove and continued her conversation with Yolanda. It was the first time in months that she'd had an overnight guest. "Girl, I'm so glad you two came."

"I should be thanking you. I'm kind of glad to get out of Dentonville."

"Why? What's up?"

"Well, for one thing, this is Momma's first Christmas with Richard. I didn't want to impose on them. Then there's this guy named Kelan—"

"A *man?*"

"Yes, a man," Yolanda said evenly.

"I'm just saying, I didn't know you were in the dating mood, Miss I-don't-need-anybody." Dianne eyeballed Yolanda.

Yolanda rolled her eyes and continued. "Anyway, he keeps trying to make me commit, but I'm not ready for all that right now. Then there's this whole thing with Regina. One day she's doing fine; the next day she's hardly speaking."

"Sounds to me like she's just being regular old Regina." Dianne shook her head.

"That's the problem—all these years of mood swings have been a direct result of the underlying problem. She has what the psychological community calls depressive episodes. It's like she goes into self-destruct mode."

Dianne was all too familiar with the term.

"Anyways," Yolanda continued, "Regina's got to learn to deal with life without overeating or obsessing about weight loss. And then there's the situation with your mom."

Dianne held her hands up. "Stop. I don't want to hear any more."

"I'm just telling you what's going on in Dentonville."

"I don't want to hear anything about Joyce Ann." Dianne shook her head firmly.

Yolanda chewed the insides of her cheeks as she contemplated what to do next. She could go off on Dianne as she'd done with Regina, or she could pray about it and leave it alone. Seeing that she hadn't just spent four hours holed up with Aunt Toe on the drive from Dentonville to Darson in order to end up in an argument with Dianne, she chose to keep her mouth shut for now. Yolanda exhaled and said, "Okay, Dianne. I just hope you know that you can't put this thing on the back burner forever."

"I've been on *her* back burner for over twenty years now," Dianne muttered. "What's another twenty?"

Later that Christmas evening, they gathered in the living area to exchange gifts. Aunt Toe surprised the young ladies with a gift, knowing that they wouldn't expect anything from her. Her present was only a token of the love she had for them. Aunt Toe was no fool; she knew that she was a handful in the way that strong, stubborn women with graduate degrees in common sense could be. She wanted her nieces to know that she appreciated them.

"This is beautiful," Yolanda gasped as she twirled the black angel ornament around with its shimmering, glitter-laced wings.

"Thanks, Aunt Toe." Dianne took her angel straight to the tree and hung it near the top. "This is perfect."

"Well, I figure I ain't got too many more Christmases left." Aunt Toe shrugged, pushing her glasses back up on her face.

"You'll probably outlive all of us." Yolanda draped her arm around Aunt Toe's shoulder and gave her a squeeze.

"Oh, I doubt that. Chile, I've got one foot in the grave and one foot on a banana peel. Don't push me, now."

After sunset Dianne took Yo-yo and Aunt Toe to an upscale part of town renowned for its Christmas decorations. They gave a small donation near the gated entry and joined a caravan of onlookers in gawking at the elaborate holiday scenes staged by some of Darson's wealthiest citizens to benefit the Red Cross. They bought hot chocolate from a group of drill team girls and sipped on the smooth warmth as Dianne cruised the neighborhood. There was nothing like it in Dentonville—the first time in all of Aunt Toe's years she'd seen such a display of Christmas spirit. "Well, I'll be," she remarked time and time again as lights dazzled across artificial snow and illuminated rooftops that seemed to reach the stars.

"Ooh, they light bill gon' be sky high next month," Aunt Toe laughed. "But I suppose it was worth it."

Later that night Regina called to say hello to Dianne. They talked at length, with Dianne easing into her room to converse privately. Aunt Toe took that as her opportunity to corner Yolanda. "So, is it working?"

"I don't know, Aunt Toe. It looks like Dianne has a pretty good thing going here in Darson."

"Hmph. Ain't nobody called her except Regina and Gloria. How's that a good thing?"

Yolanda shrugged and shook her head, not wanting to give Aunt Toe any ammunition.

"What's wrong with you, chile?"

"Nothing. I'm just glad to get out of the house."

"Mmm. Me, too," Aunt Toe confessed. "It's good to get out sometimes. But there's no place like home. There's nothing like being around your own peoples, you know?"

"I don't know, Aunt Toe. If Dianne moved back, we wouldn't have anybody to visit. Besides, I don't think Dianne wants to be around Aunt Joyce Ann just yet."

"*That's* the real problem." Aunt Toe wagged her finger in the air.

"I'm afraid so."

"It was an awful thing, what Joyce Ann did. I can't say I blame Dianne for feeling the way she does. She's entitled to those feelings. But deep down in my heart, I know that Joyce Ann still loves Dianne, and Dianne still loves her, too. If they didn't still love each other, it wouldn't hurt them both so much."

Yolanda put her face in her hands and spoke to Aunt Toe between her palms. "That may all be true, but I don't think that badgering Dianne about the situation is going to help anything. I think we need to give them time."

"I ain't *badgering* her!" Aunt Toe whipped her neck around and faced Yolanda. "But that thing about time healing all wounds isn't always true. Yeah, leaving some wounds to time is okay, but other wounds need to be pulled tight and stitched up before they can heal. And I do consider myself surgical thread, 'specially when it comes to my family."

Yolanda didn't argue. Actually, she was too tired to argue. A nice nap would hit the spot right about now. "Well, I'm gonna go lay down for a bit."

"I ain't through with you yet." Aunt Toe grabbed Yolanda's arm and yanked her back onto the couch.

"What did I do now, Aunt Toe?"

"It's what you ain't doin' that I'm concerned with." Aunt Toe looked at Yolanda above the rim of her glasses.

Yolanda was clueless.

"That boyfriend of yours—what's his name, Keldrick?"

"I don't have a boyfriend, but I'm assuming you're referring to Kelan."

"Well, whatever that nappy-headed boy's name is, he's a good 'un, and I think you ought to keep him," she offered her unsolicited advice. Any other time Gloria would have come in and pushed Aunt Toe out of the room, but not today. Aunt Toe had Yo-yo all to herself, and she was ready to lay down the law. "If there's one thing I can't stand, it's to see a foolish woman throw away a perfectly good man."

Yolanda figured she might as well hear Aunt Toe out one good time so maybe they wouldn't have to have this conversation again. Aunt Toe waited for Yolanda to protest. When she didn't, Aunt Toe continued, "You know, there was a time when a black woman couldn't expect to hold on to a good man, 'cause at any moment he could be taken away. My great-grandfather got sold off, left my great-grandmother's heart broke in two. She never got over it. Nowadays y'all just toss 'em out like old grease. You got no idea how much your ancestors wanted to fight to keep their marriages and families together, but they lost their families because they didn't have a choice."

Yolanda had never given it much thought. She considered for an instant what it would be like for someone to come and take Kelan away. "That's sad." Then she thought about all the black men who had intentionally abandoned their families, and countered, "But you have to understand, Aunt Toe, some of these men aren't *acting* right. Evidently, they don't know what a blessing it is to be in a position to *stay* with their wives and kids."

"That's all a part of what we're still dealing with as a people." Aunt Toe sympathized with Yolanda, but she explained herself. "See, three or four generations ago a black man couldn't keep his family together. Couldn't protect them. He couldn't stop a white man from taking his daughter's purity; white man come in and attack the girl with the daddy right over in the next bed—wasn't nothin' he could do about it. That *does* something to a race of men after a couple hundred years. Then here come the black women; we just took on both roles in the family since we couldn't count on them being there. The women stuck together and raised each other's kids, nursed for one another even. Hundred years or so of that, and I guess some of us started thinking, 'What we need these men for?'

"And even though we're past that now, we're still only a couple of generations from it. Our men want to come back home, but we have to be willing to take 'em back in and make 'em feel welcomed and needed. A man's ego is a fragile thing. Especially *our* men. A lot depends on how this generation of educated black women responds to the black men who are making an effort to come home." She pointed at Yo-yo as if

the entire African-American community rested on her shoulders. "You've got to be sensitive to their issues as well as let
them know you ain't givin' 'em another three hundred years
to get their act together. It's a fine line, Yo-yo. A very fine line.
I'll tell ya what, though: there's no substitute for a man in your
life. You can have all the female friends you want—ain't
nothin' like the hum of bass in a man's voice." Yolanda
couldn't argue with that.

She could appreciate Aunt Toe's interpretation of the battle
of the sexes, and in the case of the Rucker women, much of it
seemed to be true. If generations of African-Americans had
grown up under the same pretense that she and Regina grew
up under—that women were self-sufficient islands who neither needed nor desired a man's help—it was no wonder that
so many sisters were doing it for themselves and flat-out
kickin' brothers to the curb. Up until now, however, Yolanda
hadn't seen this as one of the endless ramifications of slavery
in America. If she thought about it long enough, she could
probably poke holes in Aunt Toe's theory. There wasn't
enough time left in all of eternity to win a debate against Aunt
Toe. Still, she couldn't help but wonder what all this had to do
with her and Kelan.

As though she'd read Yolanda's mind, Aunt Toe summa-
rized her sermon. "All I'm saying is, don't be so independent
that you won't allow for one of the best things that could ever
happen to you in your life. Your momma finally listened to
me, and I tell you, Gloria's got a smile on her face that I
haven't seen her wearin' since Willie was alive. Love is a beautiful thing, you know?"

"I guess it can be," Yolanda agreed.

Aunt Toe put her hand on Yolanda's arm. "Don't be afraid,

baby. God's got everything under control. Ain't nothin' gonna happen to you that He don't already know about."

"Hmm." Yolanda gave Aunt Toe a big hug. It wasn't often that she got the chance to sit next to her great-aunt and capture nuggets of her wisdom. She was grateful for moments like this, especially considering that she might not have many such moments left. The twinkle in Aunt Toe's eyes faded a little more each year.

Chapter 22

*Y*olanda agreed to a truce with Kelan on New Year's Eve. With her family off doing couple things, and Paulette having kicked Kelan to the curb for good, they were both down to each other. They attended watch service together on New Year's Eve. At the stroke of midnight they praised the old year out and the new year in. Yolanda was thankful for the relationship that they'd both come to rest in throughout the previous year. And whether or not she was ready to admit it to herself, she was truly falling in love with him. Not the kind where the butterflies fluttered aimlessly in your stomach—the kind where your butterflies knew what they were fluttering about. His dreadlocks were two inches longer. They'd grown on her too. Yolanda had even toyed around with the idea of getting her hair done in twists, but she could never quite set the appointment.

Yolanda considered herself to have the best of both worlds: she was comfortable enough with Kelan to assume that they'd spend some time together on the weekends now that Paulette had officially broken up with him. Yolanda conceded that they were in a romantic relationship, and Kelan seemed happy enough to introduce her as his girlfriend, and she could live with that. Some days she looked at him and he was a man, complete with biceps, powerful thighs, and the unmistakable aura of masculinity. Other days he was just artsy, quirky, plain old Kelan. Still, she had to confess: "Kelan the man" days were beginning to outnumber the others.

Kelan, on the other hand, was tired of this shallow declaration of their connection. Even with all her issues, he couldn't imagine his life without Yolanda. He knew that with time and patience she would come to realize that God was trying to love her through him. But how much time would it take?

"Happy New Year," he said to her later over waffles at an all-night pancake house.

"Same to you."

"This is going to be a blessed year." He seemed assured.

"Go on, brother, prophesy."

"Well, I don't know if you're ready to hear it." He shook his head, taunting her.

"I'm ready."

"Yolanda, I'm in love with you, and before this year is through, we're either going to make a commitment or go our separate ways."

"What?" She dropped a corner of her waffle back into its syrup.

"I told you you weren't ready."

"What are you talking about, Kelan?"

"I'm talking about *us*. I love you, Yolanda. I love everything about you. I love the spirit within you."

"Kelan," she laughed slightly, "you'll have to forgive me, but you do love every woman you meet within three weeks?"

"Okay," he traded laughs, "I'll give you that one. I used to have this wildly romantic idea about love. But our friendship has shown me the best of what God meant for Adam when he created Eve. It's just that I can't keep going with this friendship front."

"So our friendship is a fake?"

"No, the friendship is real." He stopped her. "It's built on a firm spiritual foundation."

"Right," she agreed.

"Right, and that's the great thing about us, Yolanda. We did all of the groundwork without any pressure. And I'm not trying to put pressure on you now. I'm just not interested in having a lifetime girlfriend."

"You picked a fine time to tell me about all this." She put her fork down. The part of her that was in love with Kelan was happy to hear that he wanted more than a friendship. But the part of her that held its independence and order sacred was knocking at the knees. It spoke for her. "It's now or never, huh? You know, Kelan, if you really loved me, you wouldn't push me to do something I'm not ready for."

"If you're not ready, that's okay, Yolanda. I would never ask you to do something that you're not ready for. I just need you to understand that I *am* ready to be in a committed relationship. It wouldn't be fair to either of us to carry on in a relationship that isn't filling our needs. Perhaps we simply have different desires at this point in our lives."

"Perhaps we do. Maybe it's best if we just stop this whole thing in its tracks." She bobbed her head.

"Yolanda, you don't have to get an attitude about it."

"You're just like everybody else."

"No, it's just like *you* to run from everything," he said. "I know you well enough to understand that every time something threatens to disrupt your life as you know it, you run."

"I'm not running from you."

"Well, then, what are you running from?" He sensed her despair and gently took her hands into his. Again Yolanda reveled in his touch. "Yolanda, I love you. We've spent I don't know how many hours on the phone; we check on each other

throughout the day; we're partnered on the hospitality committee; we pray together about everything; I'm a regular at
your family's dinner table. I mean, how many other symptoms
do you need before you can make this diagnosis?"

"All that doesn't mean I love you," she interrupted him. He
withdrew his hands. "At least not the way you think I do."

"Well, you tell me. What does it mean?"

It was one of those moments when you know what you
probably should say, but you just can't make the words come
out of your mouth, maybe because they sound too corny.
Maybe because they would come back to haunt you—Yolanda
couldn't be sure which. She played it safe. "I don't know what
it means."

He heaved a miserable sigh. She hoped that he was as frustrated as she was. *How dare he spring this on me?* Yes, she'd
seen it coming. She'd prayed with, for, and about Kelan, and
she knew that he was, in all honesty, a godsend. And she did
love Kelan—was crazy about him, actually. She had all the
symptoms: doodling his name over and over when she should
be working, accidentally calling other people his name in conversation, thinking in terms of *their* plans rather than hers
alone. Were it not for her upbringing, Yolanda might actually
have suggested that they move in together. She could live with
someone indefinitely. Commitment, however, was another
thing. After all, she reasoned, people could be fickle—especially men. This was one instance where being a practicing
Christian was extremely inconvenient.

Lord, what do I do? "Kelan, I'm sorry. This whole thing is
just mind-blowing, you know? I need some time to pray on it."

"May I ask when I can expect to hear from you on this?"

"I don't know." She dipped her head, annoyed with his
question. "I hope you're not trying to give me a deadline or
something."

"What about the meanwhile?"

She gave him a questioning look.

"Until you make your decision, I'll still consider myself a bachelor."

"You *are* still a bachelor. You always *have* been. We are both too old to be playing these games. You do whatever you want to do," Yolanda hissed.

"Cool." He took a sip of his ice-cold water.

Needless to say, Yolanda's New Year came in with a bang. Kelan had caught her off guard with that all-or-nothing spiel. True to his usual style, he was premature. Flattering but premature, she felt. She had a good mind to make him wait it out until December 31 before she gave him her answer—whatever that was going to be—barring that someone else might actually snatch him up before she got the chance to grace him with her answer. *What if?*

When she finally got off work the day after New Year's, Yolanda took a long bath and then pulled out her Bible. It was the first chance she'd gotten to sit down with the Lord since Kelan's semiproposal. *Lord, what do I do? I'm not ready to get married, but I don't want to lose Kelan's friendship.* She came out of that prayer and study with no reply. Usually, when that happened, it was because she already knew the answer. No, it wasn't right to expect to be able to have her cake and eat it, too. She would either have to commit to him or set him free. In the midst of the realization, however, a sense of power came over her, as though her destiny—and Kelan's—rested with her yea or nay. It was a false sense of control, however, as she was soon to learn.

Chapter 23

On the words of the late Reverend James Cleveland, nobody told Dianne that the road would be easy. She could handle a hard road, no problem. Most people could handle a few bumps and twists. But a midnight-black road with potholes deep enough to sink in, a shoulder that dropped off over a cliff, and a curve that could only be overcome with slow, painstaking maneuvers—she wasn't so sure about that. Such was this road to recovery.

"Dianne, we've had quite a bit of time to talk about the changes that God has made in your life. And maybe it's time we took things to another level. Would you join me in prayer?" Dr. Tilley offered her hands to Dianne and sat forward in her chair.

Dianne took those hands as she had done many times before, closed her eyes, and imagined that God Himself was physically touching her. She had no doubt that He had worked through Dr. Tilley to free her mind of the constant strain. Dr. Tilley said a prayer that Dianne knew was coming. "And, Lord, as we delve deeper into the work that You have laid before us, help Dianne to remain strong. Give her the courage to face the obstacles ahead and gain the victory in You. In the name of Jesus we pray, amen."

Dianne's hands were sweaty by this time, her nerves rattled by this prayer. It was time to deal with the nitty-gritty: her feelings about and against Joyce Ann. Time to let go of unforgivingness, anger, grudges, all of those things that Dianne felt she had a right to—and yes, she'd always thought that if she gave that up, Joyce Ann might actually get away with it. Though Dianne had no intentions of repaying Joyce Ann for the hurtful things she'd done, there was no way on God's green earth she could see sweeping this whole thing under the rug. Didn't her feelings mean anything?

Everything Dr. Tilley said about forgiveness went in one ear and out the other. It was a short spiel, delivered to induce talking. But for the first time, Dianne closed her lips, an impenetrable blockade.

"You understand that facing your giants is the only way to slay them?" Dr. Tilley asked by way of provocation. It didn't work.

"Yes, I understand." Dianne looked Dr. Tilley directly in the eyes.

"And you know that you must work through the pain to get to the other side."

A tear trickled down Dianne's cheek. "I know." She simply wasn't ready to talk about it yet.

"Do you think that you could write a poem about it?" Dr. Tilley made a desperate attempt to turn the pain inside out, put it on the table so they could poke at it and slowly drain it of its power in Dianne's life. She had a vision for Dianne.

"I could. I don't know how Christlike it would be." Dianne gave a pathetic laugh.

"Just write it."

At home, it took her every bit of five minutes to belt out a poem of hurt and despair. She'd cried so hard that she could barely see the words eighteen inches from her eyes. Tears smeared the ink, but she kept on writing.

How Could You?

If you loved me, how could you?
How could you?
Watch me tremble in fear at the broken body,
Join forces with your new love and pounce on my spirit,
When I already couldn't breathe. Maybe you wanted
me to suffocate.
How could you?

You don't get to watch me grow, be what you couldn't.
You don't get to feel my love, use me like ointment to
soothe your wounds.
You don't get to hear me say that everything's okay.
Why? Because it ain't.
And I can't.
How could you?

Aunt Toe scrambled through the numbers in her phone book. It was her tradition to call everyone she knew on their birthday, first thing in the morning, and pray for another good year. Dianne's birthday was easy—it was the same as Regina's. The past few years she'd only gotten Dianne's answering machine. And Dianne would call her back to thank her for the call but rush off the phone with some excuse or other. That Dianne was so busy running—the kind of running that leaves you so exhausted that when you finally do pass out, you wake to find that you haven't really gone anywhere, just used up precious energy. A mental treadmill.

She waited until the news came on with that wonderfully articulate African-American anchorwoman. She was a smart cookie, quick to pick up where the field journalists left off. She didn't skip a beat—made Aunt Toe proud to watch her. The late-breaking news was dreadful, as usual. The devil was roaming the streets, seeking whom he may devour. That was nothing new.

Dianne kicked her feet beneath the covers in temper-tantrum style. It had been another one of those nights where you plead with your brain to shut off, but it just keeps connecting the ticks to the tocks, pondering every little inkling of a thought until it's so late that it's early. It seemed like, only moments ago, she'd won the battle. Now this. *Who is calling me at this hour of the morning?* "Hello?" Dianne bit into the inconsiderate caller as though Aunt Toe could have possibly known that this had been another of Dianne's sleepless nights.

"Dianne?" Aunt Toe was sure she'd read the tone in Dianne's voice correctly.

Dianne pressed her eyelids together, hoping to squelch the irritation that had almost overcome her in a matter of seconds. "Good morning, Aunt Toe." It came softly.

Aunt Toe's brow unfurrowed. "I waited for a while before I called you—I didn't want to wake you up," she apologized indirectly.

You waited *until five-thirty to call me?* Dianne laughed a little, thinking that both she and Aunt Toe had probably been awake only an hour ago. "I appreciate that, Aunt Toe."

"Well, you know I always call and wish you happy birthday."

Dianne hadn't given the day a second thought. Hadn't even written it on her calendar, let alone her heart. Another year, compounded issues. Would she take them to her grave? "Thank you, Aunt Toe."

"Dianne, is it all right if I pray with you?" Aunt Toe wasn't really asking. Dianne needed prayer. She had been a great Christmas host, but even Yo-yo didn't seem to pick up on the loneliness. Aunt Toe had arrived at her own conclusions during their visit. A two-year-old Bible in perfect condition, no pictures of people on display, no linger of good times in the air. Dianne needed her God and her family. Problem was, that gal never came around the family.

"I don't mind."

Aunt Toe proceeded to pray, thanking God for another year in Dianne's life and, almost word for word, reiterating Dr. Tilley's request for courage and strength in the upcoming year. It seemed to Dianne that everyone must know how weak she was. *Am I that transparent?*

"In Jesus' name, amen."

"Thank you, Aunt Toe." Dianne smiled, wishing now that she hadn't scanned the caller ID for the past two years and conveniently missed Aunt Toe's calls. She could have used a good prayer a year ago today. Already she felt better about the day—but not about Joyce Ann.

"You got any plans for today?" Aunt Toe asked.

"No. Just another workday."

"Why don't you go shoppin' or somethin'? Splurge a little," Aunt Toe suggested.

"I don't know . . ." Dianne sat up in bed and turned off the alarm clock. No need to wait for the irritating beep-beep now. "I might go out after work."

"Dianne, when are you going to talk to Joyce Ann?" Aunt Toe got straight to the point.

Dianne's defenses jolted into place. "I have nothing to say to Joyce Ann."

"Well, I have somethin' to say to you. I know that she still loves you and you still love her, too. God's already showed me that. It's about time the two of you stopped waiting for the other one to step forward. Life is too short for holding grudges." Aunt Toe let the words off her chest, feeling lighter with each word lifted. Then she waited for Dianne's response.

"Joyce Ann is no longer a part of my life. She made that decision a long time ago."

"I would let it go if I could see that the two of you made peace. I can't leave this earth without doing my best to make sure that this family buries some old hatchets."

Dianne's body hiccuped in shallow laughter. "Thanks for the birthday call, Aunt Toe. I have to go now. It's about time for me to go to work. I love you."

Aunt Toe scrunched up her lips, racking her brain to come up with the right combination of words. In the movies there was always one line, one concoction of words, that made all the difference in the world. She wished she had it now, but life had taught her better. Sometimes there were no words. Sometimes people had to hit rock bottom to get to the Rock at the bottom.

Chapter 24

Joyce Ann was going on her seventh month in Gloria's rent house. Yolanda had gone by there a few times to say hello. Always Joyce Ann was busy sewing in her bedroom, wearing that same old faded muumuu. She had a small refrigerator, a toaster oven, a television, and a portable stove all within reach of her bed. Except for her room and the adjacent bathroom, the rest of the house was dead. The drapes were drawn, with the only light coming from the tiny bulb on the sewing machine. Yolanda gathered that Joyce Ann stayed confined to her tiny quarter of the house most of the day, working and watching television. She seemed subdued, more melancholy than she'd been in recent weeks.

She had been repeatedly assaulted by her past.

Her head was wrapped in a scarf, and she wore a housecoat that looked as though it was way past repair. Her face, soft and brown, contrasted with her hard, chapped, blackened lips. Even in her rough simplicity, Aunt Joyce was more attractive than the average woman.

"Your sister hasn't come by to see me." Her lips flattened. "You think she ever will?"

"I'm sure she will, Aunt Joyce Ann," Yolanda said. "Just give her some time. Actually, I came by to ask you if you wanted to come to Momma's house and celebrate Regina's birthday with us. I guess it's kind of a birthday brunch. Not much, just whatever Momma made and some cake."

"I knew you had some reason for stopping by." She reached over and touched Yolanda's knee. "But I'm glad you did. You're my favorite niece, you know?" She looked up at Yolanda with deep-set eyes that resembled the hand-blown glass eyes of a porcelain doll. Blank. Still. Yolanda wondered where Joyce Ann was, in her head. How she processed things in her mind. How she could have abandoned her daughter. . . .

Joyce Ann returned to her sewing. Her voice took on an erratic, deeper tone, "People don't hardly want to hire you when they find out you've got a record and been to a mental hospital. That's two strikes. They think you're gonna go in and stab everybody. Little do they know, most of the really crazy people will never see the inside of an institution until they're in the penitentiary.

"This wedding place I'm working for, Ellen's Bridal, they contract the work to me. They let me use their sewing machine and their notions. I got to give it back if I quit, though, else they'll come looking for Gloria to pay for it, since she's the one that got me the job. Shame what these machines cost nowadays. This one here's probably a couple of thousand dollars, with everything on it.

"But they only give me so much work, you know? There's only so much you can do without working at the place. But a few of the brides asked about me and they've been referring their friends to me on the side. I've got quite a few weddings lined up and one of those fifteen-year-old parties for a Mexican girl. Things are really picking up."

"That's good, Aunt Joyce." The small talk became uncomfortable. "Well, I'm gonna walk on back to Momma's house—"

"Have you talked to Dianne?" She stopped her sewing but didn't look up.

"Yes."

"Did you tell her that I was here? Did you tell her I'm back and that I have a job?"

"Yes."

"What did she say?"

"Nothing, really." Yolanda shrugged.

"Oh."

Yolanda waited to see if Joyce Ann was going to ask about Dianne. She couldn't wait to tell her that she'd talked to Dianne just last week and that Dianne had a poem that was slated for publication in a national magazine, and how much better Dianne seemed to be doing. But when Joyce Ann didn't inquire about her own daughter, Yolanda had a few choice words to share. She asked, with a professional coolness, "How about *you* asking how *Dianne* is doing? How about *you* asking if *she* needs anything, is *she* in good health, does *she* have a job? You're not the only one whose life was devastated by what happened in this house, you know?"

Joyce Ann put her foot back on the sewing machine's pedal. Yolanda could barely hear her over the hum.

"What did you say?" Yolanda found herself almost yelling at Joyce Ann.

"I said I know that!" Joyce Ann looked up at Yolanda, her lips trembling.

"I'll be praying for you, Aunt Joyce Ann," Yolanda said. As far as Yolanda was concerned, Joyce Ann's lips could tremble till the cows came home; that wasn't going to change anything. "You can go to all the rehabs and all the mental clinics you want, but no one can do what God wants to do for you."

"I'll be down to your momma's house in a few minutes. You go on."

Yolanda walked back to her mother's house alone.

"Is she coming?" Gloria asked Yolanda as she came through the door.

"She said she'd be down here in a few minutes."

"What's she doing?"

"She's busy sewing. Momma, are you sure Aunt Joyce Ann should be staying there by herself? Did you know that she's got all her stuff in one room?" Yolanda sat down at the kitchen table and watched her mother smooth the icing on her famous Italian cream cake.

"Maybe that's all she can handle right now." Gloria shook her head. "I check on her every day. And she comes up here sometimes, too. I know she only looks like a shell of herself, but she's alive. And as long as she's alive, there's hope."

Yolanda shook her head, wondering how much longer her mother was going to stay in denial about Joyce Ann. Her mother always seemed to have the answers when they were growing up—why was she having such a hard time now?

"Regina's on her way," Gloria chirped. "Yeah. She'll be here any minute now. She had a doctor's appointment today. She's coming by right after she's finished." Gloria licked the last drop of icing from her fingertips and submerged the knife in the waiting dishwater.

Yolanda reluctantly followed her lead away from the topic of Joyce Ann. "What else did you make?"

"I didn't want to make a big fuss, so I just made soup and sandwiches. Oh, I need to know if you're inviting Kelan on Sunday. I want him to bring one of his pound cakes. That boy sure can cook, you know?"

"I don't know if Kelan will be coming or not. We kind of had a . . . disagreement."

"About what?" Gloria asked, suspecting the truth already.

"He just wants more out of a relationship than I do right now," Yolanda explained in generic terms.

"Mmm-hmm." Gloria wiped the countertops hard. Finally, she spoke her mind. "You can't have your cake and eat it, too. You leave it up there long enough, somebody else is gonna come and take a bite."

"I don't want to commit to Kelan just to keep him from someone else." Yolanda gave a quizzical laugh. "If I make any kind of commitment, I want it to be because I love him."

"Well, do you?"

Yolanda froze in her tracks. Thought about it. What a scary word, this "love." Love of family she knew; love of God she knew; love of profession she knew. But love of a man? No point of reference, no gauge, no database. "I don't really know what love is," she answered.

"Well, sometimes you only know it was love after it's gone," Gloria advised.

Joyce Ann banged through the front screen, announcing her arrival. "Hello. Where y'all at?"

"We're in here," Gloria called to her.

Joyce Ann walked into the kitchen wearing a white sundress and sandals. A fresh coat of red lipstick masked the crusty lips Yolanda had seen earlier. Her hair was pulled back into a neat, brisk ponytail. But it wasn't just a matter of how quickly she'd changed clothes and thrown on a few accessories. She was literally a different being: jovial, lively.

"Hey, Gloria." She hugged her sister. "Hi, Yo-yo." The name bounced off her lips like a giant beach ball. It was as though it were her first time seeing Yolanda all day. Earlier, when

Yolanda thought that Joyce Ann was "thrown off," she'd put her in the category of people who just lived in their own world. But this was different. Joyce Ann wasn't the same woman she'd been earlier. Even the look in her eye had changed. Her eyes shined with spark and definition, not the dreary lostness they'd embodied before. Her switch, her metamorphosis, was eerie.

They heard Regina let herself in the front door and readied themselves to sing "Happy Birthday." The look on Regina's face put an end to all thoughts of song.

"Hey, Regina!" Joyce Ann called from her chair at the far end of the kitchen table, waving her hand like a beauty queen in the town parade. "Happy Birthday!"

Yolanda expected Regina to give her a good eye-rolling, but she wasn't up to it. "Hi, Aunt Joyce Ann."

"Regina, what's wrong?" Gloria asked.

"Well, nothing's really wrong," she said, denying the look of concern that contradicted her words.

Gloria eyed her daughter and warned, "You better let somebody help you, girl. You can't go through your whole life keeping things to yourself."

"Hmm," Yolanda heard Joyce Ann say under her breath while Regina listened to their mother carry on, "ain't that the pot calling the kettle black?"

Okay, she is off into her own little world. Yolanda wasn't licensed to diagnose mental illness, but it was clear to her that Joyce Ann wasn't well yet. Definitely not well enough to be living on her own. *Why am I the only one who can see this?*

They ate and listened to Joyce Ann go on and on about her sewing. Like everything was normal.

Yolanda cleaned up when she got home. The hot, soapy water smelled of bleach and Pine-Sol. She submerged her gloved hands in the bucket and pulled out her cleaning towel.

The routine of it all, with its familiarity and reliable results, calmed her. Slowly, meticulously, she scoured her house, removing hints of the imperfections that came with the living that took place there: dust settling into the nooks of the baseboards, the droplets of water that found their way into the shallow drain beneath the refrigerator's water dispenser, and the tiny morsels of food that fell beneath the stove's metal catching dishes.

She cleaned and cleaned until, finally, Kelan's ultimatum seemed to disappear like the oily residue that she had discovered on the light switch panel in her garage and had attacked mercilessly, wiping, double-checking, and then wiping again to be sure. *Wouldn't it be easy if Aunt Joyce Ann's problem could be sucked out like the invisible dirt being violently extracted from beneath the surface of these carpeted floors?* She mopped and scrubbed until everything was perfect and in order, just as it should be.

When she saw Kelan's name on the caller ID display at eight o'clock that evening, she breathed a sigh of relief.

"How was your day?" he asked her.

"Fine. I went to the my mom's house for brunch; then I came home and cleaned my house. Then I took a little nap. I just got up a few minutes ago."

"I told you, you're working yourself too much. Nobody needs to clean their house from the front door to the back porch every single week," he fussed. "I could see if you had a houseful of people, but it's just you. You don't have to do all that."

Yolanda was glad that he still took the liberty to express his concern.

"How did the thing go with Mr. Preston—Richard's friend?"

"Oh, he called and rescheduled. I'm meeting with him early next week to show him some of my pieces."

"I know you're going to do great."

"Thanks for the vote of confidence. I meant to ask, did your aunt Joyce Ann come to Regina's brunch?"

"Yeah, she came. But you know, Kelan, after talking to her at my mom's house, I think that she should be admitted. I mean, she had one kind of persona when I saw her at the rent house. She was cynical and subdued. But by the time she got to my mom's house, she was Ms. Congeniality. I think she's got some kind of bipolar thing going. It's like she snaps in and out of herself."

Yolanda had filled enough prescriptions for antidepressants and other mind-regulating drugs to know that the brain could malfunction just like any other part of the body—especially under duress, bending and straining beyond what the average psyche encountered.

"Is there anything I can do to help?" he asked.

"No," she declined, "I can handle it, don't worry."

"You know, sometimes I can't tell about you." He held his breath and then spewed out the contents of his heart. "I can't imagine my life with you day in and day out; then again, I can't imagine my life without you. You keep me in line where I would stay perpetually out of line, at the same time you make me realign everything that I thought I knew about life and love itself. I want to be a part of your life, but then you do these little things to kick me out."

Yolanda agreed with him and, for once, thought she'd give him that pleasure. "I feel the same way."

"Then why don't you say so?"

"You just said it for me."

"This is a classic," he said. "I think I know where this whole thing is going. Sooner or later you're going to say that I'm too good for you and that I should find someone else who will treat me better."

"No. I wasn't about to say that."

"That's what usually comes next."

"Well, this isn't the *usual* relationship."

"I agree with you, Yolanda. But I have to tell you, I feel very rejected when you tell me that you care about our relationship but you can't commit to me, all in the same breath. I'm man enough to admit that. But what upsets me even more is that you're not woman enough to admit that you are afraid. I—"

"You know what, Kelan," Yolanda cut him off, "I'm tired of going around and around in circles with you about this. I really don't want to talk about it anymore."

"Yolanda, I've been . . . having lunch with someone at work."

Yolanda's heart fell to her stomach. She was glad that he'd told her over the phone, so he wouldn't get the chance to see her lower lip drop. She let the thought sink in and pulled her jaw up before she said, "Oh. Okay. That was quick. It was only, what, a month ago that you practically asked me to marry you. It's interesting to know that I can be replaced so easily."

"Yolanda, I'm not going to apologize to you for refusing to be your man in waiting. But don't worry, we can still be friends."

She wanted to slam that phone down in his face. "We always have been. So why are you telling me about this woman now?"

"Because I was thinking of inviting her to church on Sunday."

"You don't have to ask my permission to invite a guest to church. It's a free world."

"I'm not asking you for your permission. I just didn't want it to be an awkward situation for either one of us, in case we bump into each other."

The thought was sickening. Kelan at church with another woman, nudging her when the preacher made a striking point. Passing her a Tic Tac. Would he bake her a pound cake for dinner after service? Probably. Jealousy got the best of her. "Oh, and I guess you'll tell her that you love her, too, in another week or so?"

"No. Honestly, Yolanda, I didn't know what love was supposed to be until God built it up between me and you. But if you're too stubborn to recognize what we have between us, what choice do I have?"

I know he ain't waiting on me *to give him the green light.* "Well, I don't know what to tell you, Kelan. A man's gotta do what a man's gotta do."

"Okay," he said against his will. "I think that the best thing for us to do is to break it off. I can't play buddy with you anymore, Yolanda. I can't keep going back and forth with this thing. One night we're holding hands at the movie theater; the next night I'm trying to convince you that we should take it to the next level. It's wearing me down."

"What are you saying?" she asked him.

"I'm saying that until we're both going in the same direction, we're only going to keep growing apart. So before we start saying or doing things that we'll regret, I think it's best if we stop seeing each other."

Yolanda didn't know how to respond. Her cake was sliding off the platter right before her very eyes. She wasn't going to get to have it or eat it. She felt herself, once again, in that peculiar place where her heart screamed one thing but strong, independent Yo-yo said another. "Okay. If that's the way you want it."

"That's *not* the way I want it." Kelan made it clear.

"Whatever, Kelan."

"Do you *really* mean that?" he asked.

Yolanda didn't respond. They both held on to their phones. Yolanda ran her tongue across her teeth, checking for signs of buildup to scrub away. Kelan was speechless. Surely these wouldn't be their last words. Yolanda waited for him to cave in, to say something—anything—and keep the conversation going.

"Good-bye, Yolanda." He hung up.

Yolanda stared at the receiver in amazement. *Did he just hang up on me?* She held on to the phone through the silence, the dial tone, and the message, "If you'd like to make a call, please hang up and dial the number . . ."

Yolanda had always prided herself on the fact that she didn't lose sleep over men. True to her game, she pulled out her Bible and attempted to close out the evening as she always did. *I knew men were nothing but trouble. I shouldn't be surprised.* She opened her devotional guide to the marker that held her place. Things had turned out just the way they always did. She was back in her bedroom. *Me, myself, and I.* Back to the efficient, predictable, steady way of her life.

Yolanda's Scripture for the evening was Philippians 3:13 and 14: *Brethren, I count not myself to have apprehended: but this one thing I do, forgetting those things which are behind, and reaching forth unto those things which are before, I press toward the mark for the prize of the high calling of God in Christ Jesus.* She read Kelan all through these verses, her anger allowing for the misinterpretation of the message. *Maybe I do need to leave Kelan behind.*

To her dismay, she couldn't turn her brain off. She *did* lose sleep that night.

Chapter 25

*O*f all the weekends Gloria could have picked, she happened upon the coldest Saturday of all winter to clear out her garage. She didn't have much of a choice, though, because Richard's friend Jerry wanted to start working on the garage conversion right away.

"The home improvement business gets pretty slow during the winter," he'd said. In exchange for the off-season work, Jerry gave them a discount. Gloria had immediately called her daughters and Joyce Ann to help with the efforts.

"In the garage?" Joyce Ann had balked.

"Yeah, me and the girls are gonna clean it out. We're gonna have it made into a den." Gloria hoped to get Joyce Ann over, run a comb through her hair, and make her presentable so that Yo-yo could get off her back about it for a while—at least for today.

"Are you trying to kill me or something!"

Gloria offered a calm tone. "What are you talking about?"

"I can't stand to be trapped!" She slammed the phone onto the receiver.

Well, maybe this wasn't the best day to establish Joyce Ann's sanity.

Gloria asked Yolanda to go and pick up Aunt Toe so that

she could get out of the house. Aunt Toe complained about being dragged out of her home on what she termed "a day that'd make a snowman shiver," but she was happy to be in their company. Though Aunt Toe couldn't do much in the way of lifting or pulling, having her there to sift through the cherished family memoirs would certainly make it a memorable day. Gloria warmed up some apple cider and made an event of the task.

"Okay, we need to try and save all the stuff that you two might want to pass on," Aunt Toe had ordered. Regina and Yolanda pinched each other at Aunt Toe's directives. Somehow she'd fallen under the impression that she was to supervise this garage clearing from her wheelchair.

Aunt Toe threw on two blankets, grabbed a cup of warm cider, and parked herself near the kitchen door and talked up a storm the whole time, commenting on every item they pulled from the chest of old clothes beneath a steel shelf. "Ooh, chile, I remember when your aunt Joyce Ann bought that purse." Regina displayed the patent leather bag for them all to see. Yolanda gave it a quick glance and got back to business. Aunt Toe continued, "She paid an arm and a leg for that thing, just 'cause it came from Sanger-Harris, and the handle popped off after 'bout a week or so. Ha! Ha! Ha! I tried to tell her that bag wasn't nothin', but you know some people ain't satisfied till they spend a quarter for a nickel."

The working crew continued with Aunt Toe's commentary serving as white noise. "Ooh!" she shrieked. "Hand me my gown!"

"This old thing, Aunt Toe?" Yolanda stood up, stretching her back and holding up a flannel nightgown with paisley print.

"That's my *cotton* gown." Aunt Toe snatched the gown from Yolanda. "Yes, I've been looking for this for *years*. Gloria May Rucker, I got a mind to whip you for takin' my gown."

"I didn't know I—" Gloria started to apologize, but Aunt Toe continued her rampage.

"I mean, I looked high and low for my cotton gown, and here you are with it in your garage. Well, I'll be. Everybody needs a cotton gown. Cotton panties, too. Cotton breathes. But you don't wear panties to bed—I've never worn panties to bed. Can't sleep with 'em on. Seem like I ain't *free* when I wear panties to bed."

They all stopped and looked at Aunt Toe. Finally, Regina spoke. "That is way too much information."

"I'm just tellin' you," Aunt Toe mumbled. "You should not be wearing panties to bed at night. As for me and *my* house, no panties at night, praise the Lord. I'm going back in the house with my cotton gown."

Halfway through the morning, Aunt Toe conked out in Yolanda's old bedroom. Thus far, Gloria and Yolanda had only managed to get through the old workout equipment, a crate of grade school awards, and a chest of drawers filled with eight-track cassettes. "Yeah," Gloria remarked as she held up vintage Al Green toward the single lightbulb dangling from the garage's ceiling. "Your daddy used to love these eight-tracks. That was back when every song had to be good, 'cause you couldn't skip through anything on an eight-track."

Yolanda found it impossible to follow her mother's memories of Willie. There was nothing down that path for her to remember.

Yolanda had given up on her efforts to expedite the cleanup process. Every time Gloria's hands found something she hadn't touched in decades, she had to relive it. "Look, Regina, you remember this?" Gloria climbed onto a brown exercise bike and began pedaling. The creaky old bike's wheels revolved, rust falling to the concrete as Gloria forced the motion. "Ooh-wee, y'all. I really thought I was gonna get *super fine* with this thing."

"You look fine now," Regina told Gloria.

"So do you," Yolanda said to her sister.

Regina sighed, rolled her eyes, and let them land on her mother again.

Yolanda was satisfied now that Orlando was on her team. He'd make sure Regina didn't do irreversible damage to herself. But Yolanda noticed that when Regina sat down to eat on Sundays, she seemed to detest the undertaking. Closing her eyes as she brought the fork to her mouth, chewing like a child eating a mandatory serving of carrots at the dinner table. Yolanda knew that Regina was only biding her time, crossing off the days on her calendar until she could get back to the laxatives or whatever else she had in mind.

"Let's just get this over with." Gloria called a truce between her daughters.

"I'm hungry," Regina broadcast. "You cook anything, Momma?"

"Now, that's what I like to hear." Gloria jumped off the bike and rubbed her hands on her sweatshirt. "I didn't cook today. We could go out and get something. What do you want, Yo-yo?"

"I'll take a burger and fries if it'll get us out of here quicker." Yolanda looked up from her stool with tired eyes. She'd worked until a little after midnight reconciling inventory at the pharmacy.

"You okay?"

"Yes, Momma. You two just go get something to eat." Yolanda wanted her mother out of that garage.

"Okay. Let me go get my purse." Gloria stepped back into the warmth of the house and welcomed the distinct smell of her home. She'd raised a family there: three girls, who had all gone on to make something of themselves. And now she had Richard.

Back in the garage, Yolanda asked Regina to take the long route. "I don't have all day to freeze in this garage, so I'm gonna get through as much of this as I can while you're out with her."

"Got it."

With her mother and sister gone, Yolanda was left to sort through the garage, determining what should be saved or discarded. She got busy throwing out expired cans of ant spray, dried-up gallons of paint, a toaster that was beyond repair. Yolanda consolidated six boxes into two and stored them in the vacant closet of her old bedroom. She was tempted to stop and thumb through the photo albums but decided it was best to wait for another day. Besides, her hands were too numb from the cold to thumb through anything.

Yolanda thought of how much easier the job might have been with a man's help. Richard was away on business; Orlando was home with the baby. She thought of Kelan and how he would have been intrigued by the relics in her mother's garage. Then she laughed, thinking that she probably would have sent him out for food with her mother and Regina because he would have been in the way, too.

After giving her hands a chance to thaw out, Yolanda made her way back to the garage and gave her attention to a box that had been conspicuously covered by a scrappy vinyl tablecloth. She uncovered the dusty old hatbox and read the top: "W. A. J."

"What's waj?" Yolanda asked herself out loud.

Yolanda lifted the lid off the box and suddenly realized that she'd discovered a box of Willie Amos Jordan memorabilia. She was face-to-face with her father—a shadow in her mind, maybe a silhouette at best. All Yolanda had ever heard about her father, Willie Amos Jordan, was "yeah" and "amen." From what she gathered, he was a hardworking man who served his family and his church faithfully. The prospect of going through this, what was left of him, sent an unnerving flush of emotion through her. She wanted to put the lid back on, but she couldn't. Yolanda forgot all about her mission to hasten the clearing, forgot about the coldness seeping through her jacket, and pieced through this, what was left of her father.

For the next half hour, Yolanda got lost in a whirlwind of sentiment and discovery. There were envelopes filled with pictures of her father and mother in happier days. Regina's face appeared in several of the pictures, too, and suddenly Yolanda felt the pang of grief. She had never gotten the chance to know her father. Wasn't even sure if he'd known about her at the time of his death. The pictures showed a man she should have been proud of. Someone who should have packed her on his shoulders and carried her around the house against her mother's wishes. Someone who should have grabbed hold of her arms and swung her around and around in circles until she got dizzy. But none of that TV stuff had happened for Yolanda.

There were letters that Willie had written to her mother, presumably when they were dating. He talked of raising a family, growing old together. Yolanda was careful to wipe the tears from her eyes before they fell to the page and caused smudges.

Next she came across the death certificate and autopsy results. Yolanda knew that Gloria wouldn't have wanted her to see those records, but Yolanda's curiosity was further piqued by the official seal of Dentonville County. She opened the envelope and read the documents. Her eyes settled on the cause of death: drowning. Yolanda wanted to add the rest of the story onto the cause. The story was that Willie Amos Jordan died after he jumped off the boat to save his friend Rayford Shelby, who had fallen out of the boat on a fishing expedition. Rayford Shelby lived, but Willie went under. Some people said that Willie got caught by one of those strong undertows, the kind that can suck you beneath the surface without warning. Some people said that maybe Willie caught a cramp and couldn't recover. Still others said that he was simply exhausted from hauling big old Rayford Shelby's behind into the boat. *Should have let him drown!* she'd heard a neighbor say. Whatever the reason, Willie went under and didn't surface again by his own power.

Yolanda sifted through the medical jargon with her professional expertise at the forefront of her mind. Maybe she could find something that the examiner had overlooked, something to explain why her father, apparently a healthy man, had drowned. After several minutes of combing through the papers, she gave up trying to find another cause. It was just one of those things. The same mystery.

She looked up toward the ceiling, closed her eyes, and let the warm tears fall so far down her neck that they turned cold. "Lord, I wish I could have known my father." But it was too late for that. Yolanda folded the record along its original creases and prepared to put it back into the envelope when, like a lightning bolt, it jolted her. She opened the document again.

Yolanda waited in the living room and met her mother at the front door with one demand. "Tell me about my father."

"Your father was a wonderful man." Gloria pushed past Yolanda and walked into the kitchen. She didn't talk much about Willie, never wanting to upset the girls.

Regina followed her mother into the kitchen, hoping to hear more about her daddy, the grandfather her son would never know.

Yolanda followed, with the autopsy results in hand, though Gloria had failed to notice.

"He was wonderful. Everybody loved him. You would have loved him, too. And I'm sure your daddy is loving us all in whatever way God allows in heaven." Gloria beamed as she placed the bags of food on the table.

Yolanda surprised herself by what she did next. Maybe it was anger; maybe it was desperation, but Yolanda took firm hold of Gloria's shoulders and forced a point-blank dialogue. Yolanda was determined that Gloria wouldn't wiggle out of this as she did with Joyce Ann or with Regina's eating disorder. Not this time.

"Momma, I'm not asking about Willie Amos Jordan. I'm asking you *who* my father is."

Gloria twitched free and occupied herself with coupling the burgers and fries. Yolanda continued her line of questioning, knowing that she had her mother cornered. There was nowhere to run. "My blood type is O, and Willie Amos Jordan was an AB. It's impossible for an AB to be the biological parent of an O. An AB can have anything but an O. It's one of the first things we learn when we study blood types."

Regina stood still, too stunned to speak. Yo-yo was serious, and her mother was acting strangely.

Watching Gloria's trembling hands was enough to confirm what science had already declared. Willie Amos Jordan, deceased, was not her father. Yolanda covered her ears and screamed with everything in her, "Answer me!"

Gloria plopped down in a chair, slumped over onto the table, and realized that she would now have to begin to unbury her head from the sand.

Hearing the commotion, Aunt Toe crept into the kitchen. Her wheelchair stopped at Yolanda's feet. It was one of the last things she wanted to see cleared up before she left this earth. "Willie wasn't your father, Yo-yo." She would leave the rest to Gloria.

"What!" Regina asked.

Gloria looked up at her oldest. "He's *your* father, but not Yo-yo's."

"What do you mean, he's not *my* father?" Yolanda asked with the innocence of a small child—the logistics hadn't even entered her mind yet. Telling her that Willie Amos Jordan wasn't her father was like telling Yolanda that she wasn't black, she wasn't female, she wasn't Yolanda Jordan.

"Willie was already dead when I got pregnant with you. It . . . it just happened a few days after he died. I was so distraught . . . I was so out of my mind." Gloria waved her arms in the air at nothing.

"What do you mean, he's *not my* father?"

Gloria looked Yolanda in the eyes, finally. "He's not your father."

"Who *is* my father, Mother?" Yolanda terrified herself, yelling at Gloria as if she hadn't been taught better. But at that moment Yolanda could feel herself coming apart, like her life had caught a snag long ago and she'd unraveled—only no one had told her that she'd been walking around all this time with her entire backside exposed. *I'm not me. My whole life has been a lie?* "Why didn't you tell me? Where is he?"

"Your father's name is Bernard Livingston. He was living in Parker City, the last I heard," Gloria said, her eyes fixed in a trance.

Regina bristled. *Yolanda has a father? Living?*

"You don't even know him?" Yolanda accused her. "How do you just sleep with somebody, have a baby with somebody—"

"Yo-yo, don't, okay? I've already been through the guilt

trip. You have no idea what it feels like to lose—" She spoke softly, but Yolanda was not feeling one bit sorry for her.

"This family is so sick!" Yolanda screamed, clasping her hands and resting them on top of her head. "Is that the excuse for everything? Every time somebody dies, people just lose their minds? That gives you the right to leave your kids, jump into bed with strangers—"

"Please." Gloria's eyes begged. "Please don't, Yolanda. You can't say anything to me that I haven't already said to myself."

Aunt Toe bit her tongue, willed it to stay still. Gloria should have had this conversation with Yo-yo a long time ago. Yolanda and Gloria just sat there for a moment, staring at each other, Yolanda fuming, Gloria melting. Regina stood against the counter, wondering what all this meant for her. Yolanda wondered, *How could she let me live my whole life thinking that I didn't have a father? How could she let me suffer the pain of his absence needlessly? Doesn't she know that every little girl wants a daddy?*

Yolanda couldn't ask her those questions without an attitude, so she decided it best to leave. Regina grabbed her purse as well.

"Sit down—both of you," Gloria commanded. Slowly, they obeyed, waiting to hear the answers.

"Yo-yo, you have to understand the position that I was in," she began, shedding tears she'd kept at bay for a number of years. "When your father died—I mean, when Willie died— my whole life stopped. I was bred, born, and raised to be a wife. I know you don't understand that, because I raised you, Dianne, and Regina to stand on your own two feet, but that's not the way your grandma Neal raised us. God rest her soul, she meant well. But me and your aunt Joyce Ann came up thinking that we were nothing without a man. So when Willie died, I felt like the rug was pulled right out from under me. I was so lost, I thought about killing myself. If it wasn't for Regina, I would have." Regina clasped on to that attention, but Yolanda felt that she could vomit any minute now.

"The day after the funeral Bernard came over to tell me how sorry he was about the loss. Bernard was one of Willie's coworkers. He had taken up a collection from the other men down at the plant and then brought it to me. I knew him well enough to invite him in. Joyce Ann had taken Regina down to the rent house for a few hours and given me some time alone. Anyway, Bernard came in and we started talking. I started crying, leaning on him. He hugged me, held me in his arms. And I started thinking, 'What if I never get held like this again? What if this is *it* for me? I felt so weak, and he felt so strong. I kissed him. He looked at me like . . . like he was just as confused as I was. I asked him to . . . to kiss me. He started to say no, but I kissed him before he could get the word out. We kept waiting for the other one to say 'stop' or 'we shouldn't be doing this.' But neither of us said a word the entire time.

"For weeks he called to tell me how sorry he was for what happened, for taking advantage of me. I told him that it was just as much my fault as it was his and not to worry about it. He gave me his number and told me to call him if I ever needed anything for myself or for Regina, or if I ever needed someone to talk to."

"Does he know about me?" Yolanda interrupted her.

"No. Not really." Yolanda waited for Gloria to explain this answer. "He knows I had a baby, the same as everybody else in Dentonville knew that I had a baby nine months after Willie died. I guess he just assumed that you were Willie's. But I knew. A woman *knows* these things. You take one look at Bernard and you'll know without a doubt that you're his." She nodded.

"Who else knows?" Yolanda asked.

"Grandma Neal knew. Joyce Ann knows. Aunt Toe knows. Hmph, probably Dr. Hamilton."

"Great!" Yolanda replied sarcastically. "Why is it that everybody else knows except me, Momma? Don't you think I would have liked to know that I had a father?"

"You're not a mother yet, Yo-yo. I really . . . I don't expect you to understand."

"There's nothing to understand!" Yo-yo put it in black and white. "You lied to me. Why, Momma? It makes no sense!"

Gloria did her best to explain. "When you're a single mom and you're doing your best to raise your kids in the best atmosphere possible, you try to cut down on all the problems you can. Times were different back then. People didn't have this outcry of support for single mothers, let alone a mother with children who have different fathers. I didn't want to put you and Regina through a whole lot of mess—one daughter having a father and the other one not. One child getting extra Christmas gifts and the other one not. Aunts, uncles, and cousins for one but not for the other. I just didn't want a lot of drama and rejection for you if people in Dentonville found out that you weren't Willie's, or if Bernard got married and had other kids. I just wanted you and Regina to grow up as normal as possible—grow up with few disruptions. That's a mother's prerogative."

"Well, it wasn't fair." Yolanda shook her head. "I have a right to know my family."

"We *are* your family. We've been enough until now."

"You got your nerve."

Gloria braced herself. "Go on, Yo-yo. Say what's on your mind."

"You raised me, and I know you care about me. But it wasn't right for you to keep the truth from me for *your* convenience, so that everything would be perfect and proper and painless. It might have been easier for you, but it wasn't easy for me.

"And did you ever think that maybe Bernard Livingston would have turned out to be a great father to me? That he might have been a good male figure in my life—maybe even in Regina's life, too? Did it ever occur to you that maybe my father is a good man?"

"I never said that he wasn't a good man."

She looked down at her thumbs. Yolanda almost felt sorry for her. Almost. The man that she'd always loved as her father, Willie Amos Jordan, was not her father at all. All the dreams she had about him, where she imagined that he somehow knew about her before he died. All the times Gloria told Yolanda that "Daddy would always be in her heart," when *her* daddy was alive and kickin'. How could Gloria sit there and watch Yolanda cry and pray to God that she would see her daddy again in heaven when, the whole time, her *real* daddy was just a few towns away?

"Just when were you planning on telling me this? When were you gonna tell me, Momma? Were you gonna take this to your grave? What about Richard? Does he know?"

Gloria shook her head.

"I took this to the Lord a long time ago. You know, some things are better left in the past, Yo-yo."

"Evidently, the Lord didn't agree with you about *this* thing." Yolanda fetched her bag and headed for the door.

Gloria called behind her. "Wait, Yolanda. You don't understand how hard it was. I . . . I never meant to hurt you, baby, but once you tell the first lie, the rest get easier."

Yolanda slammed the car door shut, ignoring Gloria as she pounded on the window. "Yo-yo, wait! Wait!"

Yolanda gave her mother a look of utter disgust. There it

was. The dark, smoky look of anger that Gloria had spent a great part of her life avoiding. Now she had it. Deserved it, too—more than Yolanda knew.

Gloria stepped back from the car.

There really wasn't anything Gloria could have told Yolanda that day to quell the fury. The excuses and apologies simply overloaded Yolanda's brain. As far as Yolanda was concerned, Gloria was dead wrong and there was no justification for what she'd done. Yolanda screamed out loud in the car. "Crazy! This whole *family* is crazy!"

Chapter 26

*T*he news of Yolanda's father split their relationship right down the middle. Half sisters: same momma, different daddy. It was disgraceful; cheapened the family. It was downright ghetto, as far as Regina was concerned. But for all the bad things it was, the fact still remained: Yo-yo had a father and she didn't. When and if Yo-yo decided to get married, the possibility of someone escorting her down the aisle did exist. Someone her kids could call "Grandpa."

When Orlando came home from working out, he peeled off his sweaty clothes at the laundry room and walked to the kitchen wearing only a smile. He wished that he could lick his index finger and then hold it up in the air to test which way Regina's attitude was blowing today. He could gather nothing from the way she hovered over the kitchen counter, preparing the baby's bottles for the day. It was a routine, standardized. He'd try words. "Hey, baby. How did things go at your mom's?"

Regina glared at his naked body, perfect enough to model any underwear label. "Do you have to walk around the house like that?"

"You know, I'm really sick of your attitude." He stormed out of the kitchen and off to their master suite to shower. As water pulsed from the showerhead, Orlando tried to wash away his frustrations. He wondered how much more of this he could take. He could give her some slack on account of the fact that she was supposedly going through a depression. Everybody knew that with the sudden hormonal changes, new moms could be cranky. But given the fact that Regina's attitude needed an adjustment *before* the birth of their son, her temperament was double-bad. Worse than any one person should have to put up with.

Back when they were dating, Orlando had liked Regina's smart mouth. She kept him on his toes. Unlike the women he'd dated prior to meeting Regina, she didn't put up with his playboy lifestyle in exchange for the picture of a handsome man in her purse. He'd bent over backward for Regina, and would continue to do so if she'd give him a little credit. Things were different now. They'd moved up in their careers, had bills and a child. He couldn't give her his undivided attention anymore—not that Regina would have appreciated it anyway.

And that eating disorder thing—which he still wasn't sure he'd seen the end of—what was that all about? Would she go back to it after she went back to work? Would her attitude improve? What would he do if she were worse off than before? The word "divorce" skipped through his mind, a subtle suggestion. Orlando slammed his fist against the ceramic tiles on the shower wall. *There is no way on earth I'll leave my wife and child.* He couldn't do it. On the other hand, he couldn't see himself married to someone who was in a perpetual state of misery and in turn pulled their child—and eventually him—into the well of despair.

He closed his eyes and stood there. *What am I going to do?* Orlando thought of the advice his father gave him the day before he married Regina. "Son, when you get married, it's for life. I know folks who've been married three and four times, and I'll tell you this: the only choice you have is to be happily married or unhappily married. Either way, you're gonna be married. So you might as well choose to make this one a happy marriage, 'cause no matter who you marry, the choice is still the same."

At the time, it all sounded like gibberish. Now it made sense. The choice was to be happily married or unhappily married. Problem was, he couldn't make choices for Regina. His father hadn't mentioned what to do about that.

Maybe I could pray. All he knew to say was, "Sorry I haven't talked to you in a while, God, but can you help? Please? Amen." It was clumsy, and it wasn't pretty. Nonetheless, it was a prayer.

Orlando turned the water off and caught the sound of a whimper through the closed shower and bathroom doors. At first he thought it was the baby. But it came through stronger the second time. He wrapped a towel around his waist and rushed back to the kitchen to check on his wife. She rocked a sleeping Orlando Jr. in her arms and cried into his baby blue cotton onesie.

"Baby, what's wrong?" He sat holding both Regina and Orlando Jr. now.

"I don't know what to do," she cried.

For as long as he had known Regina, Orlando had never heard these words from his wife. Even when she didn't know what to do, Regina would jump into her attorney suit and trump up some kind of solution. Be it reasonable or wacky, she was never found without an answer or an explanation. Seeing her like this, helpless and hopeless, made Orlando both afraid and angry. Was she coming undone right before his very eyes, or was this just another one of her pity parties? Probably both, he decided. Either way, she needed him now, and he would be there for her.

"What do you mean?" he asked her guardedly.

"There's so much going wrong." Regina's tears fell on the sleeping baby's cheeks. How he could sleep through drama, she didn't know. "My mother lied to me and Yo-yo. Willie wasn't her father. He was mine, but he wasn't hers."

"I'm sorry to hear that." Orlando held her tighter, stopped her from rocking. "Did she say what happened? Why she didn't tell you?"

"She didn't want me to suffer, I guess."

"Well, can you blame her?" Orlando asked, calming her with the tenderness in his voice.

"Yeah, I can blame her." Regina softened in her husband's arms. He was larger, stronger than her weakened frame. She sank into his bare chest and rested. Today would be the day that it all came out, for better or for worse. "I blame her for getting pregnant by this whoever-he-was. I blame her for keeping this secret for all this time, and for letting the secret get out now. I'm going through a lot right now. How could she do this to me?"

It never ceased to amaze Orlando how Regina could take anything, any statement, and make it about her. She was a great attorney, but sometimes she didn't know when to turn it off. "Baby, I understand what you're saying. But what makes you think this is all about you?" Orlando decided to confront her. He'd had just about enough of this Regina world. It was time she grew up and recognized that the sun didn't rise and set for her. Orlando knew that he'd helped to create this monster, but he wasn't about to let Regina ruin this family, because he certainly didn't feel like going out and finding another one. "The situation between Yo-yo, your mother, and her father doesn't have to be a problem for you unless you *make* it your problem."

Regina looked at him as if he were crazy. He looked at her the same way. One of them was right, and the other was wrong. It occurred to her just then that she might be, well, mistaken. She switched gears suddenly and decided to let it all out.

"You know what else? I want to be a good mother, but I don't like myself. I don't like what I see in the mirror. If I don't like me, how can anyone else like me?"

"If you don't like you, there are two things you can do: you can change you, or you can learn to like you. I personally think you ought to do the latter because, baby, there is nothing wrong with the way you look. You look even more beautiful now than you did when we met. I wish you could see that." Orlando rubbed their baby's soft head. "But if you don't see that, then I think you should maybe join a support group since you don't think I'm enough support for you."

"I never said that you didn't support me," she said, shaking her head.

"It's not what you say, it's how you act. How you push me away, how your attitude gets worse and worse over time. How much more stress do you think our family can take?"

She whipped her body to an upright position, causing the baby to stir. "Oh, is that it? You're going to leave me now?"

Orlando felt the abrupt shift of the winds. "Regina, I never said that."

"That's what you're implying."

"Stop putting words in my mouth." How many times had he said that over the years?

"No! Go ahead and leave! You're obviously working out to keep in shape for your next wife, anyway," said Regina, poking at his emotions.

Orlando Jr. opened his eyes, awakened by his mother's jerky movements. Orlando had words, and Regina had words, until finally she stood over her husband, hurling accusations of everything from adultery to abandonment. Orlando countered every one of her charges with one of his own, from her acting downright crazy to being a drama queen.

"Oh, so I'm a drama queen now?"

"I didn't stutter!"

"You think I like being fat and finding out that my sister has a father but I don't? How would you like it if you found out that your momma slept with a man who wasn't your daddy?"

"That would not be my problem! Regina, you have enough to deal with here in our home without bringing in all of these other issues. What's the big deal, Regina? The fact that you and Yo-yo have different fathers is not the end of the world. Get over it! You are not the first woman in the world to have a different father than your sister. And you are definitely not the first woman to put on a few pounds after having a baby. Join the club! Get the T-shirt! This is life!"

"It's not *my* life. This is *not* what I want for *my* life!" She rocked the baby now to keep him from crying.

"What is your life supposed to be like? Perfect?"

"Yes. Perfect. And it *would* be perfect if people like you would quit excusing mediocrity."

"You know, that's your problem. You're a perfectionist. And when things don't go your perfect little way, you have a special knack for blaming everybody else and making yourself into poor little Regina. Hwaa! Hwaa! My sister's dad is still alive!" He balled his fists and rubbed his eyes. "Hwaa! I'm big fat Regina!"

Those words tore into her soul. Instantly, she was back on the playground with a circle of her peers dancing merrily about her, teasing her, her sense of worth dwindling. Regina balled up all the anger inside of her and threw it at Orlando. "I want you out!"

"Not a problem!"

The baby let out a cry that traveled throughout the house, and Regina kissed him profusely as she watched Orlando march to their bedroom.

Orlando threw clothes into an overnight bag, wondering

what on earth he was doing. This was his house, too. But if any-one had to leave, he would rather it be himself than his wife and son.

Orlando hated these arguments. Hated the way that only Regina could push his buttons and make him hurl these words that he could never take back. Words that she would probably hold over his head for months and years to come, long after the argument was over. He couldn't help it, though. Somebody had to tell her. She was beautiful, even when she was angry. He wished she could see that.

He walked out the door without saying good-bye, got into his car, and drove. It was still early in the day. Maybe he'd call her again before sundown. They could talk, and he'd be back to sleep in his own home. Maybe not in his bed, but he could at least be there.

Regina went to the refrigerator and pulled out a bottle for the baby. After warming it, she propped him up on the couch with the bottle positioned over his head. Then she went to the pantry, pulling out a bag of oatmeal cookies and devouring them two at a time. The food was an instant salve, calming her nerves for the moment. And even as she crammed them into her mouth, she thought of all the harm she was doing. She knew that she was in self-destruct mode, sabotaging her marriage and herself. Problem was, she didn't know how to turn off the switch. She wanted to fold up all these problems and just tuck them away, but it wasn't that easy.

When she'd finished eating the entire package, she sat down on the couch next to the baby and cried. She was fat, her hus-band was gone, and she'd just eaten well over fifteen hundred calories in one sitting. *What have I done? Does life ever take a re-cess?*

Chapter 27

Dianne left a message with Dr. Tilley's answering service a little after four a.m. "Just tell her that I'll . . . I'll call to reschedule." It was her second consecutive cancellation. She gently placed the phone on the receiver, as though any noise might wake Dr. Tilley from her sleep. Worse, she might wake the hunk of flesh lying in her bedroom. Unlike most decent one-night stands, Marvin insisted on hanging around until the next morning.

"Just lay here next to me," he'd said as he rubbed his hand along her thigh. Maybe, if she didn't know better, she could have returned this intimate gesture with one of her own. She might have curled up beside him, rested her back against the prickly hairs on his chest.

Problem was, she *did* know better.

Halfway through the night, she'd been startled into consciousness. For the third night in a row, she had the horrendous dream. She'd pulled herself closer to Marvin, only to be repelled by the sound of elephants charging from his nose and throat. She'd poked and prodded him as long as she could before finally leaving her own bedroom for the discomfort of her couch. She wrapped herself in a blanket, propped her head up on the armrest, and tried to get some sleep.

An hour later she was still counting sheep. *Why are the night-mares back again?* She'd been doing so well in counseling and with poetry. Why now? Dianne wished that she had some-one to talk to. This was one of those times that people talked about, wrote songs about. Even with a man in the next room, the loneliness was insufferable on nights like tonight, when she was up while the rest of the world slept . . . snored . . . carried on like everything was okay. Well, maybe it was with them. But this relapse made open wounds throb harder. She never would have started the journey if she had known things could get worse before they got better.

Just a few weeks ago, Dr. Tilley was a bit concerned with the way Dianne approached the topic of Joyce Ann. "I sense a great deal of anger, Dianne. Tell me about the source of that anger."

"I'm not mad." Dianne twitched her nose like Samantha on *Bewitched*.

"Do you really believe that?" Dr. Tilley asked as she scrib-bled on her notepad.

"If I say I'm not mad, I'm not mad." Dianne got up from the comfy couch and walked toward the window. Three floors below, cars stopped and started at the intersection, living nor-mal lives. *All those people out there are living regular lives. Why did mine have to be so messed up?*

"Dianne, I think that you really need to examine yourself on this one. If you can go from zero to sixty in two seconds when we discuss your mother, I think—I *know*—that this is an area that we really need to handle with a lot of talking and a lot of prayer. A vast part of your healing must deal with some very strong feelings that you have about your mother."

"Her name is *Joyce Ann,* and I would appreciate it if you would *not* refer to her as my mother." Dianne turned around, acting as if *she* were the expert. And she was, in a way. An expert in pain. Probably more hurt than people like Dr. Tilley ever felt. For all Dianne knew, Dr. Tilley would hop into her little European-made luxury vehicle, stop briefly at the light, and then pass on through the intersection into her perfect little doctor life, too, leaving every bit of Dianne behind.

In her heart, Dianne knew that wasn't true. But she had to entertain the scenario long enough to get out of that office.

"I'm leaving now." Dianne had grabbed her coat and handbag.

"I don't advise it."

"Yeah, well . . . just pray for me."

Dianne flicked the channels on her television now and laughed at herself for having believed that her life could be anything but crazy.

The one thing she still held on to was poetry, though she'd been blocked lately. Nothing seemed to flow now, and Dianne interpreted her block as another of the deceptions: that she'd been kidding herself about being a poet as well. She'd decided to make Saturday night her last meeting with the group. Maybe she could tell them that she was moonlighting.

Keisha's house was on the wrong side of town, but you couldn't tell it from the inside. Dianne was amazed at Keisha's decorating talents—it was nothing short of an hour-long design show. Coral picture frames, beaded lampshades, satin and tassel-cornered throw pillows. Classic eccentricity.

Keisha welcomed Dianne into her home, embracing her as a sister. "Girl, you're running late. We've already started." She glanced down and noticed Dianne's empty hands. "Where's your notebook?"

Dianne gave her her best ditzy look and said, "Oh, I . . . I don't have anything to share."

Keisha let Dianne into the foyer but stopped her, placing a hand on her arm. "Are you okay?"

"Yeah, yeah." Dianne flung her hair back nervously.

"No, you are *not* okay." Keisha spoke with certainty, bending down to look directly into Dianne's eyes. "You are *not* okay."

Juanita bounded toward to door to greet Dianne but stopped in her tracks at the sight of Dianne crying. Juanita's chest tightened as she relived nightmares of her own. "What's wrong?"

"It's Joyce Ann," Dianne blurted out. "It's about Joyce Ann."

"Who's Joyce Ann?" Keisha asked, never having heard the name.

"It's my . . . my mother." Dianne fell into Juanita's arms, drawn almost magnetically to her shoulder.

Keisha looked at Juanita above Dianne's head quizzically. When Juanita's face went blank, they both knew that it was time to pray. Juanita helped Dianne to the living room and sat her down on the love seat. "Slowly, Dianne, tell us what's going on."

"It was my fault."

"*What* was your fault?" Keisha asked softly.

"My sister died." Dianne closed her eyes and, piece by piece, strung together the line that separated her existence into two parts.

For the first time in her entire life, Dianne told somebody.

The sewing machine stopped humming long enough for Joyce Ann to reposition the fabric. Her sewing was fluid, automatic. Somewhere in the part of her mind that operated involuntarily, she made split-second calculations, adjusted the fabric at angles that no sewing book could describe. Each of her crafts was a work of art. Regardless of her mental state, Joyce Ann's gift for sewing was never in question. She could sew a masterpiece on her worst day.

"Mmm," Joyce Ann hummed, too involved to hear the doorbell.

If you had been a better mother, it wouldn't have happened. You're the cause of Shannon's death, you know?

"Yeah, you right." Joyce Ann placed her foot on the pedal and stitched another row.

Well, you can't stay here under Gloria's thumb forever. She's married now. Her husband ain't gonna put up with this for long. She's gonna send you back to the funny farm.

"I sure ain't going back there. I'll leave before I let that happen."

What you waitin' on?

"I don't know. I guess was hoping I could see Sugarbee."

Please! Sugarbee ain't thinkin' about you. What makes you think Dianne wants to see you again? After what you did, you really don't deserve to live. You should have ended it a long time ago.

"Maybe."

It's not too late.

"Well, I've got to finish this order at least. Gloria May got me this job; I don't want to leave her name in the mud."

Why you worryin' about Gloria? She never worried about you! You two made a huge mess out of everything!

"I said I already know that. Didn't you hear me?"

Regina rapped her knuckles on Joyce Ann's bedroom door and entered cautiously. "Aunt Joyce Ann?" Regina saw her aunt and searched the room for a visitor.

"Ya." Joyce Ann didn't look up, kept her eyes on the ruby taffeta.

"Were you talking to somebody?"

"No."

Regina could have sworn she heard Joyce Ann talking to somebody. Regina rolled her eyes and forced the invitation out of her mouth. "Momma told me to come down and let you know that we'll be eating in about half an hour."

"Is everybody already at Gloria's?"

"No. I don't think Yo-yo's coming."

"Why not?"

"She found out about her father yesterday."

Joyce Ann froze at the machine. "Oh. I guess . . . I guess it was about time."

"You knew?"

"Of course I knew. Your mother and I *were* close once upon a time."

Regina wanted to ask: So what's wrong with you *now*? But there was no use. Furthermore, she didn't want to sit around here any longer, exposing herself to whatever Joyce Ann might have floating around the rent house. For all she knew, Joyce Ann might have been smoking or inhaling or doing whatever it is that crazy nuts did.

It was beyond Regina why her mother would put up with Joyce Ann and all her issues for all these years. People like Joyce Ann, who spent their whole lives feeling sorry for themselves and not doing anything about their problems, made Regina sick. When things weren't going your way, you found some kind of way to fix them. Granted, the way Regina fixed her own problems might not have been the safest method, but it worked for her. Why couldn't Joyce Ann get her act together and do one of two things: spend the rest of her life begging for Dianne's forgiveness or spend the rest of her life back beneath whatever rock she'd been under for all these years? Really, it was all Regina could do to remain in the presence of a woman who had abandoned her child.

Regina gladly left Joyce Ann and walked the short trek back to her mother's house, soaking up the good that came with memories of the old neighborhood. Miss Doublin's dog barked its usual squeaky little bark as he'd done for probably the past fifteen years, putting Miss Doublin on gossip alert. Three seconds, maybe four, before, Miss Doublin cleared an inch between the curtains and the wall to see what was going on outside.

Chapter 28

Yolanda was glad to work a few hours for Brooke-lynn on Sunday morning. It gave her an excuse to miss Regina and Kelan at church and skip dinner with the family—assuming that there were no more of these family secrets waiting to ambush her without a moment's notice. She couldn't sleep or eat, barely could think, and her heart ached from something she couldn't describe. Whether she was better off now that she had a father was anybody's guess—assuming that Bernard Livingston was still alive. Who was she kidding? She couldn't assume anything. If she couldn't even trust her own mother, where did that put her? Just one more testament to the fact that people couldn't be trusted.

Then there was this whole thing with Kelan. The plain truth: she missed him. Maybe if she'd never started dating him, she wouldn't have known how it felt to look forward to his call or share a banana split with him. She wouldn't have all these burdensome happy memories. And she certainly wouldn't have spent her time looking up on the screen every five minutes at church, trying to scout him out in the audience. It seemed now that everyone was gone, busy about the business of their lives. All Yolanda had was God, and really she hadn't talked to Him in a few days.

"Thanks." Brookelynn breezed into the pharmacy at a quarter after twelve. "I hope you haven't missed your meal with your family." She was obviously running on caffeine, her voice a squeak above a bird's.

"Oh, I'm not going."

"I'm sorry," Brookelynn apologized, her eyes artificially alert. "I tried to get here in time for you to make it."

"Don't worry about it. I wasn't going anyway."

"Is everything okay?" she asked.

"No, it's not." Yolanda thought she might as well put it all out there. If Dr. Hamilton knew, there was bound to be someone else out there in the field who knew more about her heritage than she did. "I just found out yesterday that my dad wasn't my dad."

Brookelynn's face was a big hole. She asked tentatively, "Is that . . . I mean, is that a *good* thing or a bad thing?"

Yolanda laughed. "I don't know."

"Who *is* your dad?"

"Someone named Bernard Livingston." Yolanda shrugged like a preschooler lost in an amusement park.

"Where does he live?" Brookelynn sat down at the computer and went to the World Wide Web.

"Parker City, but that was a long time ago."

"We'll look him up on the Internet. There's a site I subscribe to; I think I told you about it. They do a background check. It'll tell us everything about him." She got busy entering all they knew. "Okay, they'll e-mail me the results of the search in a couple of hours. I'll call you. Will you be at home?"

"Where else am I gonna be?" Yolanda smiled.

"With your Prince Charming." Brookelynn sat up straight and batted her eyelashes.

"Kelan and I are through." Yolanda gathered her belongings, not wanting to discuss the matter further. "I'll be at home, waiting to hear from you."

Yolanda returned the messages left on her answering machine, starting with Dianne's. It had been a while since they talked, so Yolanda pulled a sandwich and chips to her side for fuel throughout the conversation. She had a lot to tell Dianne, now that they had so much more in common than they ever imagined.

"Girl, I got your message."

Dianne took in a deep, cleansing breath and then let it out. She'd had quite a few of those breaths since laying down her burdens at Keisha's house the night before. Sharing the terror of her memory seemed somehow to divide the load, as though she'd given pieces of it away, never to own them again. "I just wanted to thank you. I know that you and Regina and everybody back home have been praying for me. I got a breakthrough last night."

"With your doctor?"

"No. With the Lord. He prescribed confession the same way a doctor prescribes medicine."

"Bless God, girl. And thanks for telling me. I really needed to hear a praise report today."

"Why? What's up?"

Yolanda could hardly get the words out, but she explained the situation to Dianne, including how she ran across the clue that blew her mother's secret. Dianne couldn't imagine that her aunt Gloria would deceive them all since childhood. It wasn't like her to lie—but on second thought, it *was* like her to guard her girls at all costs. "Maybe she just wanted to protect you."

"Protect me from what? From having a positive male figure in my life?"

"How do you know he's positive? He can't be too positive

if he doesn't even check up on his own child." Dianne thought of how she'd dismissed the thought of her father from her mind many years ago. From what she understood, he was way too old to be dating her mother in the first place—in his thirties when Joyce Ann was a teenager. Probably should have been locked up. The thought of him disgusted her, but for some reason Dianne had released him from her anger long ago. There was only Joyce Ann left to deal with.

They talked for another half hour, with Dianne assuming the strong role. Yes, her heart still ached, and she still had miles to go before facing Joyce Ann, but the prayers of the righteous availeth much. Keisha and Juanita had laid hands and prayed over Dianne until the power of the Holy Spirit comforted her, buffered her against the razor-sharp memories. The facts still remained, but they didn't jab with quite the same severity as before. She was ready to resume sessions with Dr. Tilley.

"Hold on," Yolanda said to Dianne as she broke their conversation to answer her other line. "Hello."

"Yo-yo, where are you?" Aunt Toe demanded.

"I'm at home."

"Why aren't you over here at your mother's?"

"I'm not coming today, Aunt Toe."

"Oh, yes, you are," Aunt Toe contradicted Yolanda as though Yolanda had no control over her own life. "We're all waiting on ya."

"Y'all might as well go ahead and eat, Aunt Toe, 'cause I'm not coming today." Yolanda couldn't quite believe she'd just said that to Aunt Toe. She almost expected to see a belt pop through that phone.

"Chile, I do believe I just saw your life flash before my eyes. Now, *I* say you're coming over to eat with your family, and I *mean* you need to get your behind over here like yesterday. You hear me? I got a lot to say to all of y'all, and I mean for you to hear it, too." For as much as Aunt Toe wanted to drum up sympathy for her great-niece, it just wasn't happening. People had lived through worse than this, and Yo-yo would be no exception. Granted, this wouldn't be one of her better days, but Yo-yo had far more good days than bad in her life.

Yolanda rolled her eyes in dismay, wondering if she *really* had to do what Aunt Toe said. She'd never crossed her great-aunt before. There was something about her that commanded obedience—as though, if you didn't do what she said, something bad might happen to you. Not a curse, more like a prophecy. Or maybe it was just that Gloria had so thoroughly trained them to respect their elders that disregarding Aunt Toe was irreverent.

Yolanda sidestepped the issue for now. "I'm on the other line with Dianne."

"That's even better. Tell her you'll call her back when you get here. I need to talk to all of y'all. I've got some things I want to put in motion in this family."

Aunt Toe hung up the phone and rolled herself back to the kitchen. She was so mad at the devil, she could eat scorpions. She'd been thinking about her girls. Looking at them, seeing them suffer over the past several months. Seemed like since Gloria's wedding, they'd all been on a downward spiral. Aunt Toe had made a decision to fast until three in the afternoon twice a week, and from what she heard, Dianne might be getting better. But there was still Regina. And now Yo-yo and Gloria were at odds. *Lord, if I die and come to heaven now, it'll take another two generations to straighten out this mess.*

"Is she coming?" Gloria set the Crock-Pot to warm, holding the dial and her breath.

"She will if she knows what's best for her." Aunt Toe was busy praying, knocking the devil off all his platforms in this spiritual battle for her family. Enough of this talk about psychiatrists and psychologists and counseling and support groups. There was no harm in it, she knew. But there was no substitute for Dr. Jesus.

Yolanda clicked back over and let Dianne know that she'd call her later. "Aunt Toe's about to give me a beatdown if I don't get over there. And she says she wants to talk to you, too. I'll call you when I get to my momma's."

"I'll be here. Bye."

Yolanda put the phone down and bunched up her face in a frustrated scowl. She used to feel that same pestering sensation when Aunt Toe volunteered her, Regina, and Dianne to sing at the sewing circle's annual program. Aunt Toe used to send a little note up to the pulpit, and the MC would announce, "We have a special request for an A selection." And even if the service had gone on way past time to dismiss, the MC would make room for Aunt Toe's request.

"Ooh!" Yolanda stomped her feet. Well, Aunt Toe didn't say what *time* she had to be there. Yolanda decided to boycott the dinner for another ten minutes. That was how long it would be before Aunt Toe called back.

Ten minutes passed, and Yolanda grabbed her keys from the kitchen counter as the phone rang. She just knew it was Aunt Toe. Yolanda stood over the answering machine, fully aware that she'd better not let Aunt Toe catch her still at home. Yolanda danced over the machine, sticking out her tongue like a child whose parent just disappeared behind the bedroom door.

"Hi, Yolanda, it's me." Brookelynn's voice halted the dance, and Yolanda couldn't help but laugh at herself.

Yolanda fumbled the receiver for a second. "Hey, Brookelynn, I'm here."

"Oh . . . well, um, I've got information on Bernard Livingston. Do you want it?"

Do I want it? Exactly what am I supposed to do with it? Yolanda grabbed a pencil and wrote down the information Brookelynn gave her, as if performing a professional task. After recording the address and phone number, she thanked Brookelynn for the search.

"There's more. Do you want to know?"

"I guess so."

"He owns a small bookstore there in town. His residence is valued at one hundred forty-eight thousand dollars, and he owns two other properties in Parker City. Hm, pretty good credit. He's been married once, divorced several years ago. Um, files taxes quarterly, no dependents, never been arrested. He's lived in Parker City since he left Dentonville thirty-two years ago."

"Brookelynn . . ." Yolanda's mouth was wide open.

"Hmm?"

"What kind of a stalker-friendly Internet service is this?"

"I told you, it's a background check service for the single woman. You can never be too careful these days," she warned.

"This is crazy, girl."

"Well, are you gonna call him or what?" Brookelynn asked.

"I don't know."

"Oh, please, Yolanda. I think this is so awesome. He's an old man who's never claimed any dependents, which means that he probably doesn't have any kids. And here you are—

Dr. Yolanda Jordan—finding the father you never knew you had. This is like a movie of the week."

"It's a bunch of drama, all right," Yolanda agreed.

"I didn't mean it like *that*."

"I know, Brookelynn. Thanks for your help."

Chapter 29

*Y*olanda trudged into her mother's house with an attitude in tow. If she could just eat and leave, that would be great. Highly unlikely, but great. Gloria hadn't slept much. After telling Yolanda the truth, she'd told Richard. He wasn't angry, just puzzled. He wanted to know if there was anything else she hadn't told him. When she laid it all out for him, he'd said that he needed some time to think. "You need to come clean," was all he could say. He spent the night in the guest room. They sat next to each other at church, but no words had been said. And now he was noticeably absent from Sunday dinner. Said he was going to ride around, clear his head.

Though Orlando was back in the house, he and Regina still weren't speaking. And Joyce Ann had just come out on the losing end of a two-hour bitter argument with the voices of ac-cusation.

The clang of pots and pans rang through the house, but Yolanda sat herself right down on the couch in the living room. Were it not for Aunt Toe's evil eye, she might have stayed there. She knew better. Yolanda plodded into the kitchen to help with the remaining preparations. The sooner they got finished eating, the better things would be. She dropped her purse on Richard's new lounge chair in the living room and made her way to the kitchen. The table was spread with all things unhealthy—and some that were meant to be healthy but got smothered in oil and salt in the traditional southern cooking process.

"When are we gonna have some healthy stuff to eat for Sunday dinner?" Yolanda asked.

"When you start hosting Sunday dinner at your house," Gloria replied, giving Yolanda that don't-mess-with-me look as she removed the ham from the oven.

Yolanda stuffed her mouth with a dinner roll to keep herself from going off. Regina nudged Yolanda out of her way, reaching past her to place a steaming hot dish of macaroni and cheese on the table.

"You could say 'excuse me,'" Yolanda said, stepping aside. Regina didn't respond.

The doorbell rang. "Make yourself useful." Regina looked at Yolanda.

Yolanda rolled her eyes and left the kitchen.

"It's me," Joyce Ann sang.

Who invited her? Regina wondered.

"Hey, Yo-yo." Joyce Ann hugged her niece's neck tightly.

She smelled of Shower to Shower packed on top of body odor: powder on funk. Yolanda held her nose and thought to herself, *This is ridiculous. She needs help.*

Joyce Ann had enough sense not to get too close to Aunt Toe. A little wave, and she was off to the kitchen. Once she was out of sight, Aunt Toe asked Yolanda, "Is that Joyce Ann smellin' like that?"

"Yes, Aunt Toe." Yolanda bugged her eyes, glad she wasn't the only one to notice that there was something seriously wrong.

"Gloria May!" Aunt Toe yelled toward the kitchen.

"Yes?"

"Could you come here, please?"

"What?" she answered again, walking into the living room. "What is it that can't wait?"

Aunt Toe poked her lips out, closed her eyes, and, with a point of her finger, directed Gloria's attention to Yolanda.

"Somebody needs to be taking care of Aunt Joyce Ann. This is getting out of control. She's not even bathing anymore," Yolanda whispered.

"I'll talk to her." Gloria looked back toward the kitchen, making sure that Joyce Ann was out of hearing distance.

"You betta listen to this girl," Aunt Toe reiterated. "Joyce Ann just came through here smellin' like an armpit factory."

"Aunt Toe, ain't no such thing as an armpit factory," Gloria rerouted the comment.

"Well, we got the first one on the map right in this house. Didn't you smell her?" Aunt Toe asked.

"She just needs a bath," Gloria said between clenched teeth.

"She's sick." Yolanda matched Gloria's anger. "You can't keep walking around the elephants in your life, Momma. She's not getting any better."

"What do you want me to do, treat her like a baby? She's got her pride, you know," Gloria argued.

"But she ain't got her head on straight, Gloria. Anybody can see that." Aunt Toe spoke the truth far more candidly than Yolanda could.

"People said I was crazy, too, when Willie died."

"You was." Aunt Toe bobbed her head up and down. "Grief and hurt and pain can do that to anybody—for a little while. But most peoples learn to move on. Joyce Ann ain't doin' that. She been down for too long now. I didn't realize how bad off she was until she moved back home. She ain't doin' too hot, Gloria."

"Aunt Toe, I've committed her before, and every time she comes out crazier than when she went in, I think." Gloria put her hand over her mouth.

"Maybe she could get some outpatient treatment," Yolanda suggested even as she wondered exactly when Joyce Ann had been committed. "That way she could live at the rent house and still get help. Face it, Momma, Aunt Joyce Ann needs help—the kind of help that you can't give her. The kind of help that God sends through professionals who routinely help people sort through their grief. Something has to be done."

"Can we talk about this after dinner?" Gloria asked.

"Yes," Yolanda said. "We need to make some concrete arrangements—today."

"And I've got a plan of my own that needs to be put into effect, too," Aunt Toe added.

Gloria nodded her head and went back toward the kitchen. She stopped in mid step, making a U-turn and catching Aunt Toe and Yolanda up to speed on a few things. "Richard is busy . . . doing some things. Orlando and the baby aren't here. He and Regina are having a little problem. Don't ask no questions."

"Not even questions about my father?" Yolanda looked her mother squarely in the eyes.

"What else do you want to know, Yo-yo? I told you everything I could. I tried my best to do right by you girls."

"This is crazy! Is that how this family does things—just pick up and go? You think it's that easy? I have a father out there, Momma. Doesn't that mean something to you?"

Gloria thought about the current affair of her life. Her husband was gone. One daughter sick, one daughter angry with her. "I can't talk about this today." Gloria clutched the towel harder and left the room.

"When *can* you talk about it?" Yolanda yelled.

"Y'all quit all this hollerin'!" Aunt Toe thundered. "Sit down and let me bless the table!" She prayed an angry prayer. Angry with the enemy.

They assembled around the table—Yolanda, Regina, Gloria, Joyce Ann, and Aunt Toe—and ate without a word except for the "amen" uttered after the prayer.

"Is anybody going to say something?" Aunt Toe asked after her second helping of dessert.

"I got something to say." Aunt Joyce Ann stood as though she were giving a speech. That's when they all noticed her breasts, braless, barely sheathed beneath her sheer white blouse. Joyce Ann looked like a contestant in a wet T-shirt contest. Sweat poured down her neck as she became more and more unglued with every breath she took. "I'm not going to no funny farm!"

"Joyce Ann?" Gloria stroked her arm.

"Don't Joyce Ann me." She jerked her arm from Gloria's reach. "I heard y'all talking just a few minutes ago. Y'all must think I'm deaf, too, huh?"

"Joyce Ann, we're just trying to do what's best for you," said Gloria, trying to calm Joyce Ann.

"We've been doing what's best for *you* since we were kids! It's all about Princess Gloria!"

Aunt Toe was tired of this foolishness. "Joyce Ann, you—"

"Shut up!" Joyce Ann screamed at her aunt.

"Oh, no. Now I *know* you crazy." Aunt Toe unlocked the wheels of her wheelchair and began rolling toward Joyce Ann. Regina grabbed the handles on the back of the wheelchair. "Naw, let me go! This child got enough nerve to tell *me* to shut up, she must got somethin' over there to back it up. Let me go, Regina."

"Aunt Toe, just calm down." Gloria stood up, walked behind Joyce Ann, and locked Aunt Toe's wheels again.

"Joyce Ann."

Yolanda watched her mother restrain her emotions in an attempt to reason with her sister. "I know it's been hard for you living all alone. And I know it's been very isolating. But I think it's time we—"

Joyce Ann plopped back into her seat with her mouth wide open and a look of amusement on her face. "Well, ain't that a pickle! That sounds like exactly what I told you before you went off and slept with that . . . what was his name—Bernard? *Hmph.*"

Gloria squinted her eyes and drew her lips in tightly. "This isn't the same thing, Joyce Ann. This is on another level and you know it."

"Oh, so if I just go out and get pregnant and then lie to everybody about it, will that make everything okay? You got a habit of doing that, you know." She cocked her head and splashed a sinister smile across her face.

"Get out of here." Regina pointed a butter knife at Joyce Ann, speaking as though she were the authority. "I've been wanting to kick you out of our lives since the moment you brought your sorry behind to the wedding. Too sorry to even call your own daughter and say 'Hello, Dianne—just wanted to speak to you. Hello, Dianne, just wanted to make sure you were alive.' Anything! She would do *anything* to hear from you! How can you sit here and ridicule the woman who took over *your* job and raised *your* child for you? Just get out!"

Yolanda jumped in. "Regina, wait. We do need to talk with Aunt Joyce Ann about the arrangements."

"You . . . just . . . don't even worry about this." Regina directed her anger toward Yolanda now. "I'm sure you've got a lot of other stuff on your plate, with your new family and all."

"Look, I don't know what Orlando did to you, but—"

"How could you?" Regina stamped her foot, looking daggers at Gloria.

"I haven't said anything." Gloria looked back at Yolanda and shook her head. "Ooh, you got a big mouth."

"Me? *She's* the one who's bringing up irrelevant issues," Yolanda argued like a teenager caught in battle with a sibling.

"I'm not going anywhere," Aunt Joyce Ann said, cutting herself a healthy slice of double chocolate cake. "This is my sister's house, and I'm gonna stay here until she tells me to leave."

"Right now I want you *all* to leave." Gloria wiped the corners of her mouth with a napkin and began collecting dishes for the sink. In unison, Regina and Yolanda gladly rose to their feet.

"Ain't nobody goin' nowhere!" Aunt Toe finally spoke. "Every last one of y'all has lost your ever-lovin' minds! Everybody sit down, and shut up! Lord, help me."

One by one, they sat down and scraped their chairs back into place. Eyes rollin', nostrils flaring. Gloria's hands shaking like a leaf.

"Gloria, you've been right about a lot of things over the years, but you were wrong about this one. When you gave birth to this child thirty-something-odd years ago, I told you she would find out. You made us all promise that we wouldn't tell her, and we respected your wishes, but the good Lord saw different."

Gloria looked at her lap.

"Regina, I don't know exactly what your problem is, but I *do* know that you need to deal with it, because you gonna fool around and single-handedly ruin your entire family. You think you're so much better than Joyce Ann—well, you're about to do the same thing to *your* child, tearin' up a home."

Regina traced her hairline and wondered, *What if I were too ill to raise my own child?*

"And as for you," she laid into Yolanda, "I know it came as a shock to you to find out that your daddy wasn't Willie Jordan. But you got to understand the situation Gloria was in at the time. Put yourself in her shoes for a minute. Maybe it wasn't the best choice she made; I'll give you that. But the bottom line is, you grew up in a home where you were loved. That's more than what a lot of folks had.

"And as for that nappy-headed boyfriend of yours, you got a lot of book sense, but you'd be an educated fool if you don't give him the chance to love you. I know your momma didn't have many men around you, but that was to keep you from freaks and perverts. I can't half-blame her. It was the seventies—people were coming down off their sixties high, and we had those murders in Atlanta. It was a crazy time to be a single black mother. But you done made a mountain out of a molehill. You better let somebody love you, gal. Long as you goin' around lookin' for *you* in suspenders, it ain't gonna happen."

Yolanda looked away from Aunt Toe.

"And, Joyce Ann, don't even get me started on you. You are going to somebody's hospital, I don't care what you say. You ain't runnin' nothin' here but your mouth.

"Now, we're all here together 'cause we're family. And we're gonna stay family till the end of time. I'm calling a prayer chain right here right now. I don't care what comes our way, the Rucker women have always stuck together and we have always been prayerful. I blame myself for letting this go on so long. Yeah, I'm wrong, too. We're all wrong. But it's time we dusted ourselves off, got up, and kept going. Yo-yo, get Dianne on the phone; she needs to be in on it, too. I'll start the prayer chain at five o'clock. Who'll pray at six?"

"I'm not prayin'," Joyce Ann declared.

"Since when do you turn down prayer?" Aunt Toe asked, a look of horror crossing her face.

"Since it stopped working." Joyce Ann loaded her fork with cake and shoved the mass into her mouth.

"How can you say that, Joyce Ann? God listening to my prayers is what's kept you alive *this* long," Aunt Toe acknowledged.

Joyce Ann licked the tines of her fork. "So it's *your* fault that I'm still alive?"

"Call Dianne," Aunt Toe ordered Yolanda. "Jesus said he stands at the door and knocks, but He can't get in until we unlock it from the inside. If Joyce Ann wants to sit here and act a fool, that's on her. She can't stop us from praying for her, and she *is* gonna get some help some kind of way."

Yolanda dialed Dianne's number, and Joyce Ann left the room. She plopped herself down on the couch in the living room and turned up the volume on the television.

One by one, they obliged Aunt Toe's wishes and signed up for the prayer chain. Dianne took the last slot. Both Gloria and Regina signed their husbands up for half an hour. Aunt Toe asked Yolanda if she thought Kelan would take a time slot. "I don't know. I haven't talked to him in a while."

"Well, *talk* to him," she instructed, bugging her eyes at Yolanda.

Once again, Yolanda felt the conviction of Aunt Toe's words. The question now was whether Kelan would give *her* another chance.

Despite the fact that the chain links had been assigned, everyone was still angry and ready to leave. Gloria hastily assisted them all in making to-go plates and rushed them out of her kitchen. Yolanda was the first one out of the kitchen, and almost immediately on crossing the threshold, she felt the air lose its rigidity. That was until she saw Joyce Ann bent over the couch, rummaging through Yolanda's purse. A cat digging through trash. "What are you doing?"

Joyce Ann looked over her shoulder, scampering to put the contents back inside. "I . . . I just needed something."

"What were you going through my purse for, Aunt Joyce Ann?" Yolanda's voice went up an octave. "Why were you in my purse?"

"I wasn't even in your purse!" she cried.

"Yes, you were!"

"Y'all need to quit lyin' on me! Been lying to me since I was seventeen years old!" Joyce Ann wailed, as though she'd been falsely accused. Real, live tears streamed down her face. *Where did those come from?*

"I wasn't in her purse—I swear to God!" Joyce Ann plummeted into Gloria's chest, sobbing like a child. "I swear to God! Y'all been trickin' me since I was seventeen."

"I know, I know," Gloria shushed Joyce Ann.

Yolanda grabbed her bag and checked her wallet. All forty dollars present. Nothing else was missing, as far as she could tell. "It's all here."

"That's 'cause I wasn't in your stupid old purse." Joyce Ann rose off Gloria's shoulder long enough to lie, then resumed her childlike tantrum, complete with snot dripping down between her quivering lips.

"I'll call you first thing in the morning about this," Yolanda said, pointing toward Joyce Ann's back. "I mean *first* thing in the morning."

"I'll keep her here tonight," Gloria said, rubbing Joyce Ann's back, comforting her as she heaved from her endless crying. Gloria's eyes were filled with tears and fears. She understood, finally, the severity of Joyce Ann's condition. Even beyond that, she had agreed to partner with Yolanda and get help for Joyce Ann. It was the second good thing to come of that horrible meal.

Yolanda took the short route home and decided that Kelan's call would have to wait. She needed some time with the Lord and with herself. She hurt for the angry, ugly blows that had flown across her mother's kitchen table in the form of words. They had all been blindsided, fueled to rage by flames flickering before they ever sat down to eat.

Father, forgive me for neglecting to meet with You every day. Time away from You is time away from my source. I need You, Lord. Especially now. Help. As she went through the motions of straightening up her bedroom, Yolanda began to feel the love of God envelop her again. He had always been faithful to forgive her for these times that she went about living her life without Him. And always, when she'd finished making a complete mess of things, He was there to pick up the pieces and put her back together again. How unfair it was. But that was love.

After she dusted, Yolanda pulled out her Bible study notes again and revisited those verses in Philippians. This time she *got* it. She understood that the past she needed to leave behind wasn't Kelan. It wasn't even a person. It was a feeling, a fear—a spiritual stronghold that had hooked on to her soul long, long ago and caused her to shut out anything that didn't align to the neat little plans she'd laid out for her life. Yolanda laughed at herself now as she realized that the elephant woman sermon had been meant for her after all. *I am turning out to be just like Gloria May.* Maybe Gloria wasn't so bad after all.

Gloria called later that evening to clear up the purse fiasco. "Yo-yo, I just want you to know, Joyce Ann wasn't trying to steal anything from you. She was looking for Dianne's phone number."

"Mmm. You didn't let her call Dianne, did you?" Joyce Ann was in no shape to be calling anybody, let alone Dianne.

"I haven't let her do anything but take a bath and lie down in the front bedroom. I haven't heard anything else from her tonight," Gloria said softly. "Have you got some kind of a treatment facility in mind that we can look into tomorrow?"

"I know a few reputable doctors just outside of Dallas. I'll put in a few calls, but we don't have too much time to spend looking into things. We're checking her in someplace tomorrow, and she needs to stay there until they can get her stabilized, on medication, in treatment, and determine that she's not a threat to herself or society."

"Yeah," Gloria sniffled, "I know. We're checking her in tomorrow." Sadness.

With Joyce Ann's situation settled, there was only the matter of Bernard Livingston to resolve. Yolanda wanted something more from her mother, and what that something was, she didn't know.

Gloria didn't know exactly what that something was, either, but she knew where to start. "Yo-yo, I'm so sorry, baby. I never meant to hurt you. I never meant for you to find out about your father this way. It's just that sometimes you have these intentions, but then time goes on and on, and the lie almost turns into the truth in your head, and you never get around to fixing it. And—"

"It's okay, Momma." Yolanda stopped her there. After all the good Gloria had done, she knew that the last thing Gloria owed her was an explanation for the things she *hadn't* done. "I don't agree with your decision, but I know that you have always been in my corner."

"Are you going to get in touch with your father?" Gloria wanted to know.

"I might. Would you have a problem with that?"

"I guess not. It's up to you."

Yolanda searched her mother's voice for a trace of antipathy. There was none. "What about Regina?"

"She says she's happy for you, about your father and all."

"I don't think she means it."

"It's too hard for her right now, Yo-yo. You know your sister better than anybody. Just give her some time. She's got a lot on her mind right now."

"I feel bad for her. I feel like I have something that she'll never have. It's never been like that between us. You always made sure we were treated the same—it was all or nothing," Yolanda tried to explain herself to Gloria, but the more she talked, the more she realized that her excuses sounded a lot like Gloria's reasons for keeping Bernard a secret.

"Regina is strong. She's got things that you don't have. It'll all be even in her mind after a while."

"I think that's the problem, Momma. We don't both have to be in the same situation for things to be 'even.' This isn't a competition. It's life."

"Yo-yo, you are so much smarter than I was when I was your age. If I knew then what I know now, things would have been different. If I'd had someone thirty something ago to tell me what you told me just now, I wouldn't have spent so much time running around like a chicken with my head cut off trying to handle things that I needed to turn over to God. You don't know how blessed you are, learning all this while you're so young. I know it was crazy how all this came about, but I also know that all things work together for the good of them that love the Lord. And this is just another one of those *things.*"

Yolanda hung up with her mother in peace.

Sunday evening's Bible study was preempted by the annual young adult choir's musical, and Yolanda dressed for the service. She'd had some time to think about what Aunt Toe had said. Kelan was valuable, and she didn't have any business throwing him away. Miraculously, she saw him on the monitor and took note that he'd come to the service without female companionship. She could only hope that she wasn't too late.

It was almost dusk, and Yolanda was hoping that she wouldn't miss him on his way out the door. She rushed to the main entrance, hoping that Kelan was a creature of habit who would enter and exit using the same doors as when they had attended church together. But as the masses pushed through the doors, Yolanda realized that her efforts were futile. No way could she distinguish him in that crowd. She walked on toward her car.

The bright red metallic paint of his pickup truck seemed to call her name, not three rows over from where she stood. *Thank you, Lord.* Yolanda waited for him.

Okay, be calm, Yo-yo. And she was calm—right up until the moment she spotted him, his shoulders, squared and broad, his tie flapping in the wind as he moved steadily toward her. Aside from the beautiful, caring person that Kelan was on the inside, he was also something very nice to look at. *Why didn't I see all this before?*

She gave him an awkward wave, signaling a truce. Yolanda expected him to stop and wave back. Say hello or something. But he just kept coming. Walking, striding toward her with certain, purposeful paces. He got right up on her, towering above.

"Hi," she barely whispered, staring up at his expressionless face. All at once, she was confused and afraid. Was Kelan angry with her? He had every right to be, of course, but was he? Yolanda looked down and found herself face-to-face with the third button on his shirt. White. Round. Four-holed. *Once again I've made a fool of myself.* Her defenses jumped to the forefront, and she pulled out an attitude with her usual quick-ness, crossing her arms and looking up at him again. "Kelan, we need to talk."

It took him only a second to tear down her wall. And he did it with a quick, endearing kiss to her cheek. Yolanda closed her eyes and let the rush spread throughout her whole body. "I'm sorry, Kelan. I'm sorry for pushing you out."

Without a word, he ushered her to the passenger side of his truck and then walked around to his side. For once, it didn't matter to her that Sunday morning's newspaper was un-derneath her feet instead of in the proper recycling bin. She was in the car with her man—well, she hoped he was her man. He'd kissed her, all right, but she knew better. Kisses didn't have the power to turn back time, allow people to pick up right where they left off; and actually, she thought maybe that was a pretty good thing. Yolanda didn't want to go back to the old Kelan and Yolanda. She'd changed during their hia-tus, and she wanted Kelan to know that she was a better woman for the obstacles and tests that God had carefully al-lowed into her life.

He got in, turned the key slightly, and let the windows down. A brisk breeze blew through his window and out hers. Yolanda slid her heels off and rested her right arm on the door panel.

"I just want you to know, Kelan, that I had some other is-sues I had to deal with," she explained. "I didn't grow up around men. Only women. So having you in my life is . . . it's weird. It makes me feel weak. It makes me feel like I have to depend on you and I don't like it."

"So why are you here?" he asked.

She thought about the question, considered pulling the handle and jumping out of the truck. *But isn't that the prob-lem now?* "I'm here because . . . because I think that being vulnerable has its rewards. Closing the door keeps me safe, but it also keeps me from being loved. Keeps me from enjoying you, enjoying my life. You showed me that. I was wrong and you were right, okay?" She sighed heavily and threw her hands in the air.

"I never wanted you to be wrong. I just wanted to love you," Kelan said as he squeezed one of her hands and repeated, "I just wanted to love you."

"That might mean being hurt." Yolanda couldn't look at him.

"I know exactly what you mean."

Yolanda realized that he was referring to the pain she'd caused him. "I'm sorry, Kelan." Yolanda reached over and hugged him. "I didn't mean to hurt you. I just got so scared."

"I know, I know." Kelan relaxed his hold on Yolanda but reinforced his efforts when he realized that she was holding on for a reason. "What's the matter?"

"Willie wasn't my father. My father is alive."

"What!" He slid back to read her face.

"He's alive. He lives in Parker City. It's a long story."

"Well, I knew something was going on. I've been praying for you and your family."

"Why would you do all that for me?" she asked.

As if he read her mind, Kelan answered, "Because I love you whether you're right or wrong—perfect or not, Yolanda. Sometimes I think I love you in spite of you."

"Hmmm . . ." She reveled in his words. "Thank you." She wiped her face dry.

Another gust swept through the car.

"Kelan, can we . . . I just want to . . . spend time with you again. I miss you." Yolanda knew exactly what she was feeling, but she'd gotten so used to suppressing her feelings that she wasn't even sure how to express them anymore. The words faltered out of her like those from a toddler speaking its broken first sentences.

"I've missed you, too," he assented.

"Do you think that maybe we could go somewhere and talk? The bookstore maybe?" She strapped on her seat belt, the adrenaline from their embrace still pumping strongly through her body.

He looked away from her and adjusted his rearview mirror. "Actually, I have plans for this evening. But I'll call you tomorrow."

Plans? What plans? She unlocked her seat belt, shocked that he'd declined her invitation. She knew Kelan well enough to understand that he wasn't one to play games. He really did have something or someone more important than her baby-I'm-back self on his agenda. Yolanda wanted to cry, but she knew it would only make things worse for both of them. She, too, was beyond games. Maybe things weren't going to work out for them after all. She'd have to settle for a call. "I look forward to hearing from you."

"Okay." He walked Yolanda to her car, got back into his vehicle, and waited for her to pull out of the parking lot ahead of him. He followed her all the way to the highway and then went east as they approached the ramp. He honked his horn twice and sped off to wherever he was going. Yolanda let a few tears escape on the way back home. Maybe she was too late. Maybe she would have to live with the fact that she'd loved and lost. The thought was unbearable. Yet she had to admit that if she had it to do all over again, she would choose love.

That night Yolanda tossed and turned in bed. Who was Kelan seeing? Where had he been? What if she lost her one big shot? She played hide-and-seek with sleep for two hours and finally gave up the chase. She couldn't sleep without praying. She slid out of bed and approached her Father, the One she had known and depended on all her life. And, like always, He was there.

Unlike most of her prayers, where she felt she knew all the answers before she even went to Him, Yolanda knelt at the throne in utter confusion. "Lord, this is one big mess that I've created for myself. I know it's not fair; I know it's not right. I should have asked you sooner, but I didn't, and I'm sorry. Would You please show me what to do?"

And, just as with Paul, the scales fell from her eyes.

She loved Kelan.

Chapter 30

Get up! Get up!

Joyce Ann bolted straight up in Regina's old bed. It took her a second to recognize her surroundings. She wasn't at the rent house. She was in Gloria's home, but the voices had followed her. They were everywhere.

Get up before they come get you!

Joyce Ann scrambled out of bed, obeying the instructions as they came. Her clothes, her purse. The phone number.

Put you on some clothes and go get your stuff from the rent house. Shhh! They gon' get you!

Joyce Ann carefully slipped out of her sister's house and jogged barefoot down the street under the blanket of darkness. She had to leave before they came to get her. Miss Doublin's poodle appeared behind the curtains of her front room and barked as Joyce Ann passed by. His high-pitched yapping would be one thing that Joyce Ann wouldn't miss. "I gotta go," she chanted with the voices. "I gotta go."

Joyce Ann pulled the key from her purse with the intent to rush into her bedroom and pack in ten minutes flat, as she had done so many times before. But this time things were different. When she opened the door, the entire house was furnished. It was filled with all the things she and Otis had purchased. Everything was just as it was back then. Yellow shag carpet so long and stringy, she could feel the fibers between her toes. Gold elephants, a lime green lava lamp. Two little pairs of shoes on the tile so they wouldn't track mud through the house. Startled by the illusion, Joyce Ann dropped her purse at the door. *Shannon? Sugarbee?*

Joyce Ann rounded the corner to the kitchen, calling, "Shannon! Are you here? Sugarbee? Are you here, baby?"

The kitchen glowed red, flaming hot, pulsing like a lake of fire. It breathed, in and out, in and out, the walls expanding and contracting right along with Joyce Ann's breath. She had seen this in her dreams, this dwelling that had taken her life away. These walls, this space. It had stolen her essence, snuffed out her soul.

Kill it! Kill this house!

Joyce Ann made a dash toward the bedroom, plugged in the hot plate, and turned the dial to ten. "You gonna die tonight, house. Die tonight." As she waited for the hot plate to reach its maximum heat, Joyce Ann threw her things into the only constant in her life: the chest. Her purse went in last. And there was the phone number she'd managed to get from Yolanda's purse, sticking out at her like a finger of accusation

936-555-8725. Sugarbee. Call her and tell her what a stupid thing you've done! Tell her how you hope she can live with the guilt for the rest of her life! Tell them all how it's all their fault! Tell her the truth about Gloria! Leave her with the bags for once!

Again Joyce Ann obeyed the voice of damnation. She dialed Sugarbee's number. But when she heard Dianne's voice on the answering machine, she couldn't say the words that the voices gave her. Though Dianne was a grown woman, there was still that sweetness in her tone, that innocence. Joyce Ann left a different message.

The plate was hot enough now. Joyce Ann grabbed the plate's plastic platform and held it to the bottom of the drapery. Smoke first. Then the spark came, brought a smile to Joyce Ann's face. It was time for the house to die. She watched the flames lick their way up the draperies and then onto the walls. A beautiful dance of yellow and orange butterflies fluttering. Captured the imagination, carried it higher inch by inch. This force, this element of life. Watching it flow was hypnotic.

Were it not for the smoke, she would have marveled longer.

Stay! Stay a little longer!

Joyce Ann covered her face with both hands, closed her eyes for a second because the smoke was starting to sting her eyes, nose, and throat. She groped the floor for her bag but couldn't find it in the darkness behind her eyelids. Every time she tried to get a view of the floor, the smoke overcame her and she shut her eyes tight again. She needed her purse for bus money so that she could be gone before Gloria found her. Once again Joyce Ann tried to find her things, but she couldn't. It was too hot now.

Joyce Ann crawled out of the house with nothing but the clothes on her back. Gloria would wake up soon and everything would be gone. She had killed the house and now she'd have to face the music. There was nowhere to hide in Dentonville. Nowhere she could go that Gloria wouldn't find her.

The sewing machine! Gloria got that for you! You have to go back and get it!

"What!" Joyce Ann stopped in the middle of the street. She shook her hands like a rag doll's, and screamed, "The sewing machine! The sewing machine!"

And she went back to get it.

* * *

Yolanda was awakened by the phone's piercing ring. At first she thought she was dreaming, suspended between fantasy and reality. But by the third ring, Yolanda realized that she was in real time. As she read the digital number on her alarm clock, "1:38," a wave of anxiety coursed through her body. No one called at 1:38 in the morning with good news.

"Hello?"

"Yo-yo!" Gloria screamed and then yelled out something else inaudible.

"What? Momma, what are you saying?"

She sobbed uncontrollably. "Joyce Ann, Joyce Ann! It's Joyce Ann!"

Aunt Joyce Ann? Funny how, when you don't know what's wrong with someone, you suddenly realize the constancy of the position they have held in your life: how you first came to know them, your first experiences with them. Yolanda's whole life with Aunt Joyce Ann, even in her absence, ran its tape in her head; it took only a fraction of a second.

"It's burned down in the rent house!" Gloria cried, her thoughts obviously jumbled.

"The rent house is burning?"

"Yes—and Joyce Ann! I can't find her! The rent house—her house—I think she burned it down."

"Is she okay?" Yolanda asked.

"No! I don't know—I said we can't find her!"

"I'm on my way, Momma."

Chapter 31

$\mathscr{H}$ello?"

"Dianne."

Dianne knew the voice and the tone right away. It was Yolanda.

"It's about your mother. There's been an . . . accident."

"She's killed herself, hasn't she?" Dianne said.

"Well, no, she's not dead. We're not sure what happened. There was a fire at the rent house, and—"

"She tried to?"

"We think so."

"Is anybody else hurt?"

"No."

"How is Joyce Ann?"

"Your mother is burned pretty badly."

"Stop calling her my mother." Dianne shook her head as though Yolanda could see her.

"She *is* your mother, Dianne." Yolanda accosted her with words. "She needs you. We all need you here with the family. Just yesterday we'd agreed to get her some help, and now . . . I don't know. You'd better hurry and get here, Dianne. They're saying she might not make it through the night."

"Let me . . . I'll call you back."

"You have my cell number?"

"Yes." Dianne fumbled to turn on the night-light. "I'll call you back."

"Hurry, Dianne." Yo-yo's last words resounded in her soul's ear like a pair of clashing symbols. *Hurry, Dianne. Hurry, Sugarbee.*

Dianne called Dr. Tilley's answering service and asked them to request a callback. She'd never requested a callback outside of office hours the way she imagined that only the most troubled, close-to-the-edge patients did. But who was she kidding? Her toes *were* hanging over the edge. *What if Joyce Ann dies?*

At first the anger was diminutive, like the aftertaste following an unsweetened beverage. But the more Dianne chewed on the thought—tasted the news, swallowed what she feared was the truth—the more revolting and infuriating it became. *How dare she kill herself! After all she owed me!* Dianne opened the top drawer in her bureau and pulled out a handful of undergarments, stuffed them into an overnight bag. She heard herself mumbling, "You think you can just die, Joyce Ann? You don't *deserve* to die." She bundled up a pair of jeans and a few long-sleeved casual shirts and threw them in on top of her tennis shoes. "You don't *get* to die—not after what you made me live through." Dianne reeled off a list of cuss words she hadn't used in a long time.

There's something about losing someone, even if it's someone you can't stand. When there's always the chance or distant hope that you'll have one more argument or one more go-round with them, even that provides some kind of comfort. But when they're not alive anymore, something changes. Suddenly, you can't even so much as hate them anymore. They're gone. And whether you liked them or couldn't stand them doesn't really matter. No matter how decayed something is, you still miss it after it's been amputated.

Dianne was so far into her own thoughts that she almost missed Dr. Tilley's call.

"Dianne?" Dr. Tilley's voice sounded woozy, though she had tried her best to disguise her drowsiness. Dr. Tilley knew that if Dianne had called, it was serious. "What's going on?"

"I have to cancel tomorrow's appointment."

"Dianne, I thought you said you were ready to keep going." Dr. Tilley wiped her eyes. Canceling an appointment didn't warrant a callback. "What's *really* going on?"

"My crazy—Joyce Ann."

"Your mother?"

"What kind of mother tries to kill herself before apologizing to her child? She's Joyce Ann, *not* my mother," Dianne told her quite frankly. She didn't appreciate Dr. Tilley referring to Joyce Ann as her mother. They'd discussed that plenty of times in session.

"I'm sorry, Dianne. Joyce Ann. What happened with Joyce Ann?"

"She . . . she might be dead. She might have killed herself in a fire. I'm not sure. I think I'm going back to Dentonville in the morning."

"Are you sure about any of this—about the fire, about whether or not she's alive?" Dr. Tilley seemed to be grasping for a handle on all this. Dianne didn't have one to give her.

"I don't know. My cousin just called me and told me what she knows. Joyce Ann is hurt; she's in the hospital, I guess. I'm going to Dentonville in the morning," Dianne rattled off what she knew, wondering if she had done the right thing by calling Dr. Tilley. All this talking was wearing down her anger.

"Dianne, listen to me. If she is dead, you have to know that who you are and what you are has nothing to do with Joyce

Ann. You are a wonderful, vibrant, divinely created child of God, and there's nothing anyone can say or do to cancel what God did when He gave you life."

The empty hole in Dianne's heart opened wide and almost wrung her through from the inside out. "But why?" Dianne slammed her backside against the closet door and slowly sank to the floor, inch by inch. "Why didn't she even say good-bye? That's the least she could have done."

"Maybe she didn't know how, Dianne."

"She could have said good-bye," Dianne cried, her behind finally hitting the bottom of the floor.

"What would that have meant to you, Dianne?" Dr. Tilley's voice softened.

Suddenly, she cried out loud, "I would know that in the end she loved me."

"Would that make up for everything?" Dr. Tilley asked.

Her question struck Dianne at the core—that all she ever really wanted was a mother's love. Something about a mother's love seemed irreplaceable, incapable of substitution. Perhaps, if Dianne hadn't known Joyce Ann before drugs, she would have been better off. She wouldn't know then that she could call out "Momma" in the middle of the night and have Joyce Ann come to her bedside and run her hand across her forehead to see if she felt warm. Dianne wouldn't know the familiarity of her voice. Or the spark in her eyes that confirmed, "I am her baby. Her Sugarbee." Maybe if Dianne hadn't known all that, it wouldn't have hurt so bad.

Dianne allowed Dr. Tilley to pray for her emotional wellness as she traveled back to Dentonville. "Dianne," the doctor said in her closing words, "remember what we've talked about for all these weeks now: what you did not get from your parents, you can still get from God."

Dianne hoped that God was awake.

A few sleepless hours later, Dianne raised her bag to her shoulder and picked up her purse. "Ooh!" She remembered her cell phone, mounted on its charger in the bedroom. She pulled the cord and stuffed the charging system into her purse, then turned the phone on and stuffed it in as well. The vibration signaling that she had a message startled her. She thought for an instant that the phone had a life of its own.

On the way out the door, Dianne dialed her voice message retrieval code and listened to the only new message she had.

"Voice message one, received Monday . . . at . . . one twenty a.m.: 'Sugarbee . . .'"

Her body went numb, and she stopped dead in her tracks, with the front door locking just behind her. "Sugarbee, it's me. I . . . can't even tell you what I want to say, 'cause it doesn't sound like something with sense. Sometimes you just can't run from it no more. Get tired of dealin' with it. Made such a big mess of my life. About what happened to Shannon. I . . . it wasn't your fault, Sugarbee. You were a good mother to Shannon and a good daughter to me. I love you—always have and always will. Loved all of y'all—Yo-yo, Regina, Shannon, everybody—but I'm leaving Dentonville for good tonight. I can't stay here no more. But before I leave, I have to tell you the truth. I know you been hating me all these years and you been upset 'cause you didn't have a mother. Sugarbee, that's not true. I'm . . ." There was hesitation in her voice. "I'm not your mother. Gloria is your mother."

"End of message. To replay this message, press one. To erase it, press two. To save it, press three. For more options, press four."

One. She listened again. *One.* Again. *Three.*

Dianne held on to the wall to stop herself from collapsing into a mere heap of madness and confusion. She would never be able to actually recall walking to her car, pulling out her car keys, and closing the door, but she must have done so because she found herself crying behind the steering wheel, clutching its worn leather grip.

She'd gotten what she asked for. An apology. An "I love you." An admission of guilt. A mother who had taken care of her all these years. Still, she didn't feel any better about the whole thing. Seemed like the anger just shifted from Joyce Ann to Gloria, in which case Dianne was destined to lose another chunk of her life to that same roller coaster.

"No," Dianne said as she sat trembling in her car. "No, no, no." She pulled a Kleenex from the travel pack in her purse. "No, Dianne, no." As crazy as it had sounded when Dr. Tilley suggested it, Dianne knew that this was one of those pick-yourself-up-with-the-help-of-the-Lord moments.

Then she saw it as clear as day. She had come to that instant, that sliver of time in her life, when she had to make a vital resolution. No matter what Joyce Ann did or said, no matter what happened in that rent house years ago or on this night, Dianne had to decide. She, too, was tired of the past beating her up day in and day out. She was sick of not knowing if she was going to wake up in the middle of the night in a panic or spend the next day seeing Shannon's face.

Dianne's forehead hit the steering wheel, and she prayed what she knew would either be the last prayer or the first prayer, depending . . . She knew then that this must have been what Joyce Ann felt. And now, only a few hours later, here she was at that same crux. Dianne would either die because of her past or thrive in spite of it. The middle ground was nothing but sinking sand, a constant, vain expenditure of energy. A waste of life. She would get off this emotional seesaw now or never. Every angel assigned to her life stopped and heard Dianne's cry.

God, it's me. I can't do it any more, Lord; I just can't. There is nothing left but You and if You don't move in me, I can't go any further. I'm tired of crying; I'm tired of the nightmares, Lord; I've been hurting almost all my life, and I'm drained. I'm bringing myself and this whole mess to You. I'm through with it. If You don't fix it, it won't get fixed, because I'm not dealing with it anymore. Please forgive me for not forgiving Joyce Ann, and give me the strength and courage to know that I can live the rest of my life in peace, in love, and in Your will. Thank You for everyone You've used to hold me together up until now. In Jesus' name I pray. Amen.

Dianne opened her eyes, and in one heaving motion, she finally released the guilt-ridden words Otis had given her so many years ago as her sister lay dead. They flew from her soul, expelled by the power of God. In His excellence, He knew that Dianne was too close to the edge to teeter much longer. Life is timed; Dianne's new time had come.

The sky looked the same as it had when she stepped out of the apartment. The car still smelled like the strawberry-scented trinket hanging from the rearview mirror. Her hands still clutched the steering wheel. But they weren't shaking anymore. She had laid down that burden for the last time.

Chapter 32

$\mathcal{I}$t was selfish, she knew, to call him before the sun came up. He had a life of his own, and that life might not include her. But if anyone could be there for her now, it was Kelan. While in the waiting room, she dialed his number from her cell phone, a second apology ready on her lips if necessary.

"H . . . hello?"

"Kelan?"

"Yeah. Who's this?"

He doesn't remember my voice. "It's Yolanda."

"Yolanda. Are you okay? Is everything okay?" The bass in his voice caressed her, made her feel comfortable in the incomparable way that Aunt Toe said only a male companion could do. Yolanda understood now why God put Adam and Eve together.

"No. It's not. My aunt Joyce Ann started a fire in my mother's rent house."

"Oh, Yolanda, I'm so sorry. What can I do?"

"Can you just . . ." Yolanda's voice squeaked to a halt. "Could you just be here for me?"

His immediate reply: "Yes." He turned on his night lamp, fired up his laptop to send an e-mail to his students and the dean. Thirty minutes later he met Yolanda at the hospital.

Forty minutes later he gave her the shoulder she needed after Joyce Ann was pronounced dead.

Of all the people who could have told Dianne that Aunt Joyce Ann was dead, Yolanda had to be the one. Even Regina had been too torn up to come with her to the airport. Just what was Yolanda supposed to tell Dianne? They were sure that Aunt Joyce Ann had set the fire, but whether she meant to kill herself in the process was still unclear. It was anyone's guess.

From the hospital Kelan drove Yolanda to Dallas Love Field, where they waited for Dianne at the baggage claim area for the passengers exiting from gate twelve. The sun was in full bloom, still marvelous on a day like today. "Look at that," Yolanda said to Kelan.

"What?"

"The sun. God brings it up every morning no matter what happened the day before. Even if we can't see it directly, its light still reaches us, gives us what we need to see every day."

Kelan rubbed her hand. "You're starting to sound like the artsy type."

Yolanda looked at him out of the corner of her eye and felt the frown on her face turn upside down. "Thank you."

"For what?" he asked.

"For making me smile on a day like today." She blotted the corners of her eyes. "I needed that."

Yolanda stood near baggage claim and waited for Dianne to emerge from the throng of Monday morning business travelers dressed in suits, carrying briefcases, and talking rapidly on cell phones. Business as usual for them.

She almost overlooked her. *Dianne?* Dianne's eyes were red and puffy from crying, but her face was radiant. Where Yolanda had expected to see a crumpled frame of an already fragile Dianne, there was a sturdy woman.

Dianne was the woman she had been that night on the stage, reading her poetry. That night she'd been sure of herself. In her element. Alive. The prayer, the counseling, the poetry—all used to build her up, to sustain her in such a time as this. *Thank You, Lord*. She had help.

They hugged for what seemed like a long time, but not long enough. Yolanda knew that when she did see Dianne's face again, she'd have to tell her that Joyce Ann was dead, if her expression didn't do it first. But Dianne was stronger, Yolanda could tell—perhaps the stronger of the two.

Yolanda pulled herself off Dianne and gave her the news. "She passed, Dianne. About an hour ago."

Dianne nodded, wiping her eyes. "I can't explain how, but I already knew that."

"I'm sorry. We should have taken better care of her," Yolanda apologized to Dianne, feeling like a failure for the first time in her life. Yolanda had seen all the warning signs. She was around sick people all the time. If anyone should have acted sooner, it was she. She was sure of it. *How I could have been so negligent as a Christian, a family member, and a professional?*

"Don't." Dianne squeezed her arm and spoke slowly. "Don't go down that road, Yo-yo. It's nothing but a loop that goes round and round and comes back to square one every time."

Yolanda knew exactly what Dianne was talking about. She picked her head up and gave her another hug.

Kelan took their body language as his cue to come over and be introduced. "Oh, Dianne, this is Kelan, my significant other," Yolanda stepped back and gave them room to get acquainted.

"Hi, Kelan."

"Hi, Dianne. I'm so sorry for your loss," he said.

"Thanks for your condolences, Kelan."

Kelan offered to carry Dianne's bag to the car, and she took him up on it. "Up at six in the morning to be with the family? He's good," Dianne said in the few seconds they had to do the girl thing before Kelan returned from putting her bag in the trunk. "Cute, too."

"Girl, I almost let him go."

Back at the house, Gloria, Regina, and Aunt Toe sat weeping in the living room when Dianne, Kelan, and Yolanda walked through the door. They all rose to hug Dianne. She stood in the center of a group hug, smiling.

"Hey," Dianne said, physically supporting Gloria, "it's okay."

"Oh, sweetie"—Gloria wiped her face clumsily—"here, come sit down."

Dianne sat between Gloria and Aunt Toe and comforted them. Aunt Toe wept deeply, summoning the pain in Yolanda that she'd set aside at the airport—but not the guilt. They would never see Joyce Ann again.

"Aunt Gloria . . ." Dianne looked her mother in the eyes and whispered, "I need to talk to you. Alone."

Everyone in the room looked Dianne's way, but they all understood that maybe she needed some time alone with Gloria. After all, if anyone could recap Joyce Ann's last days and release Dianne from the mystery of her mother's life, it was Gloria.

Gloria stood, offered her hand to help Dianne up from the couch, and led her to the guest room. They sat next to each other at the foot of the bed. There was such a long silence that Gloria knew. But Dianne spoke first.

"Aunt Gloria, she called me."

"Who?"

"My mom—I mean, Joyce Ann. She called me and told me before she died."

"Oh, baby . . ." Gloria threw her arms around her daughter and felt a weight fly from her shoulders. "I'm so sorry. I just . . . I was in college." Gloria looked into Dianne's eyes and searched for accusation. There was none. All Dianne wanted at this point was to fill in the blanks.

Somehow, Gloria found her help in Dianne. She continued, "My freshman year in college. I was young; I was naive; I felt out of place because I was one of the few blacks at a campus hundreds of miles away from my home. Anyway, *he* was the only African-American professor on staff. I did my work-study in his department, and we often met after class to discuss notes and things like that. Before I knew it, I was caught up in this *thing* with him. I wouldn't call it a relationship. It was more like a circumstantial acquaintance, and I didn't really know how to maneuver through it at the time. I take full responsibility for my actions, but I would be lying if I said that I didn't feel pressured.

"Anyway, I got pregnant. I told the professor, and he did the right thing. He told the powers that be what was going on, thinking that we'd both be asked to leave the university. I remember him telling me that he never meant to hurt me—that at some level he'd felt just as trapped at the university as I did. Anyway, the board of directors didn't ask him to leave the university—they only asked *me* to leave. I didn't know what to do. Aside from the fact that I was a small-town girl with a big-city problem, the professor and I were both black, and I knew that this situation could make it more difficult for black students and professors at the university in the future. I felt like the whole world was riding on my shoulders.

"My initial reaction to their request was to oblige. I remembered that in our freshman orientation, they had said that one in every three people would not finish. I couldn't believe *I* was the one. So there I was, all packed and ready to come back when I made that tearful call home to tell my family that I was coming home from college. Instead of Aunt Toe or my mother, I got Joyce Ann on the phone. I explained the situation to her, and she told me in no uncertain terms that I would *not* be coming home—that those people at that college would *not* make me the scapegoat, and that they had better figure out some kind of way to keep me there, because I was *not* going to take the fall by myself." Gloria nodded her head, thinking fondly of that conversation. "Joyce Ann was always bucking authority. This was right up her alley, thank God." It was as though Joyce Ann had given Gloria a shot of you-better-stand-up-for-yourself all those years ago—a shot that saved her life and renewed her hopes and dreams.

"I went back to the administration office, and we pushed and shoved until we had it all worked out. They said that if I would either sit out a semester or have an abortion, they would pay for the rest of my college education so long as I kept my mouth shut. It was strange—I mean, they even had a *contract* for this agreement. I wondered how many other contracts they had on file for other professors."

"Why didn't you just sue them?" Dianne asked.

"We didn't sue for everything back then. People just figured that women got what they deserved. I know it all sounds crazy to you now, but things were different then."

"Why didn't Grandma Rucker or Aunt Toe get involved? Couldn't they have demanded the removal of the professor . . . I mean, my father?" Dianne was outraged and ashamed. Her father, the professor, had seduced her mother and then left her out to dry.

"Oh, no." Gloria shook her head vehemently. "Joyce Ann

and I never told them the whole truth. Far as they're concerned, I got pregnant by someone on the basketball team. They would have hit the roof if they had known everything, and I could not afford to let happen. Aunt Toe and your grandmother were a force to be reckoned with, for sure, but this was a different game. These were the good ol' boys, and they had their system. At that point, I had all of my college expenses paid for, I would be able to support my child in a few years, and I figured that was more than I deserved.

"I just needed to make a decision about you. So I asked Joyce Ann if she'd do me the biggest favor a woman can ask of another woman: take care of my child. My momma said it was the best thing, since Joyce Ann wasn't doing anything with her life anyway. She'd dropped out of school and gotten a job at one of the factories like everyone else did back then."

Dianne encouraged Gloria to go on. "That was very brave of you."

"Well, I didn't feel so brave when I skipped that semester and went back to Craw Prairie to finish out my pregnancy and give birth to you. Joyce Ann came with me. She quit her job, and we both went to Aunt Toe's old stomping grounds so I wouldn't have to go through the pregnancy alone. Folks in Dentonville thought I was still in college, so there were no questions about me. But they would have wondered how Joyce Ann popped up with a baby when her stomach was flat as a pancake the other day. We stayed gone for months and came back with a beautiful little baby.

"Craw Prairie is so backwards—back then black people still used midwives. Didn't take much to make Joyce Ann your official mother."

"But why didn't you just finish college and then come get me, Aunt Gloria?" Again, Dianne was sincere, not accusatory, in her quest for knowledge.

Gloria replayed the decision she'd made while Dianne was still a toddler. "Well, right after I graduated and moved back home from college, I met Willie. Sometime during the transition period of weaning you from Joyce Ann's house back to mine, Willie and I fell in love and decided to get married. I didn't think he'd do it if he knew I had a baby already. Times were different; things were different back then. I should have known that I could tell him, though. He was such a good man." Gloria's face beamed at his name. "I told him before we got married, though, because I wanted to come clean. He said that he still loved me and that he wanted to adopt you— give you his name—but we couldn't do it right away because, legally, you weren't mine. There was a lot of *costly* red tape. We were saving up the money to get this whole thing straightened out. In the meanwhile, we got married and I had Regina. You and Joyce Ann and Shannon came over almost every day, and life went on. You got so attached to Shannon, God knows we would have had to adopt her, too. And Willie was fine with that except, by the time we got ready to go to the courts, Joyce Ann had started doing drugs and she was getting food stamps for having both you and Shannon in the house, and she was using you to raise Shannon. Everything just spiraled out of control so quickly. Before I knew it, it was all a big mess. I fixed things the best I could. I made Joyce Ann move into the rent house down the street so I could watch over you like a hawk.

"But I must have blinked." Gloria paused. Though she leaned her head back and closed her eyes, the tears broke through and made shiny streaks down her face. "When Shannon died, I wanted to crawl in the casket with her, but I couldn't, because you needed me then more than ever. I always blamed myself for that."

"Why?" Dianne wondered. *Who breathed such life into this monster?*

"Because if I had been there, it wouldn't have happened." Gloria smacked an open palm on her forehead. "Shannon wouldn't have died, and you wouldn't have had to go through a lifetime of pain if I hadn't been so busy worrying about one child over the other one. And all I put Joyce Ann through, everybody thinking she was the one with all the problems. God, help me! Help me!" she repeated, now beating her brow with closed fists.

Dianne grabbed Gloria's hand and stopped her. "Momma." The term caught Dianne off guard. She hadn't called anyone by that name since the day her beloved Shannon died. "You did your best." Dianne let her mother cry into her shirt, and in turn, Dianne cried her own tears. She did have a mother, and that mother had loved her all along. These lies that had been nothing but smoke before her eyes all these years suddenly dissipated, and the child within turned a hundred cartwheels, popped a thousand wheelies, scooped up a million jacks in one bounce, and screamed for joy. She had a mother.

"I do have another question." Dianne wondered if she really wanted to know the answer, but she asked anyway. "Where is my father?"

"He passed away about ten years ago. Cancer. I read about it in the alumni news."

Dianne's gaze landed on the floor.

"You know," Gloria confessed, "your father really was a good person. I think that if we hadn't been professor and student, things might have worked out differently. I don't know. It was a very complicated situation."

"Let's tell Regina and Yo-yo." Dianne took another step toward restoration.

Gloria nodded in submission. Two shameful secrets down, none to go. Back in the living room, Regina and Yolanda listened with a mix of bewilderment and satisfaction. Dianne always did belong to them.

Aunt Toe was liberated, too.

Orlando and Richard came through the front door, their hands blackened from soot. "There's nothing left, Gloria." Richard shook his head. "It's all gone."

Gloria sniffed and wiped her nose. "I didn't think there was anything left, but I couldn't see much with the firemen everywhere. Are the last flames out?"

"Yes, ma'am," Orlando assured her, "they put them all out."

The men stood around helplessly, uncomfortable. "I'm gonna go put on a pot of coffee," Richard said. Orlando and Kelan followed him to the kitchen.

Aunt Toe started wiggling her foot, rocking her whole body back and forth from the bottom up. "Joyce Ann would have had a birthday next week. *Hmph*. She sure was a pretty little girl. Had all that long hair—till you cut off her ponytail."

Gloria blinked back her tears and put a hand on Aunt Toe's knee. "She told me to."

"Since when did you ever listen to Joyce Ann?" Aunt Toe laughed through a sob. "The two of you got into more trouble together than that Nancy Drew and the Hardy boys. I swear, I could have wrote a book about the two of you—Joyce Ann, Gloria, and the whippin's."

"You mean the beatings." Gloria lowered her chin and looked at Aunt Toe.

"Did you have your clothes on when you got the whippin'?"

"Yes, Aunt Toe. Momma never—"

"Well, it wasn't no beatin', then," Aunt Toe said to Gloria.

"Aunt Toe, you saying that Grandma Rucker whipped you naked?"

"Might as well. By the time the clothes got to me, there was more holes than thread left." Aunt Toe chuckled at her own joke.

"Come on now, Aunt Toe. I've got that old picture of you and my momma, and you were both in pretty white dresses." Gloria pushed herself up from the couch. She came back from her bedroom with three photo albums and two shoe boxes full of pictures.

They spent the next two hours laughing and crying over old pictures. Regina, Dianne, and Shannon in matching plaid bell-bottom outfits that Joyce Ann made for them. She was a wonderful seamstress. Gloria and Joyce Ann as young adults Hula Hoop-ing with Afro puffs. Joyce Ann's smile was contagious. She was beautiful. A picture of Joyce Ann with Dianne on one hip and Shannon on the other, all of them dressed in pink skirts and halter tops. Finally, a picture of Joyce Ann and Gloria holding Dianne up to the table so that she could blow out the candle on her first birthday cake. All of them bearing smiles that showed no hint of the pain to come. Gently Dianne asked Gloria for that priceless photo.

Gloria peeled back the clear film, releasing years of pent-up secrets into the hands of her oldest daughter, her beloved Sugarbee.

They had lunch, spent some time at the funeral home, contacted church officials, and then made dozens of phone calls to get out the word about Joyce Ann's funeral. Yolanda was weak, exhausted from the past twenty-four hours. Under the circumstances, she could have called in to work, but she didn't want to. Monday was always a busy day at the pharmacy—people having been to the emergency rooms over the weekends and gotten prescriptions, along with a myriad of other scenarios that caused people to handle much of their business on Mondays. With that kind of rush, the hours passed quickly. She worked her eight hours and came straight home.

Dianne met her at the door and made sandwiches while Yolanda ran bathwater and got undressed. There was no need to cook anything. If the church folk were still up to their old traditions, the family would have enough food to last a week by the time they got finished burying Joyce Ann.

"You want mayonnaise?" Dianne called from the kitchen.

"Mustard," Yolanda answered. It was nice to have someone to talk to when she came in.

Yolanda devoured the sandwich Dianne made for her, took a bath, and lay down on the couch across from her while they switched channels between old *Happy Days* reruns and the BET network. Yolanda planned on taking a little catnap but ended up crashing for the night in the living room.

The next morning, they dressed and went to Gloria's house, greeting other family members and talking out funeral plans. It was odd, laughing one minute, crying the next, eating all the while. So much goodness in the pain.

Regina, Dianne, and Yolanda took a walk down to the rent house late Tuesday afternoon. It was the first time the sisters had seen it since the morning of the fire—yellow tape surrounding the property as if it were some kind of crime scene. The three of them held hands like kindergartners assigned to buddies on a field trip, not wanting to get lost or separated. It wasn't safe to go inside the house; that was for sure. But just standing there, with the smell of burned wood still fresh in the air, was therapeutic. Smelled like a fireplace almost, as though, if you closed your eyes, you might be in a cozy living room snuggled up under a warm blanket.

They walked around to the backyard and took in the view

from behind. "Remember when we used to sit on this back porch and eat orange push-ups?" Regina asked.

Dianne wiped her cheek on her shoulder, still holding their hands, and nodded. "Me, you, and Yo-yo."

"Mmm-hmm."

"Joyce Ann called me," Dianne uttered.

"When?" Yolanda asked, not looking away from the porch.

"I guess just before she started the fire. She said she loved me. Loved all of us," Dianne sighed a deep, cleansing sigh. "Said she just couldn't take it anymore."

"Well . . ." Regina bit her unsteady lip. "I know I wasn't much help to her. I was too busy kicking her while she was down. I didn't realize that she was already at the bottom." The tears fell freely from her eyes, and she made no effort to stop them.

"Stop blaming yourself, Regina," Dianne said sternly with the same conviction she'd exhibited at the airport with Yolanda. "What's done is done. You were angry, you were hurt, and you didn't know what to do. I'm sure every one of us would have done things differently if we'd known then what we know now. But that's not the way life works. You have to move on with what you understand now, and ask God to give you more wisdom and keep you from making the same mistakes twice. That's all anybody can do."

They stood there for a little while longer, letting the reality of the situation sink in.

The evening's chill crept from the shadows of the house. "We'd better get on back to Momma's house," Yolanda said. Their feet made soft, simple noises as they carefully tiptoed around the house. The ground, with its new spring buds amid soot-laden debris, seemed awkwardly sacred. At the side of the house, they stopped and let Dianne close the gate. A necessity.

As the three walked back to Gloria's house, they mentally

prepared themselves to greet the host of family and friends that had come by after getting off work. But what Yolanda really wanted, above all else, was to be left alone. To go to a room and sit down and have herself a good cry. "I . . . I think I'm gonna go on home," she voiced her preference.

"Why?" Dianne inquired.

Why is she asking me why? "I just . . . I just want to go home."

"To be alone?" Dianne took the words right out of Yolanda's mouth.

"Yeah. I just feel like squeezing into a small space, curling up into a ball, and crying," she explained.

"That's how it all starts, you know?" Dianne nodded and threw her head back, giving the laugh of a wiser, much older person talking to a young heart. "You think you're doing the right thing by isolating yourself. But you know what?"

"What?" Regina asked.

"When you're going through, that's when you need other people the most. Your family. Your friends. Whew! I wish I had known all this twenty years ago." She shook her head. "I wish Joyce Ann had known all this. When you're hurting, it seems like the most natural thing to do—go off to yourself. Gather your thoughts. But once you get there, the longer you stay, the harder it is to get back to who you were before."

Regina pulled Dianne's hand close to her heart. "Dianne, you have come a long way, my sister."

"Bless God." Dianne gave Him the glory. "Bless God."

Miss Doublin sat in the living room, giving everyone an account of Joyce Ann's death from the moment the first flame flickered to the time the last firefighter left. Yolanda sat down for a moment, not really wanting to hear all the horrid details, but needing to rest her feet. Yolanda thought about getting up, but the tone of Miss Doublin's voice drew her into the conversation.

She spoke in a low whisper. "I heard her." Miss Doublin's third chin wiggled with her recounting of the night's events. "She ran out of that house just hollerin'. I looked out my window—she was almost back up to this here house when she turned back around and ran back to the other house. She was screamin' somethin' 'bout a sewing machine. 'Two thousand dollars,' she said. She ran back into that house screamin' 'bout the sewing machine. Next thing I knew, the firetruck and the policemens pulled up."

She went back to save the sewing machine? "Miss Doublin, have you told my mother what you told us all just now?"

"I . . . I told the firemen, but I haven't told your momma," she whispered. "Bad enough your aunt died. Worse that she could have made it out alive but went back inside for a silly old sewing machine."

"Well, don't you think my momma ought to know before everyone else on the street does?" Yolanda truly didn't mean to disrespect Miss Doublin, but she couldn't hide her resentment.

Yolanda pulled herself up from the chair and went to the kitchen to gather Gloria, Aunt Toe, Regina, and Dianne and tell them what Miss Doublin had revealed. Aunt Toe didn't quite understand the significance of the events. "Aunt Joyce Ann went back for the sewing machine because Momma was liable for what happened to it while it was in Aunt Joyce Ann's care. She went back for it so that Momma wouldn't have to pay for it."

"We have insurance that would have replaced the machine," Gloria cried. "She didn't have to do that for me."

"Aunt Gloria," Dianne said, "she wasn't in her right mind."

Chapter 33

Regina woke in the afternoon, wondering if it all had really happened. For a moment she thought it might have been a horrible dream. But one look around her old bedroom confirmed that the horror was reality. *Joyce Ann is dead.* She remembered now. With the exception of Orlando, everyone else had gone to the funeral home while Regina crashed from the sheer exhaustion of it all. How she managed to sleep at a time like this could only be attributed to the fact that she wasn't eating much.

She could have gone home, but she needed to be with the women in her family. Separately they might fall. But standing back to back, they could support each other, hold each other up.

Regina imagined that it must have been that way when her father died. She couldn't remember exactly what happened following Willie's death, but she did remember the way that everyone banded together when Aunt Toe's husband died. Gloria had helped Aunt Toe with the arrangements and saw to it that the memorial was a fitting homegoing celebration for a man who had suffered from diabetes for many, many years. Yolanda conducted the flow of traffic in Aunt Toe's house, greeting the mourners, insulating Aunt Toe. Dianne made arrangements for an automatic transfer of funds from her Bank of America account to Aunt Toe's once a month, something she still did. Regina herself handled the legalities of death, though she'd already crossed the "T's" and dotted the "I's" in the years leading up to Uncle Albert's death.

And always, there was prayer.

Regina remembered what it was like to pray; the feeling that God was watching over her, the peace that enveloped her when she knelt beside her bed, closed her eyes, and pushed the "pause" button on her life. In this hour, Regina wished that she could push "rewind" and go back twenty-four hours. She wouldn't yell at Joyce Ann. She wouldn't be disgusted with her presence. She would hold Joyce Ann and assure her that things would work out.

Too late now.

Regina lay in bed with her thoughts. If she got up, Orlando would surely come in the room, asking if there was anything he could do. He was, after all, a good man. *So why am I pushing him away?* Regina wondered exactly where she'd gone wrong. She was an attorney, a member of a loving family, and married to a wonderful man. Yet happiness seemed to slip through her fingers like water sometimes. She might have it in her grip for a little while, but never for long, because the minute she tried to enjoy her happiness—wash her face in it, spread it all over herself—it slipped away. Regina could hold on to happiness only under certain austere conditions, one of those being that she stay under 120 pounds. Another being that her life line up with her ideal. Without alignment, there was no happiness.

Regina wondered if this was how the rest of her life would be. *Will I always have to be thin and in control in order to have happiness?* Certainly, the events of the past several months had taken her weight and her entire life out of her control. It was a sad understanding: that her life wasn't in her control. Never had been, she realized now. No, she hadn't taken the time to call a time-out in her life. So, evidently, God had.

Orlando peeked into her room and saw the reflection of the hallway light on her eyes. "You okay?" he asked as he tip-toed across the eggshells, approaching her bedside.

"No. I'm not okay."

"You need something to drink? Eat?" he asked.

"I mean I'm *not* okay. Something is wrong with me and I don't know what it is, but I don't want to keep belittling every-one around me because I can't cope with life on God's terms. I don't want to end up like Joyce Ann, and I don't want to hurt anyone else the way I hurt her yesterday." Regina spoke as though she were reading a philosophical essay out loud.

Orlando hugged his wife and silently thanked God for the revelation. He expected her to go into one of her dramatic cry-ing spells, but she didn't this time. Regina had cried so much in the past eighteen hours that her tear ducts simply couldn't produce any more. Joyce Ann was dead.

Gloria, Yolanda, Aunt Toe, Richard, and Kelan returned from the funeral home in utter and complete fatigue. Regina and Orlando joined them in the family living room. Someone turned on the lamp to combat the darkness, and they all draped themselves throughout the room, coupled on the sec-tional sofa with Aunt Toe pulled up next to Gloria's side. The ceiling fan's blades beat a steady whisk above. Five women, three men. And for a moment they deliberated in silence.

Each of the men wondered what he could have done to prevent Joyce Ann's death. Maybe if they'd been more as-sertive, attentive, or adamant about the necessary changes— anything to keep the women they loved from getting hurt. If only they had taken the risk, "butted in," Joyce Ann might still be alive. But they hadn't, and now one of their own was dead.

Aunt Toe's heart was so heavy, it felt like lead. She'd seen it coming just the same as everyone else, but what could she have done? Called the prayer chain sooner, that was for sure. She'd waited too late to pray. She also could have moved in with Joyce Ann herself and kept that gal from burning the place down. Maybe she could have called the State on Joyce Ann, told them she was a danger to herself. But she didn't have any proof. It was a sticky situation when somebody's mind was sick. Aunt Toe had learned that the hard way—twice over now.

When Ruth ran off behind a man and left the girls for two days, Aunt Toe had called the police. She could have taken in Gloria and Joyce Ann. In fact, she intended to. Calling the police was just a matter of getting Ruth to face up to her responsibilities. But Ruth never saw it that way. She and Aunt Toe were never close again, because she'd opened her mouth and gotten "white folks" involved—that's what Ruth had said. Aunt Toe hadn't actually approached Ruth face-to-face again until Ruth was faceup in a casket. That hurt like nothing else. Now Ruth's youngest daughter had taken the same route: died too soon. If anybody should have known better, Aunt Toe figured, it should have been she.

Gloria was beside herself. None of it seemed real just yet. It *couldn't* be real, because if it were, she was to blame. She didn't find the right clinic, the right doctor, the right counselor. She had completely discounted everybody's warnings about Joyce Ann. But Joyce Ann was more like a daughter than a sister to Gloria, and it was hard to admit defeat and throw in the towel on your own. It was a heartbreak that lasted nearly two decades. Gloria fought for Joyce Ann the way Joyce Ann had fought for her when Willie died. No matter how crazy every-one else thought Gloria was, Joyce Ann stood up for her. She'd covered for Gloria about Bernard Livingston, and Gloria owed it to Joyce Ann to cover for her. But in her effort to con-ceal Joyce Ann's crisis, Gloria had failed. And all this time she thought *Joyce Ann* was the one with the problem. Well, at least Joyce Ann didn't let Gloria kill herself. What kind of a woman ignored her sister's mental illness? In her mind, Gloria an-swered: "A bad woman like me."

Yolanda rested her head on Kelan's shoulder as tears rolled from her eyes onto his denim button-down shirt. Her brain pounded against the inside of her forehead, and her eyes burned raw from the endless crying. How could she have let this happen? Aunt Joyce Ann was dead because of her, she was sure. It was a textbook case of a disassociative disorder, and no one in their right mind would have allowed Joyce Ann to live alone. She should have stood up to Gloria. Maybe if she hadn't been so busy worrying about Bernard Livingston, she could have paid more attention to Joyce Ann and they could have admitted her hours sooner—on Saturday night instead of putting off the final discussion. But it was too late. Things like this just didn't happen to Yolanda unless she hadn't planned well enough. When she really thought about it, this whole thing was her fault.

There is a feeling, a distinct tone, that permanently fastens to a finite number of occurrences in your life, such that just thinking of a particular event, the tiniest inkling of it, trans-ports your soul back to that very same spot at that very same time even years after the fact. In a flash, you play the mental videotape, smell the smells, and feel the sensation of that timeless instant engulfing you as though it had happened only yesterday. You relive it—to your detriment or benefit—at will, sometimes *against* your will.

What you do with that memory makes all the difference. Dianne knew this well, better than anyone else in the room. As she looked at the faces of her loved ones, she recognized their despair. In their eyes, pools of woe, she saw a reflection of her old self: guilt, regret, self-degradation, making herself pay the price for sins that Jesus already bore on the cross—in Dianne's case, wrongdoings that she had pinned on herself. And now, just as Dianne accepted freedom and vowed to slay this penance monster, its heart was still beating. It had lived just long enough to find other hosts and be transferred to her loved ones.

Not as long as the power of the Holy Spirit within Dianne could help it.

All the way to Dentonville, Dianne had prayed and read the Scriptures that Dr. Tilley gave her weeks earlier—the ones she'd put away and refused to look at in her anger. They gave her the strength and comfort of a million mothers rocking her to sleep and a million fathers tucking her into bed. Dianne could stand on the word of God, and if the others couldn't stand on it with her, they could at least lean on it until they found the strength.

All that morning at the hospital and the funeral home, Dianne had been quiet. She listened only to the Scriptures as they played over and over again in her mind. Now it was time to declare them. She reached down to her feet and pulled the brown leather organizer from her oversize purse. As she flipped through the notes section she saw herself in a different light. All her bad days were being used by Him for this time. She sat up straight on the sunken couch and took center stage as she read His message from the tablet of her heart.

"I'm sitting here looking at everybody and I'm thinking: if anyone ought to be sad, it should be me. I should have reached out to her. And I'm sure that looking back, we can all think of many shoulda-woulda-couldas. I think we've all been convicted of something or another when it comes to Joyce Ann, and there is a lesson to be learned, as in everything else in life. But there's a difference between constructive conviction and guilt. When God convicts us, it's because He wants us to grow stronger. He wants to take that lesson, take that misery, and make it our ministry. But the enemy comes to steal, kill, and destroy. He is the accuser who only reminds us of our shortcomings in order to beat us over the soul with them. He wants us to doubt and discount everything that Jesus did on the cross.

"I can't tell you exactly how you can turn that guilt around, and actually, I don't know that you can. It takes God and His word to change a heart. A mind. A spirit. So, that's what I'm gonna share with you for just a moment. And then we'll pray," Dianne commanded as she closed her eyes and recited the verses from memory. "Galatians five and one: 'It is for freedom that Christ has set us free. Stand firm, then, and do not let yourselves be burdened again by a yoke of slavery.' First Peter two and twenty-four: 'He himself bore our sins in his body on the tree, so that we might die to sins and live for righteousness; by his wounds you have been healed.' John eight and thirty-six: 'So if the Son sets you free, you will be free indeed.'

"Now let's pray."

Whimpers turned to sobs as Dianne wrestled guilt to the ground. Aunt Toe's body heaved up and down. Gloria buried her face in her hands. Regina hung her head, and Yolanda cried while holding tightly to Kelan's hand.

"Father, we're hurting," Dianne prayed. "We're hurting so badly, Lord, that it seems almost unbearable. We don't understand it, Father, but You do. You loved Joyce Ann more than any one of us did, so we don't question You. We only hope and pray that we will see Joyce Ann again on the other side.

"But now, Lord, guilt, shame, and despair have come to bear down on us because of Joyce Ann's death. The accuser has come to destroy us, but we ask that You would give each and every one of us the strength to learn the lesson without taking on the guilt that the enemy brings to us. We simply bring these burdens to You and leave them there.

"Father, we praise You already for the deliverance." Dianne stood and clapped her hands in praise. Within moments, Dianne's family, old and new, surrounded her and joined her in praise. "Lord we praise You for deliverance; we give You glory. Be magnified; be exalted in our lives." The room transformed from a space of sorrow to a space of glory as they lifted the name of the Lord on high in the midst of their pain. With their minds open, their hands lifted, and their hearts broken, the spirit of God gingerly planted a seed of healing into their fertile hearts.

And so it happened that the one known as Joyce Ann's girl, the one who had been the most fragile, the least stable, held out her hand to help those who had always helped her. It wasn't a cure-all or an instant solution. Yet, it takes only a second to start looking forward instead of looking back.

Chapter 34

*Y*olanda had been holding on to information about Mr. Bernard Livingston of Parker City, Texas, for days now. Though she was busy with getting things squared away for Joyce Ann's funeral, Yolanda's eyes rolled across that number at least three or four times a day. By now she'd memorized his phone number and address. Calling her long-lost father was the kind of feat that got increasingly difficult as each day went on. She had a good excuse to procrastinate, with Joyce Ann's death still fresh on her mind. However, the fact still remained: if she didn't call him now, she might not ever lift her fingers to do it.

The phone rang two times before an answering machine picked up. "Hello!" His voice was distinct, jovial—as if he might bust out whistling the tune to the *Andy Griffith Show* at any moment. "Sorry we missed your call. Leave a message and we'll get back to you as soon as possible. If you want to leave a message for Candace, press one. For Bernard, press two. For the both of us, stay on the line. Have a great day!"

Yolanda pressed "2" and waited for the beep. What was she supposed to say? She didn't want to leave a bombshell message on an answering machine. The beep caught her unprepared. She held on to the phone, breathing. Okay, she couldn't leave a heavy-breathing message. She had to say something. "Hello, Mr. Livingston, this is Yolanda Jordan. From Dentonville. Could you please return my phone call? My number is five five five, one oh eight seven. It's important. Thank you."

Yolanda hung up the phone and waited. Would he call back? Would he erase it so that Candace wouldn't hear it, whoever she was? Yolanda was certain that he was divorced. Was he living with someone? Hours passed. Still no call. She had to get up and get ready for work. What if he was out of town? *I should have called him sooner.*

On her way to the garage, the phone rang. "Hello."

"Hello, is this Yolanda Jordan?" It was him.

"Yes, this is Yolanda Jordan."

"This is Bernard Livingston. I'm returning your call. How can I help you?"

"Mr. Bernard, I'm . . . I'm . . . well, Gloria Jordan, Willie Amos Jordan's widow . . . I'm their daughter. You worked with Willie at J. T. Plastics before he died in a boating accident."

"Oh, right, Yolanda"—he sparked with fondness—"with the cute little button nose. Your father talked about you all the time. How are you? How's your mother? How's your family? I was just thinking about Willie the other day."

He obviously had her confused with Regina. "No, Mr. Livingston, you're talking about my sister Regina. I'm Yolanda. I . . . I'm *your* daughter."

Dead silence.

"Hello?"

"Yes. I'm still here," he barely spoke.

"I'm sorry to have to tell you like this, but I don't have much time."

"Time?"

"Mr. Livingston, I . . . I have to go to work now. I'm sorry to just dump all this on you and then leave, but—"

"What do you do?" he asked.

"I'm a pharmacist."

"A pharmacist, huh?" Yolanda heard him beam with pride. "A pharmacist."

"I'm sorry. I'll have to get back with you later." Yolanda hung up the phone.

On her way to work, Yolanda replayed the way he'd said "pharmacist" over and over again in her head. *My father is proud of me.* All at once she felt guilty. What about Daddy—Willie? What about the place he held in her heart? It seemed simple enough. She should have been able just to forget about all that and be happy about Mr. Livingston. Willie was dead and there was nothing she could do to change that. But when you've mourned for the one you thought was the missing piece for thirty-one years, it's not so simple. How many times had she pulled out pictures of him and talked to them? How often had the images of him that she gathered from old photos appeared in her dreams?

Everything was further complicated by the fact that this was one life-changing event she could not experience alongside Regina.

Those five hours at work seemed like a full shift that night. Between calls from Gloria and Regina about Joyce Ann's funeral arrangements, Yolanda's mind drifted to thoughts of her father. In all honesty, Yolanda couldn't wait to talk to Mr. Livingston again. She made up a list of things she wanted to know:

1. Do I have any brothers or sisters?
2. Who is Candace?
3. Did you have any idea about me?
4. What have you been doing all this time?

After work, Yolanda's curiosity got the best of her. She could hardly wait to call Mr. Livingston when she got home. He readily answered her questions. "No, you don't have any brothers or sisters this way," he laughed openly. "You're the only child. My ex-wife, Dorothy, and I tried for many years to have a child, but it never happened."

"Who's Candace?" Yolanda jumped to her next question.

"She's my lady friend. We've been together, oh, about four years now."

"You're not married?"

"No. How about you?" he returned the question.

"No."

"Any grandchildren I should know about?"

"No. No kids here, either," she laughed.

She held off on the third question. It just didn't seem to be the right time. Mr. Livingston seemed cordial enough on the phone, but she wasn't interested in hearing what might be his sorry excuse for not following up on the birth of a child nine months after he slept with the child's mother. Simple math. Maybe he just didn't care.

Yolanda wondered why she'd even called. "Well, it was nice talking to you, Mr. Livingston."

"Yolanda," he stopped her. "I . . . I would like to meet you. If that's okay."

"It's really not a good time for me. My aunt just died and—"

"Oh, I'm so sorry. Was she ill?"

"Yes, she was," Yolanda said.

"My condolences."

"Thank you." She could only whisper now. "I'll call you . . . some other time."

*   *   *

The women sat arm in arm on the front pew, holding on to each other for support. Aunt Toe thought it would be a good idea if the immediate family wore pink, Joyce Anne's favorite color. It seemed odd at first, but when they all stood together near the church entrance, the soft pastel colors made a great tribute to Joyce Ann. Despite all the bad in her life, she was a beautiful blossom. In the end, they were all glad they had paid heed to Aunt Toe's suggestion.

They buried her next to Shannon, in Dentonville's only cemetery. Here again the four women sat on the front row, mourning. Kelan remained a strong pillar, a ready shoulder. He cried with the family, saying good-bye to a woman he'd never known. Yolanda wished that he had known Joyce Ann. Gloria wished that everyone could have known how good she was. Perhaps it was the good in her that had cost Joyce Ann her life. Maybe the part of her that never truly wanted to cause harm was what had made her go back into the house to salvage a sewing machine.

Property of Ellen's Bridal.

Regina never thought saying good-bye to her aunt Joyce Ann would be so difficult. It was the hardest thing in the world to bid farewell to someone she'd mistreated. Even if it wasn't her fault that Joyce Ann was dead, Regina knew that she'd missed the opportunity to be kind to her. If only she had known that the words she had used to fuss at Joyce Ann for being sick would be the last ones, she wouldn't have said them.

"Ashes to ashes; dust to dust," the minister said as he sprinkled dirt on the top of Joyce Ann's casket.

Yolanda was so smothered by grief, she could hardly breathe. "Just take a deep breath," she heard Kelan say as her eyes became fixated on the white, shiny casket trimmed in lavender and pink roses. She took deep breaths, giving herself room to resolve, then forced herself to focus on something else. She looked up and saw that she was sitting next to one of the largest floral arrangements at the grave site: a beautiful array of spring flowers, trimmed in greenery, accented by pink ribbons. The outside of the card was blank. Yolanda leaned forward, just enough to read the inside. "May God Bless You and Keep You. The Livingston Family." Yolanda wanted to process the feelings she had about her father, but she couldn't do it. Not then.

Leaving her sister's body at that cemetery felt like a crime. Gloria kept telling herself over and over that Joyce Ann was dead. She'd known that for several days now. But when she walked away from Joyce Ann, left her there in that casket, that's when Gloria knew that she was gone. Gloria's legs went limp. Richard and Kelan helped her back to the car, her weak legs making the motions like an infant who instinctively knows the moves but doesn't have the strength to actually walk.

Aunt Toe led the congregation in song. "Bye and bye, when the morning comes . . ." With everything in her, she sang the words as clearly and as purposefully as anything she'd ever given her sweet voice to. It was all she could do to get through the day, hoping that when she got to heaven she'd know why there was so much pain in life. "For we'll understand it better bye and bye."

Chapter 35

$\mathcal{T}$he two days following the funeral had been draining. They seemed to be taking turns going up and down the emotional roller coaster following Joyce Ann's funeral. Members from congregations across the Metroplex sent food or dropped by. The outpouring was comforting and eased the pain considerably. It was then that Dianne realized how much she missed the church, the "saints and friends," as Aunt Toe would say.

Dianne decided to stay with Yolanda for the rest of the week. Dentonville did her good with its laid-back lifestyle. In her new position at work Dianne could telecommute four days a week, and if she talked with her supervisor, she might even be able to get away with conducting teleconferences rather than coming into the office, much as her predecessor had done. That would cut her office time down to three or four days a month. Maybe she could coordinate those office days with her visits to Dr. Tilley. And she could keep in touch with her poetry group via the Internet. They would understand that she wanted—no, needed—to be around her kinfolks. Flying back to Dentonville every couple of weeks would be worth every cent.

"Someone called for you a few hours ago," Dianne informed Yolanda as she walked through the door after work. "I think it was your father. Is his name Bernard?"

"Yeah. What did he say?"

"Said he'd call back later tonight."

"Thanks." Yolanda stood still before the door to her closet for a second, thinking. *My father called.* If he waited too much later, he might miss her altogether. She and Dianne were planning to head into Dallas, catch a movie, and do some shopping. Yolanda decided to call him back. "Hello. Is Mr. Livingston in?"

"Yeah, sweetie, who's calling?"

"This is Yolanda."

"Oh, hello, Yolanda. I'm Candace, your father's girlfriend. It's nice to finally get to speak with you. I tell you, your father is so proud of you, sweetie. He's been telling everyone we know about you," she laughed one of those "tickled pink" laughs.

"Oh, that's nice to know," Yolanda said.

"Hold on, Yolanda, let me get him on the phone for ya."

A few seconds later, his cheerful voice was on the other end. "Hello, Yolanda. How are you?"

"I'm fine, and you?"

"Mighty fine, mighty fine."

"Thanks so much for the floral arrangement. It was beautiful."

"Well, I know how hard it is when you lose a loved one. Every little bit of support helps."

"I agree." Yolanda pictured a chubby, gray-haired man wearing glasses, but it was difficult to form a picture from just words. She decided that what she had in mind was more or less a black Santa Claus. *No, he's not that old. How silly not to know what your own father looks like.* "You called me?"

"Yes, I was just wondering if you'd like to meet sometime. Maybe not right away, but I just wanted to . . . to ask."

Yolanda held on to the receiver, wondering exactly what should be said. She knew that he was waiting, that he would follow her cue, whatever it was. Part of her wanted to say, "Why didn't you call and ask me that thirty years ago?" You know, let him sweat to see if he'd ever get the chance to parade her around the Livingston family. What did he think she was anyway, some kind of child trophy? And then there was the side of her that had learned its lesson. *Life is too short to play these games. Either let the man in or don't.* "How about this weekend?"

"I'm throwing Candace a birthday party on Saturday afternoon," he whispered. "You could come by before, during, or after. Just depends on whether or not you feel up to meeting the entire Livingston family. We'll all be here."

To be perfectly honest, she wanted to have a crowd. Maybe it would relieve her anxiety, take the pressure off this one-on-one meeting with a father she didn't even know. "I'd love to come to the party. Do you mind if I bring someone with me?"

"The more the merrier," he bounced back. "I can't wait for you to meet everyone. Most of the family will be here. I'm really looking forward to meeting you."

"Same here."

Yolanda's hand trembled as she placed the phone back on the receiver. Dianne was waiting to hear an instant replay of the whole conversation, but she wasn't quite sure that Yo-yo was ready. So much had happened so quickly.

"You ready to go shopping?" Yolanda asked, jumping up from the couch.

"Wait a minute, Yo-yo. We need to talk."

"About what?"

"Actually, *you* need to talk." Dianne patted the empty cushion next to her, inviting Yolanda to have a good old-fashioned heart-to-heart.

Yolanda plopped herself down. "What?"

"Okay, let's talk about your father. You haven't had two words to say about him. It's time you talked to somebody."

Yolanda let her hair down and confessed that she was scared to death to meet her father. With Joyce Ann's death and this reconciliation with Kelan, she felt like a mass of raw nerves, sensitive to everything and everyone. It wasn't like her to be this open. "What am I gonna do? I mean, what if I start crying or something?"

"Okay, so what if you do start crying? You think they're gonna say, 'She's crying because she just saw her father for the first time—get her out of here!'?" Dianne asked.

"No." Yolanda rolled her eyes. "I just don't want to lose my composure."

"God forbid that you should appear human." Dianne sang her sarcastic remark.

"I *am* human."

"Then don't be afraid of it. You're never gonna get anywhere by denying that you have feelings."

Yolanda wondered where this sudden surge of Dr. Phil or Dr. Laura or Dr. Whoever had come from. It wasn't too long ago that Dianne was sitting in the backseat, crying because she couldn't bear to see Joyce Ann. "How do you know so much about all of this?"

"It's been a long, hard road, Yo-yo. Longer and harder than anything I've ever done. And I'm sure I've still got miles to go. But God is good. He sent me friends; He gave me a gift; He put people in my path to help me recover; He rekindled my relationship with my family. I realize now that He was there all the time."

"What about things with Joyce Ann? I mean, how are you

going to deal with this now that you'll never get the chance to reconcile with her?" Yolanda didn't mean to pry, but she saw no need in being shy now.

"You know, at this point I have forgiven her. I have released her of all she owed me. My feelings haven't gotten the message yet, but I've made a decision to forgive Joyce Ann. It helps that she called me, you know?"

"I always knew she loved you," Yolanda said. "Even when she was in that zone of hers, she asked about you. She did love you like her own daughter. I don't think she ever forgave herself for what she did to you. That guilt ate her alive."

"It almost ate me, too." Dianne came clean. "There were days when I thought I would rather be dead than live with the memory of what happened to Shannon, and the pain of Joyce Ann leaving me. And I do regret that I wasn't strong enough to put my arms around her while she was still alive. That's something else I've got to work through now. But you know what I learned in counseling?"

Yolanda shook her head.

"I found out that I can't expect people to give me what only God can give. We just don't have it in us. Nobody else can make me happy, keep me satisfied, fulfill that desire to love and be loved like God can and does every day. It is my responsibility to seek Him out every day in an effort to maintain my sanity. We may come from a family of broken women, but it stops right here right now with me, you, and Regina."

Yolanda blew air upward. "I don't know about Regina, Dianne. I've been praying for her, but I don't see her attitude getting any better."

"Well, that was the whole purpose of the prayer chain." Dianne looked at her watch. "And speaking of the prayer chain, it's my time to pray."

"Mind if I join you?"

"I was hoping you'd ask. It's been a long time since we prayed together."

"Too long."

Kelan and Yolanda made a stop at the Super Wal-Mart between Dentonville and Parker City. She had no earthly idea of what Candace might want for her birthday. As a matter of fact, Yolanda was still trying to figure out exactly what was going on between herself and Mr. Livingston, not to mention this live-in thing with Candace. He obviously cared for her. The family must have cared for Candace, too, or else they wouldn't come to the party. What's up with the commitment? *Hmph. Maybe this fear of commitment runs on both sides of my family tree.*

They narrowed down the gift down to two choices: lavender-scented bath gel with lotion and body spray, or a candle.

"We've got to think generic, here," Kelan said. "Everybody takes a bath. I think we should go with the bath stuff."

"Okay," Yolanda said, "bath stuff it is."

"That was almost too easy." He looked at her suspiciously. "What?"

"Since when do you agree with me the first time?"

He was right—that was not the way it used to be. Somehow, at some point, her heart and soul had stopped fighting him. Stopped fighting his love, his appointed place in her life. Yolanda put her arm around his waist. "I don't know. It just happened."

"What happened?" He seemed to be searching for an express answer.

Yolanda shook her head and looked down, taking a few steps and hoping to see his feet follow suit. But they didn't. Yolanda was too far ahead to hold on to his waist anymore. "What?"

"Say it," he said.

"Say what?"

"Say what you feel for once, Yolanda."

"I just . . . I just agreed with you." Remnants of the wall that used to keep her from hurt began to assemble themselves, weakly, at the base of her heart. *How come there's nobody else coming down this aisle?*

"No. I asked you what happened. What happened that caused you to stop arguing with me about every little thing?" He tore through the wall, pushed the icy blocks away.

"Okay, we're in Wal-Mart, Kelan. We don't have to go here now."

"Hey, this is the great American store. If we can't talk in Wal-Mart, we can't talk anywhere." He turned up the corners of his mouth just enough to melt the foundation.

Yolanda took two steps toward him. Her arm reclaimed the place along his waist that she'd abandoned only moments before. His arm slid across her shoulder and then pulled her into him. She stole one hug, for strength, before backing out of his embrace and facing him head-on. He deserved to know the truth.

"Kelan, I love you." His eyes softened. "I don't know how you've put up with me this long, but I thank God that you have. I'm not going to waste any more energy trying to deny what God has put between us. Life's too short for that. I've learned that the hard way this year. *That's* what happened."

"That is sooo cute, ain't it, girl?"

Yolanda turned around to find two teenage girls standing behind her, holding on to each other and smiling at her and Kelan as though they knew the whole story.

"Uh-huh," the other agreed in a giggly tone. "This is just like the movies."

They were dressed in gothic: silver chains, black hair, flesh pierced, faces stark white, and nails painted purple. Trying to find themselves, Yolanda figured. But for all that, they were too funny and innocent to be annoying. Yolanda stood next to Kelan, and they laughed at themselves and at the girls for a second.

"Here. Y'all take a picture," the taller one said. She pulled a Polaroid camera from her backpack.

"You carry that thing around with you?" Kelan asked her.

"Oh, yeah. I take pictures of everything: animals, cute clothes—"

"Fine guys," the shorter one added.

"Okay, y'all, get together. Smile!"

She snapped the picture and handed it to Yolanda when it slid out of the camera. "Here you go. Y'all have to invite us to your wedding, okay? My name is Mandy; this is Elizabeth. We live over at the girls' home, on South Street. Invite us, okay?"

"Okay." Yolanda got caught up in their excitement and agreed.

"Okay, bye," Elizabeth squealed. "Oh—cool dreads, sir."

"Thanks," Kelan said.

And they bounded off to catch their next picture.

"We're having a wedding?" Kelan raised an eyebrow.

"According to Mandy and Elizabeth we are." Yolanda laid the blame elsewhere.

"But you agreed with them." He pulled her in.

"Yeah. I guess I did, didn't I?"

He kissed her on the cheek and left her to ponder what she'd gotten herself into. As she watched the film develop, she had to admit, *We do look good together.*

The drive to Parker City took longer than she'd anticipated. Or maybe it was that she was so nervous. What do you say to a stranger who happens to be your father? She focused her attention on the scenery. With the country boom, as they called it, Parker City had its share of construction and renovation to clog its vessels as well. Mr. Livingston's home was located in a newer section of town. His was a planned senior community, complete with a clubhouse and community pool for its golden-aged residents. It was an unseasonably warm March afternoon, allowing for a pleasant lunchtime stroll. Elderly couples lined the streets, many hand in hand, and took advantage of the weather. Watching them saunter down the streets of Mr. Livingston's community, Yolanda's mind formed questions that their smiling faces and warm glances answered. They were happy. They'd been together for years and were settling into these last sacred ones together.

Kelan was impressed with Parker City, the rolling hills and relaxed community lifestyle in which Mr. Livingston resided. "This is the life." His own parents were so busy roaming the country, he rarely saw them. Maybe in a couple of years they'd sit down somewhere in a place like this.

As they pulled into Mr. Livingston's driveway, Yolanda noticed that there was only one other car at the residence. She thought of asking Kelan to drive around, stalling for more people—distractions, actually. That's when she saw him come out of the front door. Mr. Bernard Livingston. Her father. The first thing she noticed about him was herself. After looking at her face for all of her life, seeing his was eerie. His bone structure, the way his nose flattened out. His eyebrows—thick and bushy, the way hers would look without waxing. His lips, full in the center and thin at the corners. And the way he walked with his feet turned slightly inward. Yolanda could still remember wearing those foot braces to bed at night. *This is my father.*

"Hey." He met her as she climbed down from Kelan's truck.

"You look a lot like me, stranger." His sense of humor was corny but cozy, and very much welcomed.

"Hello," Yolanda said—not sure how to address him. "It's nice to meet you."

He reached out for Yolanda and took her into an embrace. The smell of men's cologne filled her nose as she fought to withhold her emotions. She could count on one hand the times she'd laid her head on a man's chest. *And this was the one that I should have had to lean on all along.* Her head seemed to belong there, as if she fit there in a hollow made especially for her.

"It's nice to meet you, too, Yolanda." He hugged her still. Then he stood back, looking at her again. "No, you look better than me. You've got your mother's eyes." He winked.

"Um, this is my good friend Kelan." Yolanda took the attention off herself.

"Nice to meet you, young man."

"Same here, sir."

"Come on inside. Everybody's on their way." Bernard placed a hand on Yolanda's back and escorted them into the house. The front room had a relaxing southwestern motif. Comfortable for actually sitting and conversing. They stopped there for a second as Bernard went down the row of pictures lining the mantel, naming off family members and their relation to Yolanda. There was such a strong family resemblance between the Livingstons that Yolanda saw herself in each of their faces. She was part of one of those families where everybody looked the same. The more she saw of them, the less she saw of Gloria's side. They Livingstons all belonged to her, and it showed.

"These are Carolyn's kids—your first cousins, Pamela and Patricia. They're twins, about your age. Pam plays in the WNBA. Patricia is a teacher. We've got lots of overachievers in the family," he boasted proudly. "Yep, these are my sister's kids. I'm proud of 'em, but I can't wait to show them a picture of you—the doctor."

Yolanda smiled shyly and lowered her head—something that she hadn't planned on doing. *Why am I feeling like a . . . a little girl?* Then he showed her a picture of himself at his fiftieth birthday party. The life in him—his nature, his easygoing demeanor, his broad smile—showed in the same way that his voice echoed his character. He was good people, and she'd missed out on him all her life. He looked like someone she should know. Someone she should be proud of. Someone whose picture should have been in her wallet all these years. But it wasn't. *Whose fault is this? Whose fault is this?* She screamed it over and over in her head.

In another room, Earth, Wind and Fire's "September" started playing. Seconds later, a woman who, Yolanda assumed, was Candace brightened up the front room with her red jumpsuit and red heels to match. She was obviously way beyond caring what people thought of her. Why else would she be wearing those earrings all down to her shoulders? Just the type for Mr. Livingston, Yolanda thought.

"You must be Yolanda," Candace shrieked.

"Yes. And this is my friend Kelan."

"Oh!" Candace pulled them both into an earthquake, jolting up and down like a showcase showdown winner on *The Price Is Right.* "I am so happy to meet you—the both of you. Don't you two look great together! Oh, Bernard, go get the camera. This is wonderful!"

All at once a caravan of Livingstons arrived, and the party was on. Everybody kept saying how much Yolanda looked like someone they called "Nanny," who was long gone. From what Yolanda could gather, that was a compliment. "Nanny" was the beloved matriarch of the family, who had passed a few years earlier.

The house was alive with music and people moving about. Snapping fingers, dancing a bit, eating, talking loud, drinking, laughing, and enjoying the company. Yolanda could smell smoke from a cigar—smooth and rich. Not overbearing. The setting was different from any family gathering she'd ever known, but the feel wasn't. They were a loving family, too. As an adult, Yolanda could see that. But she couldn't imagine how she would have handled it as a child—hearing from her mother's side that smokers and drinkers were hell-bound sinners and then coming to her father's house to see the other side smoking and drinking and loving her.

Mr. Livingston took them all over the house, introducing Yolanda as his daughter and Kelan as her friend. During this round-the-house tour, Yolanda heard a slew of what she gathered were supposed to be welcome-to-the-family remarks. "She's definitely a Livingston" . . . "Look just like Denita's girl" . . . "Bernard, you couldn't deny her if you wanted to." Okay, that last one got to her. Yeah, yeah, yeah, she knew it was just one of those things people said. But hearing it over and over again was . . . making her think. *Did he* want *to deny me?*

"I'm ready to leave," Yolanda whispered to Kelan when she got the chance.

"But we just got here," he whined. This was his type of event: people gathered, eating, just hanging out. Good music, from back when music was still treated like art.

"I don't want to stay here any longer. I'm ready to leave," she repeated.

Kelan pulled himself away from his hot wings long enough to read her face. "Baby, what's wrong?"

"There's are a lot of issues that my father—I mean, Mr. Livingston—and I need to discuss. I shouldn't have come here without settling those things with him first," she said.

"Well, why don't you go over there and talk to him. They say there's a whole other bunch of folks that haven't even arrived yet. I'm sure no one would mind if your father took out some time talk to his daughter." Kelan motioned for Yolanda to join her father near the kitchen sink.

He *was* all alone at the sink, washing and seasoning another tray of meat to put on the grill. "Go on," Kelan prodded her, taking another bite of potato salad. "And bring me back some ribs." His humor, as ill-placed as it was, lightened her.

She approached Mr. Livingston, almost tiptoed to his side. "Hi."

"Hey, Yolanda. What you know about seasoning meat?" he asked.

"I'm pretty good."

"Naw, you sound like an amateur. Here, wash this last piece of meat. I'll season it."

She took a place next to him. Almost like at Gloria's house, only this time she was with a man. Her father. Should have been here next to him years ago. The chicken breast felt squashy in her hands as she rinsed it, turned it over again and again.

"You think you got that one clean enough?" Mr. Livingston interrupted her train of thought.

"Oh, yes. Here you go."

The lyrics from Al Green's "Let's Stay Together" filled the house.

"What you got on your mind, Yolanda?" he asked her.

Yolanda felt cornered, like she had felt at Wal-Mart. Pushed up against the wall, ready either to be subdued or to come out swinging. *Stop fighting.* "I've got a lot on my mind, Mr. Livingston."

"Grab that barbecue sauce and that brush. Let's go outside. It's a little chilly, but we should be okay."

She followed him to the porch. He lifted the lid of the pit and stood back, letting the smoke fill the air. Probably teased some hungry strays somewhere. He took the wieners from the grill and placed them in a foil tray. He walked back to the door and yelled into the house, "Got the hot dogs ready for the kids!"

Then he came back outside again. He was dressed in denim shorts and a navy blue sweatshirt. His legs, scrawny—a lot like Yolanda's, only with hair. His feet were big and clunky, with toes that begged for a pedicure. Or at least some lotion. *Maybe old people don't worry about such things.* Kelan had said that old folks knew how to live. Maybe toenails weren't so important in the scope of life.

"I know you've got a lot of questions." The chicken sizzled as it hit the hot bars of metal. "I don't know that I can answer them all, but I'll try."

"Really I just have one question to ask you." She didn't want to sound accusatory, but how else did you ask? "Did you ever think that maybe I was yours? I mean, you were with my mom and . . . she had a baby nine months later. You must have *known* that in a small town like Dentonville."

"I would be lying if I said that the thought never crossed my mind," he admitted, closing the top to the grill and taking a seat next to her. He faced her now, with no intention of side-stepping her question. "It *did* cross my mind. But your mother was an upstanding church member and a good woman. I didn't want to ruin her reputation. Besides, I was young, broke, and I didn't know what to do with myself, let alone a daughter.

"That next year, I moved to Parker City and married Dorothy. We tried for years to have a child, but never could.

Dorothy felt like less of a woman because she couldn't carry a baby, and the last thing I wanted to do was slap her in the face with the possibility that there was another woman out there who might have given me what she couldn't.

"We divorced in ninety. Irreconcilable differences. Now, looking back on it, I should have asked your mother. I've missed out on so much in your life."

"Yes, you have. But it's not all your fault. My mother should have told you." Yolanda searched for some way to make sense of things.

"Yolanda, everybody has their reasons," he said to her in the deep, earthy tone of an aged man. "People do what they think is best at the time."

He was right.

"I guess I'm looking for someone to blame. It just doesn't seem right," she said.

"Well, for my part, I can say that I'm sorry. I'm sorry that I never checked up on you. I'm sorry that I left and never looked back. I thank God that you have grown up to be a beautiful, beautiful person, and I hate that I missed it all because I was too scared. I should have been there, but I wasn't. And I'm sorry."

His heart was so transparent, so easy. Nothing like Yolanda's. She'd wanted to fuss at him a little more—draw blood. But she couldn't. Really, what else was there to argue about after someone had admitted fault and an apology had been offered? "I accept your apology."

"Thank you." He jumped up and hugged her tightly.

They sat back in their seats and continued talking while the chicken smoked. "How's your mother? Your family?"

"They're all fine," Yolanda said with confidence.

"And who's this fella you brought over here?"

"Kelan—he's my, I don't know." She was embarrassed to

be discussing this with her father. "He's my man friend—kind of like Candace?"

"Oh, Candace won't be my lady friend after today." He stood up to turn the meat over. "You're the first to know. I'm going to propose to her today."

"Really?"

"Yeah. I figure we've been playing house long enough. It's time I made an honest woman out of her," he said.

"That is so sexist." Yolanda joined him at the grill.

"Probably so," he agreed, "but it's the truth. Can't fight that."

Candace cried for a good ten minutes after Bernard put the ring on her. Her full head of hair seemed to spring up and down with her heavy sobs. She couldn't have been much older than forty, but she had an older texture about her. As if she, too, had learned to slow down and enjoy the journey.

After she finished crying, the women in the family took turns looking at her diamond. She held her plump, light brown hand out for all to see. The house was filled with "It's about time" . . . "Don't know what they were waiting on" . . . "They ain't gettin' no younger"—things people say.

When Yolanda got home, she returned a phone call from Regina. "Hey, you called?"

"Yeah, I called you at work but they said you were off. Where'd you go?"

"I went to meet my father," Yolanda said.

"Oh."

"He's really nice," Yolanda added before it dawned on her that she shouldn't have elaborated.

"That's good. Well, I'll speak to you later," she said quickly.

"Did you want something?" Yolanda asked.

"No." Regina hung up the phone.

Chapter 36

$\mathcal{Y}$olanda wondered how long it would take for her mother to bawl her out about the situation with Regina. It took a little over a week, but Gloria finally called Yolanda and gave her two cents. "Look, Yo-yo, you and Regina have been carrying on long enough with this situation with your father. It's about time you quit actin' high and mighty and remember the family you grew up with."

"Momma, I haven't done anything to Regina."

"That's the problem. You ain't called her. You ain't asked her nothin' about the baby. When's the last time you went and picked up your nephew?" she added for effect.

Totally irrelevant. "Okay, I'll call her."

"You will?"

"Yes, ma'am."

"Call her right now, too."

"I will, Momma. As soon as we hang up."

"Bye."

Lord, don't let me be so bossy when I become somebody's momma. Yolanda laced her fingers, closed her eyes, and put her hands on top of her head. Only Gloria could talk to her like that—well, Gloria and Aunt Toe. Maybe Kelan could, too. But that was it. *How did he get so high up on the list?*

Yolanda prayed before she called Regina at work to ask her if they could meet for lunch. It wasn't as if she were afraid of Regina. She also prayed that Regina would be in a good mood. It was a long shot, but she prayed it anyway.

When she did call, Regina sounded too tired to put up a fight and agreed to meet her at Papa's Bar-B-Q Shack. Yolanda thanked God for working it out in His way. The restaurant was crowded with white-collar workers who looked out of place at such a down-home, hole-in-the-wall restaurant on the wrong side of the tracks. The leather on every chair was peeling, and the tables wobbled on uneven legs. The decor was straight out of the sixties, seventies, and eighties—maybe even a few treasures among them worth many times what the owners had paid for them decades ago. For as far back as Yolanda could remember, the autographed picture of Tony Dorsett had been hanging over the cash register. Nothing had changed, not even the people who worked there. Same attitudes: Speak up and say what you want. Have your money ready. But the sweet smell (not to mention the taste) of smoked meats kept everybody coming back to Papa's Bar-B-Q Shack.

"Girl, they need to make a *candle* out of this scent," Yolanda joked as they entered Papa's, testing Regina's mood.

"People wouldn't be able to think straight." She offered a smirk.

I've caught her at a good time. Regina got in line behind her sister, but Yolanda insisted that Regina go ahead and hold a booth for them. "What do you want—a chopped beef sandwich with baked beans?"

"Yeah, and get me some potato salad and sweet tea too," Regina said as she turned to walk away.

"Ooh!" Yolanda touched Regina's shoulder and pointed toward a booth in the back corner of the restaurant. "Those people over there are getting up."

"Okay. I'm all over it."

Yolanda was never so glad to get dirty and sloppy with her sister as when they ate that day. They ate as if they didn't have good sense—just as hard as they wanted to. No pretensions. *Thank You, Father, for opening this door already.* Felt like old times—before any of this happened with Aunt Joyce Ann, Regina's eating disorder, or the business with Yolanda's father.

"I take it Momma called you?" Regina asked, licking barbecue sauce from her fingertips.

"Yeah."

"What she say?"

"A bunch of stuff. And let me be the first to say I'm sorry."

"For what?"

"I'm sorry if I made you feel like I was putting you on the back burner with this thing about Mr. Livingston." Yolanda threw it out there, making it seem insignificant for Regina's sake. Then she put her fork down and talked to Regina. Yolanda knew that she would never get an "I was hurt" out of Regina, so she went on before Regina could deny her feelings. "I feel almost . . . guilty. I mean, we've been through *every-thing* together. We've always had the same things—the same clothes, same rules, same opportunities. And now here I am with a father that I don't share with you."

"*Hmph.*" Regina put her hand over her mouth to keep from losing food. "I felt the same way when I got married."

"Mmm." The memory of Regina's wedding was bittersweet for Yolanda. On one hand, she was happy for Regina's love and fulfillment; on the other, sad for the empty space it created in Yolanda. Give and take. Regina cared about her sister, all right, but Regina had funny ways. Yolanda wouldn't ever have guessed that Regina felt the slightest bit guilty.

She went on. "When I really thought about it, I was sad,

too. I guess, when you share a bedroom with someone for most of your life and then, poof, you're out of there, it's weird. Almost scary. At least when I was away at college, I knew I'd come home and have you to talk to if I wanted to."

We didn't talk that much. Okay, Yo-yo, don't go there. This is as close as you're gonna get to reality with Regina. "Yeah. It was nice to talk sometimes," Yolanda agreed with her.

"Now that you've got a father, though, it's like all that time we spent bonding in our misery was a lie. Like it never happened," she squinted and leaned in toward Yolanda, as if to say, "You know what I mean?"

"Now, imagine what it would be like if your whole life was a lie—not just the part you shared with someone else, but the whole thing." Yolanda challenged her sad little story. *Hold my mule.* "And don't forget, I grew up without a father, too. He might have been alive, but I sure didn't have access to him. Like you, I only knew one Father: God."

Regina nodded in agreement. Even in a man's absence, they never went without their Heavenly Father. He had *always* been more than sufficient. A father to the fatherless.

"Look, Regina, I can't apologize for having a natural father any more than I can apologize for being born and robbing you of your only-child status," Yolanda teased her.

She relented, letting the corners of her lips break upward. It was no secret that four-year-old Regina had not been happy to learn that she would have a little brother or sister.

"I can give account for myself," Yolanda continued. "For the record, I apologize if I have done anything to make you feel ostracized. And the fact that we don't have the same father has not diminished my feelings about you. No matter what happened with Momma or Daddy or Mr. Livingston, we still have the same heavenly Father and you will always be my sister—flesh, blood, and Blood."

"I feel you." Regina blinked rapidly.

Yolanda's soul cried out, *Hallelujah!*

Just when her life was getting back to a reasonably comfortable routine, Kelan jolted Yolanda into an upright position when he announced that he was going to meet his parents in Oklahoma for the Fourth of July and wanted her to join him.

"It's not often that they're this close to Dallas. I really want them to meet you," he stated one Sunday after church, on their way to Gloria's house for dinner.

Yolanda turned up the volume on his radio. She didn't know why, but this meet-the-parents thing caught her off guard. Kelan didn't talk much about his parents or his family. Yolanda knew that his mother and father were retired and traveled a lot. She knew he had a much older brother who was a missionary overseas, but that was about it. Frankly, Yolanda rather liked the idea of an in-law-less relationship.

"I don't know." Yolanda rolled her lips in between her teeth and pretended to think hard. "Let me see how the calendar at work looks. It seems like I've been taking off for everything under the sun since Momma's wedding, and that was just a little over a year ago."

"What's wrong *now*, Yolanda?" Kelan asked, propping his elbow on the door frame. Annoyed. "How are we supposed to have this wedding if you haven't even met my parents?"

"We are not even officially engaged yet, Kelan," Yolanda reminded him.

"Is that what you're waiting on—a question? A ring?"

"That's usually the way it's done." *Hello!*

He shook his head and started humming a tune. An old saints song. One that Yolanda thought she recognized, but wasn't sure of until he started the second round. "Don't let the devil ride. Don't let the devil ride. If you let him ride, he'll surely want to drive. Don't let him ride . . ."

"I know you're not talking about me!" Yolanda pointed at herself, using every available muscle to keep from giving in to his humor.

"I haven't said a word." His lips struggled to stay straight. Humming again.

"Look, Kelan, I'm not the one who started all this marriage business," Yolanda lectured him. "You're the one who said you wanted to have a commitment by December thirty-first."

"And then there was the chain of events, right?"

He could be so brutal with the truth. "Yes, the Lord allowed a lot in my life to help me see what's really important. But the fact still remains, you said that you were ready to move to the next level in this relationship. I already told you how I felt—at Wal-Mart, of all places. Now I'm wondering, which one of us has the coldest feet here?"

"You know what we haven't done?" He bolted upright as he parked the car in Gloria's driveway and turned off the ignition.

"What?"

"We haven't prayed about this. Together, I mean." His index finger rose in the air, and he prayed right then and there for both of them, grabbing Yolanda's hand. Squeezing it. "Lord, we thank You for who You are in our lives and how You've brought us together through Your divine plan. We thank You for teaching us and showing us even now to seek Your face in everything we do, because it's not just about me or Yolanda, Lord. It's about You. It's about Your love that continues to grow and develop us in Your will. Father, let this be the first and the last time we try to make decisions without You in the midst. Teach us what it means to be one—to pray on one accord, not in our own separate corners with separate agendas. Thank You for that uneasy feeling we both felt before we sought Your final word as one. Keep us in Your will, o God, both now and forever. In the name of Jesus we pray. Amen."

Yolanda opened her eyes, leaned across the center of Kelan's car, and kissed her man of God. She lost her fingers in his dreads and wished never to see her nails again if she could just stay there. With him. And in His presence with the man she loved. Inwardly, Yolanda thanked God for bringing Kelan in through the back door—the only way he could have gotten in. And she thanked God for covering Kelan with His love so that he blended in, imperceptible to her radar. Yolanda received Kelan's love because they both knew the undeniable, life-giving love of God. It couldn't have happened any other way. *You are so good, Father.*

Chapter 37

The doorbell rang just as Gloria May bent over the cake to light the candles. "Who's that?" She blew out the match and ordered Yo-yo to answer the door. On the other side, Dianne waited, teeth gleaming, bouncing from the cold, her heart full with anticipation. Love.

Yo-yo looked through the peephole and gasped with disbelief. She swung the door open, yelling, "It's Dianne!" The two fell into each other, the same as they had at the airport. With the same connection, only less inhibited. Dianne with her whole heart healed, Yo-yo with hers less guarded. Both able to freely give and receive what had been struggling inside for years. Some things need to flow.

"Dianne!" Regina strode into the living room to embrace her cousin.

"Girl, look at you," Dianne stood back and marveled at Regina's figure. "Got your shirt all tucked in. You're looking good, girl."

"God is good," Regina said. "So are sit-ups, crunches, and weights," she added. In all honesty, Regina still hadn't figured out how to stay away from her favorite foods. Every once in a while she broke down and ate a whole lot more than she should. But seeing a counselor had been helpful. More than that, signing up for the aerobics class at Master's Tabernacle was what she had needed to get on a healthy track. It was hard, but the women in her class held one another up in prayer twice a week. Between the counselor, her exercise partners, and Aunt Toe's continuing prayer chain, Regina found herself praying for her own needs as well as the needs of others several times a day.

One day at a time.

"Mmm." Dianne took note of Regina's attitude—better than she'd seen in a long time.

Next Gloria hugged Dianne and pulled off her coat before leading Dianne into the kitchen to greet the rest of the family. Orlando, Kelan, and Richard took backseats to the women's reunion, watching. Adoring. "Aunt Toe, look who dropped by for your birthday."

"Dianne!" The loose skin on Aunt Toe's face rode up. "What a wonderful surprise!" Her eyes traveled the full length of Dianne's body once over. She looked good. Solid.

"Where's your man, gal?" Aunt Toe scolded her.

"I'm still single, Aunt Toe. Where's *your* man?" Dianne taunted her.

"Don't you worry about *my* man." Aunt Toe rose to the occasion. "I got me a jet black man with big white teeth."

"Wooo!" Regina reached past Orlando and slapped hands with Aunt Toe.

"That's enough." Gloria smiled, too.

"Oh, Gloria, please. What I'mo do with a man? I'd keel over the minute he kissed me," Aunt Toe laughed at herself.

"Yeah, right." Yo-yo pushed Aunt Toe's joke from her mind.

"You drove up all by yourself, Dianne?" Regina asked.

"Yeah. I'll be leaving out on Sunday, after church."

"Can I spend the night at your house, Yo-yo? I *know* it's already spic and span."

"Girl, I caught her with some dishes in the sink the other day," Regina said with amazement.

"That was a rare occasion." Yo-yo rolled her eyes. "Of course you can stay with me."

"Dianne, you be careful drivin' long distances by yourself. You hear?" Aunt Toe said. "You might do yourself some good movin' up this way instead of doin' all this drivin' and flyin'."

"Well, I think I may be able to put an end to all this travel soon. I'm meeting with my boss next week to see about telecommuting ninety percent of the time," Dianne announced.

"What's that?" Aunt Toe asked.

"It's when I do my work on the computer and by telephone," she said.

"That would be great, Dianne," Yolanda said. "I can't wait to have you move back to Dentonville."

"Hey," Dianne announced, "I've got a big gig coming up, a national conference on the use of writing as a tool for healing. My doctor submitted a few of my poems for consideration, and I was invited to speak."

"That's great, Dianne," Regina congratulated her. "This could be a new career for you, you know?"

Dianne shook her head in amazement. God was indeed opening doors for her. "Now I understand what people mean when they talk about the story behind the glory. It cost what you paid to be who you are."

"Dianne, that's deep." Kelan nodded. "No wonder you're the poet."

"That's my Sugarbee," Gloria agreed.

Gloria ordered Yolanda and Regina to take Dianne into the new den. "Go show her how I've fixed it up."

Yolanda and Regina led Dianne to what used to be the garage. Dianne happily huffed and puffed at the sight. What was once a cluttered, dark, stuffy garage had been transformed into a bright, airy living room. Fresh carpeting and wood paneling covered the planes, while traditional furniture gave the appearance of many good times past in the room. Cleverly placed shelving displayed several of the pictures they'd rummaged through following Joyce Ann's death. Dianne was drawn to one picture in particular, though: one of Joyce Ann in happier days. It was the way Dianne wanted to remember Joyce Ann.

And then the idea hit her. "You know what?"

"What?" Regina asked.

"Why don't we establish a scholarship or something in Joyce Ann's name? We could award it to a college freshman who's overcome and managed to push forward despite a rocky beginning."

"That's a great idea," Yolanda agreed. "We didn't go through all this pain all this time for nothing."

"I know that's right," Regina agreed.

They discussed the idea with their larger family over dinner, and everyone agreed to help establish the Joyce Ann Rucker scholarship fund. Richard volunteered his connections with the community, Kelan volunteered his artistic skills to create a logo, and Orlando offered to set up a Web site. Where Dianne, Regina, and Yolanda had envisioned a women-only operation, they found that the men in their lives had something to contribute. Rather than being *in* the way, they made the way a little easier.

Gloria lit the birthday candles, and Aunt Toe blew them out just as quickly. In years past, Aunt Toe had wished that she would live to see her girls reunited. She'd received that. Aunt Toe didn't have any more wishes—or birthdays—left. She knew that this would be her last one. Sometimes people know. And she was fine with that now.